BLOOD CIRCUS

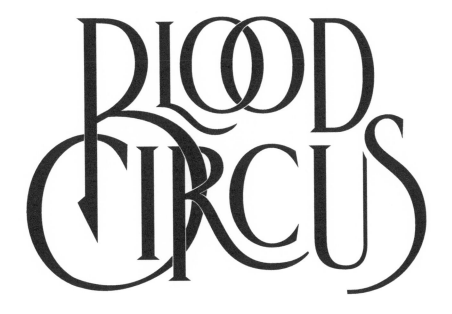

CAMILA VICTOIRE

**BLACK
STONE**
PUBLISHING

Printed in the United States of America

First edition: 2023
ISBN 979-8-200-81608-8
Young Adult Fiction / Fantasy / General

Version 1

Blackstone Publishing
31 Mistletoe Rd.
Ashland, OR 97520

www.BlackstonePublishing.com

To muck & paps & midi
my family, my stand

N

DEEPER WOODS

K L U J N   T E R R I T O R Y

RED RIVER

Orphanage

T R E M B L E   H I L L S

Loudhouse

BLACK MOUNTAIN

JUSTICE FALLS

ASCENSION

Mine Alley

MT. DOMINION

*TWO HOURS FROM RED RIVER TO MISSION CREEK

cir·cus *noun* \ ˈsər-kəs

1. **a** : a traveling company of entertainers, such as clowns, acrobats, animal trainers, trapeze artists, and musicians, who typically perform under a large tent

2. **a** : a circular arena lined with tiers of seats, used especially for sports and games, such as Gladiatorial combats, races, mock battles, and blood sports

   b : the exploitation or slaughter of animals for spectacle

—**cir·cusy** *adjective* \ ˈsər-kə-sē

From *A Brief History of Klujns*
by Catrina Sherman

Klujns (pronounced *kloonz;* Latin *Homo arcanum*) are dangerous, human-eating predators that live in wild, remote areas, from the icy tundras of the Northern Boreal to the swamplands and burning forests of the South. Klujns are so adept at camouflage that they managed to evade humans for millennia, until their discovery in 2071. While it is unclear how they stayed undetected for so long, some speculate that Klujn tribes have barriers that produce electromagnetic pulses that confound human technology and make them virtually invisible to the naked eye.

After his rise to power in 2088, North American President Atoll Grouse sent missions into the deep wilderness in an attempt to uncover more about these beasts and their way of life. The Explorers who returned told of the remarkable properties of Klujn meat (which has ten times the protein of animal flesh), and Klujn claws (a precious crystal with the ability to turn barren soil arable). They also told of the Blood Race—a macabre tribal tradition that takes place every year at the October Blood Moon, where young human hostages are slaughtered in an arena setting.

In response to this unsettling discovery, Grouse ordered for the erection of electrified fences around human townships. Grouse's Military and its department of Hunters began to hunt Klujns for their meat and claws, which began to transform North American society. In 2090, the calendars were reset and Year Zero was born as a reminder of this new enemy that forever changed our culture. Now, in the new era, dubbed *AK (After Klujns)*, any creature who wanders on the wrong side of a fence can be shot dead on sight.

While much about this species remains a mystery, one thing is unequivocal: no human captured by a Klujn tribe has ever returned.

Editor's Note

Catrina Sherman was an anthropologist, author, explorer, and scientist who devoted her life to the study of Klujns. After the death of her wife, Sherman went to live in the wild. She disappeared in 16 AK while researching the fallen Estrella tribe, where she was likely killed and eaten by Klujns.

RED RIVER,
NORTH AMERICAN TERRITORY

October 1, 31 AK

1

I hear a woman's heartbeat, racing fast, like an ominous drum. Boom, boom, boom. I'm tucked inside a blanket, nuzzled against her chest. My eyes are open, gazing up at a dark moonless sky. It hangs above my head like a lake in the night. Deep, still, devoid of life.

As she runs, I hear her breathing—rapid, sharp. A prey animal being chased by a predator. But where are we? And what are we running from?

The forest is almost pitch-black. Thick, pungent smoke fills my lungs and stings my eyes. I cry. The shrill, terrified cry of a baby who doesn't understand.

"Shhh," the woman says quietly. Nevertheless, her voice is frantic, desperate.

We reach a small clearing by the edge of a cliff and the woman comes to a stop. Down below, a river rages—a deafening soundtrack of white whirling water. She speaks again, this time to someone else, then leans down toward me, her face coming closer but never in focus. I take in the hood of her coat, her long brown hair, her dark blue eyes and curved eyebrows. The woman's lips press against my forehead in an abbreviated kiss. Then, she throws me over the edge, deep into the jowls of the waiting current.

I'm falling.

* * *

I awake to find I'm in my room. It's dark. A moon lamp glows on the wall, the only source of light. My pajama shirt is drenched in sweat, my bare legs tangled in bedsheets. *A nightmare.* Haven't had one of those in a while.

I get out of bed, walk over to the window, and draw open the blackout curtains. Bright light floods in, blinding me, sharp and unexpected. After a moment, my eyes adjust to the new day outside. It can't be morning already; I still feel so tired.

The sun is strong but hidden behind gray clouds. In the summer the clouds are always darker, pregnant with ash, as the burning season devastates the south. Winds carry the evidence north to where we are. It's why the trees in the woods look the way they do, wearing coats of cinder like the mourning wear black.

Our house faces north. Down in the front yard, Diana, my adoptive mother, is already hard at work in her glass-walled greenhouse, her natural hair pulled back into a ponytail. The greenhouse is shaped like a hexagon, filled with ponds of algae, small trees, and wilted plants of different kinds. A little white robot rolls around the dry earth, pollinating flowers. Diana had designed it when she got tired of the tedious labor. There used to be insects whose job it was to do that—*bees*, they were called—but they went extinct long before I was born. Luckily, science has an answer to almost any problem.

Behind the greenhouse, a few hundred feet into the charcoal forest and across the river, stands the tall electric barbed-wire wall that separates us from the Deeper Woods. Klujn territory. A region of the Boreal— North America's largest remaining forest—that stretches across the entire continent and up to Arctica. When my brother Mercy and I used to play hide-and-seek as kids, I would always hide down there. On our side of the fence, of course. Mercy was too scared to even venture past the yard. After a while, when he got really upset, I would emerge from the forest—sporting black palms, a black dress, and a triumphant grin on my face. Then Mercy would tell on me and I would get the usual lecture. My childhood was one big cautionary tale. *Don't go too far. Don't touch the fence. If you so much as take one step on the other side . . .*

Like a hungry Klujn was waiting with an open mouth.

I watch Diana as she rakes the soil, mixes in compost, and carefully plants seedlings. Then she whispers under her breath. I've heard her; it's almost like a prayer, begging the earth to respond, to nurture plants where plants can no longer grow.

When soil dies, it becomes dirt, and dirt can't foster life. It's as barren as an ocean without fish or a sky without stars. By the time humans realized the importance of sustainable farming—that only healthy, living soil could yield crops and feed the planet—it was already too late. Food couldn't grow anymore, and famine prevailed. Almost everything has to be grown indoors now, in big industrial Greenhouses with precious fertile soil, away from bugs and thieves and volatile weather. They grow meat there, as well.

There is only one thing that can bring it all back to life: pulverized Klujn claws and bones. Mixed with the dead earth, it rejuvenates the soil and makes it arable again. But only Grouse's Military has access. Klujns are still too rare, and their precious land dangles out of reach; so close and yet so difficult to find.

None of this matters to Diana, who is vegetarian, and who insists that we eat only what we grow ourselves. My seitan sandwiches and misshapen apples and popped quinoa make me a laughingstock at school, where everyone eats the same foods from the Greenhouses: pigs in a blanket, cured meat sandwiches, and cream-filled donuts. The salty and sweet and delicious tastes.

Diana finishes her morning ritual, wipes her hands on her patchwork overalls, and picks up her wicker basket. She leaves the greenhouse and closes the door, locks all three locks on her way out, rights the crooked *Thieves Will Be Shot* sign, and heads toward the porch. Past the outdoor staircase to her left that descends into George's basement study—a cabinet of curiosities with its old yellowed maps and dusty books and strange artifacts. The front door creaks open and she's inside.

"Ava!" Diana calls. "Time to get up!"

I walk into the bathroom I share with Mercy and turn on the shower. The same reflection as always greets me in the mirror. Short brown curly hair. Olive skin. Brown eyes, speckled like a connect-the-dots puzzle.

The sleeves of the nightshirt cover my arms; everything I own has long sleeves. I look at the familiar scar on my right hand, the outline of a wolf bite that's been there for as long as I can remember.

The shower, as always, is lukewarm. The water-level indicator next to the shampoo rack reads *low*. I set the timer to three minutes, the longest we're allowed. It's never enough. I zone out, my mind goes *dans la lune*, as Diana calls it, which in her native French means "in the moon."

I dream of travel. But where would I go? You need permits to get through Military checkpoints. Even then, I don't know anyone outside Red River.

All logic aside, I like to fantasize about the ocean. About burying my toes in warm sand and letting the sun bronze my skin. Breathing in that salty air. Then the timer sounds, my water allowance runs out, and the cold hits me like a tidal wave.

My room is even colder.

First period is Combat class, so I slip into my gym uniform. Dark blue sweatpants, T-shirt, and a matching sweater with a silver triangle emblazoned on the back. Last and most important, I reach into my jewelry box for the pendant George, my adoptive father, gave me on my last birthday.

"It's the claw of a young female," he had said, clipping the rose gold chain around my neck. "Taken from its finger before it had a chance to emerge. That's why it's so clear. We call it virgin crystal."

The curved crystal is small but surprisingly heavy. Clear as a spring sky before the burning season starts. When you hold it up to the light, it's as if the crystal contains a rainbow inside it—glowing red, green, purple, and gold. "Best not show it off," George told me, and winked, an unusual mix of kindness and melancholy in his bright green eyes. "It's extremely rare. People will be jealous."

I swore that I would keep it hidden, but the promise has been difficult to keep. It is the most beautiful thing I have ever owned in all my sixteen years.

"Ava!" Diana yells again, her patience thin as an ice cap. "It's twenty to nine!"

I switch off my moon lamp and go downstairs, shrugging my backpack onto my shoulders.

When I reach the bottom landing, a delicious smell greets me. Diana stands in the kitchen, spatula in hand, as strips of a white-colored bacon sizzle in a pan. But that doesn't make sense. She doesn't eat meat, and the rest of us only eat it when we can afford it. Even then, it's usually chicken.

"Happy Hunter's Day to you, too," I say, trying to steal a piece, but Diana swats my hand away. A small TV, muted for the commercial break, glows at the end of the breakfast bar next to the telephone. "Where's Mercy?"

"He left already," Diana says. "I don't want him getting in trouble with Mr. Mogel because you can't be ready on time."

"I didn't sleep well. I started having nightmares . . ." I trail off, feeling Diana's eyes on the back of my neck. "It's nothing," I add, before she has the chance to worry. I fill up my water glass, take the purification wand and stir it around for ten seconds. *Beep. Safe to drink*, it reads in green, and I take a sip. I notice a large lump on the breakfast bar, wrapped in recycled paper. "What's with the mystery package?"

"It's for tonight. Your father's friend sent it over."

"General Santos?" I ask, but I don't need an answer. The vein in Diana's temple is a dead giveaway. It always pulses when his name is mentioned. George and Rodrigo Santos go way back—back to the three years of mandatory Military training they served before George became a Klujn expert and Santos became a Hunter. He now holds the highest rank, just under Grouse, and operates a Loudhouse on the other side of Tremble Hills—those black brick buildings where Klujns are bred and harvested. He generously sends us kanum now and then—that's Klujn meat—because my dad had to retire from the Military before he could get his pension. He teaches now, and there aren't a whole lot of luxuries you can afford on a teacher's salary.

I look back at the bacon in the pan, realizing what it is.

"Rodrigo's going to drop by later, before your father and Mercy leave for Hunter's Camp," Diana continues. "And you know what they say—it's rude to send gifts back."

The commercial break ends and she unmutes the TV. It's Sabah Strongman's morning show. A guest speaker dissects a diagram of the moon's cycles like a weather forecaster describing an imminent storm.

"Everybody should be on high alert tonight," says the expert, in his smart blue suit. "Klujn activity usually heightens around the waxing gibbous phase in the days leading up to the October Blood Moon. I know it's easy to get caught up in Hunter's Day celebrations, but tonight isn't the night to drink too much homemade lumber liquor and go wandering in the woods. Not that there is ever a good time for that."

"Surely *they* won't cross over onto our side of the fence?" Sabah says dramatically, as her audience members shift uncomfortably in their seats. "I mean, it's happened before."

"These tend to be isolated cases," says the expert. "In the last few decades, Klujns have mostly respected the fences. However, people should remain on the safer side of caution."

"Waxing gibbous," the words roll off my tongue. Last year, we learned about the moon's phases in our Klujnology prep class. We learned about the Blood Race, too—a gruesome fight to the death between a human and a Klujn. Apparently, more girls get captured every year than boys; the ratio is almost ten to one. Nobody knows why Klujns prefer girls. Some say it's because we're easier to catch. That we put up less of a fight.

On TV, they move on to news about Atoll Grouse who, after thirty-three years of presidency, denies a fresh wave of rumors concerning his declining health. He was inaugurated at a young age, after his father died, and for the last three decades he has been hard at work. Grouse addresses the media and a crowd of his loyal supporters outside the Silver House in Mission Creek, a few hours southeast of Red River. He is a handsome man in his midfifties, with graying chestnut curls and sparkling auburn eyes that radiate warmth like a fireplace in a log cabin.

"In the last hundred years, we were abandoned by God," he says, his warm voice full of a conviction that puts me at ease. "When God turned the weather on us, we were forced to abandon religious faith and pick up weapons. Ever since, we have fought a constant war against Mother

Nature, and more recently, against Klujns. Today, we celebrate the last Hunt before the long winter. More importantly, we celebrate the strength and resilience of man, the most successful species who has ever walked the earth. Because we are our own gods now." The crowd cheers. A reporter inquires about the lack of profitable raids in the last few months. "We are ready to launch new technology that has been in development for years," Grouse announces with a grin that exposes straight white teeth. A crystal stud decorates each of his canines. "It will be crucial in infiltrating Klujn tribes and getting past their complex camouflage. Another raid means more soil, more crystals, and more meat. More meat means *repopulation*; it means no more one-child policy. Our economy will soar, soar, soar . . ."

At these words, the crowd goes wild. It's pandemonium.

"They're like babies excited by flashing lights," Diana says flatly. "Without understanding the mechanics of electricity." She turns off the TV.

"I was watching that," I tell her. Instead of answering, she turns to the kitchen counter, unwraps the mass of recycled paper and a bald lump falls out. It looks like a headless turkey, but with softer skin. It's young kanum, a delicacy.

Diana slices the kanum open and fills it with the white bacon she'd already cooked up, along with a buttery herb stuffing. She closes it back up with a needle and edible thread, glazes it with oil, and slides the pan into the oven.

"It looks disgusting raw," I say.

"It's your saving grace," she answers, tight-lipped. "It's worth a season's wages, and your father's fortunate enough to get it for free." She has a sour look on her face, or maybe it's sadness. I realize I don't know which Diana I prefer: the one who's on my case about being late for school, or the one who vanishes inside herself, forgetting I'm even there at all.

Diana takes off her rubber gloves, wipes down the breakfast bar, and reaches for the wicker basket. She looks inside, and her shoulders slump. The harvest is small and lacks vibrancy: a few carrots, potatoes, onions, radishes, mustard greens, and a small handful of berries.

"To think there was a day when our blueberries came from Peru and our mangoes from India," she sighs.

"Where's Peru?"

"It was a country in the South American Territory. Don't you take geography?"

"The maps we study in class don't go down that far." I reach for the berries, but Diana swats my hand away.

"They're for tonight."

"Mercy and I are going to the fair," I tell her.

"Mercy has to pack," she says, with the usual edge. "The buses leave at nine."

"He packed a week ago."

"I don't want you out after dark. It's not safe."

"Everyone in this township owns a gun," I say.

"This time of the moon cycle, you shouldn't be taking any chances." Diana begins to peel an onion.

"Hunter's Day only happens once a year," I plead, not telling her the real reason I'm so keen to go: rumor has it there's going to be a real live Klujn at the festival this year.

"*I don't care!*" Diana's yell brings me back to earth, like a lasso around a Klujn's neck. Her words pull me down to the ground and leave me there. Her eyes are fixed on the cutting board. They're not looking *at* it, but *beyond* it. At what? *Dans la lune.*

"I want you back before sundown," she says after a moment, her voice eerily low now, the warning in it more present than ever. "Have I made myself clear?"

"Crystal," I mutter. I grab my electric longboard and head out. Stop at the door and turn around. Diana begins to chop her onion. There are tears in her eyes.

"What's gotten into you?" I ask.

"Onions," she mutters, but she refuses to look me in the eyes.

2

It's a five-minute ride to school along the Military road, ten if I take the path along the river. It's too bumpy to ride my longboard, but I usually opt for the detour even though it's longer. I like to look at the trees—identical cherry trees with black trunks, standing straight like soldiers. They are grown to be cut down, their lumber used to make everything from alcohol to houses to beds to coffins. Although I guess coffins are a type of bed, and you use them for a longer time.

I find the narrow path that edges along the river's bank with the temperate slopes of a children's roller coaster. This time of year you can sometimes glimpse bronze and yellow leaves poking out from ash-covered branches. When the wind blows, they rain down like confetti.

My board is heavy under my arm. Diana built it using a skateboard deck, a spare motor, and an old wheelbarrow tire. There's a hole cut into the middle for the tire, and a place for my feet on either side. The motor achieves more in the way of noise than speed, but it gets me where I need to go, granted I'm not in a rush. Over the years, I've painted the deck with bright symbols and patterns. I love any excuse to create using my hands. Casual color is uncommon in our world, where most things are silver, blue, and gray—the shades of Grouse's family, his Military, and his Hunters—but it sparks something in me. No one else has anything like it.

On my morning walks, I like to listen for birds and insects. Today, like most days, the path is quiet, with only the dark-violet blackberry shrubs and the river's soundtrack to keep me entertained. The river is relatively dormant here, its surface stained a reddish-brown by the trees that are logged up north and carried downriver to the timber farms. The fence towers on the other side, signs posted every few feet shouting their usual warnings: *Beware! Danger! Do Not Enter! Authorized Personnel Only.* My morning walks are occasionally rewarded with exciting finds—a flower growing through dead soil, a butterfly, a streak of blue in the sky. These are anomalies.

I sense eyes watching me. I look around, but there's no one there. The river continues upstream to the northwest, toward the orphanage where George found me, a child with no family or history, only a name sewn into a threadbare blanket.

Again, I feel someone—or something—watching me. I turn around and there, behind the fence, I see it.

A flash of white. Black markings. Blue eyes. It's a spotted wolf. I recognize it from the *Dangerous Predator* posters at school. Illegal poachers risk the penalties of traversing the fence to hunt them because their meat is delicious and their pelt extremely warm, or so it's said.

I freeze, even though I know I am safe on this side. As the beast continues to watch me, silent and unmoving, a strange familiarity sweeps through my body. It's almost as if I know the animal from somewhere. *Don't be stupid*, I think.

Then the leaves rustle, and the wolf is gone.

The rush of nostalgia goes with it.

* * *

It's the last day before Fall Break, and first up is Combat class. I'm late. From the doorway of the gymnasium, I spot Mercy sitting in the front row. My brother is the exact combination of our parents, like the result of mixing two primary colors. His skin is golden, with Diana's tight black curls and George's bright eyes, his build on the smaller side of average. I try to catch his attention but those eyes are focused on the front, where our teacher Mr. Mogel demonstrates on a Klujn dummy—a vaguely humanoid female made of silicone, its eyes glowing an electric orange. The thing would be frightening if not for the gym uniform thrown over its naked body.

"The amount of force required to rip off an ear is about the same as turning a doorknob," Mr. Mogel says. "Not a lot. But our brain's defense mechanism prevents us from being able to do it to ourselves or to our friends." He grabs the dummy's ear and twists, ripping it off easily. Underneath is the dark cave of an ear canal. "And to sever a finger—we're talking the same amount of pressure it takes to bite into a carrot." He lifts the dummy's hand, bites down, and the finger comes off clean, revealing plastic bones and ligaments. He spits it out. "You need to be prepared. You're juniors now. When you graduate and go off to Military training, it won't all be fun and games. Sure, some of you have been going to Camp since you were children, or doing Scouts, but the wild is something else. If you come across a real live Klujn out there, these skills can and will save your life."

The gym floor creaks as I enter. Mr. Mogel stops talking and looks at me, a gesture that's mirrored by twenty pairs of eyes. In the sea of identical uniforms, girls and boys are alike. I can't help but notice Coll—Mr. Mogel's nephew. He dwarfs everyone else, stocky and strong, with blond hair and a sadistic look in his pale-blue eyes. Next to Coll are his thugs, Dayn and Justine, who retain the look of their Indigenous heritage, not that there remains a whisper of their culture. They, like everyone else, are North American through and through. Both wear ruthless snarls and pendants of silver triangles around their necks.

Mr. Mogel leers at me. "Ava, glad you could make it. And thanks for volunteering to help me with the next part of the demonstration." I don't have a choice; I walk to the front of the room, backpack in hand. "Now, if you want to keep it clean and don't have a gun handy, most people go straight for the wrist, forcing the animal to drop whatever deadly weapon it may be holding." Mr. Mogel strikes my wrist and I drop my backpack. Out of the corner of my eye, I notice Mercy flinch.

"Or for the knees," continues Mr. Mogel, "making the creature crumple." The teacher kicks me below the knees and I fall on all fours, my face inches from the ground. He leans down and whispers in my ear, his breath hot on my neck. "Next time, if you don't want me to make an example out of you, don't be late."

My cheeks flush with embarrassment. And then, a wave of anger washes over me. Warm, prickly, uncontrollable. Before I can stop myself, I swing my legs around and knock the teacher down.

Mr. Mogel falls on his ass. The class is stunned into silence. The teacher takes a moment to recover, but the recovery isn't a physical one.

"I should fail you for that," he finally says, teeth clenched.

"Tiger Tail Sweep. Last week's homework," I tell him. "You can't fail me for learning."

* * *

We spend the rest of the class practicing new moves on each other. The fights are always safe. We stay inside the triangles of silver tape on the blue spring floor. There's no blood allowed and no broken bones. We wear red jerseys or blue ones, divided into sides, and rotate whenever Mr. Mogel blows his whistle. Most of the time Mercy and I pair off.

Mercy flips me on my back and the springy floor shudders beneath me. He straddles me and pins my arms down above my head. I act surprised, as though I didn't see this coming—truth is, I could fight him in my sleep. Behind the confident front, there's a boyish softness in his eyes. A trickle of self-doubt. It's as though he's flipping through the pages of the textbook in his mind. He's not in the present moment, reading me, his opponent, allowing his body to feel and react.

I make the most of his hesitancy. Buck my hips up, then swing my arms down with force. Mercy loses his grip and crumples on top of me. I grab his right arm, tug, and flip him onto his back. My hand finds his throat, my knee his crotch. I don't hurt him, even though I could.

"Aren't you hot?" Mercy asks me, nodding at my sweater. I'm damp at the pits and along my spine. We usually wear them in winter when we play sports outside. But it's easier to pretend my wardrobe is a choice, not a necessity.

"Worry about you. I'll worry about me," I say, jabbing my hand deeper into Mercy's throat. He splutters. I dig a little more, and his face turns the color of red cabbage.

"Okay, okay," he wheezes. "You win." I loosen my grip and let Mercy go. We stand back up, panting. My arms feel like jelly. Mercy looks faint. It takes a moment for the blood to return to the rest of his body.

Mr. Mogel walks past us. "Beaten by a girl," he smirks. Any joy I had over this fight extinguishes like a campfire in the rain. Mercy's cheeks flush with embarrassment.

"She's not a girl," he says. "She's a machine. She could take any of the guys here." The veins in my teacher's neck pulse. He looks around at the class, then blows his whistle. A clockwise rotation, and a wiry boy steps into my triangle. Mr. Mogel blows his whistle again. People look confused but oblige. Another rotation, and Coll takes the boy's place.

No. Not Coll. Anyone but him. I catch Mr. Mogel's eyes and curl my lip.

"This should be easy for you," Mr. Mogel says dryly. "Since you're made of metal." The rest of the class stops to watch. There's a flicker of fear in Mercy's eyes, a touch of guilt.

Coll is only a few inches taller than my five three, but what he lacks in height he makes up for in size, his blue jersey straining against fat and muscle. He gives a crooked twitch of a smile. So far this year I've managed to avoid getting him as my opponent, but there's no escaping him now.

"You want me to go easy on you?" he asks, wiping his sweaty brow on his sleeve. *Right. Like there's a charitable bone in your body.* Behind Coll, his sidekicks look on with voracious excitement.

"Please don't," I answer.

"Good. 'Cause I wasn't gonna."

"Ready?" says Mr. Mogel. "And . . . begin."

The only sound comes from the nervous shuffling of feet. My heart pounds in my chest, pumping adrenaline through my veins.

"Come on," Coll says. "I'll let you have the first hit." But I know better. The best self-defense is, after all, no fight at all.

He throws a swing at me and I duck out of the way. Another, and his knuckles graze my face. I throw a high kick at his ribs and he grabs my leg, twists me around, and whips me down like battle rope. My head smashes against the gymnasium floor, chin-first. I taste blood on my lips. Warm, metallic.

I sneak a glance at Mr. Mogel, wondering if his "no blood" rule still applies. He watches with an amused smile. *Guess not.*

"Don't make it too easy on me," Coll jests. He steps on the fingers of my left hand and presses down, hard. My knuckles crack. I grimace. It feels like my bones are shattering into a thousand pieces. "Did you break a nail?" he taunts, and the class laughs. He may be popular, that much is clear, but he's only popular because he's feared.

Coll increases the pressure, and blood rushes to the tips of my fingers. He grinds down with the tip of his shoe, and the nail on my left middle finger peels away from the skin. My face contorts in agony, but I don't want to give him the satisfaction of a scream, the glory of tears.

Mercy watches, arms crossed, shoulders hunched, nervously rocking onto the balls of his feet. He gives a cautionary shake of the head—*Don't do it, it's not worth it.* But I refuse to let Coll win.

I twist on my back and kick up, striking Coll between the legs. *Thud.* My foot sinks into soft flesh—he's so sure of himself, he didn't even wear a jockstrap. He doubles over with a curse, cupping his family jewels.

I manage to free my hand from under his shoe and stand up to face him. The pain continues to gnaw at my finger with sharp teeth.

Coll circles me like a shark. There's a look in his flat, blue eyes—like he hates me down to his core. Like he could kill me if we were alone. Maybe it's not me he hates, but the idea of losing. To a girl.

"You know what I want to know?" he asks, moving toward me. "Why you always wear that ugly sweater, even though it's like a million degrees in here." I ball my hands into protective fists. My nailless finger throbs with its own heartbeat as blood pools in my palm.

With surprising speed, Coll grabs my wrist and pulls me into him.

My back is forced against his front. He hooks his arm around my torso, crushing my stomach and breasts, and before I can defend myself he yanks up the sleeves of my sweater.

By the time I realize what's happening, it's already too late.

I face the wall of watching teens, exposed like a zoo animal without the luxury of a glass display. I see the fear and shock and disgust ripple across everyone's faces—even the teacher's. Words and whispers catch like a fire; small crackling flames at first, then burning fierce and hot and vulgar. They are staring at my forearms, which are covered in lurid scars, marking my skin like a tangle of ugly vines.

Compulsions. That was the diagnosis I received as a child. When I'd wake up in the middle of the night, kicking, screaming, and bloodied, having clawed the skin off my arms.

I was always picking, fidgeting, pulling at things, my hands full of this anxious, destructive energy. Doing art with Diana helped, but it was never enough. There was no cure, the doctors said, aside from ample sleep and exercise and *self-control.* But self-control was easier prescribed than done.

The laughter and the insults continue to fly, building in volume, hitting me with the force of a thousand punches. I catch the words *freak* and *sick* and *vile.* Mr. Mogel looks amused. Mercy, on the other hand, is mortified. He knows about my compulsions, but he hasn't seen my arms in years.

Another wave of anger washes over me.

I manage to break free from Coll's grip. He lunges, but this time I'm ready. I duck under him, then pull his shoulders back and send one strong kick into his butt. He flies through the barricade of our snickering classmates—which parts—and crashes straight into the Klujn dummy. In an attempt to regain balance, he grabs at it, and they stumble together in an awkward dance before landing on the floor, Coll on top of the dummy, looking like they've been caught doing what most teenagers do behind closed doors. *Everyone except me*, I think.

The class explodes. Now Coll's at the center of the solar system, and I'm grateful to have escaped unharmed. The only pair of eyes still on me are my brother's—sad, frightened. The kind of sad and frightened that walks hand in hand with love and worry. I wish he'd mind his own business.

I pull my sleeves back down and grab my backpack. Don't care that the class isn't over. If I stay, or if I so much as open my mouth, I might burst out crying, and emotion isn't something you should ever show in public.

No one says a word as I leave, except Coll. He sits up, rubbing his ribs. His forehead is bruised, his ego even more so. "I'll get you back for that," he says. And the look on his face tells me he means it.

I walk down the hallway, past a row of identical navy blue posters with silver words:

REPORT UNUSUAL BEHAVIOR

A message from the Department of Societal Order

Finally, I reach the girls' restroom. It's empty. With the stall door closed and locked behind me, I let out the sob I was keeping in. Better to show your weakness to four walls and a toilet, because, around here, the strong prey on the weak.

3

Pull yourself together. I wrap my finger in toilet paper, change into my regular school uniform and slap cold water on my face, wiping away all traces of the fight. I manage to make it through Science unscathed. Whatever people have heard about my scars, I stay far enough away that their whispers don't reach me.

Next is Home Studies, a girls-only class, where we learn about child care and how to sew things with different stitches. Cross-stitch, zigzag stitch, blanket stitch. Today, we bake nourishing cakes for the boys to take with them to Hunter's Camp. It's a tradition, and traditions don't change.

In fourth period History, Mr. Verywell reads monotonously from a textbook by the pioneers of our modern world, *Quest, Logic, and Frost: A Brief History of Our Territory.* The teacher has a cloud of shockingly white hair on his head that contrasts his dark skin, and he wears the same blue turtleneck no matter the season. He tells us for the hundredth time that the United States and Canada used to be separate countries. That the land on which we stand once belonged to Québec—the French-speaking province of Canada—with the US border about a three-hour drive from here, just south of the capital, Mission Creek. When soil became fallow and food became scarce, the One World Treaty was created—a global incentive that vouched to put the environment before the economy—but it was too little, too late. The United States withdrew and merged with Canada, joining forces and resources and severing ties with the outside world.

But, as it turns out, the enemy can also come from within. What followed was a period that people have since dubbed "A War against God," because only God is powerful enough to do such things. God's wrath led to rising temperatures, warming oceans, dying reefs, melting ice, the thawing of the permafrost, and a mass extinction that wiped out most of the animal kingdom and their habitats. New viruses, wildfires, tornadoes, floods, and droughts made the headlines on a weekly basis. Things were so dire that they stopped registering—news of death tolls in the millions earned only a shrug of the shoulders and a roll of the eyes.

Religious groups abandoned their faith and churches were burned down. People began fighting over the most basic resources, like clean water and arable soil. The price of meat, dairy, and produce skyrocketed. When the cities' water supplies became restricted, most people fled to rural areas, where, if they were lucky, they could claim a plot of land with its own water source.

To prevent cyberattacks from the outside world, internet use was confined to the government, and technology returned to its origins: televisions, radios, landline telephones. There were no more credit cards, and a new currency was created: tokens.

Scarcity led to famine, which led to fear: fear of a changing world, fear of thieves, fear of outsiders with different *ideas*. Small townships were formed, like Red River, but even then it was every family for themselves. Every mouth for itself. Death tolls reached the hundreds of millions. Bodies were left in the street or tossed into unmarked graves. Humanity teetered on the brink of extinction—a walking skeleton with a hunger as big as mountains.

And then we discovered Klujns.

I say "we," but I'm just quoting the textbook, because all this happened decades ago, when Diana and George were my age.

Klujns had the power to save us.

Township squares became the new temples, Executioners the new priests, and spit roasts a mass that everyone attended when a Klujn was found wandering on the wrong side of the fences.

Without Klujns, humans would be long gone by now. We have Grouse to thank for giving our species a second chance. Day by day, raid by raid, he is saving us from famine, and they say famine is a pretty terrible way to die. Because it happens slowly, long enough to bring out the darkest in mankind. Soon—*repopulation.*

Naturally, Klujns have become a Territory-wide obsession, something that people both venerate and fear, because so much about them remains shrouded in mystery. Are they like archaic humans—Neanderthals or *Homo floresiensis*—or are they more like animals? A morbid hybrid of the two, perhaps. And what are their claws *really* used for? Why are their eyes colored like that?

"Most technological advances halted in the aftermath of Klujn discovery," Mr. Verywell says now. "Or, rather, technology focused on the exploration of this new, elusive species."

The bell rings.

* * *

It's last period. We are all restless in our seats. Mercy and I sit three rows back from the front.

Words on the board read: *Professor Sparrow. Klujnology 101.*

Klujnology has quickly become my favorite class because, in the sanctuary of George's domain, I am safe from the Colls and Mr. Mogels of the world. Even though we're not related by blood, he has always treated me like a daughter.

"Klujns are nomadic creatures," says George from the front of the classroom. "They live in settlements of a few hundred. They move seasonally, sometimes annually, and need to do so for survival. However, the fences have limited Klujn migrations—called *karavans*—and, as a result, their behavior has become more unpredictable."

As my father speaks, I doodle in my notebook with coloring pens—a red sun perched above a forest, mirroring the one outside the window.

I press a little too hard and the tip of my pen bursts like an aneurysm, leaking a big glob of ink on my hand.

"Klujns are highly adaptable creatures," continues George. My father has shaggy brown hair, streaks of gray in his beard, and an almost-imperceptible limp that he got from a rogue bullet to his right Achilles tendon—and just like that, his days of fieldwork were over. His cane leans against the desk, within reach. His eyes sparkle like a green lagoon, hinting at hidden depths. "They can make a home in almost any environment—at high altitudes, in hot deserts, humid jungles, freezing-cold tundra and taiga, perched on high treetops, even underground. They build infrastructures that blend meticulously with their surroundings, and can cultivate plants in any climate and much more rapidly than we can, thanks in large part to the minerals in their claws—their *viațăs*." He pronounces the word *vee-AH-tah*.

Mercy passes me his notebook, where he has started a game of Hanging Klujn: five dashes on a white page, like a running stitch of black thread. We've been avoiding what happened in first period, but I know the matter is still very much on my brother's mind. I dread the moment he decides to say these uncomfortable things out loud. Some dark rooms should not be filled with light.

"You shouldn't have challenged Coll like that," mutters Mercy. "Who knows what that thug is capable of."

"He deserved it," I mutter back.

"That's what bullies want. They want you to fight back."

"So what was I meant to do?" I ask. "Lie there like a beached whale?" I pick a new pen—this one magenta—and draw an *A*. Mercy draws the outline of a Klujn hanging upside down.

"All I'm saying is . . . it's a dangerous game." I write a *C* and Mercy draws a rope around the Klujn's ankles. Next, an *E*, and he scratches the letter above the first and third dashes.

"Enemy," I say, and my brother defeatedly fills in the blanks. A moment passes. The silence between us feels tense, the way it does when the weight of unsaid things remains.

Then, he finally says it: "I thought your episodes had stopped."

"They did," I say quickly. "Sometimes they come back, but they're under control."

"That didn't look under control to me."

Mind your own business, I think. A boy like Mercy could never understand what it's like to be in my skin—a boy so grounded and good.

"Eyes to the front," says George, giving us a look that says, *No special treatment just because you're mine.* I'm grateful for the interruption.

Just to irritate Mercy, I press my ink-stained hand on his notebook page, leaving a perfect red handprint. He snaps the notebook shut in retaliation, and we turn back to face our father.

George dims the lights and a projector buzzes to life, casting him in a spectral glow. Images of Klujns stare at us from the front of the room, with their sharp crystal claws and hypnotic colored eyes.

"Let's recap what we covered last month: the peculiar anatomy of Klujns. Their strong bodies, distinct cheekbones, and—who could forget—their notorious claws. Klujns are born without fingernails. Their baby claws grow during adolescence, at around sixteen or seventeen years of age, when they begin to transition into adulthood. After a few months these fall out, like milk teeth, and their adult claws take their place."

Next slide.

"We went over the diversity found among Klujn tribes," George says. "From their unusual customs to their skin pigmentation and eye color. Like species of trees in a forest, different tribes have different characteristics. Unlike *Homo sapiens*, who all originate from the African Territory, *Homo arcanum*—Klujns—are believed to have come from the Carpathian mountain range in the European Territory."

"Then how did they get here?" asks a girl behind me. Without even turning around, I know it's Reesa, the class know-it-all. The cadence of her voice gets on my nerves.

"How did humans?" George answers. "This happened over twenty thousand years ago, during the last glacial maximum when sea levels were lower. It's presumed that Klujns crossed over the Laurentide Ice sheet, migrating first to Greenland, then descending into the Boreal and the rest of the Americas. Where most *Homo sapiens* built cities and developed sedentary agricultural societies, Klujns remained nomadic, staying far away from any human community. Even separate tribes rarely mix, which is why you can tell where a Klujn is from based on its features.

"How they managed to remain hidden for so long and why they didn't make contact with us are questions we constantly ask ourselves." His voice is charged with excitement. "Some evidence actually suggests that Klujns may have been discovered earlier than we think. That they had contact with the French and the Indigenous Peoples who lived here, decades before the North American Territory was founded by Grouse's father, Pepito Silver, but that it was the arrival of the new colonists—*us*—that drove them deeper into the wild, far away from any human footprint."

George trails off as a blue fly buzzes in front of him.

"Where was I?" he asks, as the insect flies off and settles on a nearby windowpane. "Oh, yes, Klujn interaction with French and Indigenous Peoples. But this is just hearsay," he adds. "Propaganda." The excitement he had only a moment ago is gone. George moves to the next slide, the clicker clenched in his hand, his knuckles white.

"In our last class, we talked about some of President Grouse's most famous Klujn raids—Estrella, an island tribe with violet eyes, discovered off the eastern tip of the Gaspesia peninsula. Zonia's bright-green-eyed swamp Klujns, and Raynn's yellow-eyed desert Klujns. Before the break, we're going to be looking at—any guesses?"

Silence. George clicks to the next slide, a hand-drawn but incredibly lifelike illustration of a Klujn settlement. It looks beautiful but sinister. Tents are scattered over a pine-forested hill, at the top of which looms a large black arena that looks like an old circus big top. It glows menacingly under a red full moon.

"This is Circo. A cold-climate tribe in the Deeper Woods, home to light-skinned, red-eyed mountain Klujns. Rumored to be one of the largest and most vicious human-eating tribes in the Boreal, but no one can be sure, because no one has even gotten *close* to finding it."

Click. An image of a round circus ring in a black-and-red striped tent. The black ground is covered in human remains. A few students shield their eyes, but I lean in closer.

"Even with advancements in cyborg-dog and cyborg-horse technology, drones, and more Hunting missions than ever, Circo has always managed to evade us," continues George. "They, like all Klujn tribes, are moon-worshippers. They live by the moon's cycles, which is why the Blood Race always happens in the days leading up to the October Blood Moon or, as we humans call it, the Hunter's Moon."

Next, a map of the North American Territory. The devastating inferno of the South, the swamplands and floodlands of the East, the dust bowls of the West. Just northeast of the Great Lakes is the habitable land we call home. Around the Territory, dashed lines show pockets of human settlements. Above us is one long fence, dividing us from that vast expanse of Klujn land still unexplored. The Boreal.

George uses his cane as a pointer. "Circo is believed to originate from the upper Boreal, slowly migrating south."

"Where are they now?" Reesa butts in.

"If I had the answer to that question, I would be a very rich man," George smiles. "No one knows for sure, but we can speculate." He moves his cane down, settling on an expanse of mountains in the Deeper Woods, not too far from Red River. "They may be closer than we think," he says, and the class buzzes with nervous excitement.

"What makes them so hard to find?" the girl next to Reesa asks.

"They're masters of disguise," George tells her. "Some experts believe that Klujns' unique eyesight enables them to see colors that humans can't. That they use these 'invisible colors' to hide in plain sight."

"How can a color be invisible?" Reesa wants to know.

"All animals see the world a little differently. Human eyes contain three types of color-detecting cells, called cones, while Klujns have four. The function of these extra cones is unknown, but it may have something to do with night vision. Where human eyes see only shades of gray at night, Klujn eyesight possibly enables them to see bright colors even in the dark. Leading scientists to the popular belief that they are nocturnal—"

"If they're so hard to find, how do we know so much about them?" a boy cuts in.

"They have nomadic tendencies, meaning they move around. Aside from the raids, everything we know about Klujns comes from the clues they've left behind. This is how we've been able to know what they call their tribes. It's also how we know that Circo is one of the most violent tribes; in their abandoned settlements we've found evidence of cannibalism, macabre altars, and human sacrifice." Someone gasps.

"In this class, we'll take a look at what makes Circo Klujns unique," continues George. "Their strength and athleticism, their bloodlust, as well as their impressive memories . . ."

"Can a Klujn reproduce with a human?" Reesa's friend asks.

"Pretty sure that's bestiality," Reesa chides.

"A legitimate question, Lilly," says my father. "But the answer is a definitive *no*. If a human and a Klujn could produce fertile offspring, that would mean they belonged to the same species. Now, we won't cover mating rituals until later this year. And unless you want to stay here over the holidays, there will be no more questions until the end of class."

Everyone settles down, and George continues the lesson.

"A belief shared by many people is that circuses, old-fashioned freak shows, and werewolf mythology were inspired by ancient contact with Klujns," says George. "This is due to their love of spectacle and their nomadic ways, as well as their relationship with animals and the moon. Fun fact: the name 'Circo' comes from the Latin *circus*, and the Greek *kirkos*, which shows us that Klujns are curious about human languages."

"My boyfriend just started Military training," I hear Reesa say in an undertone. "He went on his first mission last week. They saw a Carniflora."

"What's that?" Lilly asks, rapt.

"They're these black trees in the Deeper Woods that eat humans alive," says Reesa. People nearby start to listen in, and she enjoys the attention. "If you get too close, they trap you with their roots. Their thorny branches have roses that release a toxin that basically digests humans alive. It's like getting slow-cooked by acid."

Lilly shudders. "That's sick."

"It's the truth," Reesa answers matter-of-factly.

I turn my head a fraction and look out the window. Three stories down, the Klujn Fair is being set up in the streets surrounding Hunter's Square. We have one every year on Hunter's Day. In the middle of the square—which shouldn't be called a square because it's shaped like a triangle—there's a gargantuan statue of Grouse. A bird has shit on his head, so there must be birds hiding away somewhere. The statue overlooks a gallows on a podium where Klujns are hung if they're caught on our land. I've never been to a live execution, only seen them on television, but I've heard there's nothing quite like it; after the Klujn is set ablaze, the township's people feast all night.

"Because of their European origins, Klujn dialects resemble some of the human romance languages, namely French, Romanian, and Esperanto, which all have roots in Latin."

My father's voice continues, but nothing he says is of much interest to me. I want to hear the real facts. The things they teach at Military training, or that Hunters get to see *out there*. What could be so shocking? Is the forest as scary as they say it is?

In the distance, the canopy of the forest sways in the wind. I can almost hear it, the papery brush of the leaves, like voices whispering secrets.

The moon is rising now. It looks like a dull gray coin in the afternoon sky. I can tell by its shape that it's about five days away from being full. I feel a tugging inside me, like a magnet moving into range and pulling me—but where, toward what?

George continues. "Although these fascinating specimens can speak, we cannot forget that our distant cousins are fierce, merciless beasts. We may have the same genus, *Homo*, which places us in the same family, biologically speaking. But families are very large. We have about as much in common with Klujns as we had with chimpanzees before they went extinct. Klujns are—in one word—savage. They don't feel love or empathy like we do. And, if you were standing in front of one, it wouldn't hesitate to kill you."

4

Hunter's Square is crowded with families, the adults and teenagers dressed in the traditional Hunter's garb—bomber jackets, dark gray shirts tucked into matching camouflage pants, and curved knives in their belts. There's the fanfare of carnival music and rides. Children run around, chasing one another, wearing scary Klujn masks that glow in the dark and fake plastic claws clipped to the tips of their fingers.

It's not even six, but the sun is already low, the sky beginning to darken. Hundreds of colored lights flicker on. I lock my longboard at the entrance near the buses being loaded with Camp supplies, and Mercy and I go down a row of identical gray tents.

I've changed out of my school uniform; now my skin can breathe. I wear a soft white sweater that Diana knitted, a blue corduroy skirt with gold vintage buttons, brown tights, and my favorite pumpkin-leather boots, made from last year's jack-o'-lanterns.

"We shouldn't be here," Mercy says.

"We don't have to stay long," I answer, pulling my brother into one of the tents. The inside is a wonderland of Klujn merchandise. They have everything from masks to heat-activated mugs to starry lamps that project the real night sky. There are Klujn-detecting binoculars and walkie-talkies and crystal trinkets. The crystals must be fake though, because real ones are too precious and rare to be exhibited at a township fair. A candy rack sells maple popcorn and spun caramel and chocolates shaped like eyeballs, wrapped in shiny cellophane.

"Check this out." I show Mercy a little bottle of eye drops. *Now in seven colors*, the label reads. I take the lid off and squeeze a few drops into my eyes, then look into the small mirror they've hung on the wall. Mercy peers over my shoulder. I blink once, and my eyes turn neon red. Again; they turn yellow. Once more, and they turn bright green. Then I blink twice, and they go back to brown. "That's so cool," I say excitedly.

"It's creepy, that's what it is. Save your tokens for something else." He walks out of the tent. Deflated, I place the bottle back on the shelf and follow him.

We walk down Sideshow Alley, where people play games for prizes. A boy shoots at Klujn holograms that glow in an ultraviolet forest. A burly woman throws an ax at a large stuffed bear. A middle-aged man swings a bat down at a target and a pulse of light shoots up a tower, measuring his strength. It lands somewhere between *Human* and *Klujn*.

I notice Coll and his thugs at another sideshow booth, along with his parents and Mr. Mogel. They all wear the Hunter's uniform, and the men have rifles strapped around their shoulders. In the booth, little birds are tied to strings. They flap their wings furiously, trying to escape, to no avail. Coll cocks his right arm, then hurls the knife with impressive speed. It hits a bird and pins it to the backboard in a puff of blood and feathers.

"Did you see that?" Coll crows. "Got it right in the neck!"

"We should go home," Mercy tells me. "It's almost sundown. Dinner will be ready soon, and I still have to finish packing."

"A bit longer," I plead. "I'm going to be so bored when you leave." Mercy doesn't answer. He looks distracted. "Are you excited for Camp?" I ask him.

"Sure." There's a shadow across his face. I know my brother, know when his mind is elsewhere.

"What's wrong?"

"I wish I didn't have to go," he admits. "I want to join the Military when I grow up, not be a Hunter. But everyone goes to Hunter's Camp, so if I don't go, I look like I'm afraid or something."

"Every *boy* goes," I correct him. "In case you forgot, girls aren't allowed."

"Girls can be Scouts," Mercy says.

"Scouts hardly ever get to leave the township. And even then, Diana and George won't let me sign up."

"You're lucky. I wish I could spend the next week at home doing nothing." The words hit me like cold water. Like my staying home is a choice, or cowardice? I would give my right arm to leave this township for one day. To see even just a small sliver of the Territory, but I can't, because I'm a girl. I didn't choose this body, but the Territory has chosen for me every single day.

"There's something else," Mercy says. He looks around then lowers his voice. "I heard Mom and Dad arguing. There's a rumor . . . that we might be going on a real mission. Out *there*." He nods in the direction of the fence. "Apparently there's a raid attempt coming up and the Hunters need all the help they can get."

"Really?" All of my senses are on alert. Mercy nods distractedly, but I can tell that he's afraid. More afraid than he'll ever admit. "You just turned seventeen," I say. "You haven't even passed your rifle test."

Yes, I'm worried for him, but I'm jealous, too. I wish we could trade places. While he and George are away, doing something meaningful and exciting, I'll be spending the next week alone with Diana and the aura of despair that follows her around. Gardening and cooking and canning our preserves, making enough apple-rosemary jam and pickled jalapeños and beetroot-leaf pesto to last through the winter.

"You're lucky," he says again.

"Yeah," I mutter. "Lucky me."

A breeze touches us, its crisp undertones signaling the beginning of fall. We still have four seasons, but only just—the summers are long and hot, the winters equally long and cold, with ephemeral shoulder seasons in between. The leaves have barely started changing color, but the first snow will fall in no more than a few weeks.

"Food?" I ask my brother, eager to lighten the mood. Mercy nods, although he's still far away, like his anxiety is its own island surrounded by waves the size of abandoned high-rises. He follows me into Hunter's Square, where rows of trucks sell street food, mainly small game caught by local poachers in Tremble Hills—the small natural reservoir on our side of the fences. There's squirrel-on-a-stick, stuffed frog legs, sweet-and-salty sparrow, pulled porcupine, and skewers of roasted chipmunks and deep-fried chicken hearts.

I walk up to a food truck and order bug fries. The clerk hands me a paper bouquet, oil seeping through the black-and-white motif of grass-hoppers.

"Mom's going to be mad if you spoil your appetite," says Mercy.

"Please," I retort. "Whatever I do, she's always mad." I pop a crunchy golden fry into my mouth. It tastes so good, unlike the healthy food Diana always has us eating. Mercy and I continue down the brightly lit alley, past a Klujn photo booth where two teenagers come out, laughing at the little images in their hands. Mercy steals one of my fries. I shove him away and he comes in for a second. "Get your own!" I say, pulling the bouquet away from him. He finally manages a smile.

I look around at the families and the kids our age. Coll drifts into my vision, clutching a giant plush toy he won at the bird stand. He throws it in a trash can as he and his friends walk up to a food truck selling fox ribs.

"I can't wait to get out of here," I sigh.

"And go where?" asks Mercy.

"Don't you feel suffocated?"

He looks at me like I'm speaking a foreign language. "Why would I feel suffocated? This is home."

"*Your* home," I correct him. "I've never felt at home here."

"Maybe if you weren't so shy, you'd have more friends."

"I'm not shy," I snap. "I just don't feel like myself around these people." It frustrates me, the word *shy*. An easy label to slap on someone who doesn't take up as much room as everybody else. I know I'm not as social as some of the kids in our class, but I'm hardly a fragile feather that the wind can blow around. I feel confident in movement—in Combat class, or walking in the woods by our house, or when I'm making art. It's only around people that I shrink into myself. I don't remember much about my life before George brought me home from the orphanage six years ago, but it's not a series of images that remain. Rather, it's a feeling, like opening up is something that must be done with caution.

"I don't need any friends," I say.

"That's what people who don't have friends say to make themselves feel better about being alone."

"That's mean."

"It's true."

"I just don't have anything in common with anyone here."

"Because you're *different*." That word. It hurts more than *shy*. It crushes me like a tumbling boulder, but how can I blame my brother? This is the language that he has grown up speaking, where *different* means bad and dangerous, because one must protect their little plot of land—at all costs.

This is why I hide my arms.

The moon glows a muddied gray, the color of mist and indecision. It always seems blurry, like it's behind fogged glass. I don't know what it is about tonight that's got me thinking about the future, but the question mark of the future has been on my mind a lot lately. Maybe it's the cyclical nature of the seasons; the death that fall brings. Another year almost gone, and this feeling of discontent only continues to grow inside me. Seeing everyone here, gathered around and celebrating, only echoes the loneliness I feel. I want my branches to grow higher, want my roots to spread deeper. But this sandbox of a town is just too small, my growth stunted by dirt roads and dead forests that only lead to barbed wire.

Not a day goes by where I don't wake up yearning for adventure. There's a constant tightness in my chest, an itch in my legs like they're not legs but colonies of ants.

"Don't you want more?" I ask my brother.

"More than what?" he asks.

"Than this," I say, gesturing to the fair, our town, its inhabitants. "Than school and marriage and a lifetime of hard work. Than one kid and retirement and *happily ever after* until we die."

"I can have two kids if I work a Military job. And everyone dies eventually." He just doesn't get it.

"But we're not robots!" I tell him. "It's like our whole lives are a series of boxes waiting to be ticked. For example: What am I going to do after I graduate?"

"Military training."

"What if I don't want to do that?"

It's clear from his face that now I'm the one who doesn't get it. "Ava— you don't have a choice. It's mandatory. Plus, the Military has loads of options that are safe for girls."

"I don't want *safe*," I bark. "And I don't want to spend my life in a uniform."

"Then work in a Greenhouse or a Loudhouse, like Mom did."

"And spend my days scrubbing blood off the floors? No thanks."

"Maybe you could work in the Breedingroom. I heard it's really interesting. And you get to take young kanum home sometimes."

I don't want to end up like Diana. Joyless, sour Diana. Not that I'm particularly joyful now.

"If you work for Grouse until you're fifty you can retire with a good pension," Mercy says. "You get organ coverage, limb replacement in case of accidents, cyborg service dogs. And the dental insurance is great."

"I like my teeth the way they are," I say. I hate that I can count my non-Military, non-Hunter options on one hand: Home Studies teacher, nurse, Greenhouse worker, child carer, mother.

What else is there? Coll's mother is a butcher. I could run a little shop in the township. Sell candy or fireworks. The idea of doing any of these things makes me want to gouge my eyes out with a freshly sharpened pencil. Am I being unreasonable in wanting more?

"Maybe I'll apply for a travel permit," I say dreamily. "Move to the coast. Be a painter, or an archaeologist, or a marine biologist . . ."

"Ava."

"What?"

"Those last two aren't jobs for girls. And painting isn't a job at all." Mercy looks around, suddenly on edge. "You shouldn't speak like that. 'Specially not with so many people around." Then, he adds, "We shouldn't even be here."

We've come to a stop outside a small box office. A rectangle of yellow lightbulbs frame a sign that reads: COLISÉA. Beneath it, more words: *Come inside and see a real live Klujn! Admission: 18+ only.* Behind the box office is the entrance of a passageway that leads to an impressive blue pyramid. A few people trickle in, pushing through a turnstile.

This is, perhaps subconsciously, where my feet were leading me ever since we got here. We've never had a Coliséa in Red River. They usually visit the larger townships to the southeast, along the river. Ours is too small and too far north, at the end of the road, right before the electricity blinks out.

"We're underage," says Mercy, recognizing the dangerous expression on my face. "We're not allowed in there."

"They probably don't even check ID," I say, refusing to let him kill my excitement. "Come on. There's no harm in trying."

I go to the box office, my heart thumping in my chest. I wonder if the rumors are true. If there's a real live Klujn in there. "One, please," I tell the clerk.

"Twenty tokens." I try to stop my hands from trembling as I reach into my pocket and pull out a twenty-token bill. Grouse's face smiles at me from the silver-colored note. I hand the clerk my entire month's allowance, but he's already bored with me. He stamps my wrist. "Show starts in five."

I turn to look at Mercy, who hasn't moved a muscle. "You know Mom would ground you forever if she knew," he tells me.

"Who's going to tell her?" I ask. "You?" Then I add, "Aren't you the least bit curious?"

"Not really, no."

"Don't be a coward," I tease. Mercy's demeanor shifts at that word. "That's mean."

"It's true," I throw his line back at him. Mercy doesn't answer. "Oh, come on. I'm only joking," I say, but it's too late. When Mercy gets offended, he withdraws inside himself, somewhere irretrievable, like a coin dropped down a storm drain. I wish he didn't have to take every-thing so seriously.

"Do what you want," he says, his voice flat. "I'll see you at home."

"Mercy!" I call out, but he's already disappearing into the crowd. *Let him brood*, I think. I know I should follow him, but my curiosity is too strong, so I push through the turnstile and step inside.

5

My eyes take a moment to adjust to the dark. Exhibits hang on either side, glowing like jewels in glass boxes. The people that entered before me are already halfway down the passageway. I know I shouldn't be here, that I'm too young, but the thought of having all this knowledge at my fingertips is too exciting a notion to resist.

I peer into the first display, where a costume hangs. The costume is crimson, embedded with what looks like rubies. A golden sun crown is perched above it. A nearby plaque reads:

> A traditional costume worn by a female Klujn
> during the Blood Race, which takes place on the
> first Blood Moon after its first claws come in.

I catch a glimpse of my reflection—for a split second, it almost looks like I'm wearing the costume. I take a small step back, then stop, lean in again. The image on the glass is not grotesque like I would have imagined. There's something almost . . . *regal* about it.

I realize that I am completely alone in the tunnel now. Time is slipping by. There's still a lot to see and not much time.

I hurry on, peering in at the other exhibits. There are copper-colored moon masks, wax models of hands with claw replicas, and photographs of dark forest scenes. There are dried flowers and wooden utensils and other curious items—objects belonging to strange animals. As I walk down the tunnel, I read up about the Deeper Woods and occult rituals and secret trails. One placard explains that Klujns mark their territory by blocking paths with dried entrails. *A place no human should ever wander*, the description reads, *unless they desire never to return.*

Then, from down the end of the corridor, a voice booms: "Ladies and *gentlemen!*"

Not wanting to miss the show, I walk quickly past the remaining exhibits with regret, emerging into the brightly lit Coliséa.

I blink a few times until I get my bearings. Packed bleachers surround the sandy triangular stage, which is easily eighty feet across. Most of Red River's adults are here, and some from the neighboring townships as well. Several hundred people, drinking beer and eating beaver dogs, their fingers stained with grease, mustard dripping onto their shirts. Even though I just ate, the smell of popcorn and salted pretzels makes my mouth water. Vendors walk around selling Klujn-tamer figurines and clear latex balls on sticks wrapped in multi-colored lights. Others twist long, thin, colorful balloons into hands with exaggerated claws.

I try to keep a low profile, not wanting to be recognized, even though I doubt anyone here knows who I am. A woman bumps into me, forcing me against the wooden railing that separates the crowd from the stage.

A male ringmaster in a blue costume stands at a podium with a microphone. "I give you"—a drumroll sounds—"Elios Tonnerre!"

The crowd erupts as the man steps out on stage. He wears a silky gray Klujn-taming suit, his face covered by an Executioner's expressionless mask: blue with silver triangles under the eyes. In his scarred hand, he holds a long spear with a wickedly sharp crystal tip. If it's real, like my pendant, it must be worth a fortune.

The Klujn tamer circles the arena, raising his spear to the eager crowd.

"And his opponent," continues the ringmaster, and the crowd's cheering lowers to a simmer. "From the tropical island tribe of Estrella . . .

hungry as ever for the meat on your bones . . . ladies and gentlemen—
BONAVENTURA!!!"

An assistant comes out, pulling on a metal leash that clanks. At the
end of which is a . . .

Real.

Live.

Klujn.

My jaw hangs open. *It's nothing like the dummy from Combat class.*

The Klujn is female. Its body is of average human proportions, thin
but muscular, with torrential brown hair the color of hazelnuts, tangled
in knots. It has pronounced cheekbones and piercing purple eyes that
glow brighter than any human color. Its skin is a pale pecan brown, darkly
freckled; its claws are long and clear with a murky shimmer to them,
sharper than any knife in Diana's kitchen. Draped in scruffy rags, its body
isn't hairy, but its spine is slightly curved, like a werewolf midtransition.
Unlike the Klujn tamer, it doesn't wear a mask. One scar leaks from the
middle of each eye, like permanent tears, marring its smooth face.

It's not the creature's anatomy that makes it look pure animal, but
the wildness in its eyes.

Purple eyes—that's Estrella.

Now I understand what George was saying in class: we may share
the same genus, but the thing in front of me is not human at all.

I'm filled with an exhilarating sort of terror—my palms are wet, my
mouth dry, my mind thrown into confusion. It doesn't feel real, and yet
it's unfolding before my very eyes. I begin to regret where I am standing. If it decides to charge, there isn't a whole lot I can do other than
brace myself for impact.

The assistant tugs on the leash, which is tied to a transparent collar
around the Klujn's neck. When they reach center stage, the assistant un-
hooks the chain and presses a button on the collar, which floods with
a rippling green current.

Elios Tonnerre faces the animal, his chest broad with machismo and
confidence. His costume is striking and elegant in comparison to the
creature's rags. His eerie mask has two black holes for eyes.

The ringmaster announces that the fight will consist of three rounds of three minutes, in which the Klujn tamer must try to kill the beast in any way possible, or he can aim for an infinitesimal point on its collar for bonus points. A mechanical horn sounds and a timer begins to count down from three minutes. The crowd is abuzz.

I shouldn't be here, I think, feeling the cold grip of anxiety tighten around my heart, wringing it like a wet towel. But I can't leave. Not now.

The three minutes unfold in a blur. The Klujn tamer circles his opponent, trying to stab it with his spear. He aims for the collar but misses. With every attempt, the Klujn becomes more agitated until, finally, it snaps.

In a burst of astonishing strength, the creature pounces on the Klujn tamer and knocks the spear out of his hand. Elios Tonnerre is thrown to the ground. The animal's jaw snaps open, showing razor-sharp teeth made for cutting through thick flesh. *Human* flesh. With a swipe of its claws, the Klujn splits the warrior's mask. The crowd gasps. With a ravenous bite, the Klujn takes a sizable chunk out of the man's unprotected forearm. Veins and muscles are exposed to the horrified crowd.

The creature is so wild, like nothing I have ever seen. Its strength, its animosity—both live up to every story I have ever heard about their kind. I shouldn't watch, but I can't stop. I don't want to see what happens next, yet I must.

The attack continues, but the Klujn tamer is losing. The crowd begins to chant: "Finish it, finish it, finish it . . ."

Elios Tonnerre's blood-slick fingers reach out and fumble for his spear. Then, as the timer on the wall shows that the first three minutes are soon to expire, it happens.

The Klujn tamer's hand closes around the spear. He drives the tip up into the creature's collar, locking into the exact spot he needed to strike.

As the spear makes contact, the band of green light turns an angry, violent red. An electric current shoots into the Klujn's body and the beast is thrown into the air in an impressive arc toward me. I shield myself, but the creature crashes to the ground about twenty feet away. It writhes, the electric current so strong that its skin begins to sizzle, bubbling and popping like molten lava. A hair-raising shriek escapes its lips. It is the most violent thing I have ever seen. And from so close.

My excitement wanes and nausea rushes in.

I try to push out of the crowd, but there are too many bodies, all yelling, all chanting, possessed in their excitement. They shove me forward again, crushing me against the barrier. My eyes are drawn back to the sandy pit, where the still-twitching thing's head flops to the side. Its expression is no longer malicious, but that of an animal that is far past distress—one that wishes to be put out of its misery.

I feel trapped, like the crowd is squashing me. Like the walls are closing in.

I fight my way out, not taking no for an answer this time, pushing through until I'm finally outside. The fresh night air and moonlight whip my face. I inhale, feeling soothed by it, grateful to be out and away and alone again.

The sun has set and the sky is already dark. "Shit," I mutter, remembering Diana's curfew. I hurry until I've left the crowds of families and the cacophony of children's screams behind, until I've reached the exit and the buses and the Military road that leads out of town.

I unlock my longboard and step aboard, one foot at a time, a balancing act. A tap with my foot in front and the board's blue LED lights illuminate the road. The motor hums to life.

As I travel down the dark road toward home, I'm calmed by the vibrations that run through my legs. The wheel spins and the motor makes a loud rattle, but it's not loud enough to drown out the memory of the cheering crowd and the look in the Klujn's eyes. The image returns—its thrashing, blistering body. *Not it*, I think. *She.*

I tap my board twice to pick up speed, but it's barely faster than a brisk walk. My lungs feel shallow, like no matter how much air I breathe in, I can never get enough. I thought it would be exciting to see a Klujn. Now I find myself wishing I'd listened to Diana.

I continue down the road, the headlights of my board barely penetrating the thick dark. I lean my weight backward and the tire swerves left, down the private gravel road that leads toward my house.

I have almost reached the driveway when my headlights illuminate three bodies.

I tap my foot and the board stops moving. The motor sputters and dies. The three figures are dressed in matching Hunter's clothes, wearing glow-in-the-dark Klujn masks that show only their eyes and mouths. The one in the middle smirks. I recognize his lips, his teeth, that crooked twitch of a smile. It's Coll.

And we are alone now.

6

The night is silent. There are no streetlights and it's almost pitch-black. I glance behind me, wondering if I can go the other way, go back where I came from, but my board is battered and slow and any attempt would only make them laugh. I can't ride around them, because the road dips down into a ditch where there are dense weeds, stinging nettles, and other poisonous plants.

"What do you want?" I ask, trying to keep my voice steady, but there's a quiver there, something high-pitched that makes me sound younger than my age. Coll lifts his mask and the others do the same. Dayn. Justine. No surprises there. They stand shoulder to shoulder with their ringleader, all of them built like bison.

"Didn't anyone ever tell you it's dangerous to ride alone in the dark?" Coll says. He must've seen me at the fair, and plotted his revenge for Combat class. Even though he humiliated me, I got the last laugh.

"Can you get to the point?" I try to sound bolder this time but I realize that I am afraid, I'm terrified. "I don't want violence."

Coll's smirk evaporates. He and his friends exchange brief whispers, then walk toward me. I hop off my board and hold it up in front of myself like a shield.

"Look at her," Justine taunts, her mocking smile parting her lips to reveal a set of broken teeth. "Like that piece of junk would protect you against the wind." She pries the board out of my hands and throws it against a tree. It snaps in half. Falls on a sharp rock, which punctures the tire. The headlights flicker and die.

We are in near-complete darkness now, save for the faint glow of the moon and the lights of my house in the distance. It's too far away, though. Even if I yelled, no one would hear me.

Justine grabs me by the nape and drags me down into the ditch. Poison plants brush against my tights. A tingling begins to creep through the fabric. I try to break free, but Dayn grabs my other arm and pins me to a tree. The bark digs into my back.

"Don't resist," he says. "It'll hurt more if you try."

Pressure builds behind my eyes. *Don't cry*, I think. *Don't let them see your weakness.* I blink, begging the tears to go back down, please, to not expose my fear because that's what people like Coll and his thugs feed on, the fear of the weak.

Coll walks up to me, taking center stage between his scornful acolytes.

"What did I ever do to you?" I ask.

"You were born," he answers, "and you're a freak." He pulls a knife from his belt and raises it to my eyes. The blade catches a lone ray of moonlight, glowing white. "You know what this is? It's a 3D-printed Klujn knife. Designed for all your butchering tasks. Handle made of plastic. Blade made of crystal bones. But that's only decoration. This," he says, revealing a hidden compartment at the base of the handle, from which he pulls out a set of nasty-looking pliers, "is what my parents use to rip their filthy claws out."

"You mean your *adoptive* parents," I snarl. Coll's eyes flicker menacingly at that. He traces the pliers along my collarbone. "You're an animal."

"You're the animal," Coll answers. "With your weird food and clothes and your ugly scars." He slides the pliers down my arm, all the way to my fingertips. "Whenever my dad catches one of them Klujns, I make sure I have a front-row seat. I love to see the look in its eyes when the claws are pulled out. That screechy sound they make, like pigs having their throats cut. They say fear makes the crystal more powerful or something."

He grabs my hand and pinches my fingernail with the pliers. Bends it back, smirking as the nail begins to separate from the skin. I screw my face up and close my eyes, bracing myself for the pain of having another nail ripped off, but it doesn't come.

Then, I hear Coll laugh. "The look on her face," he says, dropping my hand, and his laughter grows louder and louder until it becomes a cackle. His friends join in, imitating my scrunched expression.

"It's not funny," I say.

"You're right," Coll answers derisively. "That wasn't funny at all." The three of them continue to howl with laughter. I try to break free, but he blocks me. His arm catches the fabric of my sweater, pulling it down, exposing the rose gold chain of my pendant.

"Well, what do we have here?" He scrapes his finger against my chest and lifts the crystal to the light.

"Bet you it's not even real," Justine says, but she looks transfixed.

"I wonder how much I could get for this?" Coll asks his friends, his expression greedy like the fortune is already his. "Five thousand tokens? Maybe ten?"

My cheeks burn with rage. *No.* He can have my board, but he's not taking my pendant.

Then Coll and his sidekicks stop grinning. They stare at me like they've seen a ghost. From somewhere behind me, something pounces. A flash of white. It knocks Coll to the ground. It's a wolf. A big one. It turns to look at me, and I recognize it—the one I saw this morning.

The wolf turns back to Coll, who had begun to rise, and pushes him flat on his back, its front paws squarely on his chest. Dayn and Justine drop me and stare, horrified, their feet rooted to the ground.

"Aaaahhhh!" Coll cries out, shielding his face with his arms. The wolf clamps down on one of his forearms with a sickening *squelch*. Between screams Coll manages to say, "Get help!"

With dumb looks on their panicked faces, Dayn and Justine run back toward the fair.

The wolf continues to attack Coll, swiping his belly with its claws, making a gash so deep I can see the abdominal muscles beneath the fat. It bites Coll's neck with its glossy teeth, and blood spurts from the wound in a dozen identical fountains.

I should run, but instead I watch, frozen in fear and fascination. Finally, I come to my senses, edging cautiously forward. The wolf bares its teeth at me—now a glistening scarlet—in warning, then resumes its attack on Coll.

"Stop! You're killing him," I say, but the words feel stupid. It's an animal, after all, and animals don't understand. The wolf bites down on Coll's wrist, which almost severs from the rest of his arm—a pulp of flesh and bone, like a hand that slipped into a meat grinder.

I make a decision.

I spring forward and grab the wolf around its muscular shoulders. I manage to wrangle it off and we both fall down into a tangle of weeds, burrs catching in the animal's fur and latching onto my clothes. The wolf tries to break free, but I keep it trapped in my arms in a deadlock.

"It's okay," I say, pressing the animal's warm body into mine. My arms tremble from the effort of restraining such a wild, strong thing. My fingers stroke the thick fur around its neck. With its belly exposed, I see that it's a boy. Then, something strange happens. The wolf seems to calm under my touch. The storm in his deep blue eyes abates. The muscles in his face relax. Slowly, carefully, I begin to loosen my grip. The animal doesn't try to escape. I let the wolf go completely and he stays there, panting, but not in a ferocious way. Simply . . . out of breath.

I look over at Coll, who's still conscious but alarmingly pale. I slowly stand and walk over to him, my eyes drinking in his terrible injuries. The gash in his belly reveals layers of skin and fat and muscle like a particularly unappetizing slice of tri-colored cake. His neck is bleeding profusely, but the bite marks seem to have avoided any major artery. *Will he live?*

I reach down to try to suppress the bleeding.

Then, voices.

"Over here!" Justine yells. She and Dayn run over, followed by Mr. Mogel and his sister, who rushes to her son's side. Mr. Mogel's eyes dart from Coll to the wolf to me, connecting rather obvious dots. He raises his gun. Aims it at the wolf.

"No!" I say, standing between Mr. Mogel and the wolf. "Don't shoot him. He was trying to protect me." I regret the words at once.

"*Him?*" Justine says suspiciously. "Listen to her. Talking about a beast like it cares about her feelings."

"Coll was attacking me," I say. "He had a knife."

"Move out of the way," says Mr. Mogel.

"Don't kill it," I plead, careful of my choice of words. "It doesn't deserve to die."

Mr. Mogel points his rifle and fires. I feel the *whoosh* of the bullet as it flies past, then a wet *thud* as it makes contact with flesh. But I don't feel any pain, and I know the flesh isn't mine. When I turn around, the wolf's massive body is already on the ground.

"No." The word leaves my lips in a rush of air. I drop to my knees and hold the wolf's body in my arms, forgetting that the others are there. His warm blood stains my sweater, forming a wet patch that grows bigger and bigger. There's an ache in my heart, in the same place he's been shot, and my breathing feels shaky. But it's the wolf who took the bullet, not me.

The wolf howls sadly. He looks at me, not understanding why something as natural as instinct warrants punishment. His soulful eyes reflect my own face back at me, my brow knitted in sadness, and the four people towering behind me. In that moment, he appears more human than all those souls combined.

The wolf lets out a final breath, the air escaping his lungs like a deflating balloon, and then he's gone. His eyes stay open, but a milky film covers them. The glazed gaze of the dead.

"You didn't have to kill it," I say, turning to Mr. Mogel.

"The law is the law," the man answers with a sick, hungry grin. In his mind, he's already warming the oven. Setting the table. Polishing his finest cutlery.

"What happened?" Mrs. Mogel-Newhouse asks Coll, who looks even paler now, and clammy.

Coll looks at me with hatred and says, "She's one of *them*."

"What are you talking about?" I stammer, standing up, facing them. I feel naked under the burning midday heat of their stares.

"I saw it," Coll manages through the pain, his voice laced with blood and venom. He sucks in a sharp breath through clenched teeth, then: "I don't know how it's possible, but her eyes . . . they changed color."

"I saw it too," Justine chimes in, taking a threatening step toward me. I realize that this is their twisted idea of revenge.

"Then, when Dayn and Justine went to get you, she tried to finish me off," Coll says.

"I was trying to help," I tell Mr. Mogel. "He's lying. They all are. They're just saying that to get back at me . . ." I take a step back. *Why would Coll make up such a vindictive lie?* Then, I remember something. "It's the eye drops. I tried these eye drops at the fair."

Mr. Mogel takes another step forward; I take another step back. "Please. I'm telling the truth." But the more I proclaim my innocence, the guiltier I sound.

Mr. Mogel's finger tightens around the trigger. It's Coll's word against mine. I realize there's nothing I can do to convince them, so I turn on my heel and run.

7

I run faster than I've ever run, the cold air burning my lungs.

"She's getting away!" yells Justine. I don't know how far they are behind me, but I know enough to understand that they won't let me go. They will capture me, and who knows what will happen then. Tears cloud my vision as I remember the wolf, his eyes, and all the things they seemed to be trying to tell me. If only I could understand. That beautiful beast, dead. And now his blood is turning cold on my chest, marking me like a target.

Finally, my house! I race up the gravel driveway and into the front yard, where an automatic light comes on. I sprint up to the porch and try the front door, but the handle won't turn. Through the screen I see what's blocking it—a tall rifle with a crystal bayonet; one that belongs to a Hunter of high rank. General Santos is here.

I bang on the door. "Open up!" I yell.

I try the handle again, but it's jammed. The television blares from the room behind the kitchen. They might be having dinner in there, watching the Hunter's Day fireworks in Mission Creek, oblivious to what's going on outside. Or maybe George is downstairs in his study, packing for Camp, and Diana went out to look for me.

"Help!" I yell, banging louder this time.

That's when I hear them. Mr. Mogel, Justine, and Dayn, stalking up the driveway.

"Shit!" I dart off the porch and look around. I see in a glance that I'm cornered between the house and greenhouse and the woods, with the others approaching from the driveway.

Mr. Mogel points his rifle and fires. The bullet narrowly misses me, crashing into the greenhouse, and the glass cracks into a spiderweb.

That's when I notice that, at the bottom of the outdoor staircase, a light is on in George's basement study. I race down the rickety stairs and hammer on the door. "George!" I yell. "Are you in there? Open up, please!"

I bang and bang, but no one answers. Then I peer through the frosted-glass window, but all I can make out are the blurry outlines of gadgets and artifacts. Nothing moving, nothing animate.

"Ava?" I hear from above. I tear back up the stairs and see Diana, standing on the porch now, with Mercy behind her. "What's wrong?" she asks, noticing the circle of blood on my chest. "Are you hurt?"

"It's not mine," I say, gasping for breath, and with a pang of sorrow. "Where's George?"

"With Rodrigo. They went to patch a hole in the fence. Ava, what happened?"

"They're coming," I manage. "Coll attacked me. Then a wolf came and attacked him. I tried to stop it, but they killed it."

Diana's eyes narrow. "Why are they after you?"

Before I can answer, I hear footsteps behind me, a muted rustle like a Hunter's boots creeping up on their prey. And then, I feel the sting. I reach up to my neck and pull out a little dart with a tail of blue feathers, like a fisherman's lure.

That's strange, I think. My mind is clouding. Great exhaustion sweeps through me. Whatever poison is in my blood, it's acting fast. As it races through my veins, everything else slows down. Images come in and out of focus, faces floating in the darkness.

Diana, who is no longer on the porch but next to me. Mercy, framed by the doorway, clutching a rifle. Mr. Mogel, Dayn, Justine, closer than they were but standing still.

What is happening?

My eyelids begin to flutter. The last thing I manage to focus on is Mercy's face and his expression. Shock, confusion, horror.

Then, the lights in the backyard begin to pixelate, and the earth tilts up and takes the place of the sky. My head hits the ground with a thud. As my attacker's heavy boots come toward me, everything goes black.

* * *

"Little brittle girlie walked into the woods
Out came a creature and snatched the girlie up
Then came a Hunter, who bravely shot the Klujn
Took his trophy home and now we sing this tune . . ."

I'm in the orphanage courtyard, a rectangle of cement where the more outgoing boys and girls play games while the quiet children are banished to the outskirts, contenting themselves with a piece of chalk and their imaginations. In the center, a game of Kill the Klujn is underway. The children's nursery rhyme drifts over to where I am—

"Catch the Klujn! Catch the Klujn!
Beat its body all around;
Take its claws, and with its claws
We'll fertilize the ground!
Take its skin; make some shoes.
Take its bones and eyeballs too.
With its blood, we'll make a stew;
Kanum blood is good for you!
Kill the Klujn! Kill the Klujn—
Whichever way you choose!
Then send it to the gallows and
We'll have a bar-be-cue . . ."

I must be nine or ten, though I am small for my age. Wearing a crown of colorful leaves on my head, I am a princess—in my imagination, at least.

I sit close to the fence, as far away from the others as I can. It isn't the real fence—the Military fence—but a smaller one to keep the younger children from waddling into the river to their deaths. I've never had this dream before, but somehow I know all the details—like I have lived this before.

It's not a dream, I realize, but a memory. A view that was shrouded in fog, and now the fog is clearing.

Here, in my favorite spot, I dig in the dirt, scavenging for worms or insects. Sometimes I like to dig for digging's sake, pretending that if I dig long enough I might reach the other side of the earth. Occasionally, after rainfall, I find bright red ladybugs drowning in puddles. I like to rescue them, blowing on their wet wings. I love to watch them come back to life, using the tip of my finger to gently right them onto their wobbly legs. Today, the earth is dry and there are no ladybugs for me to save.

I look up. The playground is crowded with children in matching overalls and the common slew of birth defects. Too skinny, too fat. Their faces full of scabs, malformed limbs, thinning hair, or blackened teeth. It seems as if everyone is a reject, a non-Military family's accidental second child. Or someone else's first; if you can only have one child, better make sure it's a healthy one.

The game of Kill the Klujn has turned into a mass of jeering children standing on the perimeter of a chalk triangle, with Coll in the center. We're the same age, but he's already twice my size, with hands that love to rip the wings off butterflies and feet that crush the homes off snails' backs. Coll fights another kid—a little girl with clumps of missing hair and a stump for a left hand. They both clutch sharpened sticks, but that's the only even thing about the fight.

With one blow, Coll knocks her down. She lies on the ground, whimpering, as he laughs. Blood covers her upper lip, which has split open.

Miss Hidgins, the orphanage director, goes over to her. "Get up, Orphan," she scolds. "You stay down, you die."

There's a rustle in the bushes on the other side of the fence. I turn and notice a pair of eyes. Blue, unafraid. They belong to a young white wolf, handsome and majestic even in his small size. There are three large black spots on his back plus a speckle of smaller ones on his face and paws, like someone dipped their fingers in black ink and flicked them at him. He's older than a pup, but not quite a teenager. On the wrong side of the river.

That's when I notice blood on the wolf's right paw. A lot, going all the way up to the elbow, as though he stepped in a tin of red paint. I check that Miss Hidgins isn't watching, then edge toward the fence.

At a safe distance, but close enough to take in the extent of the wolf's injury, I see a jagged piece of metal sticking out of his elbow. The origin of the blood. The wolf whimpers again. I consider turning around, forgetting about him to avoid trouble, but I can't bring myself to ignore the pain in his eyes.

I kneel and carefully work my hand through a hole in the barbed wire. "Please don't bite my hand off." I realize I've never been this close to a wild animal before. Even though he is small, his frame is muscular. He could chomp my fingers off with one snap of his strong jaw, but something tells me he won't. If the wolf is smart, he will know that I'm trying to help him.

I reach for his leg and he lets me. "Hold still," I tell him, and he does. I close my fingers around the piece of metal and pull, pull, pull. There's the thick, slippery sound of an object moving through flesh. Slowly, reluctantly, the metal slides out. It looks like the tooth of a trap. The wolf lets out another whimper, but there's a flush of relief behind his glacier-blue eyes. He bows his head to me as though in thanks.

"You need to go," I tell him. The wolf hesitates. His gaze turns toward the woods, then back to me, like an invitation. Then, a figure looms behind me, casting the world in shadow.

"NOW!" I hiss. With a swish of leaves, he's gone.

Miss Hidgins is there, blocking the sun. She wears a blue utilitarian jumpsuit tucked into large boots. A line of triangular crystal pins glimmer on her lapel, showing medals and honors won over years of Military service.

"How many times do I have to tell you?" she snarls, bits of spit flying from her mouth like wet sparks. I hold my breath, wondering how I can talk my way out of this one. "You are not to be this close to the fence. And digging . . ." She notices the dirt on my hands and clothes. "Do you have any idea what monstrosities you could have let in here?" She didn't see the wolf. Thank goodness for that. "Who do you think will ever want to adopt you if you keep behaving like an animal?"

"No one, Miss Hidgins."

"And why is that?"

"Because animals are food, not friends."

The orphanage director snatches the crown from my head and crushes it under her boot. "This is for your own good. You are not special. You are just like everybody else. What are you?"

I suppose the right answer is the one she wants to hear.

"An orphan."

"And what are you most certainly not?"

"A princess."

"Good," says Miss Hidgins with a satisfied smile. "You can't keep going around with your head in the clouds. In this world, only the strong survive."

8

My eyelids drift open. As the dream fades, an ache in my body sets in. The forest floor is cold beneath me, and I sit up slowly, gingerly, blinking the sleep crust from my eyes.

The darkness is thick, but there's a luminosity in the air. As my eyes adjust, I realize that the glow comes from the night sky, which is filled with thousands and thousands of glimmering stars. *Stars?* I haven't seen stars in months, not since spring, before the burning season. Even then, they are never this bright. There's always pollution in the air from the Greenhouses and factories and power plants. But here, the sky is dripping in them. Fat, shimmering stars and planets, like someone threw glitter into the heavens and it never rained back down.

I can see the Milky Way, a dreamy purple-gray, but the moon is hiding behind silver clouds. I turn my gaze to my surroundings. Under the chandelier of outer space, the colors of the night become more pronounced.

There are towering pines teeming with green needles and rich brown trunks so thick you'd need at least four people with outstretched arms to wrap all the way around. Other trees have white trunks and bright crimson crowns. I see smaller trees, too, bent by the wind, curled around one another like drunken acrobats. At my ankles are small purple bushes that look more like coral than plants. Little glow-in-the-dark flowers dot the ground like resting dragonflies. Everything looks enchanted—and *alive*.

I do a double take. Observe the diversity of the trees, the brightness of the stars, the fact that nothing is black and uniform like the woods by my house. Then, the possibility of my surroundings begins to creep in, filling me with a deep, unsettling feeling. *Am I in the Deeper Woods? Klujn territory?*

But it can't be. Who would bring me here . . . and why?

I reach for my pendant and am relieved to find it still around my neck. The crystal is cold, but its presence is reassuring. Then, a puzzling thought—whoever brought me here didn't steal it. *So it wasn't Coll and his thugs? Was it Mr. Mogel, or his sister? Why wouldn't they take such a valuable thing?*

I look around and my eyes settle on a nearby path. A small road, overgrown with weeds. Its entrance is blocked by a garland of something that looks awfully like . . . dried intestines. They connect two tall sticks that are planted in the earth, a skull perched atop each one. A silent warning that screams: *Go no farther.*

It's a secret trail.

No. No. *No!* The word pounds through my brain like a second heartbeat. It's impossible. Was defending a wolf so wrong that it warranted banishment or death? Couldn't Diana stop whoever did this to me? And who shot me? I rack my brain, trying to fill in the blanks, but it's all a blur.

I stand up, stretch my stiff body, and shake blood into my sleeping legs. When the feeling in them begins to return, I set off in the opposite direction, wanting to put as much distance as I can between myself and that secret trail.

As I walk, my eyes dart around, taking in every unfamiliar detail. I can barely see more than a few feet in front of me, but with time and lots of squinting, more colors and details begin to emerge. The leaves of the trees contain an artist's palette's worth of hues: everything from light yellow to burgundy to mauve. The soil is rich and brown, not at all like dirt, but healthy and crawling with insects. There are mushrooms and moss-covered rocks and a smell that hangs in the air, like wet earth, like rain, but without rain's chemical edge.

My surroundings are beautiful—enchanted, almost—but I know that I cannot trust any of it. Everything is but a tantalizing illusion, like poisoned candy. One misstep could be deadly. *Not to mention the animals that live here. Is anything watching me right now?*

I shiver. It's a few degrees colder than Red River, and I'm underdressed. The chill pierces straight through my sweater, my stockings, and makes a nest in my bones. I look around for signs of human life—footprints, litter, barbed wire, anything. There is nothing around, nothing man-made, anyway. *How far am I from the fence?* Surely whoever brought me here didn't venture out too deep. It would be dangerous for them, too.

I notice a tree with lots of branches that reaches into the sky, above all others. *Maybe I could climb it*, I think, high enough to get a decent view. Find my way back to the fence. Then I remember my last Klujnology class—Reesa and her chilling words: "*The black trees in the Deeper Woods that eat humans alive.*"

Carnifloras.

I gulp. Is that a Carniflora? The tree might be raven or ebony, but aren't those all just shades of black? I don't feel like taking any chances. Instead, I stick to the middle of the path, watching my feet, careful not to step on any exposed roots. It's difficult, because the ground is covered in a mulch of leaves. I continue and the path narrows until the purple coral-bushes on either side lick my calves.

I suppress the urge to cry, or to yell out in anger at whoever did this to me. Whoever put me here, without giving me the chance to explain myself, defend myself. I have no idea where I am or where I am going. I have no point of reference, no map, no compass, no supplies.

What am I supposed to do now? My eyes fill with tears and this time, there's no holding them back. They trickle down my cheeks and distort my vision until I can hardly see. *I'm lost*, I realize. *Lost in the Deeper Woods.*

It feels like a dream, as if I'll wake up in my warm bed, safe, with Fall Break ahead of me. A week where I can rock in the hammock on the back balcony listening to the wind, or help Diana in the greenhouse when she needs me. Suddenly, the prospect of spending the next seven days alone with Diana as she schools me about the many benefits of compost doesn't seem like such a punishment after all.

The path I'm on forks into two. The one on the right looks more unkempt, and there are too many suspicious roots, so I opt for the left.

Keep walking. I think for a minute about the fact that perhaps I could use the stars as a guide—after all, the Boreal is north of Red River, and everything else for that matter. But the foliage is so thick that the night sky has disappeared from view. There's no telling which direction I'm walking. I could be going farther in.

I'm so preoccupied with my thoughts that I lose focus on where I'm going. I step forward, and my right foot sinks into a concealed hollow. A crunch echoes in the dark—the sound of metal on flesh. I look down, and see that the sharp teeth of an animal trap have sunken into my boot. The pain is delayed by a few seconds, like thunder after lightning. But when it comes, it's worse than death.

I scream so loud that it rattles the branches above my head and birds fly out of the trees. The pain is intense, but shock and adrenaline quickly flood me, making it perhaps not as bad as it should be.

The front of my boot is shredded, and blood pours slowly from the holes. The orange pumpkin-leather stains a dark red. I didn't think I was squeamish, but there's so much blood—*my* blood—and my head spins. *Don't pass out*, I think. *Whatever set the trap may be watching.*

I need to be pragmatic, although all I want to do is wail. I inspect the trap: it's attached to a heavy chain that's anchored into the soft ground. I try to pry it open, but its jaws are clenched tight, like a tenacious beast unwilling to give up its catch. I pull at the trap again, but it won't budge. My toes are sealed in its unrelenting mouth.

And the pain! There's so much pain. I feel lightheaded. I blink rapidly several times and shake my head, trying to keep it clear so I can focus.

There's a vibration deep in the earth, like a buried storm. Sound follows: a swoosh, a rustle. The crunch of footfall on leaves. Judging by the rhythm, there isn't only one set of feet, but many. Lantern light shimmers on the trees, gilding the leaves. My breath quickens, and I feel even dizzier, but I need to know, to see.

A thrown shadow—the silhouette of a tall, monstrous thing. A voice speaks in an unintelligible language. Raspy, rough, but oddly melodic. Other voices join in. There are bits of English, I think, although I no longer feel sure of anything. *What Territory is that from?* I wonder.

"I heard a scream," a voice says, definitely in English now but with a thick accent. "I think it was human."

A surge of panic floods through me. I freeze, placing my hand over my mouth because I can't trust my lips to keep the sound in. The footsteps grow louder. The group is getting closer. Their lanterns move toward me like floating orbs of light. I glimpse a flash of purpley-blue. The sweep of a cloak. Only a few trees separate us now.

I notice the corpse of a tree lying across the forest floor. Its trunk should be big enough to hide behind. I pull at the chain of the trap with everything I have and slowly, begrudgingly, it begins to slide. I scream in silence as the sharp metal teeth bite deeper into my foot, threatening to touch the bone. But it's either temporary agony or sticking around and waiting for the group to reach me, and the latter option doesn't hold much appeal.

I make it to the tree in time. The chain reaches its full extension, and my leg is still exposed. I brush dead leaves over it—could do better, but there isn't any time. The group comes closer. And closer.

And then they break into the clearing.

I see a group of human hostages, all in their teens, in rows of two. They are dirty and disheveled, cuffed to each other with manacles that look like some kind of twisted vine. Their faces are hard to make out, but I see that they are mostly girls, all in different states of trauma. Some cry, while others are silent. Some murmur prayers under their breaths while others simply appear out of sorts.

My eyes move to the guards. Five of them, surrounding the group, distinguishable by their long hooded cloaks. The cloaks are a metallic indigo. Some of the guards hold weapons—spiky bats, crystal daggers, and other brutal objects I don't recognize.

At the head of the solemn processional, the leader keeps the pace, his steps as consistent as a metronome. He is male, I presume, judging by his size, and his eyes stay glued to the path ahead. The hood of his cloak casts his face in shadow, making it hard for me to read his features.

Behind him, a male dwarf speaks to a female of equal height. "Females-only," he singsongs, drawing from a glass pipe that emits a strange green smoke. "There's another trap around here, Poppet, I'm sure of it. I can smell her from here."

"You've been smoking too much of that Klandestine," answers the female, the one he called Poppet. She carries a tall wooden scythe with a rusty nail sticking out of the end. Nothing about her is as sweet-sounding as her name. "It's got you smellin' things. Plus, we've already got fourteen. The king said that's all the performers we need, Oak. Thirteen, with an extra for the opening ceremony."

The head guard turns around—irritated, impatient. Lantern light illuminates his face. That's when I see it. His eyes. They're violet.

This can't be happening.

9

Behind the head guard, the two smaller Klujns try to keep up. In the light of the lanterns, I see that their eyes are yellow, their skin sallow. At the back, two guards of average height complete the strange parade, both with pale white skin and fierce red eyes. *These Klujns are from different tribes,* I realize, confused by what George said about Klujns not mixing.

They have almost passed my hiding spot when a high-pitched shriek fills the night.

The group stalls. At the front, directly behind the head guard, a human girl has collapsed, her wrist still in the vine-like shackle that binds her to another girl. A few of the hostages cry out, but most look too tired to fully comprehend what's going on.

"She's dead," says the girl's partner, her voice emotionless, scratching the back of her shaved head. Her skin is as black as the night, with cool blue undertones.

"What do you mean, 'she's dead'?" snaps the short male, Oak, tucking away his pipe. "We can't use the dead ones."

In the second row, a purple-haired girl speaks up. "If you wanted us healthy, you could have fed us a little more," she spits. "We haven't eaten anything since Justice Falls." She's dressed for a night out. Leather jacket. A miniskirt made from the wings of butterflies. I suspect this was not the way she expected her night to end.

A few of the braver girls mumble in agreement.

Poppet holds up her scythe, the rusty nail close to the girl's eyeball.

"Eenie meenie miney moe," she sneers, twisting the stick from nail end to blunt end and back again. "Catch a human by the toe." It lands on the blunt end. Poppet clubs the purple-haired girl in the kneecap. "Next time, I'll use the sharp end." Purple Hair buckles over, her expression more wrathful than wounded.

The head guard looks at Oak. "They are your responsibility," he says. It's the first time he's spoken. His voice is not a growl, but rich and deep. It's weird to think of Klujns as having voices, speaking English.

"It's not my fault these fat, lazy humans can't handle a fast," Oak grumbles in his defense. "They're used to eating and eating and eating all the time." Without answering, the head guard walks over and unshackles the dead girl. "What are you doing? We need fourteen."

"Fourteen *living*," the head guard answers. "If you want to keep her as a souvenir, you can carry her the rest of the way." Oak takes a step back.

The leader unties the girl's body, picks her up easily, and tosses her next to my hiding spot. She lands on the leaves that conceal the trap's chain, which jerks its teeth deeper into my foot. Metal scrapes against bone.

A gasp escapes my lips before I can stifle it. I cover my mouth again, but it's too late. The sound is out, the damage done.

The head guard stops, his senses alerted. His eyes search the darkness and land on the pile of leaves, which are now thin beneath the dead girl's body, revealing the chain of the trap. His eyes follow its length until they reach the spot where my foot is hidden. Once there, they stop moving.

I close my eyes, praying he hasn't seen me. Trying so hard to keep another scream inside that my head feels like a pressure cooker.

"What is it, Diablo, sir?" says Poppet. There's a crunch of footsteps. The sound of something clearing away the leaves. Then, a warm hand wraps around my ankle and hauls me out from behind the tree.

It's over. I am now exposed for everyone to see, strewn on the forest floor like meat scraps for vultures.

I open my eyes slowly. The leader looms over me, hands on his hips, a severe and impregnable wall. Poppet peers through the gap between his arm and body on one side, and Oak leers at me through the other, rubbing his hands together ravenously.

"Looks like we found a new performer," he chirps. "Told you I could smell her."

"Should we check her?" asks Poppet.

"No need for that," says the leader. "It's obvious what she is." The trio studies me like a freak show oddity, like a particularly delicious meal.

The head guard—Diablo—reaches toward me. I recoil. His hands are large and powerful machines. About an inch and a half of pure crystal protrudes from each fingertip, the ends so sharp they could split my veins open with a tickle. Slice open my abdomen like a scalpel. Empty my innards onto the forest floor. But they don't.

Instead, the guard's hands close around the trap. His strong fingers grab hold of both sides and, with one easy tug, he pulls it open, releasing my foot. A guttural scream fills the night.

Mine.

10

Oak binds my wrist in the vine shackle and attaches me to the girl in front, the one whose partner just died. There are no introductions.

As we walk, I try to keep myself from crying out, but every time I place my right foot down it feels like I'm stepping on the necks of broken bottles. After one particularly vicious stride, my mangled foot gives way and I collapse. The leafy ground cushions the blow, but it's not bruised knees I'm worried about.

We stop. I feel the girls' eyes boring into me, probably wondering if there's been another casualty. *I can't go on*, I think. *There's only so much pain a person can take.* The head guard turns around. Only a sliver of his face is visible beneath his hood—one dark, impatient eye. I try to stand up, but a renewed pain slashes through my foot like a hot stake, and I crumple again.

For a moment, I wonder what the guard will do. Then, he detaches me from my partner and addresses the other guards in a hiss of words with lots of *k*'s and *j*'s and *a*'s. The sound is almost musical, something covert and mysterious but elegant, too.

The other guards respond by taking the rest of the prisoners a little farther down the path, into a clearing. Their lantern light grows smaller, diluted by darkness, and in its absence I realize just how dark these woods are and how harrowing the night is without electricity.

I wonder which is worse: to go with them—wherever they're going—or to be left behind.

The group sits on fallen logs. I watch as strange food and gourds of water are passed from Klujn hands to human ones. Some of the captives throw themselves at the food while others cross their arms over their chests, out of protest or distrust, refusing to touch anything that is given to them.

The guard sets his lantern down on the forest floor next to me, casting a spiral of light onto the fallen leaves. I'm jolted back to the present and my predicament with the Klujn guard leader whose intentions are still unclear. He walks outside the range of light, barely visible as he searches for something. He returns with a few large leaves edged in dark green with purple markings at the center. The pattern is beautiful and intricate.

The guard kneels by my right foot, closing the gap between us. It's not his size or strength I'm afraid of, nor his dreadful claws, but the authority that emanates from him, the aura of confidence. I am a little moon, caught in Jupiter's shadow. And, although he mustn't be that much older than me, I feel every bit the weak, quivering human he thinks I am.

The light of his lantern washes across his face, illuminating the hemisphere that was previously in shadow. My first impulse is to look away, but interest wins and I find myself gazing directly at him. His eyes burn into me, like two noxious planets.

I'm not thrown off my feet and sucked into a vortex of violent turbulence, not burned or stung or assaulted by their menace. Nothing happens. In a second that feels much longer than a real second, I absorb as many details as I can: the color of his eyes isn't homogenous; it's layered and textured, the most shockingly vivid shade of violet I've ever seen. The expression in them is deep as a sunken island. His skin is light brown and freckled, his cheekbones well-defined, and his nose and jaw are human-sized. He's not unlike the creature in the Coliséa but—oddly enough, based on our surroundings—he doesn't appear as wild.

Without warning, the guard pulls off my boot. The pain that was condensed to one spot is now granted permission to run free, and it sprints up my leg, like a fire discovering new oxygen. The fire turns to water when it reaches my eyes, and I feel the pressure of impending tears.

The guard's own eyes flicker, perhaps deriving pleasure from my pain. However, his touch is gentle. He pinches the fabric of my stocking at the ankle and nips it with his claw. The material tears, and he pulls it away. When he takes hold of my bare heel, I'm surprised to realize that his hands are soft.

He inspects the wound. I sneak a peek—it's not pretty.

There are five holes on the top of my foot curved like a bite mark, where the teeth of the trap plunged in. Thick, viscous blood oozes from each one, the skin around them red as sunburn. Unfazed, the guard begins to wrap the large leaves around my foot like a bandage. I wince, but within seconds a pleasant, numbing sensation begins to travel into my foot and up my body. After a few more shaky breaths, the pain is almost gone entirely.

"What was that?" I ask. My voice comes out as a croak. He ignores me, continuing to wrap my foot. When he has finished, he crushes a flower between his fingers and wipes the pulp on the edge of the last bandage-leaf, sticking it down against the others. Then, he replaces my boot.

My wound is bound tight, and the pain is gone completely.

"Thank you," I say, relieved by how good the absence of pain can feel. His eyebrows raise slightly at my words, but his surprise is a ripple and not a wave.

I don't know what I expected next—a hand to help me up or some crutches made of sticks—but I don't get it. All I get is a simple "Keep up," and before I know it, he is already heading toward the clearing.

I get up slowly, left foot first, followed by the right. I set my right boot down gently, seeing how much weight I can get away with. The injury hurts no more than a dull ache. I won't be running races any time soon, but at least there's no more pain. I take a few steps; only a slight limp.

I stop. I could make a run for it. But if the guard left me on my own, he must assume that I won't get far. Injured animals are usually the first to get eaten, aren't they?

I decide to follow him into the clearing. *Best I stay with them for now, until I can figure out where we're going.*

As I join them, I feel someone watching me—I've caught Purple Hair's attention. Her eyes track me, alive with questions.

Oak and Poppet place us back in our vine shackles, some girls moaning and whining about their tired feet. Poppet raises her rusty nail–weapon, and they fall quiet. After that, I don't feel like asking about a snack. Anyway, can't say I'm hungry.

* * *

We walk for hours. The darkness is as thick as a summer ash storm. The canopy of trees blocks out the stars, and it's almost impossible to see where we're going. The air becomes crisper, the incline of the forest floor steeper. There's the smell of turned earth and pines or firs, or is it spruces? I can't tell the difference. Despite the pleasing scent of the forest, we are far from Red River now, and the security of townships and Military roads and the law is now far behind. With every step I take, a deep disquiet spreads through me. *This is not a place where humans were ever meant to be.*

The head guard's light bounces off the darkness, revealing only tiny glimpses of the forest at a time—enormous trees and plants and flowers the likes of which I've never seen. We pass ponds where animals are drinking. They stop to watch us, their eyes reflecting a demonic green. *Wolves? Bears? Moose? Elk?* It's hard to tell, but at least they keep to themselves. *Such big game.*

On certain trees, there are drawings smudged across the bark. Mandalas of perfect geometry. Moons, stars, circles, squares. Dashes, dots, squiggles, and other rune-like symbols, bleeding into one another in a complex labyrinth of shapes. They glow a luminous red that pulses in the dark. *Trail markers, perhaps, or some other navigational tool?* But these symbols are unlike anything I've ever seen. Are they warnings, written in a language I don't understand?

Tree by tree, the leader follows a symbol like a mountain top with three vertical dots drawn above the crest. Occasionally, the symbol is accompanied by an *X* that has a tiny circle to its left.

For the most part, the humans don't speak—not with voices, anyway. That doesn't stop their eyes from darting around, asking silent questions. My partner keeps hers trained on the ground. Through a few discreet glances, I notice her heavy boots, baggy gray camouflage pants, and bomber jacket. She's dressed like a Hunter, only she's a girl. Despite her stern countenance, she flinches at the crack of twigs her own boots make.

"How's your foot?" a voice whispers. It takes a moment before I realize someone's talking to me. I turn around and see, next to Purple Hair—two tangled black pigtails bordering a round face. Horn-rimmed glasses magnify black eyes that look permanently afraid. The girl is plump, wearing a worn-out Scout uniform with too many pockets. A name is stitched across her left breast: *Wendy.*

"Still attached," I answer, both polite and cautious, not sure what to make of her kindness.

"How did they get you guys?" the girl called Wendy asks. The other girls don't answer. "I went orienteering with my sister. A part of the fence must have been broken and we walked right through it. My compass stopped working," she goes on. It's like speaking one sentence has given her the confidence to keep going. "Next thing you know, I'm hanging in a net thirty feet above the ground. It's a miracle I still have my glasses," she adds. "My eyes are so bad. If I was an animal in the wild, I wouldn't have made it past infancy."

"Touching story, *Pockets*," says Purple Hair sardonically. "But I prefer silence." Wendy goes quiet. Swallows like she has a lump stuck in her throat. I throw her an apologetic smile, which she catches, and she smiles back timidly.

I turn my focus to the front, and the head guard's back. His name is Diablo, I remember one of the Klujns saying. Such a human name. Diablo's posture is straight, not bent like the creature in the Coliséa. His robes end an inch above the forest floor, and his feet are bare. They are large and flat, but not hairy or gnarly like I would have imagined.

Five toes on each, like human feet. No claws or vulnerable toenails, just tough skin made for walking. As Diablo's feet navigate the path, I realize he is following some kind of deliberate pattern, the way he steps around certain piles of leaves or plants. He must know where the traps are hidden. I'm careful to imitate his steps as we continue in silence for a few more minutes.

Then Wendy's stomach emits a loud growl. "I'm so hungry I could eat a tribe," she mutters.

"We literally just ate," snaps Purple Hair.

"So? Whatever that weird stuff was went right through me. It was like eating air."

We pass a shrub with fuchsia-pink berries. Wendy plucks a few, sniffs them, then brings them to her mouth.

Purple Hair cuts in. "I wouldn't eat that if I was you."

"Why not?"

"It's Wilderweed. They call it 'insect venom.' It's a poison, and not a nice one."

"We haven't studied that in Scouts." Wendy ditches the berries and wipes her hands on her uniform. "We don't have plants like this in Justice Falls. We don't have *any* of this in Justice Falls," she gulps, stepping around a set of large footprints. "Where do you think they're taking us?" Her question hangs in the night, unanswered.

The sound of a river becomes audible in the distance. The path we're on begins to narrow until it's barely large enough for us to walk side by side. To my left, the hill slopes down into a deep chasm where a river roars like a beast before mealtime. It's a steep, dizzying drop. My comfort zone begins and ends at sea level. The path continues upward, winding into the jagged mountains. I look to my right at my partner, who hasn't uttered a word this entire time.

"Are you okay?" I ask, my voice neutral, not wanting to sound too nice. Nice means naive, and that means you can be walked right over. My partner doesn't reply. Finally, after a few long seconds, she answers without looking me in the eyes.

"My dad's a Hunter," she says, almost like a threat.

"Animals?" Wendy inquires, wanting to be part of the conversation.

"Klujns," answers my partner, trying to appear confident, but I hear the quiver in her voice. "He's friends with Grouse. They're coming for me, I know it, and when they do they'll slaughter all these vile creatures."

"You shouldn't say things like that, 'specially not here," says Wendy. "You'll be in big trouble."

"Look around you, Pockets," Purple Hair says. "This *is* big trouble."

All of a sudden, the head guard comes to a stop. He lifts his lantern and peers into the darkness ahead, where a section of the path is gone. A long branch has been placed across it, connecting both sides like a precarious tightrope. Beneath it . . . a vertical drop.

He turns to face the mountain wall. The lantern illuminates something on the side of the path, positioned right before the crossing. It looks like a dollhouse and stands at about knee height. Skulls are stacked in a small pile, and there are flowers, leaves, and a plethora of colorful crystals stuffed into their mouths and hollow eyes. Other objects are scattered on the ground around it like offerings at pious feet. Some of the girls gasp. The structure looks like an altar, but an altar for what?

The skulls look . . . *human*. Even though they have no eyeballs, it feels like they're *watching*.

Oak pushes his way forward and takes in the bottomless drop. "How do we cross?" he asks. Without answering, Diablo reaches into the depths of his cloak and pulls out a fat black crystal the size of an egg. He lays it down amid the other offerings. Then, as though this is warranty enough for him, he steps out onto the branch. It creaks beneath his weight, but he doesn't seem fazed. His toes curl around the wood as he expertly balances across, the lantern still dangling from his hand.

When the head guard reaches the safety of the other side, about twenty feet away, he turns toward us. His eyes land on me. Even though he doesn't say a word, I understand. A question. *Who's next?*

"Performers first," announces Oak, stepping aside and clearing the way for us. I look down at the branch, which is decayed and damp. The chasm seems to stretch out infinitely below like a mine shaft. But, if I don't cross, what will they do to me? Leave me behind? Throw me over the side of the cliff, into the river's waiting mouth? What choice do I have?

"We should face in," I tell my partner. "So we can lean against the wall." She nods, her gesture mechanical. *That means I'm first*, I realize. I set my left foot tentatively on the branch, then place my hands on the cliff wall for support. Drag my bandaged right foot out to meet it. It's heavy, and balancing on it is hard.

My partner steps out after me. We shuffle along, side by side, taking tiny steps along our makeshift tightrope. *Step left, drag right. Step left, drag right.* The branch wobbles, rocking front and back. I grip the rocky wall tightly, but there isn't much of a handhold.

"I'm guessing this isn't a good time to tell you that I'm afraid of heights," I say, trying to ease the tension. The girl ignores my comment. Mercy often says that I'm antisocial, but this girl makes me look like a chatterbox. *I guess I'm in this alone*, I think, deciding that, as usual, silence is probably the better option.

As I continue along the branch, my legs begin to tremble. Muscles I've never had to use before awaken with a scream. "Try not to shake," she hisses.

"I'm not exactly doing it on purpose," I hiss back. We're almost halfway now. Behind us, the other girls don't blink. We are setting the example for what or what not to do.

I hazard a quick look at Diablo. He watches from the other side, stern but with curiosity in his eyes like he's eager to see what will happen. Although I'm pretty sure he doesn't want any more of us to die. *Fourteen living*, he said. We are all supposed to reach wherever it is that we're going.

As we inch forward, my mind drifts to the Klujn Fair. To the dark road and Coll's attack. To my broken longboard. To the wolf and the look in his eyes as he died. It was like he was trying to tell me something, but what? *Don't be ridiculous*, I think. *Wolves don't communicate. Not like humans.*

Red River feels so far away. If I'd gone home with Mercy, none of this would have happened. I'd be slipping my legs between warm flannel sheets, my belly bursting from the meal Diana was preparing, my only chore to fall asleep and dream. My mouth waters at the thought of the Forest Cake she makes—on special occasions, of course—served with whipped cream made from chickpea juice, and berries on the side.

Instead I'm here, trekking across a ravine with a group of strangers, going somewhere—*where are we going?* I guess the destination won't matter much if I can't get off this beam alive.

"Almost there," I say, trying to sound reassuring. We're about three-quarters of the way across, so it's not a total lie. *Step left, drag right. Step left, drag right.* I'm beginning to feel confident that we might make it.

Then my partner's shoe slips. Her arms flail and she knocks me in the chest, knocking me backward. I don't have time to cry out. We are already plummeting toward the ground.

11

A sudden jolt stops me midflight. There's the taste of blood on my tongue from having bitten it. My right arm stretches above my head, like a doll carried by a careless child. My shoulder could dislocate at any moment. But at least I'm alive, and my partner's whimper tells me she is, too.

I look down at my boots, which dangle over the chasm and the rush of water below. That's when I realize what happened.

The handcuff stopped our fall.

The girl and I dangle on either side of the branch, our cuffed arms yanked up above our heads, a thin vine the only thing that stops us from falling to our deaths.

"We're going to die!" she shrieks.

What a useless thing to say. I might have just been thinking the same thing, but you don't give those thoughts the courtesy of words. I'm no leader, and I have no desire to be one, but a leader is what this situation needs. So far, she's not stepping up to the challenge.

"We're not going to die," I tell her. "Not today. Now, we have to pull ourselves up. On my count, okay?" In my periphery I see her nod, eyes closed, nose crinkled. "One, two, three!" I say. In unison, we reach up and grab the branch. I hook my left leg over, then pull myself up the rest of the way. I straddle the branch, but it's so narrow that it's a balancing act.

Meanwhile, my partner is struggling.

"You've got it," I say. She manages to hoist herself up, but her arms tremble. I reach down to grab her, but her arms buckle. She drops, and this time I'm pulled down toward her side.

I lose my balance and fall, only just managing to catch myself at the last second. I hang upside down like a trapeze artist, only my right leg on the branch. My left one hangs somewhere in the void, but I can't get my bearings upside down. All I see is the dark canyon beneath us. My right arm is stretched down, trembling with the girl's weight. The branch creaks ominously.

"*No!*" the girl cries out, dangling over the chasm. "I don't want to die."

"Stay *still*!" I yell, my patience thinning. She doesn't listen. My thigh trembles. The muscle threatens to release at any moment. I try to grab the bar with my left hand, but I miss and my body lurches back down. The girl jerks like a trout on a fishing line. She closes her eyes and whispers a prayer under her breath.

"I don't know who you're praying to, but this isn't a time for prayer, it's a time for action," I yell. "You have to stop moving!" I don't know where it comes from, this burst of confidence, but it works.

The girl finally listens. She freezes and just hangs there like an ornament. *Come on*, I think, taking a steadying breath. *You've got this.* I take another breath, readying myself, then swing up again, abs crunching, almost ripping, as I bend in half, adrenaline or maybe shear willpower allowing me to lift both her weight and mine. This time, my free hand manages to grab the branch and I squeeze tight. My palm is slippery with sweat, but I bring my second leg up just in time and wrap it around, squeezing the limb between my thighs. Then I readjust my left hand so that I have a firmer grasp. I'm much steadier now, but I only have one hand on the branch.

"Almost there," I say, continuing along the branch. It wobbles and creaks beneath us. I keep my head tucked up against my chest and my shoulders hunched, my movements measured and slow. My left palm is slippery and beginning to slide again when my shoulder nudges the path on the other side. I cock my head and see Diablo's feet.

He stands, watching. He could offer to help, but something tells me he's not the helping kind.

"We made it!" I call out to my partner, who has stopped crying or praying or making any sound at all. I hoist myself up onto the path and lean back, my boots kicking dirt, pulling at the cuff with both hands. She's almost up and over the edge when something happens.

At first I think it's her wrist, slipping out of the vine shackle. Then I realize that her entire hand is still in the shackle. It's a prosthetic. And it's come off.

She grabs a root with her one good hand, but it unravels from the earth.

I throw myself down, belly on the path, and grab her wrists in time. Lock my hands around them and, with a final burst of strength, I haul her up over the edge. We collapse onto the path, exhausted, safe. My every muscle burns. The girl stuffs the stub of her hand back into the prosthetic before the others can see. The skin of the artificial hand blends with her own; no one could tell the difference. She avoids my eyes. I recognize her humiliation. I know the feeling.

"Just out of curiosity—who were you praying to?" I ask.

"Grouse, I guess," she answers, looking almost embarrassed.

"No offense, but I don't think he can hear you from here."

The girl pats her bomber jacket and looks relieved when she feels something in an inner pocket.

"Everything okay?" I ask, and she nods without looking at me.

"How did you do that?" she asks.

"Strong, I guess."

"That wasn't strong, that was superhuman."

I grin, enjoying the compliment. "I'm Ava," I say.

"Zoe," she answers. "Please don't tell anyone about . . ." she trails off, indicating her hand.

"I won't," I assure her. "But between you and me—I think we have bigger fish to fry." Zoe finally looks me in the eyes for the first time. But just as suddenly, she looks away.

On the other side of the ravine, Oak looks excited by the promise of more entertainment.

"Well, what's it going to be?" he singsongs to the girls next in line. "A balancing act or synchronized jumping?"

Wendy and Purple Hair stare at the crossing in horror.

* * *

Slowly, laboriously, everyone else makes it across, guards included.

The next few hours are less eventful, much to my relief. We put the cliffs behind us and descend into a wide valley. Out in the open, away from the thick cover of trees, the sky becomes visible again. The moon comes out from behind its silver veil and my racing heartbeat calms. Perhaps because it reminds me of home, of the safety of my room.

It ascends toward its zenith with the silent authority of a god—one that doesn't abandon its people. It's still a waxing gibbous, but here it glows a bluish-purple, not the muddied gray we see in Red River.

"It's a phenomenon I read about," Wendy says, her eyes wide, like a child seeing fireworks for the first time. "Apparently it changes hues in the days leading up to the Blood Moon, running through the full spectrum from violet to red. Since there's no pollution here, we can really see the color change." It's hard to believe it's the same moon I saw back home. I've never seen it quite so big or bright. It's as though its resolution has been amplified. You can even see the texture of its craters, the light and dark areas. It would be beautiful if it wasn't so dire. What will happen when it glows red? Does this have something to do with where they're taking us, or why?

"What shade of purple *is* that?" Wendy asks.

"Indigo," I say, just like the guards' cloaks. She counts colors on her fingers, going through the spectrum. *Blue, green, yellow, orange, red.*

"That would mean we're five days away from the Blood Moon," she says.

My whole body aches, from my cuffed wrist to my bound foot to my shins and knees. Focusing on the changing landscape proves to be a good distraction. It is rather beautiful. The valley winds between tall mountains with impressive black limestone cliffs that sparkle in the moonlight. Thankfully we don't climb them and instead keep to our moderate path. We cross a stream, walking over a log bridge. Lily pads glow on the water's surface.

I feel at ease in this valley, close to the earth, away from those treacherous mountains. Now and then, I glimpse a red trail marker carved into the earth or on a tree. There are more skull altars, too, and Diablo stops at every single one. Reaches into his cloak and pulls out a crystal. A fruit. An acorn. A seed. His pockets are full of these intriguing offerings. He deposits one at each altar without explanation before continuing. I wonder what goes through his mind. What kind of thoughts or emotions a Klujn has. If a Klujn even has emotions.

Behind us, Oak and Poppet squabble in their hissing language, with bits of English interspersed throughout.

"It's strange," Wendy whispers. "If they're wild, why do they speak a human language?"

"They probably picked it up from all the humans they caught and slaughtered," says Purple Hair sarcastically.

"I'm serious."

"So was I."

"It's just . . ." Wendy trails off, deep in thought. "I've never thought of Klujns as having actual *voices* before."

"Whales could speak," says Purple Hair. "They could even sing. So could dolphins."

"Yes. But not in *English*."

As the hours pass and the sky darkens into an inky black ocean, more and more stars appear. The air is frosty, my sweater soaked through with sweat and the wolf's blood, but as long as we keep walking, my body can generate warmth. Finally, the horizon begins to turn that striking azure blue that precedes the dawn. *L'heure bleue*, Diana calls it, her French still with that Québécois twang even after years of not speaking it regularly. *The blue hour*—that moment before the day breaks and the birds wake, when everything is peaceful and still.

Diana used to whisper other words in French when it was just the two of us, surrounded by the glass walls of her greenhouse, our hands reaching into the soil and pulling up carrots. When she was young, Grouse's father, who was the leader at the time, made English the official—and only—language; nothing else could be spoken, not even in the home.

But Diana's mother tongue was sometimes stronger than she was, like a geyser trapped underground and forced to explode. In these rare moments, it was like watching her take off a mask, transforming into an entirely different person. Like those flowers that only bloom once a year for a single night.

The others behind me are beyond exhaustion now, practically asleep on their feet. Eyes open, but not recording. Pushed along by the guards when their legs inadvertently stop and break the steady rhythm. The crying ones are now quiet. The praying ones have run out of wishes. There is nothing around us but total silence, filled by the buzz of nocturnal insects who stay close but keep a cordial distance.

Finally, we reach the base of a black mountain. I look around for an altar, but there isn't one.

Diablo steps forward. He runs his claws through empty space, as though feeling for an invisible doorknob.

"What is he doing?" I whisper, but the girls near me are too cold or weak or discouraged to pay attention.

His crystal claws begin to glow a bright reddish color. Rivulets of sparks escape their tips, spreading out over an imaginary wall, forming complex circles. Then, the current stops, and the circles slowly dissipate. The air ripples, like an invisible curtain. The image in front of me comes into focus like a Magic Eye puzzle, revealing the hidden picture beneath it.

My mouth opens. I blink, wondering if it was there all along; a trick of fatigue or unfamiliarity. That my brain deceived me into missing it. I'm staring at the same black mountain as before—only now a path of lanterns the same color as tonight's moon lead up the hill in a precipitous zigzag, to a cluster of black tents. The sight is both beautiful and sinister.

It's a Klujn settlement.

What just happened? I wonder. *Does it have something to do with electromagnetic pulses? Those invisible colors that conceal them from human eyes?* I think back to my Klujnology classes and consider the possibilities, but I don't know the scientific terms to describe whatever phenomenon I just saw.

Around me, the girls begin to stir from their somnambulism.

"Is that . . ."

"It can't be . . ."

"It is," I say, confidence stirring inside me like a bear, rousing from a long hibernation. Maybe it's because yesterday's lecture is still fresh on my mind, George's words not yet swept away by the tides of time and forgetfulness.

I know exactly where we are.

"Don't you love that," says Poppet, closing her eyes and drawing in a deep breath.

"What?" says Oak. "The smell of blood and bone?"

"No, you dumb slime. The feeling of coming home."

12

Circo. It has to be. I try to remember George's last lecture, but only a few phrases come back: *A cold-climate tribe, home to light-skinned, red-eyed mountain Klujns. One of the largest and most vicious human-eating tribes in the Boreal, but no one can be sure, because no one has even gotten close to finding it.*

Why hadn't I paid more attention in class? What other crucial information did I miss?

"Hurry along, now," says Oak, urging us up the path. As we cross the invisible barrier where the guard was a moment ago, there's a warm sensation against my chest. I reach under my sweater and pull out the crystal pendant.

"Is that real?" Zoe asks. I should lie, but something tells me that it's safe, that she won't try to steal it.

"My dad gave it to me," I say.

"You should keep it hidden," she warns me. "If they see it, they might confiscate it." I unclasp the necklace and stuff it deep into the pocket of my skirt. As I do, she glares at the back of Diablo's hooded head, and the look in her eyes is murderous.

"Hurry up," calls Poppet impatiently. We continue up the path. From up close, I notice the lanterns are made from blown glass. Inside each one, a bundle of crushed leaves is responsible for the gleam. My legs tremble with the effort of another climb. We are high in the mountains now, and the higher we go, the thinner the air feels. I gasp, trying to suck in more oxygen.

Finally, when I am close to collapsing, we arrive at the end of the path. Not completely at the top; the mountain continues upward, but the slope is not as steep as the near-vertical one we just climbed.

"I thought . . . it was . . . over," Wendy rasps from behind me, her breath as scattered as my own. "I thought . . . we were . . . there."

From here, the entirety of the settlement comes into view. Circular black tents are scattered over the mountainside, carefully blending with their surroundings. There must be two or three hundred. Narrow alleyways weave between the tents, little streets that wind from here to the top of the hillside, where the largest structure stands. It's difficult to see clearly from where we are, but it looks large and ominous, like a black temple or a burned-down church. Perhaps it's the arena where they host their most gruesome games.

The sun is beginning to rise behind the mountains to our right. As its first ray bleeds over the ridge, a horn sounds—not mechanical, but something organic and deep, like wind moving through a hollow tree.

"Right on time for bed," Oak announces happily, staying close to the front. Diablo leads us up a narrow street that slithers like a snake's trail, and I notice that the black tents are made out of something that looks like dyed canvas or cloth or smooth bark. There are small fire pits with grills over dying embers. Herb gardens, bursting with wildflowers and greens. Trees are festooned with lanterns and hanging altars and bird feeders. A smell wafts over to me on the crisp morning breeze, sweet like maple snow taffy.

Yet the tents are still and the paths are empty.

Wonder and fear sweep through me. Despite my fatigue, I take in every detail of this strange world. It feels surreal. Shocking, too, but the anesthetic of the leaves bound to my foot has somehow worked its way up to the knot in my chest, unloosing it. I feel as if I'm on a night safari on a dark river in the swamplands, watching for dangerous and exotic beasts.

We pass a tunnel that burrows into the mountain, big enough for a small human. It's so dark it's impossible to see what's there. "It smells like death," says Zoe, pinching her nose.

"How do you know what death smells like?" Wendy asks.

"It's nauseating, but sweet," Zoe replies, only half-answering the question. I catch a strong whiff of the smell. It's rancid. The odor travels down my throat and leaves an acrid taste in my mouth.

"Katacombes," Oak pipes up, following our gaze. "There are miles and miles of underground passageways beneath our feet that connect the different parts of the stand. North to south, east to west, in and out. You wouldn't want to get lost in there. You might never get out."

"What's a stan—" Wendy's interrupted by a loud growl from inside the cave.

"Oh, forgot to mention—that's where the wild dogs live," Oak remarks. "They love the smell of human blood." Wendy gulps audibly. I look over at Zoe. I remember her mentioning that her father was a Hunter, so she must have seen a few dead bodies in her life.

I can't say I know the smell of death. The wolf's body was still too fresh. The only smell that comes close is the meat we used to cook at the orphanage.

And then a name comes to me—*José*. He was one of the orphanage cooks, and we spent most of our afternoons together in the kitchen. José turned everything into a fable with a moral, even a simple story about meat. He was the only adult who spoke to me kindly, who showed any emotion beyond anger or impatience.

"We ate the world."

The words come to me but, out of context, they don't mean anything.

My eyes are open, but a new memory clouds my vision of the Klujn settlement. I see the man's face for the first time in years—tan and kind. The past rises to the surface like a sunken object with new-found buoyancy.

* * *

I am nine, José is seventy-nine, but the age gap is bridged by a mutual love of stories. He is the one who found me when I washed up on the riverbank wrapped in a blue blanket, my umbilical cord freshly healed. My skin was a deep purple, my eyelashes frosted with snow. I wasn't breathing. He said a wolf was pulling at my corpse. José managed to scare it away, then he whispered a prayer in Spanish, his native language. A prayer that was interrupted by my cries.

I came back from the dead.

We have been friends ever since. In front of others, I call him Mr. Cookmore, which is the name he was given when he first set foot in this Territory right before the borders closed, but José insists that I call him by his real name, if only in private.

He always smells like the banana cigarillos he likes to smoke. He makes them himself using the leaves of a miniature banana plant he keeps in his kitchen because it reminds him of home. The little pin José wears on his bloodied apron is a black circle with a gold symbol I don't recognize. His wrinkles are so deep you could hide small objects in them, with laugh lines that haven't been used in years. José talks about his birthplace as we chop wild dandelions to make a salad. It was an island in the Caribbean sea. As the Arctic ice melted and the ocean levels rose, his island disappeared underwater. He is a "climate refugee," he tells me, even though I don't understand what that means. He says that a refugee is someone who is forced to leave their home and make a new home elsewhere, in a place that will never live up to what they've lost, with people who will never fully make them feel at home.

Like me, José loves the ocean. The only difference is that he has seen the ocean, submerged himself in it, and I have not. He tells me about turquoise water and white sand and bright coral reefs. He teaches me about whales and dolphins and turtles and something called bioluminescence, where the sea glows like electric jellyfish.

I can almost smell the salt and taste the coconuts and feel the lap of waves at my feet. Sometimes these stories make José sad, and tears come easily. It's very rare to see a grown man cry.

When I ask more about this place he comes from, José changes the subject and tells me that my curiosity about the world will only get me into trouble. Or worse, heartbroken.

"The world isn't what it once was, princesa,*" he says. "Reality's no fairy tale."*

We go back to our chopping and grating and stirring, talking about the orphanage director and who she punished today and what new children have been dropped off on our doorstep.

José opens the week's Greenhouse delivery and a pungent odor escapes the recycled paper box. A few flies buzz around. We only ever get the food that's not good enough for everyone else—animal carcasses and canned seafood past its sell-by date, half-rotted fruit and vegetables three times larger than they should be. Sometimes they throw in insect flour and maple syrup, the artificially sweet kind, not the real stuff that comes from trees. Today's delivery includes a few crows and a broiler, which is like a poor man's chicken. And lastly, the source of the worst smell: a wild dog.

José shows me how to skin it, and I force myself to watch. The rancid smell sparks a new story, this one about meat.

"We are what we eat," he says, wielding his knife. "This wild dog here smells rotten and sick, because wild dogs feed on garbage and roadkill and it makes their meat taste rotten. See how it's black when it should be pink?" I look at the blue-black lungs and pustulating organs and my insides churn. "Then there are spotted wolves, who only eat plants and roots, so their meat is pinkish-white and tender. That's why they're a Hunter favorite. And that's why they're going extinct." He sighs. "The world has always had it in for vegetarians. Because of their diets, vegetarians are delicious."

"You mean herbivores?" I say.

"Same thing."

* * *

The memory dissolves, and I am back at Circo.

Diablo notices that we have stalled and yanks on our vine shackle. I trip in the dirt, and the dormant pain in my foot stirs. If I don't get something for it soon, it'll get infected. And if that happens, I could lose it.

Somehow, I don't think that these creatures are big on hospitals or doctors.

"Where are all the Klujns?" Wendy asks, noticing the deserted streets.

"They're nocturnal," says Purple Hair. "They're probably in bed. Or underground. However they sleep."

I wish Wendy hadn't tempted fate, because I feel something watching me. I turn to my left and there, through the small window of a tent, I see it: a pair of eyes, tracking our movements. Diablo pulls on our shackles again, and we disappear around a bend. If the dead quiet of morning is this unsettling, I hate to imagine what this place is like at night.

When we're halfway up the hillside, the path levels out. "This way," says Diablo, leading us through a circular plaza. It's small and intimate, surrounded by spruces with blood-red needles. The ground is covered in glimmering black soil, and there's a circle of stones in the center, perhaps a spot for a bonfire. Across the plaza, a steep path continues straight up toward the top of the settlement and that forbidding structure, the arena or whatever it is, but that's not where we're going. We skirt the south side of the plaza and enter an alleyway on the other side.

The flat, slender artery curves around the mountain, heading west, away from the rising sun. We walk past a tree stump, about my height, that's been sculpted into an elaborate candle holder. A green flame flickers on a bed of black melted wax. Behind the candle, a vertical line of moons, stars, and other shapes has been carved into the wood. *Is it a clock of some sort?* I wonder. *Where the symbols keep the time?*

Before I can get a proper look, the guards pull us farther along the path. After a few minutes, we reach a tall fence made of branches and vines and plants that look too colorful to be kind. There's a chill up my spine as Diablo leads us into an enclosure, and another chill as a gate closes behind us.

We are in a large, open clearing with apple trees around the outside. There are circular, charcoal-colored tents of different sizes that surround a small bonfire area with log benches; a poor, unceremonious copy of the one in the main plaza. At the back of the clearing is a training area with a fighting ring, two tire swings, and pull-up bars. I shiver again. Here, the warm rays of the morning sun don't reach.

Diablo turns to Oak and Poppet. "You may go now," he says. "The king thanks you for your service."

"What about a bonus?" Oak asks hungrily, his yellow eyes fixed on a girl behind me.

"You know the rules," says Diablo. "They're guests, not toys." Oak's shoulders slump in disappointment.

"Come on," Poppet says. "Enough sulking. There is more work to be done."

"Work?" Oak shakes his head. "I'm going straight to sleep." As they walk off, he stuffs a nugget of green herb into his pipe. The two slip out the gate and disappear into the settlement.

"These are your quarters," Diablo points to a large tent on the far right. "That's where you sleep. And that's where you eat," he says, indicating the medium-sized tent next to it. "Twice a day. Night and morning."

"What about where we . . . well, you know," Wendy pipes up. "I've been holding it in all night." He points toward a mud wall on the far left, near the gate. A few holes have been dug into the ground behind it, poorly hidden from view.

"So basically, we shit out in the open?" Purple Hair mutters, not bothering to hide her disdain. "What happens if we have our period?"

"Enough questions." Diablo is impatient. "The king will explain everything tonight at the Ceremony of Fire."

"Great. I'll be sure to ask him for a tampon."

A few of the girls snicker, but I'm too consumed by what he just said. What is the Ceremony of Fire? George never mentioned it in his lectures. Is it part of the senior curriculum? I am relieved to see that Wendy and Purple Hair look as confused as I am.

Diablo and the two remaining red-eyed guards lead us to a row of large buckets near the entrance of the mess tent. They untie our vine shackles and position us in a straight line. I rub my wrist, which is red and chafed, but this injury is the least of my concerns.

Before I have time to contemplate my newfound freedom or what I could do with it, Diablo looms over me. "Strip," he says.

"Sorry?"

"Strip," he repeats, his voice a growl that makes my molars clench.

I throw a glance down the row and see that the others are being ordered to do the same. "Now."

Diablo reaches for my sweater, but I hold up my hands and manage some words. "*All right.*"

I pull off my blood- and sweat-soaked sweater, then unbutton my blue corduroy skirt and let it drop to the ground. I step out of it, leaving it in its small crumpled circle. Then I pull off what's left of my now battered boots and stockings.

As soon as I've pushed the clothes aside, I remember the pendant in my skirt pocket.

It's irretrievable now.

I stand in front of the Klujn guard, half naked and shivering. So much of my body is on display—the tangle of scars on my arms, the bite mark, my damaged foot, the blemishes and puffy areas that are exacerbated by daylight. I regret yesterday morning's decision not to shave my bikini line. Not that any of those things matter now, but I can't help dwelling on them. No one has ever seen me this way, let alone a creature of the opposite sex.

Diablo's eyes run down my body and linger on my arms for a moment. I wonder if he'll ask me to keep going, to strip *all the way*, but he seems satisfied.

Next to me, Zoe is down to a white tank top and underwear, showing skinny legs. Wendy holds a book in front of her soft stomach—it must have been hidden inside one of her many pockets. The edges of the pages are silver, and silver words gleam from the black cover. Her guard gives it a cursory glance and tosses it onto her pile of clothes. Purple Hair's only possessions are a fading glow stick and a vape. She has one of those smooth, toned bodies with nothing to hide, not even in broad daylight.

"It's a mineral vape," Purple Hair tells one of the red-eyed guards. "I'm Vitamin D deficient. It helps with seasonal depression." She looks at him defiantly, angry, or excited, it's impossible to tell. Her guard ignores her. Throws her belongings on the ground.

My eyes continue down the row, stealing curious glances at the others. I notice that they are all female as I suspected earlier, except a scrawny redhead who has male parts visible through his underwear. However, the Klujns don't seem surprised by this.

I realize how different we all are beneath our clothes—a menagerie of curious specimens. Large, thin, strong, frail. Piercings and tattoos, birthmarks and cellulite, and the usual smorgasbord of birth defects.

I have almost finished when my eyes land on a girl I recognize. It's her, I'm sure of it, although she looks much less confident without her clothes on: Reesa, the annoying know-it-all from my Klujnology class. *Has she seen me?* She might not recognize me, either.

As I wonder how—or *where*—she got caught, Diablo dumps a ladle of frigid water over my head. The cold hits me like an avalanche, knocking the breath from my lungs. He throws a brush at me, a little round plant with spiky bristles, dry and scratchy like a loofah. The other guards are doing the same.

"Scrub," he orders, and I start to move the brush over my skin in small circles. "Harder!" I do as he tells me. The brush exfoliates dirt and dead skin, making it foam in small brown swirls. Then, another ladle of icy water crashes down over my shoulders, as painful and unexpected as the first, and the dirty water slides to the ground.

My teeth chatter. My knees knock. I'm cold. *So* cold. The kind of cold that seeps into your bones and makes you feel like you'll never be warm again. I crave the ecstasy of a hot shower, even a tepid one, like back home. It's hard to believe that only twelve hours ago I was at the Klujn Fair with Mercy, eating a bouquet of bug fries. My mouth waters at the memory of their crunchy, salty warmth on my tongue.

I realize just how hungry I am—famished, even. What I wouldn't do to eat until my stomach is full to its bursting point and then crawl into a warm bed.

As I keep scrubbing, I remember the last words I said to Mercy, about how I called him a coward, even though I meant it jokingly. Or did I? I never know how to act around him. It's like I'm treading on a frozen lake, my words like footsteps, always one comment away from catastrophe. Like I have to hold back so that I'm not too much, too weird, too me. *I always ruin things*, I think. With my actions or with my words. That's why it's easier not to make friends in the first place. Walls were invented for a reason.

Diablo throws a few more ladles of water over my head. Then, when he seems satisfied, he drops the ladle back into the bucket.

"Can we keep our things?" Purple Hair asks.

"They will be returned later."

She snorts. "Yeah, right."

The guards throw bundles of black clothes our way. "Get dressed," Diablo orders. "Then go eat."

I unfold the bundle. All black. There's a long-sleeved top, a silky high-waisted skirt that travels down to my ankles, a pair of supple shoes, and a hooded cloak. I slip the clothes over my damp underwear and bralette. They are warm and snug, like a nightgown. Then I put on the shoes, which stretch enough to accommodate my swollen right foot. It has turned the color of an old bruise. Finally, I throw on the leathery black cloak. It's like being enveloped in a heated blanket. My teeth stop chattering and the memory of the cold ebbs away.

When we are all dressed in our matching black uniforms, it's Purple Hair who speaks.

"Did he say eat? I don't know about you guys, but I'm starving." She takes off toward the mess tent and disappears inside. I watch her go, wondering if her confidence is real.

"Come on," I tell Wendy and Zoe and anyone else who will listen. "She's right. We should go eat something." I start toward the tent and am surprised to see that some of the others are following me. It's a novel feeling.

13

The interior of the mess tent is a surprise.

The ceiling is striped in reds and golds. Two crescent-shaped tables face one another, with black glass candleholders that cast miniature galaxies onto a black tablecloth. At my table are Wendy, Purple Hair, a pretty brunette wearing eyeliner, and two others who keep to themselves. They were at the back of the pack, so they must have been among the first ones to get caught. I look for Zoe, and find her seated at the other table. I don't know why this feels like a betrayal after what we went through on the mountain, but it does.

Before us is a strange, colorful buffet: fruit, vegetables, bowls of hot food, and salads garnished with flowers. Despite the variety, there isn't all that much to go around.

"What if it's poisoned?" Wendy asks, studying the exotic spread with skepticism. "The brightest plants and animals are always the most venomous." She sits next to me, a little too closely for my liking, but I can hardly tell her to move away. I don't want to hurt her feelings.

"That's not true," says Purple Hair. "The most dangerous animals are Klujns."

"And they're pretty colorful," Wendy rebukes.

"Then you try it," says Purple Hair.

Wendy looks torn between a healthy appetite and the desire not to die. *Why would they bring us all this way just to poison us?* I think.

"I don't see you making a move," Wendy says. "And I didn't catch your name."

"Elizabeth," answers Purple Hair. "Not 'Lizzie,' not 'Liz,' not 'Beth.' *Elizabeth.*" Her enunciation is crisp, impatient, and precise.

"Well, *Elizabeth*, if you're so brave, you go first." But Elizabeth doesn't budge.

"Since we're introducing ourselves, I'm Willa," the brunette with the eyeliner says. She has chipped black nail polish and a small tattoo of a five-pointed star on the inside of her left wrist.

"Where did *you* come from?" snaps Elizabeth.

Willa smiles. "Fourth row, in the cluster of crying girls."

"No one asked your name." Wendy gives this Willa a look. From what I've seen of Wendy so far—her upbeat, affable demeanor—this comment seems out of character.

My eyes go from Wendy to Willa and back again. "Wait a minute. Are you two *sisters*?"

"She's right," Elizabeth says. "They are! Military mom or dad?"

"Mom," Wendy admits.

"So why didn't you say anything before?" Elizabeth demands.

"We're not exactly on speaking terms," Willa answers coolly. "After Wendy got us captured."

Wendy gets flustered. "Why is it my fault?"

"Because it was *your* stupid idea to go out in the first place!"

"You didn't have to follow me."

"If I didn't, you'd be dead."

The sisters exchange rapid-fire insults across the table. As they do, I reach forward and pluck a glacier-colored berry from the pile of fruit. I pop it in my mouth. There's an explosion of ice-cold sweetness on my tongue.

Wendy and Willa break off and stare at me. I feel nervous with the sudden attention. They wait, wondering if I'll die a gruesome death by poison, but nothing happens. I swallow.

"They're winterberries," I say. "My adoptive mother grows them in her greenhouse. They're edible."

Before I've even finished speaking, everyone's already reaching for the food, even the other two girls, who haven't said a word. The gates of our appetites open and soon we're stuffing it into our mouths as quickly as we possibly can.

"Try the pink stuff."

"What *is* that?"

"I want to say sweet potato?"

"We don't have sweet potato in Justice Falls."

"We have everything in Mount Dominion," Elizabeth boasts.

"The apple compote is delicious," Willa says, eating what looks like brown stew. She picks a purple flower from the top and tries it. "The flowers are good too."

"I can't believe your family has their own greenhouse," Wendy tells me. "That's cool as a dead girl's kiss."

It's a little overwhelming, this chaos of girls and conversation. I need a moment of solitude, where I can lie down and close my eyes and get my thoughts in order.

"I love fresh fruit so much," continues Wendy. She takes another bite and a glob of pink oozes onto her shirt like jam. "Oh, crap. Why is that always happening?"

"Because you're a slob," Willa tells her. "You should try chewing your food, instead of inhaling it."

"I would kill for a kanum steak," Elizabeth mutters. "Or kanum bacon and blue sparrow eggs."

"I've never tried kanum," Wendy says glumly. "Dad's against it."

"Too bad for you. My mom and I eat kanum all the time."

Wendy moves on to a bowl of marigold-colored potatoes, cut in thick wedges. She looks at it inquiringly. "What is this? Plantain? Squash?"

"Those two aren't even in the same family," says Willa. "And don't eat it all. There's barely enough to go around."

"It's all just so foreign," Wendy muses, letting Willa steal the bowl away from her.

"No protein, though," Elizabeth remarks. "I guess they keep it all for themselves and give us captives the scraps."

"Plants, nuts, and legumes have protein," says Wendy. "Sometimes, in the forest, it's all we can find to sustain us."

I slice into a thick brown-and-yellow steak that looks like a grilled sunflower. The flavor is unusual, but not unpleasant. Growing up with Diana, I've become used to a wide variety of vegetables and tastes.

A few more minutes in, and we've almost cleared the table. I'm thirsty from all the different flavors and spices so I fill my glass from the nearest pitcher. I take a sip. The golden drink is sweet, fizzy, refreshing. I down the whole thing.

"Be careful with that," Wendy says. "It's sparkling dandelion wine. That stuff goes straight to your head. I drank three mugs' worth on my last Scout trip to Tremble Hills last spring and puked all over my tent. It's not an experience I would recommend."

Elizabeth takes the jar of wine and fills up her own glass, almost to the brim. "Maybe getting drunk will help us forget where we are," she says, then adds, "You know what I wish I could try?" There's a dangerous look in her eyes. "*Klandestine.*"

"That's illegal," Wendy is aghast.

"What's Klandestine?" I ask, immediately reprimanding myself for how young and inexperienced my voice sounds.

"It's the green herb that the little guard was smoking," Elizabeth says. "You can smoke it, drink it, sniff it. If you take a little bit, it makes you stronger and fiercer. It makes you more *Klujn.*"

"Like steroids," says Willa.

"Only better," Elizabeth smirks.

"What happens if you take a lot?" I ask.

"It can make you lose your mind," Wendy finishes.

I look at the three of them. "Where did you learn all that?" I ask, trying to sound more confident this time, like I don't really need the answer.

Elizabeth shrugs and points to Wendy: "Scout girl." To Willa: "Witch girl." To herself: "Me, I'm self-taught."

"I guess we'll cover it next term," I say.

"What are you, a junior?" Elizabeth asks. I nod. Her laugh is knowing, condescending. "I remember junior year. We didn't learn any-thing we couldn't see on television or read in a government textbook." Her words crush me. I hate the way she feels the need to assert her dom-inance, how small and inadequate it makes me feel. "What a waste of time," she continues. "Even senior year is a joke. If you want to know anything that matters, you have to learn it for yourself."

"Then how did you become an expert on everything?" Wendy in-quires imploringly. "Books?"

An eye roll from Elizabeth. "I've never been much into theory. I prefer to *experience* things."

Wendy looks at me; her big eyes are sympathetic. "If it makes you feel any better, I'm a junior, too."

"What about you?" I ask Willa.

"Senior," she says, almost apologetically. "But Elizabeth's right—everything I learned, I learned outside of school. In my *extracurricular* activities."

They continue to pick at the leftovers, but I've lost my appetite. The knot in my chest is back. *Why didn't George and Diana teach me anything? And why didn't they let me do Scouts like the other girls?* You'd think that having a teacher and an agriculturalist for parents would be advantageous somehow. If they had taught me things, I would be better equipped to survive here. To face . . . whatever this is.

My eyes drift to the opposite table. Most of the others look older than me, with a few exceptions. The largest is a wall of a girl. She has a black tuft of hair over her heart-shaped face, with broad shoulders and strong arms beneath her cloak. A small blue tattoo of a triangle beneath her left ear indicates she's in her first year of Military training. She must be eighteen or nineteen. Next to her are three girls with silver hair and matching headbands that read *Brave Night High*—I've heard that some of Grouse's followers dye their hair silver. They're huddled to-gether, speaking in low tones. I don't know if they were friends at school, but they sure look friendly now. Next, a mousy girl with brown braids. Her quivering lip and snotty nose suggest she's been crying. She can't be older than fourteen. Then the red-haired boy, then Zoe, and finally,

Reesa, who looks at the food with disgust. Aside from the silver-haired trio, nobody else at the table speaks.

My attention returns to my table and our empty plates. There's a question on my mind, but I don't want to ask any more questions. Thankfully, Willa beats me to it. "Why do they bother feeding us?"

"In the book I'm reading, Catrina Sherman says that—" Wendy starts.

Elizabeth cuts her off. "Isn't it obvious?" The table goes quiet. "They want us to be strong so we'll fight. If we can't hold up a weapon, what fun would that be?" Her words hit like the ladles of freezing water from before.

The food, the banter. They were all distractions to keep ourselves from asking the real question: *Why are we here?*

"Is that what we're actually going to be doing? Fighting?" Willa asks, her voice wary, as though she only wants to know the answer if it's kind.

"Why else did you think they brought us here?" says Elizabeth, with her inherent sarcasm. "A safari? A cultural exchange program? Isn't it obvious? We're contestants in the Blood Race."

14

After we finish eating, we are taken to the main tent. I fall into a deep slumber, filled only with the frantic sounds of running and panting and the feeling of vertigo ripping through my insides as I'm thrown over a cliff edge. When I open my eyes, it takes me a moment to recover. I notice a flap in the tent behind my pillow. I open it and see that it's already twilight, the sky all purples and yellows like smeared passionfruit. We must have slept at least ten hours. Somehow, I feel like I could sleep longer, could sleep right through the night, but the Klujns have other plans.

Diablo and the two red-eyed guards shake us awake and order us to change into new black outfits that lay at the foot of our beds. I haul my body upright. My muscles are sore from yesterday and my foot is still numb. I examine the leaf bandage; it's peeling off. I lick my finger and try to glue it back down but it won't stick anymore.

This new outfit looks more ceremonial than the ones we have on. More like a costume. It's a jumpsuit with long sleeves, an elegant V-neck, and a fitted bodice that descends into billowy pants. The fabric is soft and breathable. The chest is covered with black crystals that catch the half-light of the tent, casting tiny rainbows of light on the walls. It fits like a second skin. So does everyone else's. We are all dressed alike, including the redheaded boy. I overhear one of the silver-haired girls making a snide remark about him, and her friends laugh.

After we eat breakfast—*at dusk*—Diablo and the two guards lead us out into the settlement. I rub sleep from my eyes. The sun has only just disappeared behind the neighboring mountains, but night comes quick and dark. I watch as tonight's blue moon rises in the sky, moving with the speed of clouds. So clear and bright. But how can it feel that much closer, that much more luminous? The stars appear one by one, like spectators coming to a fight.

Where the streets were once empty in daylight, they are now bustling with life. Blue lanterns dangle from every available surface. Everywhere I turn, there are Klujns in colorful cloaks going about their nocturnal activities. Some make objects out of dried plants and carve weapons out of crystals. Others drink mysterious potions and cook skewers on small fires. The delicious smell of barbecue makes my mouth water. *Maybe it's human meat*, I realize with horror.

A female Klujn sits in her small garden, the tips of her claws in the dirt, muttering a chant. Green light builds at the base of her claws and escapes into the earth, making previously invisible molecules glow with bioluminescence. Another female holds a large vase of water. Her claws emit trails of blue light as they trace symbols on the water's surface, making it fizz.

As the creatures sense our presence, they stop what they're doing and watch us, like the animals in the Deeper Woods. They don't come at us, don't pounce, but there's something even more sinister about their quiet observation.

Most of the girls keep their eyes trained on the ground, but I can't help looking—it's mesmerizing.

We pass a little stall where cauldrons of glowing substances bubble and smoke like alchemical flasks—bright purple, cherry red, black. We walk by a group of Klujn children: pale, brown-haired boys and girls dressed in cloaks of different colors, some with spotted wolves at their sides. When the children see us, they don't run away or hide. Instead, they peer at us openly with sharp red eyes.

There are animals, too, perched among the trees. I catch sight of a mint-colored lizard walking along a low branch, and a flutter of teal wings.

Finally, after a few minutes that feel much longer, we reach a circular plaza. It's the same one we passed on our arrival at Circo, only it looks much more reverent now than it did in daylight.

The black soil glimmers like a night sky. Klujns are crowded around the perimeter of trees whose trunks have been painted with eerie, glowing faces. Five guards stand at equal intervals. Each has a wild dog at their feet—smaller than spotted wolves, with lithe bodies and ferocious amber eyes. A circle of black candles separates them from the stage area.

There, symbols have been traced onto the soil like numbers on a clock. Fourteen, I count. One for each of us. They resemble the ones I saw carved onto the tree stump, or smudged on the trees in the Deeper Woods. *Are these Klujn numbers? Or an alphabet of some kind?*

Diablo leads us into the glimmering black ring. The Klujns wait, they whisper, they watch, keen for the spectacle to start. It is a small, intimate, macabre outdoor theater. A setting for a ritual of some kind.

One at a time, Diablo sits us down in front of a symbol. I am third to last, after Elizabeth. I look down and see a crescent. A few feet to my left, Wendy fills the second to last seat and, finally, Reesa.

On the other side of the plaza, I notice the dwarf Klujns, Oak and Poppet, waiting on either side of the path that leads to the peak of the settlement. They are dressed more formally now. Poppet has a large necklace of white cloth and crystals around her neck and shoulders; Oak has the same in red. They each hold a wooden cylinder with skin stretched tight on one end. *Drums.*

Oak begins to play, his short fingers thrumming against the tight skin, a gentle pitter-patter that sounds like rain. Poppet joins in, hitting her drum with an open palm. The deep, unsettling rhythm reaches into the cavity of my ribs, jolting my heart in time with it. As the drums grow louder and faster, the organ quickens.

In the dark alleyway behind Oak and Poppet, the light of a lantern becomes visible. Two figures descend toward the plaza. I see a hideous red-eyed guard, his face too narrow and his chin too large. Behind him is a creature in crimson robes. He is the first Klujn I have seen—and the only one in the plaza—wearing that color.

The drums suddenly stop, but my heart keeps going. I sense the circle of watching Klujns tense in response to his arrival. Out of the corner of my eye, I see Diablo, and even he looks uncomfortable in this particular Klujn's presence.

The red-robed Klujn enters the circle of black candles. He walks barefoot, moving lightly around the ring, observing us. Candlelight casts shadows on his blistered face, illuminating every horrifying feature. The beast is tall, and even though his cloak hides his frame, I can tell he is muscular. A crown of red acorns and large crystals sits atop his head. His skin is pale, his eyes an ireful red. His most notable characteristic is his menacing claws; two inches of murky white crystal. Small teeth—*human?*—are dreaded into his long chestnut hair. *Maybe they're relics from those who were here before us*, I think. He doesn't appear to be particularly young, but he isn't elderly either. I don't know how long a Klujn lifespan is, but I would guess he's middle-aged.

Wendy lets out a little high-pitched note that sounds like a stifled scream. "Holy tsunami," she manages. "I think that's the king."

I smell urine, and I'm almost certain one of the hostages has wet themselves. Zoe, who sits across from me, keeps looking over at the path that leads downhill, as though searching for an escape route. She should know the chances of that are slim.

"Welcome to Circo," says the creature. His English is good, but not without an accent. "I am Warwick, king of this stand. A stand is what we call a group of Klujns *and* their settlements. It is an unusual name, given that we are nomadic, but I did not invent it. It is a term derived from the forests which we inhabit." Warwick smiles, with an oddly jolly, gregarious sort of charm. As he does, I notice that his teeth aren't the razor-sharp fangs I would have imagined, but they are instead very human. "Circo will be your home for the next four rotations of the earth," he continues. "I assume you've already guessed why you're here. I see that the guards have done a fine job selecting this Blood Moon's performers. Quite the assortment," he says, and grins like he's looking at a tantalizing box of chocolates. "Fresh minds."

"Fresh *meat*," Elizabeth mutters.

"Did he say *selecting?*" Wendy says from my other side. "More like *violently abducting.*"

The king pauses in front of her. Wendy freezes, blanches. The king smiles. "Here, at Circo, you surrender what you've been taught," he says. "And you learn to think for yourselves."

He stops in front of me. We take each other in. For a second, I forget that I'm dealing with a barbarous, human-eating beast. Beyond the fierce scarlet, his eyes are almost . . . kind.

"The Blood Race is one of our most sacred traditions," he continues. "Just like the trees with whom we share the forest, a young Klujn is sheltered by its elders, only allowed the most basic knowledge for most of their young lives until the moment is right—the emergence of their first viaţăs.

"Then, two days before the next Blood Moon, the newly matured Klujns set out on their Blood Race. They travel through the dangerous wilderness to a destination of our choosing, collecting proof of passage before returning home to the new location of the stand. They must make it back by the Ice Moon in January, and the order in which they return is important: it will determine who first chooses their profession and their mate. Many young Klujns are lost along the way, for Nature is a ruthless teacher. Those who return do so with a deeper understanding of the wild, themselves, and their purpose in the stand.

"Here, at Circo, you are to participate in a Blood Race of your own," he announces as if it is an honor. "Although this one will be conducted in and around the stand, you will be tested, you will fight, and—like our young Klujns—your eyes will be opened to the truths of the world. Those who show resilience and adaptability will go far. Those who resist change and cling to old beliefs will perish."

He draws himself up and his voice becomes more resonant. "But the Blood Race isn't simply a competition. Like a prism, it has many sides. It is also a grandiose, tricky game, a feast of moonlight, a festival for our gods, a dark coming-of-age, and finally—a battle between truth and lies."

"Right," Elizabeth mutters. "That, and getting brutally murdered in an arena in front of a live audience." Apparently not having heard her, the king continues around the circle to the other humans.

"Starting tomorrow, you will compete in a series of challenges," the king says delightedly, as though explaining the rules to a particularly thrilling sport. "Like any journey, you will be tested, not only physically but mentally as well. The road to the arena at the top will be difficult and unpredictable. Most of you will be eliminated by natural means."

"Natural means?" Wendy whispers. "I sure as shooting don't like the sound of that."

"But, if you respect our customs and acclimatize to our ways, you may make it farther than you ever thought. Because three of you can make it to the ultimate challenge, and three of you can earn back your freedom. If it may be of encouragement to you," says the king, "some humans have survived the Blood Race and left Circo with their lives."

"Oh yeah? Where are they now?" Reesa asks scornfully from Wendy's other side. Silence. I freeze. The others freeze. There's a tense moment as the cannibal king's red eyes sweep over us until they find Reesa. They zero in on her, like a pair of Hunter's binoculars homing in on their target. And then, when the tension cannot get any thicker, the king lets out a laugh.

"That, I'm afraid, is a question for humans," he says. "And a good one."

"What if we don't *want* to fight?" Reesa asks.

Shut up, I think. *Before you get yourself killed.* The king's smile vanishes.

"THEN DON'T!" he roars, his voice like a spurt of flame that could singe off your eyebrows. "But fighting is only one small component of a much bigger process. If you are too ignorant to see that, then perhaps you should leave now." Reesa doesn't answer. He turns to the rest of us. "You may think your culture is more sophisticated than ours and that humans are superior to all living things. You have become disconnected from the natural world. As a guest here, your feelings of superiority will only hinder you," he says, his voice now ice. "You can either embrace the challenges ahead, or you can take a wander down into the tight tunnels of the Katacombes and visit our dogs instead. When the dogs are sated, they stop growling for several hours. The citizens of Circo love a bit of peace and quiet." As he says this, a faint rumble carries on the night breeze.

"One final note," he tells us. The watching Klujns are stone silent. "When we come face to face with the truth, we do everything in our power to resist it. During the Blood Race, everything that you've tried so hard to stifle will find its way to the surface. The truth of your world and your true self will emerge. Be wary of whom you befriend. Those friends may betray you . . . or perhaps you may betray them."

I throw glances at Wendy and the others, who all avoid eye contact.

"What if we do make it?" the Military girl asks. Her voice is respectful, not supercilious like Reesa's.

"If you survive until the end, you will be granted your freedom. It's up to you what you decide to do with it."

The king holds his lantern above the circle of black stones. Suddenly, he drops it, and the glass smashes. Fire spreads rapidly, filling the black circle with blue-green flames. They lick at the air like a thousand snakes, reaching upward with their split tongues. The king reaches for one of a dozen pokers that stick out of the soil. He picks it up and holds it into the flames. Its tip glows a searing phosphorescent green. Then he nods to Diablo, who approaches the girl sitting at the first symbol. Diablo's hand closes around her arm and he brings her to the center.

"What's your name?" Warwick asks her.

"Jade," she says, not looking the king in the eyes. One of the two girls who were sitting at our table last night—or was it this morning? She looks strong enough, with tattoos on her chest and arms.

"Where are you from, Jade?"

"M-Mission Creek."

"A city girl," says the king. "My favorite kind." Jade tenses as Diablo pulls her arm from underneath her leathery cloak, exposing a patch of soft pink flesh on her right forearm. The king presses the tip of the glowing poker into the girl's arm. Jade's face contracts, but she doesn't scream.

He lifts it away to reveal a burn shaped like a horizontal wave inside a circle.

"You are Number One," Warwick tells her, "and yours is the god of the Lake."

I'm grateful I'm not first, I think, as Diablo escorts the girl back to her place, and I realize that the symbol in the soil matches the burn on her arm.

Then it's the second girl's turn. She is much less composed than her predecessor. Girl Number Two has to be dragged to the flames. The more she resists, the harder Diablo's grip becomes. The girl's name is Mabry, I discover, right before the king picks a new rod and brands her with the Klujn symbol for River. The ritual continues, and I learn the others' names and symbols. Third is the Military girl—Ying Yue, who is branded with a Seed. Fourth, fifth, and sixth are the inseparable silver-haired trio: Benilda, Rachel, and Coco. Earth, Mountains, Wind. Seventh is Zoe, who gets Forest. Next is Rory, the redhead, who gets Tundra, and ninth is Bindu, the mousy girl who's always crying, and her symbol is a Star—represented by a tiny constellation of seven dots. As she walks, she tries unsuccessfully to hide the wet patch on the back of her cloak. Willa is tenth, and she gets the god of Spirit. By the time Elizabeth sits down, nursing her mark for Fire, sweat has made swimming holes of my hands.

Diablo grabs me by the arm and leads me to the flames. For a second, it's like I've forgotten how to walk, but I don't want to be carried like some of the others. I struggle to put one foot in front of the other: *left, right, left, right.*

After an endless moment, we reach the king. He is even more terrifying from up close; his face is a mask of scars and sunspots and his claws are devilishly pointed.

"Your name?" he asks.

"Ava," I manage. My mouth is so dry that my voice rasps. I would kill for a glass of water.

King Warwick nods. "Welcome, Ava. You are Number Twelve, and yours is the god of the Moon. The queen of the night, she is duplicitous, showing both darkness and light. A favorite to some in this game." I watch as he pulls a new rod from the ground and lets it sizzle in the flames. *It'll hurt less if I don't resist.*

Diablo takes my arm, and the king raises the scorching rod. It meets my skin with a hiss and the smell of burning flesh.

Pain rips through me, cold yet hot, sharp and intense. I am sucked into a tunnel. When the poker leaves my skin, I am shooting out into the vast expanse of space, floating among the stars. Then falling, falling . . .

When I come back to this earth and my body, I am quite literally falling. Diablo catches and steadies me. His grip, no matter how vile, is a small mercy.

I return to my spot and sit down, my arm throbbing as the burn seems to spread under my skin like a flesh-eating disease. I look down at the red crescent moon seared into me, about the size of a daisy head.

Then it's Wendy's turn. Warwick greets her with the same intrigue he offered the other girls and Rory. He tells her that thirteen is a very lucky number for Klujns. Their arenas are thirteen strides across. Thirteen is the number of important constellations in the sky. And, on top of that, it's the symbol of the Sun, which in his opinion is the most powerful god of all, despite the popularity of the Moon. Color drains from her face as the poker makes contact, but she swallows her scream.

Finally, it's Reesa's turn, and she goes—not without complaint. Her symbol is Creatures.

Soon we are back in our complete circle, ordered like cattle before slaughter.

I wait, wondering what's next, but I don't have to wait long. Warwick reaches into his cloak and pulls out a thick wad of dried green plants bound together with colorful thread. He dips it in the flames. It catches fire, then he blows it out and a dense trail of black smoke rises.

Willa whispers something under her breath, "It's some kind of banishing stick. We use them in rituals to cleanse a space before performing spells. It chases the bad energy away. Like obsidian," she says, indicating the black crystals on our costumes.

Oak and Poppet resume playing their drums, only this time the rhythm is ominous and slow, punctuating the king's movements. He begins to walk around the ring, moving in a counterclockwise direction, starting with Reesa. The king fans the smoke over her head then continues. After a moment, it reaches my nostrils. I recognize the smell of sage and pine. It seems harmless enough.

By the time Warwick closes the circle, we are completely engulfed in a thick cloud of black smoke. He tosses what's left of the plant into the fire. My eyes sting, and I can't see much through the fumes.

All of a sudden, I feel myself growing very tired.

"We Klujns have many gods," intones the king, and his voice sounds far away now. "They are the gods of Nature—of Earth, Wind, Fire, Water, Moon, Sun—to name a few. They are everywhere, in everything. They inhabit our forests and rivers and the ether that binds all things. They shield us from enemies and danger, help our food to grow, and protect our animals, so long as we respect them. But right now, our gods are not happy, because the temple that is their home—the home we all share—has been destroyed by you. Tonight, those angry gods peer into your hearts and banish the one who shows the least promise of change."

The smoke clears just enough for me to see the king's face as he finishes his speech. The conviction on his features, like he really believes in the philosophy of his so-called gods. *It's nonsense*, I tell myself. Just a cautionary tale to shock us into good behavior. Gods don't exist, and even if they did, they couldn't peer into our hearts. How would they even banish us? They have no bodies, no weapons, no hands. But as I ruminate on this, a feeling of apprehension begins to flow through me; a premonition that something bad is about to happen.

A cool breeze caresses my neck, even though the night is windless.

The drums continue, and I feel myself somehow moving further and further away from the fire, back inside myself.

"Don't fall asleep," Wendy murmurs urgently, but staying awake requires too much effort. I am drifting away, slipping into dark water, both light as air and heavy as lead. I sink, and as I do, I am a baby again, tossed into a river. Caught in a maelstrom of vicious white water. It drags me up and down, up and down but never allows me to reach the surface. I am drowning, my small lungs filling with water. Then, through the ripple of bubbles, I see . . . the blue eyes of a wolf, swimming toward me.

"Ava."

I see other splintered images—sharp and ephemeral.

The touch of a wolf's fur beneath my fingers.

George, sitting on my bed, sliding a book over to me. Black cover, gold edges.

A flutter of blue wings.

The tines of a fork stabbing into a piece of pinkish-white meat.

Standing on a pebble beach, blinded by the brightest moonlight I've ever seen.

"Ava." It's Wendy's voice. I cling to it, and it lifts me out of that dark water, back to earth, back to the bonfire, until I can breathe again.

Oxygen. At last.

I have returned to my body and our circle. The smoke is slowly clearing.

The cool breeze touches my neck once more, and it feels oddly like something leaving my body. As if it was inside me, peering into my memories, turning over stones, opening doors that have been closed for years. A mind without a brain, sight without eyes, touch without hands.

The god of the Moon?

Its passage through me has left an imprint behind, like wet footsteps in an empty hallway. What was it looking for? *What did it find?*

The smoke has fully dispersed now, and I notice that some of my fellow captives are looking around like me, while others are staring straight ahead, eyes glazed as their respective gods course through them. I wait for whatever is next, wondering if I have passed this invisible test, wondering who will fail.

And then, I hear it. A shriek.

My head snaps to the left. Reesa. Only this person looks nothing like the Reesa I know. Her eyes are entirely black, inky and demonic, showing no whites. Her face morphs into a hideous mask. Her neck jerks unnaturally, her tongue snapping in and out of her mouth like a chameleon trying to catch a fly.

The god of Creatures.

Before I can fully understand what's happening—this abrupt, phantasmagorical transformation—Reesa shrieks again. One long, chilling, animal wail. She stands with the broken, twitchy movements of an animal learning to walk for the first time. Then she finds her footing and stalks toward the center circle of black stones. She leaps over it, directly into the flames. Suddenly, harrowingly, I realize where the Ceremony of Fire gets its name.

The fire turns from turquoise to red with excitement and conspiracy. Reesa's clothes catch fire, then her body. A gasp escapes my mouth, and I realize I'm standing, as is the Military girl, standing too close to the flames. But Reesa is buried so deep in the inferno that there's nothing I or anyone can do to get her out without getting hurt ourselves.

I'm unable to turn my gaze away as Reesa's body burns. I watch the fire ravage her hair until there's nothing left but melted scalp. The way her muscles wither and the heat melts fat. A drop of it falls on the bed of embers below and the fire reacts fervently, explosively. For a fraction of a second, it is like I can see the silhouettes of excited gods dancing in the flames. Their mouths open, their pointed tongues hanging out, ready to catch every single drop.

Wendy stands close behind me, both hands over her mouth. Across the circle, Zoe throws up violently. Most of the others have turned away or shielded their eyes. But I can't look away. I have to see. My eyes drink everything in, like a wanderer in the dust bowls arriving at a freshwater oasis.

Reesa's shriek continues to elapse over the longest minute of my life. It's the sound of torture, distress, agony . . . or maybe it's some kind of ecstasy. A pleasure I've never experienced. Then, finally, her shriek dies down until it stops completely. And then there are no sounds at all. What is left of her body drops like a tree succumbing to a chainsaw's blade and lies there . . . charred black like the night on the human side of the fences. The flames continue to lick at her corpse, albeit with less vigor than before. Her body no longer looks human. It looks like a spit roast, left on the fire overnight after the township's denizens have gone to bed.

Reesa might have been a know-it-all. She might have been annoying. But she didn't deserve to die like this. Or die at all.

It's my first time, I think. *Seeing a person die*. But then I remember the wolf—and even though he wasn't a person, he was just as big, and his eyes were more expressive than any human eyes. If a human gets a soul, then why doesn't an animal get one? Reesa's death echoes that recent loss. My sorrow hits like rain on already-saturated earth and bursts the riverbanks in my heart.

The king looks amused. We are sitting and standing, our perfect circle broken. "Well, that was hardly a surprise," he says with dry humor. "Our gods have little patience for ignorance. It was clear from the outset that she did not want to learn a thing."

He turns and exits the plaza, followed by his guard. They disappear into the darkness of the upper settlement—or *stand*—and my eyes return to the fire.

It has settled to a low green flicker, like a beast satisfied after a big meal. I realize I've been holding my breath. I exhale, then take in a large gulp of air. A smell fills my nostrils—nauseating but sweet. A thick, sulfurous odor, so intense I can almost taste it.

The smell of death.

15

In the dim light of our sleeping tent, I can barely see the others' faces but I can hear their cries. We lie on our thin mattresses, a few of us sitting up, wrapped in warm blankets. The tent isn't very large. Our mattresses are on the floor, so close they're almost touching. The mousy girl on my left is turned away, weeping deep, distraught tears. Across from me are Elizabeth and Willa.

We returned from the Ceremony of Fire to find our clothing and possessions at the foot of our beds. My white sweater—no longer white, covered in dirt and the wolf's blood—was something I never wished to see again, but I was happy to discover my crystal pendant in the pocket of my skirt. I slipped it around my neck and felt an unusual warmth against my skin. I vowed then to never take it off again.

In the long hours before dawn, everyone broke off into small groups—the silver-haired girls went to train on the jungle gym outside while the Military girl sat in a corner of the sleeping tent with her eyes closed, meditating and mumbling to herself. When everyone went to eat breakfast—or was it *dinner?*—I decided to skip it, which earned me a few suspicious looks from the others. I sat at the foot of an apple tree, shoulder blades pressed against the bark, alone for the first time since I was captured. Bathed in moonlight, I managed a few deep breaths, collecting my thoughts. Maybe the girls saw my aloneness as weird or unnatural, but I was too tired for conversation. With our inverted sleep schedule has come an unusual sort of jet lag.

Now everyone is in their beds.

"It's so cold I can see my breath," Wendy says from my right, lying supine, blowing little clouds of steam into the air. "I've never been so cold in all my life."

I have, I think, vaguely reminded of winters at the orphanage. I hold my crystal to my eyes, inspecting it up close. A minuscule hole, as narrow as a piece of string, runs from the round, flat base all the way to the spiky tip. Strange. I've never noticed it before.

"On the bright side," Elizabeth says, taking a puff of her vape, "it's kind of like Camp." She blows out a large cloud of smoke that smells like sunshine.

Wendy gives her a look. "I don't remember anyone crying like that at Scout Camp," she mutters, indicating the sobbing girl. Bindu, I think her name is, doesn't hear.

"I do," Elizabeth retorts. "Not that I've done Scouts since I was little, because Scouts are lame, but there was always that one girl who would get homesick on the first night."

"We need to leave." Wendy sits up, her expression suddenly conspiratorial.

"Sorry to burst your bubble, Pockets, but how exactly are we going to do that? Put on a blue cloak and dye our eyes red?"

"Indigo. That's what the guards wear. All Klujns wear different colors, depending on their role in the tribe. Or stand. Or whatever this place is called. I read it in my book," Wendy adds. "And, regarding a plan, I'm still thinking."

Elizabeth snorts. "Well, *tick-tock*. The tests start tomorrow. Four days from now, we'll all be dead."

"We can't leave," I say. They turn to me, and now I have to follow up with an explanation. I take a deep breath and let it steady me. "Even if we made it past the gate, we'd still have to get out of the stand," I begin, thinking of the invisible barrier we crossed on the way in. The way Diablo touched it with his claws, creating that web of red electricity.

How the stand had appeared like a Magic Eye puzzle. "I think this place is protected by some kind of magic," I say, and regret the word as soon as it leaves my mouth.

"Please," Elizabeth snorts. "Magic is a fabrication of the clinically insane and people with too much imagination."

"What's wrong with having imagination? Nothing in our world would exist if someone hadn't imagined it first." Elizabeth's smile fades; she's not used to being challenged. "I didn't imagine that red light that came out of the guard's claws," I say. "And I'm sure I'm not the only one who saw it."

"I was too far back," says Willa. She's sitting up in bed, some occult playing cards laid out on the blanket in front of her, wearing the T-shirt she must have been wearing when she was captured. It reads: Hex the Patriarchy.

"I didn't see anything." Wendy is apologetic. "I'm short-sighted, and my glasses are constantly foggy. I think it's the humidity. I feel like a gazelle walking blindly into a pack of lions."

"I saw," a voice chirps from behind me. I turn around and see Bindu, the crying girl, who has temporarily stopped crying, although I fear the slightest stress might push her back over the edge. She is so young. "I mean—I saw the guard do something. One second, the mountain was just a mountain, and the next this whole encampment appeared out of nowhere. But it was dark," she adds, and my gratitude disintegrates like a snowflake on a warm tongue. "Even if he did do something, that doesn't make it magic. And I didn't see any red light."

"There has to be a way out," says Willa. "If we don't at least try, we're just biding our time before an even more violent slaughter. After what happened tonight, who knows what they have planned for us."

"He said three of us can make it out," I offer.

"I think he was saying that to give us false hope," says Wendy.

"No offense, but I'm not putting my tokens on you," Willa tells her sister. Wendy looks hurt, but something tells me she's used to this.

"Have you ever heard of a human who escaped a Klujn tribe?" Elizabeth seethes. We don't answer. "No. Because no one has. People who go missing don't come back. There's only one fate for us, and that's Klujn dinner." Her words hang in the air like dense smog, and we're all too drained to argue. *What if she's right?* I think about a girl from my science class who was taken a few years back. To make a long story short, she never came back.

A girl like Reesa. A girl like *me*.

Was she here? I wonder. *Did she sleep in this bed? Or was she captured and taken somewhere else? How many stands are there in a forest?*

I lie down, tucking my blanket in on all sides, cocooning myself like a caterpillar before metamorphosis. I catch a whiff of something and realize there's a sachet under my pillow containing lavender. I find the aroma pleasant. Relaxing. The gesture feels so unexpectedly . . . *thoughtful*. The burn on my forearm itches, and it takes all of my willpower not to scratch it. Instead, I use the pad of my finger to rub around it, which is only mildly satisfying, as I look up at the tent's striped ceiling.

Again, I think of my last conversation with Mercy. *Don't you ever want more?* I asked, as though my life in Red River was a death sentence. Like I was in the tunnel of a Loudhouse, being led to the Killingroom. But I wasn't trapped, I know now. I was free. And I had taken that freedom for granted, because I wanted to get out of Red River so badly.

I'm living the definition of irony: I got what I wanted, but not in the way I thought. Now, I will die without ever finding out who my parents are or where I come from. Without having been touched in that way that someone touches you when they think you're beautiful. Having never seen the ocean. José told me a thousand stories about the ocean, but stories don't live up to the real thing.

I roll over onto my side, facing Wendy. "How are we meant to sleep?" she asks. "We were only awake for a few hours."

"I guess they think we need it," I answer. "My mom—Diana—she says that sleep is medicine." *My mom.* There's a slip of the tongue.

"My dad says the same thing." Wendy looks up at the ceiling, her eyelashes matted together, tears streaming down the sides of her face.

"Don't be upset," I tell her, but the words feel useless. What are you supposed to say to someone who will most likely be dead in a matter of days? If they're lucky enough to last that long.

"Willa's right," she sniffles. "I wouldn't bet my tokens on me either."

"You don't know what the challenges are going to be," I offer.

"Look at me," says Wendy. "Look at all of you. I don't stand a chance. Except with that girl behind you," she whispers. "But that would be like beating a child. If there's hand-to-hand combat or any kind of race . . . I'm not fit. I'm not strong. I'm not *fast*."

Part of me is flattered that she placed me in the same category as the others. *Is that how she sees me? How do the others see me?* With my combat skills, I may have a chance. A slender one, but it's still a chance. Whereas Wendy's fate seems already sealed, and we haven't even begun fighting.

"You must be good at something," I say.

"I have good aim," Wendy laughs dolefully through her tears. "From working the fire dart stand at the Klujn Fair a few years running. I can survive in the woods. Well, the human woods anyway, the ones at Tremble Hills. And I'm good with maps, directions, navigation, that sort of thing. Let's just say—I know how to pack for a trip."

"Then, who knows? Maybe one of the challenges will involve something you're good at."

"Doubt it." Wendy examines the burn on her right arm. "At least my symbol's powerful. That's what the king said."

Poor Wendy. I'm naturally strong, but I'm nothing compared to some of the girls here. Girls who've been trained to fight like men since they could walk, who have forsaken so much of themselves to prove that they're good enough, strong enough, brave enough, despite their bodies and society telling them that they aren't. Because inside them is an inherent flaw, a curse—the curse of emotions, of monthly blood, of being born the "weaker sex."

There's Rory, the only male, but he seems fragile, like something made of porcelain. It's rare to see a vulnerable boy. I imagine it's the way Mercy looks without his public mask, when he's alone in his room—just a little boy who'd rather play with trains than rifles.

It's not only their strength that I'm afraid of, but their knowledge. What do the others know that I don't? What Camps or Scout expeditions did they go on? What did their parents teach them that mine didn't?

I never thought of myself as sheltered, but being here has made me realize how little I know and it's frustrating, so frustrating, this feeling of being out of my depth, so ill-equipped to face the world. The only person I should be angry at is myself. If I was smarter, braver, I would have gone out and gotten that knowledge for myself. But I didn't know that there was more knowledge to get, and I didn't know that I could. Yes, I was free then, but free as a bird in an aviary.

"The only way we can make it out of this place is if we take it one day at a time, okay?" I say. Wendy wipes her tears on her blanket and nods.

"Ava?" she says after a moment, sounding like a frightened child waking from a nightmare, standing in her parents' doorway, clutching her favorite toy. Her vulnerability is crushing. "I know we're not meant to trust each other"—and her voice is very quiet now—"but you can trust me, you know."

I swallow. "You can trust me, too," I murmur, but these words feel dishonest. How can I mean them, when I barely trust myself?

What did that dark entity see inside me? What did the other gods see in the others? What stifled things will the Blood Race bring to the surface?

Diablo walks in and extinguishes the only remaining lantern.

"See," Elizabeth mutters from her bed. "Lights out. It's just like Camp."

16

Despite how tired I felt before, now my eyes refuse to stay shut. Around me, the others snore. Some cry or talk in their sleep. Wendy mumbles words in a foreign language.

I draw open the fold of canvas behind my pillow. A cool breeze blows in. Not as cold as I'd expect, considering how high we are in the mountains. Outside, all is quiet. The moon sits high on its throne, reflecting on the black tents of our quarters. The deep blue panorama of night is slowly being pushed upward by the arrival of a yellow dawn. It will soon be morning.

My eyes travel to the front gate, where I notice something strange. There are no guards. *Where are they?* They must be hiding somewhere.

"Close it," Wendy mutters, in English now. "You're letting in the cold." I let the flap fall back into place and look up at the striped ceiling. *Think about something nice*, I tell myself. *Anything.* I close my eyes, and then a memory comes back to me, bit by bit, like colored threads woven together to form a sprawling tapestry.

* * *

I'm in the darkened orphanage cafeteria. It's the first day of the year—called Day Zero to honor the day that the calendar was reset—and the room has been decorated accordingly. I sit alone at the end of a long table, watching Miss Hidgins, who stands at a podium in front of a white screen. On the screen, a film is projected, boasting about the resilience of Man throughout our Territory's dark history. From food shortages to God's abandonment to the environmental apocalypse that followed. Miss Hidgins mouths along with the film's narration. It's the same one every year.

An anthem plays, and a banner appears on the screen: a large triangle divided into four smaller triangles. There's a silver one on top, a blue one on the bottom left, and a gray one on the bottom right. The upside-down triangle in the center shows a mosaic of Grouse's smiling face made from the three surrounding colors. Words beneath the logo read:

GROUSE IS GOD.

When the film ends, Miss Hidgins applauds louder than the rest of us. The lights come on and she raises her glass. "To humans," she cries. "The most successful species on the planet. And to Grouse, our savior." We raise our cups of juice and echo her words, then line up at the back of the room where José scoops something onto our plates. Today was my day off from working in the kitchen, so I'm not familiar with the menu.

"What is it, Mr. Cookmore?" I ask as he serves me some kind of white meatloaf accompanied by mashed cauliflower.

"Spotted wolf," he says, his expression pained. "We caught one right by the fence. It's a shame, to catch one so young. I wanted to let him go, but the other cooks disagreed. They played dice for his pelt."

I sit down at the table, staring at my plate. The small chunk of wolf loaf stares back at me. My stomach groans with hunger, but I can't bring myself to lift my fork, wondering if it's the one I rescued that day near the fence. I take a sip of juice instead. It's bright blue. Meant to be blueberry, but it tastes too sweet.

At a table across from me, Coll shovels the food into his mouth and licks his fingers clean. At another table, the girl who Coll fought in the playground eats neatly but with intent, like a cat. The cut above her lip has healed poorly. It's going to leave a scar.

After a few minutes, Miss Hidgins walks by, inspecting empty plates. Her footsteps stop behind me. "Was the food not cooked to your liking?" she asks mockingly. I don't answer. "There is not enough food to waste on disobedient children. This is your last warning. Eat, or it's the Ice House." I gulp. "Do you know what happens to children who are sent to the Ice House?" Miss Hidgins asks.

I nod. Vivid flashes steal across my mind—children dragged out to the shed at night . . . stiff corpses carried out come morning, blue faces frozen in terror . . . tears forming icicles on their cheeks. "What happens?" she inquires, trying to pry the answer from me like a splinter from skin.

"They don't come back." I look down at my plate. "I'm sorry, Mister Wolf," I whisper. Then I pick up my fork, sink the tines into the pinkish-white meat and bring a mouthful up to my lips. I chew for a long time before I finally manage to swallow. It's tender and tastes like herbs. It is perhaps the most delicious meat I have ever tasted. And yet my stomach turns.

"Good," says Miss Hidgins, with a satisfied smile. "Now, we won't be having this problem again, will we?" she asks, but it's the kind of question that doesn't require an answer.

As she is about to leave, a wave of nausea washes over me. I fight it, but it rises up like a tidal wave. A stream of vomit gushes out, hitting Miss Hidgins's boots, bullseye. The chunks of spotted wolf are there, swimming in a blue soup.

The room goes silent. Chatter dies. There's the clang of a fork dropping onto a plate. I sense every eye in the room boring into the back of my head, but I'm too afraid to lift my eyes. They are focused, instead, on the clumpy puddle decorating the director's boots.

Finally, I look up. Miss Hidgins's expression is frighteningly calm. Like a still ocean with sharks swimming beneath the surface; like a flat field with buried land mines.

* * *

Severe, merciless hands throw me inside. A key turns in a lock. I move back against the wall and curl into a little ball.

I'm in a refrigerated shed at the back of the property. It's not much bigger than a storage closet, with the remains of skinned birds and animals hanging from the ceiling. It's so cold that my breath comes out in little puffs of steam.

The Ice House. No one who has ever been taken here has ever come out alive.

A swoosh of dirt, the splintering of wood, the sound of claws on plastic flooring. And then, through the glacial darkness, I see him.

The spotted wolf. The one from the fence! Not dead, not dinner. It must've been another one they caught.

His blue eyes find me. There is an intelligence there. Even though he is young, only a little bit larger than me, his presence commands respect. He is magnificent. And alone. I wonder where his mother is, his family.

"Where did you come from?" I ask. "You're on the wrong side of the fence." Of course, he can't answer, but there's something like understanding in his eyes. "I thought you had been killed," I tell him, confused by the relief that floods through me. He is a beast after all, a most fearsome predator.

The wolf edges toward me. His expression is not aggressive, but concerned. "How did you get in here?" I ask. The dirt on his legs and belly answers my question for me. "You like digging?" I ask. "I like digging, too."

*The wolf takes another step toward me. When I begin to wonder if this is a predatory tactic—*act calm, corner your prey, and then pounce!—*the wolf reaches me. He opens his impressive mouth and licks the tears that have gathered in the corners of my eyes. His tongue is warm on my frozen skin. His breath smells like grass and leaves and other wonderful things. I run my fingers through his fur, over the black spots on his back. Three big ones.*

"I like you, Mister Wolf," I tell him, feeling as though we are alike, he and I. The wolf howls, a low cooing sound. "Wolf?" I say, and he howls again, as discreet as a secret. "That's not a very original name." He looks at me, his blue eyes textured like a mountain range on an alien planet. "All right, then. It's your decision."

I name him even though I shouldn't, because a name is something dangerous. A name means attachment. In the same way I have a name but the elders here never use it.

I lie down on the ground, my back inches from the carcass of a reindeer. After a moment, I feel a warm weight press against my body.

Wolf is lying on top of me. His body shields me from the cold, radiating more heat than a furnace. The chill disappears. Soon my limbs stop quivering. The pins and needles of blood flow return. Painful, but promising.

Wolf stays with me all night. When I wake up in the morning, he is gone, but the warmth on my skin tells me he left only recently. I notice that he has filled in the hole he crawled through, hiding the evidence of his passage. He must have sensed that someone was coming.

Right on cue, a key turns in a lock. Miss Hidgins pushes the door open, flooding the shed with light. She notices me—sitting next to the reindeer but, unlike my roommate, perplexingly alive. The orphanage director freezes as if in a game of Statues.

"How in the . . ." she splutters, the expression on her face worth a million tokens.

I make my way out into the morning sun. Miss Hidgins is too stunned to try to stop me. As I walk across the grounds, it's hard to explain the feeling that overcomes me . . . like I've made a new friend.

I carry the feeling with me well into breakfast. Soon, though, rationality begins to creep in, making me question whether it was all a dream. I look down at my overalls and find a few white hairs. I smile.

That's all the proof I need.

17

A deep horn reverberates across the stand. My eyes open. I can't believe it's finally time to get up. That by the time I return to this bed—*if* I return to this bed—a handful of us may be dead. After the Ceremony of Fire, who knows what tonight will bring.

It feels odd to be waking up in the middle of the day, or whatever time it is now. A single ray of light pierces the canvas behind my pillow. I crawl toward it, like a newborn puppy, blind but guided by instinct, and draw open the flap. The sun is still relatively high in the sky, so it's probably early afternoon. It feels agreeable against my face. Warm, but not too hot. Peculiarly, the front gate is still unguarded.

I roll onto my back, the feeling of Wolf's warmth still on my skin. The dream has left me with a pressure in my chest, and I can still hear the sickening sound the bullet made when it sank into his flesh. *Dead. He's dead.* I hate that word; the cruel irreversibility of it. It's unfair that I'm beginning to remember him, only to wake up to the realization that he's gone. *What did Mr. Mogel do with his body? Did he eat the poor animal?* The thought makes me shudder. A chill sets in my bones, erasing the memory of Wolf's heat.

I look around the tent. Some of the captives are still sleeping, and with the amnesia of sleep, they look almost peaceful. At the other end of the tent, Rory is already awake and dressed in a white costume.

Bindu is buried under her blanket, only one foot sticking out, her toenails painted yellow. I don't know why I find this detail crushing, but I do. One day, not so long ago, she took the time to pick the perfect shade. She is not branded cattle; she is a girl, with a family back home and a favorite color.

There's a commotion in the doorway. I close my eyes, wanting to sleep a little longer, but the guards have other plans. They pull off our blankets and tell us to get dressed. The girls' eyes spring open, and suddenly their expressions aren't tranquil anymore but filled with dread and homesickness and panic.

I sit up in bed and pull my legs toward me. My injured foot is heavy and has turned the color of blackberries. The holes where the trap's teeth entered ooze thick green pus. It doesn't hurt at all, but I realize that the absence of pain may not be a good thing. Pain is a signal that something down there is still working. Now I barely feel anything. I look over at Diablo, who's waking up the last of the girls. Could I ask him for help? How would that look to the others? It's a wasted thought; the guard is out the door before I can decide whether or not to turn these thoughts to words.

We dress in the same white costumes as Rory. These jumpsuits have elbow-length sleeves that show a little more of my scars than I'm comfortable with. The chest is adorned with white crystals, and the pants end at the knees. Thin, supple, jewel-encrusted shoes have straps that curl around my ankles and calves, tickling them like a field of long grass.

Once we are dressed, we are taken to eat. I hold my arms protectively, but the other girls don't seem to notice my scars, each preoccupied with their own insecurities. Around the table, things are mostly quiet. Wendy mentions her dreams, which were lucid—but now, come to think of it, she doesn't remember what they were about. Elizabeth outs her for speaking in a foreign language, but Wendy claims that the only language she knows is English.

"It was probably just gibberish."

Willa talks about the group at the other table and the order in which they were taken. She deduces that the Klujns must have started near Mission Creek before heading northwest along the river, past Goodearth, Brave Night, Valor, Between Lakes, Ascension, Mount Dominion, and Justice Falls. When Elizabeth asks her why this matters, Willa simply says that it might explain this sense of "us" and "them" that has formed. As a general rule, the closer to Mission Creek one gets, the more standoffish people tend to be. "Brave Night girls are the *worst*," she tells us.

I have trouble imagining that anyone could be more closed off than they are in Red River. Willa is also puzzled by the fact that Zoe was caught between Justice Falls and Red River. "There are no townships there," she says. "Only Tremble Hills and Loudhouse One."

Since it's been a while since we last ate, and none of us knows what's coming, we make sure to fill our bellies. I pour hot black liquid into a small ceramic bowl, hoping for but not expecting coffee. When I taste it, my taste buds rejoice—*it is*! The coffee is bold and delicious, with an aroma of butterscotch. I need it to kick in, to banish the fog of oversleep. I need my brain to function, my reflexes to be quick.

"So this is dinner or breakfast?" Wendy asks. "Or breakfast for dinner?"

"It's food," says Willa. "Just eat."

"It's good," Bindu peeps, having unofficially joined our group after her brief contribution to the conversation last night. She hasn't cried since, which must be a record so far.

I fork up a fluffy pancake with grill marks on its surface so perfect that you could play a game of tic-tac-toe. It tastes like maple—*real* maple. When I'm done, I move on to some oatmeal, making sure to take a scoop of winterberries. There's crispy nut bread loaded with something like creamy ricotta, drizzled with caramel. Warm apple loaf that steams when sliced open. Carafes of fizzy waters and fermented drinks and colorful juices that are just the right amount of sweet. There isn't a surplus of food, but there's enough to go around.

By the time we've cleared the table, I feel satisfied. Not bloated or lethargic, but light and energized.

I nurse my cup of coffee, enjoying the warmth it feeds my hands. The way it is already beginning to make my senses sharpen. I notice Zoe at the other table, still avoiding eye contact, acting like we never spoke. Her eyes are trained on the door, but I don't know who she's hoping to see.

"What do you think the first test is going to be?" Willa asks, breaking our morning vigil. "Fights?"

"Don't know," Wendy answers, cradling a bowl of fruit salad. "Catrina Sherman wrote about it in here," she says, showing us the black book from yesterday. It's a battered copy of *A Brief History of Klujns*.

"Where did you get that?" Willa asks, outraged. "It's illegal."

"No, it's not," Wendy fires back. "This is the last book she ever wrote. It was published independently after her disappearance. It's part factual, part cautionary saga, very flattering of Grouse's Military—which is probably why it's tolerated, unlike her other works, which were all destroyed in the Burnings of the early AK years. Those ones are rumored to have been wild, dark fables inspired by her travels. In comparison, this one's a little bit vanilla, but there's still some interesting stuff in there if you read between the lines."

"How do you know this one's not illegal too?" Willa wants to know.

"The pages have silver edges," Wendy says, showing us. "Her original books—the illegal ones that were all destroyed—were *gold*."

Something sparks in me at her words, but Elizabeth chooses this moment to butt in. "Everyone knows that her books are garbage."

"Who's Catrina Sherman?" Bindu asks.

"She was an anthropologist and explorer who wrote about Klujns," Wendy explains, her eyes lighting up. "She was fascinated by their culture and wandered from tribe, er—*stand* to stand, studying their customs. That's how she knew so much about them. My dad says that her earlier books were the real deal—like, detailed mating rituals and *encounters* with Klujns." Everyone seems a bit appalled. "It was saucy and exciting stuff. Sherman wasn't afraid to go deep."

"No pun intended," from Elizabeth.

After a moment, I speak up. "Does that one say anything about the Blood Race?"

"Not much more than we already know. According to this"—Wendy taps the book—"the human Blood Race consists of five stages. Sometimes they're fights and sometimes they're games. She says the first challenge is meant to be symbolic, a leap of faith, reflecting the passage from adolescence to adulthood, when teenage Klujns grow their baby claws and go out into the wild for the first time."

"What are the challenges?" Willa wants to know.

"Dunno. There was a whole chapter on it, but it's gone." Wendy opens the book to show us. Half the pages are crumbling, the words no longer legible. "Sherman was strong on ecological practices, so she insisted on having all her works printed on compostable paper. But that's the thing about compostable paper . . . it decomposes."

"You shouldn't listen to anything she says," Elizabeth tells us. "Catrina Sherman was a fraud. It's a miracle that book was even allowed. She was a radical, an ecoterrorist, and a misanthrope who wrote nothing but propaganda. She wasn't even a real Explorer!"

"She was not a fraud," Wendy protests. "She was a *scientist*, at a time when women could still *be* scientists, and she spent years exploring Klujn stands across all thirteen territories, including Australis, which hasn't been habited by humans in years."

"She was a liar who made millions of tokens pretending she knew about Klujns, but her books are nothing but pulp fiction," Elizabeth shoots back.

Red splotches appear on Wendy's cheeks. "Catrina Sherman was a misunderstood woman," she says vehemently. "She was a talented author and Klujn advocate—"

"—and cannibal—"

"That was one time!" Wendy says. Willa chews the inside of her mouth to suppress a smile.

"—who wrote bodice rippers because she had no real literary talent," Elizabeth finishes. "It's for the brain-dead masses."

"So is television," Wendy fumes. "And her previous books weren't *bodice rippers*. She wrote about sex to educate, not entertain."

"They're all gone, so you can't prove it."

"You know something? There's a code in here." Wendy gestures to the book. "There's a message between these pages. I'm positive. I just haven't found it yet."

"It's pretty obvious what that message is." Elizabeth's voice is dry. "You should be a good *girlie* and stay out of the woods. Marry a nice Hunter or a Military man. And if you want to have a fling with a Klujn, wear a condom."

Wendy drops the book, outraged. "Catrina Sherman was *queer*," she spits. "She didn't want to write about love triangles and having intercourse with Klujns—"

"And yet she did. And that's bestiality, by the way. Sherman sold out. Even if there is some validity in her work—which there isn't—every tribe has its own set of customs. So, even if the things in that book actually happened—which they didn't—it would be completely useless to us here."

"I know I'm right," says Wendy, tapping the cover of her book so hard I'm afraid she might drill a hole through it. "I just *know* it. There's a reason why this book is different from the others. More . . . mainstream. Catrina Sherman was a fascinating person. She went on extraordinary adventures and encountered remarkable people and animals and plants. She fought against kanum farming and the claw trade. But after her books were burned, she needed a new way to get her message across."

"Right," Elizabeth says. "Through purple prose, washed-out observations, and cliché morals."

"She did it on purpose."

"What, wrote badly?"

"Actually, yes!" Wendy fizzes. "She had more to say than ever, but she wasn't allowed to say it. So she found more creative ways to get her message across. Ways that the *common folk* wouldn't understand."

Wendy's argument settles on the table between our empty plates.

"Watch who you're calling common," Elizabeth says, but even she looks mildly impressed. She hides it, though, for the sake of protecting her pride. "You're reading too much into this, Pockets."

"I don't think so," Wendy says firmly. "I believe I haven't read far enough."

"Well, hurry up, before the rest of it disintegrates."

Willa snorts. "Sorry," she says, giving her sister a sheepish grin. "It's funny because it's true."

At that moment, Diablo comes in. His arrival snaps us back to reality.

"It's time," he says. "The first challenge is about to start."

18

We leave our quarters and take a left this time, walking in our numerical order—Jade and Mabry at the very front, then the Military girl and the silver-haired girls. Behind them are Zoe and Rory, then Bindu and Willa, Elizabeth and me. Wendy is last, at the back of the pack. She seems jealous of the fact that we all have partners, but I would gladly trade her Elizabeth to walk alone.

The path winds around to the north side of the mountain, which isn't populated by tents. On the hillside, freshly turned earth has been raked into neat platforms, like salt terraces. Strange markings are drawn in the soil, which is lush and brown, crawling with worms, bugs, and small rodents. Green-cloaked Klujns tend to the mysterious fruits and vegetables with smooth white hands. The harvest is abundant, a stark contrast to the dead dirt on the other side of the fences and the miserable plants in Diana's greenhouse.

"There's so much of it," Elizabeth mutters. "You'd think they'd feed us a little more."

Unlike our trek in the Deeper Woods, we're not bound by vine shackles. I could try to escape, but I doubt I would survive long on my own. I am so small in the vastness of the wild. I didn't do Scouts like Wendy. While she was learning to tie knots and forage and build shelter, I was gardening and doing crafts with Diana.

Diana always used to say that art is essential in a way people seldom realize. Before the world turned gray, it was once filled with color, with painters and poets and dancers and dreamers. But after the North American Territory was formed, Pepito Silver dismantled the Department of Arts and Culture and poured their already-limited resources into areas where they "mattered more," like defense. Art was somehow seen as both unimportant and dangerous, if it was possible for something to have two entirely different definitions.

"You would think," Diana told me one rainy day when we were cooped up inside, making bird feeders from empty bottles of maple cider, "that if our society placed more importance on art, including the art of nutrition, there would be less need for defense. But they don't think, or they don't care. They want to be the rulers of a dead world."

She would love the colors here, I think. Nature, unrestrained, might be the greatest artwork I've ever seen.

The hill slopes down into a valley, where a wide dormant river lies. We pass a group of teenage Klujns with brand-new crystal claws, as clear as water. Some of them are distinctly male, some distinctly female, but others are somewhere in between. They sit on a patch of green grass by the riverbank, looking relatively bored. No uniforms here; their clothing is colorful, and each has a style of their own. Short hair, long hair, all shiny and smooth. Pants or skirts, makeup or none—their choices on these matters don't seem to hinge on their apparent gender. I wonder if these are the Klujns leaving shortly for their own Blood Race.

One stands out. She is regal and feminine, with sharp cheekbones, milky skin, and thick brown hair that cascades down her back in waves. A crystal headdress and gold cloak make her look like royalty. She outshines all of us—any girl or woman I have ever seen. I am surprised to realize that I find her beautiful. Beside the Klujn girl sits an impressive spotted wolf; like the beautiful Klujn, it's a teenager, with a copper coat and five black spots on its back.

The female Klujn watches as we pass. Her eyes find Diablo and she gives him a look—confident, sensual, defiant. A look that feels too private to have out in the open.

I don't know where it comes from, this pang of jealousy. I realize I feel jealous of her self-assurance, of that dark, seductive power behind her eyes. It's strange to see her wearing her femininity like a strength. Not hiding it behind pants and combat boots and war paint.

Diablo looks away. The female Klujn doesn't seem embarrassed but frustrated by the guard's lack of interest. She shifts her focus to us, perhaps sizing up her future competition. Her eyes burn doubly red with condescension. Then she looks at me and smirks, perhaps sensing my lack of experience—my virginity—like a shock of color in the wild that makes me stand out from the landscape.

I burn with shame, face hot like an oven. Is it shame, or desire? The desire to grow up, fast, and to experience everything that she surely has. *What must life be like for them?* I wonder. *Out here, in the classroom of the wild.*

We pass a row of wooden boxes on stilts. Fuzzy black and yellow insects buzz around, and a sweet smell fills the air. "Holy Mother of Bog," Wendy gapes. "They're bees."

"Bees are extinct," Elizabeth says.

"Then you tell me what those are." We all crane our necks to watch for as long as we can, but soon they're lost in the distance.

Diablo guides us farther from the stand, along a path that borders the river. We continue to head north, against the current. On the fertile banks, I notice more of those strange symbols in the soil, with the tiny green heads of plants starting to sprout, turning their faces to the sun.

"They look like sigils," Willa says.

"What are sigils?" I ask.

"They're symbols used in magic," she explains. "Like runes or glyphs. Each sigil has its own meaning, which aligns with the witch's desired outcome. So if you're casting a love spell, you would use a sigil that represents love. And if you want to attract prosperity—"

"We get it," Elizabeth interrupts. "But what does magic have to do with this?"

"I'm not sure. It's like they're casting a spell . . . to the earth. Using a language of some kind."

"That isn't magic," Elizabeth says. "It's science. It's agriculture. You plant a seed, it grows—voilà! There's no magic there. It's only growing so well because Klujns keep all the good land to themselves and know how to fertilize it."

Diablo leads us into a forest of towering evergreens, speckled with the red, orange, and yellow of deciduous trees. A late afternoon mist coats the ground. It glows a mystical greenish color, not toxic gray or ash black. The smell of pines and maples intoxicates me in the best possible way. I inhale, filling my lungs.

I feel drunk on Nature. On these fresh, crisp, autumnal smells. I've only ever been tipsy once, after Diana let me try a glass of her homemade strawberry wine, but the feeling is the same. Even so, I feel unusually alert, like my vision is sharper and my eyes absorb much more detail.

The fall foliage makes the forest look alive. Chipmunks chase one another, their rapid feet crunching on the forest floor—tiny creatures making big sounds. Raccoons bake in patches of sun that flitter through the leaves, lying on their backs with their bellies exposed. Rabbits hop in and out of burrows, not concerned about our knowing their address. There is a feeling of peace in these woods. Of . . . *balance.* I continue to look around, listening to the birdsong that trills from the higher branches.

The woods in Red River are always dead quiet. A bland monoculture of uniform trees, a complete lack of diversity. This, in comparison, is nothing short of paradise.

That's when I see it. A flutter of blue wings on a low branch. Hopping along toward its nest. *A blue sparrow!* I think, with a rush of excitement, until I realize how foolish that is. They've been extinct for years. But if there are bees . . .

A memory comes, like the one of José, even though I am wide awake. I don't resist it.

* * *

It's Adoption Day at the orphanage, which only happens once a season. I stand by a misty window that faces the grounds. I catch sight of my reflection and see that my eyes are filled with tears. But why am I crying? I lift my hand and trace a crown in the fogged window, on the head of my reflection.

It's spring, and the last of the snow is melting. Through the bits of freshly cleared glass, I see Wolf watching me. He's a few hundred feet away, across the river, and the white of his face stands out from the brown and black world around him. I can't see his expression from afar, but I know that he's concerned.

Over the past four months, since we survived the Ice House, he's visited me on the sly every chance he's gotten. Maybe he worries that if I go someplace else he'll never find me.

"Don't worry," I whisper, even though he can't hear me. In all these years, no one's ever come.

I turn from the window and look at the room full of families instead. It's a difficult thing to explain, this push and pull of forces inside me. I want a home, a family, shelter, more than anything—but I don't want those four walls to become my prison.

That's when I see him, the man with green eyes. He stands next to Miss Hidgins and a tall, commanding man in a gray uniform. The three of them speak, and the uniformed man laughs boisterously. The green-eyed man's eyes scan the room like the beacon of a lighthouse, and when they land on me, they stop. I read the words on his lips—"Who is she?"

* * *

Another memory. This one, a few days later, after the paperwork is sorted.

* * *

Mr. Sparrow—George, he says to call him—brings me home. I see the house for the first time: blackened cherrywood with a solar-paneled roof, a sprawling porch that wraps around the entire house, a large front yard that faces north, with a view of Diana's hexagonal greenhouse and the forest. The back and sides of the house are all wild vegetation—jungles of weeds that thrive no matter the soil or climate. George points toward the second story and tells me that the room facing the woods is mine. All mine. A whole room to myself.

Later, I prepare for my first night in my new room, which still smells of fresh paint. Pastel pink and purple circus stripes cover the walls. There's a canopy bed with a white mosquito net that looks fit for a princess. A breeze blows through the open window and I go over to close it. Diana's voice drifts up from the porch. She's angry. She asks George what the hell he was thinking, adopting me.

I run to the bed and hide behind the white veil, wanting to disappear. Slip into the woods and never return. I hate that my existence is an imposition on those around me. That I've been a burden ever since my birth.

Soon after, there's the creak of footsteps on the stairs, and then a gentle knock on my bedroom door. It opens a crack and George stands on the threshold. "Can I come in?" he asks. I'm not used to grown-ups asking for my permission. Privacy is not something I've ever had.

When I nod, George walks in, his movements slow and cautious, as if he doesn't want to frighten me. He sits down on the edge of the bed and reaches into the depths of his coat, which smells like the forest and smoke and other mysterious things. "I have a present for you," he says, pulling out a book. "Although it's more like a loan." He parts the net and I see that the book has a black cover, the edges of the paper gold. In gold letters, the title reads:

A VERY EXCITING QUEST
CATRINA SHERMAN

"What is it?" I ask George, taking the little book in my hands, excited by it.

"It's a book of Klujn tales," he says. "Catrina Sherman wrote just over a dozen books, but many of them were destroyed in the Burnings. They're not exactly legal, but I can keep a secret if you can."

My eyes grow wide, taking in the sight of this beautiful book. I flip through its delicate pages very carefully. Some are stiff, stuck together; others have gray flowers of mold in the corners.

"I've tried to preserve it as best I can, but eventually it'll decompose. When Man goes to war against Nature, he never wins," George says with a sad smile.

"I love it," I tell him.

"I can't give it to you," he says. "It's too dangerous for you to have. But I wanted you to know it exists. That there are stories like this one that exist. But they need to be kept private . . . for their protection. I can let you borrow it, from time to time. How does that sound?"

We shake on it.

I look down at the pages. There are color plates, images of dark-skinned Klujns with bright green eyes. Of light-skinned Klujns with pink eyes. Of brown, freckled Klujns with purple eyes. They are drinking bizarre potions and performing mysterious ceremonies—costumes and makeup and dances under the wide, wide sky.

"This is what I love about Sherman's stories," George tells me. "She tells the truth, every shadowy detail, and invites anyone who isn't ready to hear that truth to simply look away. I'll let you keep it for tonight," he adds. "But don't let Diana see it."

"Why doesn't she like me?" I ask George. He looks surprised.

"What makes you think she doesn't like you?" he asks.

I shrug.

"Diana just needs time," he tells me. "After Mercy, I wanted a daughter more than anything in the world, but Diana didn't want another child. I know that she'll come around. Once she gets to know you, she won't just like you. She'll love you."

I flip to the last page of the book, where a female Klujn in a striking costume has her eyes closed, but there's a large painted eye on her brow, just above the bridge of her nose. The last sentence of the story twinkles in an elegant gold font: "With her third eye, she can finally see who she is and who she was meant to be."

"You know," George says with a chuckle. "Most people start reading stories from the beginning."

"I wanted to make sure it has a happy ending."

George looks crushed by the innocence of my words, like a centuries-old building crumbling onto a modern pavement.

"It's not only the ending that matters," he says, "but everything in between. Life isn't only about birth and death, but how we fill the pages."

"It's still important to have a happy ending."

There is a pause.

"Do you remember anything?" George asks, his voice delicate. "About your time before the orphanage?"

"I was a baby. Babies don't have memories," I answer.

"You're right," he says, chuckling again. "I'm sorry I asked."

George gives me a friendly pat on the head and stands up. He walks over to the wall and turns on a round lamp. A creamy white crescent glows.

"It simulates moonlight," he tells me, "And reflects the actual cycles of the moon. I don't have to leave it on if you don't like it." But I don't like to sleep in complete darkness, and this room is still new to me. The moon lamp is comforting.

"I like it."

"I thought you might."

George walks over to the door and turns to look at me, his finger hovering over the main light switch. I'm still clinging to the book, afraid it'll vanish, like a precious object in a dream brought back to the waking world.

"Get some sleep. It's been a big week," he tells me. And then adds, as though reading my mind, "The book will still be there come morning."

I close the book and tuck it under my pillow. With that, George turns off the light and closes the door behind him.

The moon lamp glows in my dark room. How did I get so lucky? *I wonder, thinking of the other children going to sleep in their cold orphanage cots infested with bedbugs. But some questions are best left unanswered.*

I wait until my new parents are asleep, then sneak out into the front yard, into the woods and across the river on a fallen tree, to the Military fence where Wolf is waiting.

The fence is intimidating from up close. It's glowing silver in the night. Quiet, but something about it feels alive.

I knew he'd be here, my clever wolf. He has followed me here, followed my scent. I have this feeling . . . like he wants me to leave with him. To go on a journey, to explore uncharted territories.

Should I go? No, I think. I'm safe now, because I finally have a home— *and a better one than I could ever have asked for. If my new family sees me sneaking around in the woods talking to a wolf, they might send me back. I am so close to breaking a law. An unforgiveable law, punishable by death.*

Even though it hurts heart-deep, I shoo him away.

Wolf refuses to go at first, so I start to throw sticks and stones and whatever I can wrap my small hands around. The fence awakens, crackling and sparking. Wolf gets frightened and steps a few paces back. In my sadness and my pain and my fear for his safety, I continue to push him away, until he finally disappears, swallowed by the darkness of the Deeper Woods.

The fence returns to normal.

As soon as he's gone, I feel his absence as a physical thing. My knees sink to the cold earth, and my arms cradle the empty space that he will never again fill.

Wolf! Come back! I didn't mean it!

But it's too late.

He doesn't return.

In that first year of separation, I think of him almost every day. Our lives are like two parallel lines, like the letter H, but the stroke in the middle doesn't unite us; it divides us, like the fence.

In winter, I wonder how he'll stay warm or where he'll get his food when the forest floor is covered in deep snow. In spring, as I watch the illegal poachers leaving on their Hunts, I pray that he has somewhere safe to hide, far from the glint of their rifles. In summer, when the forest is ravaged by droughts and fires, I hope that he does not get caught in the blaze, that he can find water. And when the late summer rains hit and the scorched earth floods, I hope that the torrents don't sweep him away like the smaller animals who cannot climb trees and take refuge in the leaves. On those wet days, bundled in many layers, I still feel cold just like he must. And when fall comes—that brief, beautiful season where Nature calms and prepares for another cycle of violence and Grouse's Hunters leave on their last Hunt—I worry that if Wolf is still alive, his good fortune will soon run out.

Every chance I get, I coax Mercy into playing hide-and-seek, and I go down to the woods, across the river, knowing my new brother will never follow me there. Sometimes I glimpse a flash of white on the other side of the fence, but every time it ends up being something else, something disappointing: a bedsheet that has blown far from a clothesline, a mound of snow that's not yet melted, a garbage bag.

As time passes, and I am caught up in my new life as a Sparrow, I think of Wolf less and less. Eventually, the memory of him fades completely.

The next time I see Wolf is over six years later. The night I am cornered by Coll and his friends. The night that Wolf—sensing that I am in danger—comes back to protect me.

Six years safely in the wild; one moment on the human side.

And he dies.

No, not dies, for that implies a natural process. He is killed. Killed in a senseless, unnecessary way. But perhaps it is inevitable. Because how could a creature as spectacular, as flavorsome as him, ever survive?

* * *

Then, one final memory. I don't know how it connects to the others . . . where it's been hiding all these years, or why it chooses this moment to arrive. Maybe being in the woods has provoked it; a neural pathway, blocked for so long like a tunnel filled with crumbling rocks, now cleared away.

* * *

I'm in George's Jeep and we're driving along a Military road, heading southeast, with black woods on our left and dry fields on our right. Dotting the fields are occasional landfills, factories, power plants and mines. George is taking me to see a doctor. My night terrors have been shaking the very foundation of the house.

After the appointment, George takes me camping, just the two of us—a father-daughter weekend. It's mid-May, a crisp spring day, but soon it will be too hot and sticky to stay outside. This is my first trip with my new father since he adopted me a fortnight ago. Diana is at work at the Greenhouse and Mercy is away at Weapons Camp. We drive to Tremble Hills, which sits between Red River and Justice Falls.

Unlike the woods in Red River, the forest here is alive. George takes me so deep into them that, even though we're going south, I wonder if we're still on the human side of the fences. I smell that forest smell. It is like being born, like the umbilical cord that links me to the orphanage has been cut and I can breathe properly for the first time. My lungs are helium balloons. My feet almost lift off the ground.

I close my eyes and listen to bird sounds. What are they saying to each other in their secret language? What is it like to have wings and be able to fly? To go farther than I have gone in my entire life, in a matter of minutes? We search for birds with George's heat-sensing binoculars.

"What are we looking for?" I ask.

"Blue sparrows," he tells me, scanning the lower branches. "They're small but powerful creatures. They were discovered around the same time as Klujns and spotted wolves. It's very special to see one because there aren't a lot of them left in the wild." I ask George why, and he says it's because poachers take their eggs. Blue sparrows nest on low branches, away from strong winds and ash clouds. They are sensitive to sound and scare easily, yet humans still find ways to catch them. Since there are no protection laws, he continues, their eggs are taken more quickly than the birds can reproduce. This beautiful new species is already facing extinction. "People get tired of Greenhouse food and even carnival food. Novelty food like blue sparrow eggs goes for a small fortune."

"Can't we take fewer eggs?" I ask.

"We could, but that would require a Department of Environmental Protection to make laws and ensure that people are respecting those laws."

"We don't have one of those?"

George shakes his head. "It was abolished when the North American Territory was formed." I notice that he seems more relaxed and speaks more freely here than he does back home. As though there are invisible ears in the walls of our house and his classroom.

"You know," he says now, changing the subject, "your name—Ava— actually comes from the Latin avis, *which means* bird. *I've always loved that name."*

"But you didn't name me," I point out. "My biological parents did."

"Right. It's what we call 'serendipitous.' A happy coincidence. And you're a Sparrow now—so your name is actually Bird Bird." I giggle, and he joins in.

We scour the woods for hours but don't find any blue sparrows. George takes me down lesser-known trails. He uses paper maps and old-school gadgets, telling me that when we rely too heavily on technology, we forget how to use our six senses. Sight, hearing, smell, taste, touch—and the sixth is instinct. "The voice in our bellies," he explains. "The one that's always right. Only, so often it's drowned out by the loud 'rational' voice in our brains."

George pulls out his compass. I've never seen one; it belonged to his grandmother, an archaic thing. The needle goes berserk, spinning in all directions. He tells me it happens when you approach the fences. That Klujn land is a black hole to human technology. It's part of the reason why they are so hard to find. You can be a few hundred feet away from a settlement, with all the latest technology, and you'll never find it. Hunters will go round and round in circles, convinced they're walking in a straight line.

In some places, he tells me, the fences have been knocked down due to violent storms or tornadoes or fires. A human can be tricked into thinking they're still on the right side, and end up on the wrong one. Luckily, George knows the forest like a spider knows its web.

When he puts the compass back in his pocket, I notice a crystal on a chain around his neck. He tells me that it's made from the claw of a Klujn, which is more precious than the bones and serves a few purposes. It can keep wild dogs and wolves away, and it can also act as a magnet or a kind of Klujn-compass; the crystal is drawn to places it remembers.

"How can an object remember a place?" I ask.

"One of the many mysteries of Klujns," he says. "There are some things we do not have the senses to understand. It's like trying to watch one of those three-dimensional Explorer films that play on Friday nights on television, without the red-and-blue glasses."

I ask George if we're likely to see any birds—or even wolves or dogs for that matter. He tells me that sightings are rare. Animals that are hunted by humans evolve faster than others. They become better at camouflage and quickly learn which areas of the woods are friendly and which ones to avoid.

After a few hours of walking, we set up camp near the base of Black

Mountain. We play dice and pick spotted mushrooms by a stream and cook them over a fire. George and I have only just finished eating when two strangers arrive—a man and his son. They wear Hunters' clothes, with gray bandannas over their mouths and slick rifles strapped around their backs. The man's rifle has a crystal bayonet. The two strangers look quite intimidating, even though the boy is around my size, and George is visibly startled. But he recognizes the man—General Santos—an old friend who he hasn't seen in a while. The coincidence doesn't feel like a happy one. Santos invites us to come Hunting with them, but George says we're just here to observe. My new father uses his bad leg as an excuse, but Santos tells him it mustn't be so bad—the parking lot is a two-hour hike away.

General Santos is insistent and has a haughty sort of confidence, the kind you don't say no to. When George has no choice but to relent, Santos places a sleek rifle in my father's hand.

"The thrill of the Hunt's like a virus," he tells me. "Once it's in your blood, it's there for life."

"What are you Hunting?" I ask.

"Blue sparrows."

"They're endangered," George tells his friend.

"Following the rules now, Doc?" Santos snipes, and my father goes quiet. Before I can ask George what the other man means, they set off along the path.

George realizes I haven't followed and turns around.

"I don't want to go," I say.

"It's okay," George comforts me. "We don't have to stay long. Just long enough to make Rodrigo happy." Reassured by his kindness, I follow him deeper into the woods around the mountain. The sun begins to set, and shadows grow longer. The others put on their night vision goggles. George and I don't have any, so we tail close behind.

Finally, after an hour of walking in silence, the general's son points to a low-lying branch. Santos holds a finger to his lips—shhh. He raises his rifle toward a little blue sparrow that's barely visible in the dark. She hops toward her nest, unaware of the Hunter's gun pointed silently at her. Santos aims, his finger tightening around the trig—

Crack!

A loud sound fills the forest, but it isn't a gunshot. The bird, startled, flies away. Santos lowers his weapon and looks around, seething, searching for the source of the sound.

George steps in front of me, blocking me from view.

"I'm sorry," he says. "I just got these new boots. I'm still breaking them in." Santos removes his goggles and studies my father, sensing a lie. Then his expression softens.

"We can still get the eggs," he says. "The bird has too many bones anyway." Santos gestures to his son, and they move toward the tree. The boy starts to climb the lower branches.

George turns to look at me and the two halves of the broken twig in my hands. He kneels down so that we're the same size.

"I'm not angry," he says, making sure the others are out of earshot. He takes the pieces of the branch that I'm clutching. "But you have to be careful."

"Why?"

"A Hunt is regarded as an incredibly important, noble act," George says. "If you do anything that interferes with or sabotages a Hunt, it's sacrilegious."

"What does that mean?"

"It means . . . it's a serious violation, one that you can be punished gravely for."

"I thought General Santos was your friend," I say.

"He is," George answers. "But this is bigger than friendship. Rodrigo is a very powerful man; he runs the first Loudhouse ever built and works closely with Grouse. You don't ever want to be on his bad side."

"Am I?"

George looks at me with a sad smile. "No," he says, closing his hands around mine. "But we should be careful from now on."

I know George isn't mad at me. However, we don't go on any more camping trips after that. The only forest I am allowed to see is the dead one by our house. And as I watch the girls my age sign up for Scouts, I'm told that it's best if I stay home. When I ask why, the answer is always the same: "It's for the best. Maybe next time." I am so grateful to have a home and a family that I don't fight back, I obey. I grieve my frustrations and loneliness on my own, kept from the world I am so desperate to know.

In Home Studies, the Scouts talk about all the things they learned while they were away. And when Mercy and the boys return from Hunter's Camp, they seem to have grown a year's worth in a matter of days. The gap continues to widen, between me and everyone else my age, until it is too far away for bridges. As bodies fill out and hormones strengthen and my classmates start discussing more adult things, I feel miles behind, looking for the road sign that'll point me toward where I ought to go, who I ought to be, whoever that is. It's not relationships or love I want; the thought of that makes me feel uneasy. It's to fill my skin with confidence and adventures and life experiences.

George never tells me what I did wrong, but I assume it must have had something to do with that blue sparrow. Maybe I shouldn't have interrupted the Hunt, and let nature run its course. Let General Santos kill it. It's the food chain, after all. But I have trouble accepting that particular Hunter and his rifle are part of the natural order of the world.

A few weeks later, just days after my made-up birthday on the first of June, there's a report at the end of the news. The blue sparrow is now extinct in the wild. It joins a long list of creatures before it—the giant panda. The bee. The koala. The polar bear. The Asian elephant. The sea otter. The manatee. The white rhinoceros. The blue whale. The gorilla and the orangutan. And those are just the famous ones. Now it's official: the last recorded blue sparrow has died. A graph flashes on-screen, showing the decline in wildlife over the last one hundred years. We are down to 1 percent of the animal species we used to have. One is so fragile a number, a number that offers no second chances.

Diana stands in the doorway, arms crossed tightly over her chest, and I swear I see the sheen of tears in her eyes.

"Bientôt il ne restera plus rien," she says to George, quietly but with an edge. "J'espère que tu sais ce que tu fais."

He doesn't respond, his eyes stuck to the television, the blue light illuminating his expression—something tormented.

That night, I have nightmares. I see the general's son reaching into the nest for the exquisite blue eggs. One, two, three; he slips them into his pockets.

I wake up screaming, my arms scratched and bleeding. George consoles and bandages me, but Diana is not there. Eventually, I fall back to sleep, under guardianship of my moon lamp. Its white light strokes my skin like a mother's hands.

For weeks, I'm plagued by the same image. Every time I close my eyes I see her, the mother bird, returning to her nest only to find it empty. I feel her confusion and her pain. All she wanted was to live in the wild. To watch her babies hatch and learn to fly. To be safe.

After the news of the blue sparrow, nothing changes. No new protection laws are passed. Hunters turn their binoculars to other species, other eggs, different meat.

19

The blue sparrow is gone before I can get a proper look at it. The sun is already lowering, the afternoon light golden. After about an hour of walking, we reach a clearing in the forest. Warwick, the king, is there, accompanied by his guard. Behind them is the mouth of a cave. Giant stalactites of black crystals hang from its low ceiling like fangs dripping with glimmering tar.

"Welcome to the first test," Warwick says, back to his cheery disposition. "In the wild, our young face many challenges: poachers, traps, hunger, thirst, treacherous weather, and unforgiving landscapes. The wild is not a friendly place to those who do not speak its language. Our young must learn to adapt quickly to the harsh environment and to life without four walls. Those who cannot keep up fall behind, forced to live a life of solitude in the forest until they become wild or are caught by humans. Like the start of any great adventure, the first challenge requires a leap of faith."

"Told you it was symbolic," Wendy says.

"In the wild, a Klujn faces dark caves of different kinds," Warwick continues. "One must learn to master fear and continue on, not knowing the dangers of the road ahead. True strength lies not in the absence of fear, but in having fears and going straight toward them. For a Klujn, the only way out is through."

"This is bullshit," Elizabeth mutters. "We didn't even get to train."

"You think a few days of swinging on rope ladders and monkey bars would help you beat whatever's in there?" I reply. "Life's not like television." Beside me, I hear Wendy and Willa snickering.

We all peer past Warwick into the darkness, wondering what's waiting for us in there. Whatever it is, it probably won't be too thrilled by our presence.

"Your first task is simple," says the king. "Cross through the cave and make it to the other side. Now, here's the catch: Hidden inside the cave are thirteen hourglasses. You must retrieve an hourglass as proof of passage. It does not matter which one you take but take only one. Make it out with an hourglass, and you will move on to the next test. Fail to retrieve an hourglass or fail to exit the cave, and your time at Circo will come to an end."

"So if we don't make it out, we die," says Wendy, cleaning her glasses with the hem of her cloak. "And if we make it out without an hourglass, we still die."

"We're going to make it out," I assure her.

"Newsflash." She replaces her glasses. "We don't know what's in there!"

"Number One, the Lake," says Warwick. I watch as Diablo approaches the first girl—Jade—and gestures for her to take off her cloak. She looks more vulnerable without it, as she hugs Girl Number Two, Mabry, goodbye. They might have only known each other as long as I've known Wendy and the others—maybe a little longer, since I was the last to be caught—but time in the wild is more intense than in the human world. An hour here is like a week in Red River, and a few days must feel like years.

I hope I live long enough to find out.

Jade steps toward the cave entrance. It's like watching a mouse being deposited in a snake's tank, not knowing if the snake is sleeping or awake. She puts on a brave face and looks intently into the darkness, trying to calculate it like a mathematical equation. *Why did Diablo take her cloak?* I wonder. *Is there going to be running?*

Jade vanishes inside. After less than ten seconds, a shrill scream escapes the cave, followed by the wet patter of footsteps growing ever distant.

"I'm sure it's nothing," I say, trying to convince myself. I swallow but my mouth is a desert.

"That sure as eggs didn't sound like nothing." Wendy looks ashen.

A few minutes pass as our imaginations fill in the blanks. We won't know if Jade made it until we get to the other side. *If* we make it.

"Number Two." Mabry lives up to her symbol, a river of snot and tears as she steps forward. Hands over her cloak. When it takes her too long to find her resolve, Diablo pushes her inside.

One . . . Two . . . Three . . .

I count silently, my whole body tense. We are all so silent.

. . . Eight . . . Nine . . . *Ten*. Once again, there's a single scream that matches Jade's, followed by more wet footsteps.

One by one, the others enter. Ying Yue lets out only a small grunt. The silver-haired girls pretend to be stoic, and their entrance into the cave is quiet. When it's Zoe's turn, I try to make eye contact, but she's focused on the cave.

"Break a leg," I say. Zoe nods mechanically, accepting my comment, then goes inside. Like the silver-haired girls, she doesn't scream.

"You shouldn't have said that," Wendy tells me.

"Why not?"

"Because chances are she might actually break one."

Next is Rory, who sinks into the cave with a small gasp of surprise. After him is Bindu. The slight girl has to be dragged inside, shuddering like an animal left out in the rain. "I don't want to die," she shrieks as Diablo pulls her toward the entrance. Her heels dig parallel lines in the earth like snowmobile tracks. "Please, don't make me do this." But she doesn't have a choice, and soon she, too, disappears inside.

Ten seconds pass. Willa, chewing on her black fingernails, says, "She didn't scream. That has to be a good thing."

"Or maybe her throat was slit and she had no vocal cords left to scream with," counters Elizabeth, always one to say something controversial.

I feel grateful to be going second to last. The more I think about it, though, the more I realize that going last is a disadvantage. There were thirteen hourglasses at the beginning of the challenge. By the time it's my turn, there will only be two left. I look at Wendy, who paces nearby, wondering if she's done the same math.

After a few minutes, Diablo ushers Willa to the cave. Willa throws Wendy a quick look, but whatever sisterly meaning it was meant to convey is lost on the wind.

"I despise her," Wendy says after Willa leaves. "Always have. The way she's both protective *and* mean. But I don't want her to die."

"She won't," I offer. "Willa seems pretty athletic."

"She doesn't even do sports! She's just naturally good at everything."

"Then she'll make it."

"But I might not." Wendy looks morose. I realize that she understands what our going last means. She plucks a bunch of shimmering leaves from a small tree and balls her hands into fists. "One hourglass," she says. "That's all I get. One. Like the odds weren't stacked against me anyway."

"You're not going to die," I say.

"Says the Klujn to the other Klujn in the Loudhouse," Elizabeth puts in.

"A little tact, please," I snap. Elizabeth rolls her eyes.

"If I die, tell Willa I'm sorry," Wendy stammers. "I guess I wasn't the nicest to her either. What I hate is the fact that she always saw me as pathetic and weak. And when someone sees you as something for long enough, eventually you start to believe it."

"You can tell her that yourself," I say. Then I add, "I know how you feel." Wendy shrugs my comment away, as if I *don't* know, because how could I? Our problems are not the same.

Then it's Elizabeth's turn, and she isn't one for sentimentality.

"See you on the other side," she says. "Maybe." Even though we have no way to measure time, Elizabeth's trip into the cave feels longer than the others. She doesn't make a sound, but that's hardly a surprise. There are only three hourglasses left, and the others will have chosen the most visible ones. The last will be the hardest to find. After a few minutes, Diablo walks toward me.

I'm not ready for this. Not ready to face whatever's in that cave. I feel like I'm on a rollercoaster ride. My over-the-shoulder harness is locked in and the car jolts forward. *Click, click, click.* It climbs slowly up the tracks. When it reaches the top, it stops. Hovers there for a moment. But it's too late now . . . too late to back out.

Before the guard can reach me, Wendy takes my hands in hers. The contact makes me uneasy—I've never liked to be touched. But before I can pull away, I feel something scratchy pushed into the gap between my palm and my fingers. "It's Moonlight Leaf," Wendy whispers. "We found some last year in Scouts. It's a plant that absorbs and emits moonlight. Wait until you really need it, then rub it. Be careful, though. It only works once."

Wendy lets go. I ball my right hand into a fist. Diablo takes my cloak. Without it, the cold hits. My limbs tremble. I crave warmth. To be lying in a hammock on the back veranda, surrounded by vegetation, with nothing to do but soak in every delicious ray of sunlight like a photosynthesizing flower. Or napping in my bed during a storm, under a warm blanket. I need to get running. I need to get my heart pumping. *How am I going to do that with this dead weight at the end of my right leg?*

As Diablo guides me toward the entrance, I take one last look back. I underestimated Wendy. Maybe the smarter thing would be not to trust her. But I don't know if I can get through these next days, hours, or minutes alone. I don't think I can survive here without a friend.

I just thought of her as a friend.

Diablo nudges me forward. *The only way out is through*, I think. With that, I step inside.

20

I take a few steps forward and daylight surrenders to the dark. I'm swallowed whole, like a small fish in the belly of a shark. Black, all I see is black. The only sound comes from the *drip-drip* of water and my breathing. I try to keep quiet. Whatever's in here may hear better than it sees.

The Moonlight Leaf is balled in my right fist. I'm tempted to use it. But I don't know how deep the cave goes, nor how much darker it will get, so I tuck it in my pocket.

The air in here is damp. I reach out, feeling for walls, but my hand touches something else. Something wet. It hangs from the ceiling like a punching bag. That's when I see—it's not a bag. It's a body. Its skin peeled off, all pink muscle underneath.

The scream has barely escaped my lips and I'm flying, running as fast as I can on my numb foot. I tear through the space, wanting to put as much distance as I can between me and that hanging mass. *Was it Klujn or human?*

I round a corner and come face to face with a rocky wall. It's a dead end. From behind me, there's a scurrying sound. I whip around, but there's nothing there. When I turn back, I realize that it's not a dead end, after all—there's a small opening close to the floor. It's so low I'll have to crawl. So dark I might as well have my eyes closed. I didn't realize that I could hate small spaces even more than I hate heights, but going back to the hanging body is not an option.

I get down on my stomach. The front of my costume is instantly soaked with cold, stagnant water. I inch my way through the tunnel, trying not to think about the countless feet of heavy rock above my head. How sturdy it is. What the chances are of it falling down and crushing me.

I can only take the shallowest of breaths. My chest feels tight. There is an itching in my body, a raging discomfort—I need to get out of this place, to be back in the woods, in an open space, breathing in as much forest air as my lungs can hold.

I crawl faster. Small, sharp stalagmites scratch my hands and torso, but I keep going, keep crawling. The faster I go, the faster I'll be outside again.

Finally, the tunnel opens out into another cave. This one is more than tall enough to stand in, and there are tiny cracks of red light coming in through the ceiling above my head, but not enough to illuminate the entirety of my surroundings. I take a deep breath while I can. The air is stale, but it'll do. My eyes begin to adjust, and though it's no more than shadows, I see that I'm in a long and narrow chamber. There are no hourglasses visible. If there were, they must have already been taken. There's a puddle of something in the middle, so large that there's no way around it, and long enough that I can't see the other side.

Then, from behind me, I hear breathing. Slow, watchful, hungry, echoing. I spin around and look at the pitch black hole I just crawled from.

I continue forward, step into the puddle. It is tepid, like a neglected bowl of soup. It's also deep—deeper than I imagined—and it creeps up my shins with a tickle. That's when I realize it's not water. It's thicker, almost like . . . blood.

I run, splashing through the dark syrupy liquid, and have almost reached the other side when a hand grabs my ankle. I scream. Whip around. The creature's grip is firm as it tries to pull me down into the pool. I shake my foot, freeing it, and that's when I see—it's not a creature.

It's a boy. He has a baby face, his eyes wide with fear. He's so young, he could be Mercy. He wears a Hunter's uniform, and there are deep gashes on his chest. Claw marks. They start at the base of his throat and travel all the way down to the bottom of his ribcage. I see his exposed bones, and blue tissue that could be lungs. They expand and contract as the boy gasps for breath. Manages a word.

"Help."

The boy tries to speak again, but red bubbles escape his lips instead of words.

Then, behind him, I see it. The creature. It's a Klujn. It looks as feral as the one in the Coliséa. Like the images in our classrooms and the ones on television. Its red eyes bore into me like two scorching suns. I don't have to be telepathic to know what it's thinking.

I want to help the boy, but I can't. He's so far gone. I won't get very far if I have to carry him. Not on these legs. And then we're both as good as dead. *I'm sorry*, I think, and sprint out of the puddle, making for the exit I can now see on the other side of the chamber. I reach a tunnel and my hands feel for walls, as dizzy as a fairgoer in a Tilt-A-Whirl. A splash behind me tells me that the Klujn is likely following, but time is precious and I can't afford to turn around for confirmation.

I follow the tunnel as it bends to the left and then to the right. The soles of my shoes are thin and my working foot feels every rock and pebble beneath it. My bad foot steps on a stalagmite and it stabs into my heel. I yelp, out of reflex, but the pain is dull, like a dentist's drill on anesthetized teeth. I grab my leg and yank it off the spike.

Behind me, the creature must be closing in.

When I reach the end of the tunnel, the path veers left again. I sprint around the corner only to see that the path ends. I manage to grab the cave walls in time to stop myself from going over the edge. At my feet lies a great expanse of black emptiness.

Did I miss a fork in the path? Is this a dead end? Am I trapped? I try to rack my brain but I don't think there was another way. This was the only one. *It's a leap of faith*, I remember the king saying. Surely, they wouldn't want to kill us all in the first challenge. If young Klujns in the wild thought they were to die at every turn, they would never make it past day one.

In the tunnel behind me I hear movement. I realize, with horror, that the only way is down.

So I grit my teeth and jump.

21

I've always hated heights. That feeling like I've left my stomach in the air while my body falls. I've always felt good being close to the earth, with my two feet planted on the ground. Near water. *Water.* I hit the surface with a painful smack. Barely have time to suck in a breath before I'm sinking, swirling through dark water. I can hardly tell which way is up or down. When the little oxygen in my lungs is about to expire, my body begins to rise, and all I can do is let it. Hurry. *Hurry!* The laws of buoyancy bring me to the surface and I suck in a deep breath.

My eyes adjust again. Now I'm in a cave with a rocky ceiling. Despite the darkness, the water glows turquoise—it's freshwater, not salt. A shore of black stones leads toward the cave wall, where there's a single sliver of light.

Light? Could it be a way out?

I begin to swim toward it when I realize I still don't have an hour-glass. I dip my head underwater and look around. It's hard to see the bottom. *There's got to be an hourglass here,* I think, as panic wells. I have no way of getting back to the previous chambers, and I can't leave without one. I dive deeper and strain my eyes to see through the murk. My lungs are burning and I have to come up for a breath.

I break the surface of the water, gasping for air. Glance up at the ledge, but the creature isn't there. *Maybe it stayed to finish off . . .* I can't finish the thought.

Treading water, I scan the walls for crevices where an hourglass could be stowed. There's nothing. The remaining ones must be at the bottom of this pool somewhere. I don't have time to waste, so I suck in another breath and dive again.

This time I see something. A flash of gold, about ten feet beneath me, glimmering on the floor of the basin. I lift my head to take a deeper breath when—the creature's eyes fix on me from the top of the drop. And then, it dives!

I swim down, down toward the object, kicking my legs for dear life. Hoping against hope that it's my hourglass. My ears block as pressure builds but I keep going, keep swimming. When I'm an arm's length away, the object comes into focus and I see—it is!

The hourglass is beautiful, made from gold-rimmed glass, about the size of a goblet. I pick it up, then begin to kick back toward the surface when I notice, almost hidden from view, a minuscule hourglass, this one no larger than an eggcup. It is brown and camouflaged by algae. Too easy to miss. And it is the last one.

I don't have enough air left in my lungs, so I pierce the surface. The creature is not far away now, thrashing ferociously toward me.

Go, a voice in my head says. *You have what you need. Get out while you can.* Then I remember Wendy, who is as good as blind without her glasses. How will she see anything underwater? Even if she makes it this far, the chances of her finding that tiny hourglass are next to none. If I leave now, I am almost certainly guaranteeing her failure, sealing her fate. I can't live with that on my conscience.

The creature is getting closer. *She helped you*, says the voice in my gut. *She didn't have to.* So, against my better judgment, I dive back down. The pressure in my ears returns as I kick toward the tiny hourglass. The creature is not far away now, approaching from the other side.

I pull my arms in rapid breaststroke, but swimming with the gold hourglass in one hand slows me down. *Come on, come on. Almost there!* I finally make it before the Klujn. Grab the second hourglass and push off the rocky bottom, back toward the surface, lungs empty and contracting.

I've almost reached the surface when a hand closes around my right ankle.

The Klujn tugs on my injured foot. I swing around and smash it in the head with the gold hourglass. The creature lets go of my foot and screeches, its voice coming out as a stream of bubbles. Its face, seen from so close, is the stuff of horror museums.

I manage to break the surface and catch my breath. Blink water from my eyes. The shore is about fifteen feet away. I swim toward it, but the beast is on my heel.

I make it out of the water, scrambling over slimy rocks. I run, guided by that ray of light. *Please*, I pray. *Be a way out.*

When I get a little closer, I realize that my pleas have been answered—it's an exit.

I hear the Klujn splash out of the water behind me. I continue toward the light, but my bad foot slows me down. The beast easily closes the gap between us and tackles me.

I am helpless, pinned to the ground. The Klujn is male. Its strength is like nothing I have ever felt—all bones and muscle, no fat. Its slippery legs rub against my sides. *What is this creature?* I think. Wild like the one in the Coliséa. *Why isn't it with its stand?*

I'm paralyzed. Eyes wide like the horizon. *This is it. This is how I'm going to die.*

A stray beam of light crosses us, and I take in every frightful detail of my attacker. Its oily skin, its red eyes. I wait for it to end me. To plunge its claws into my eye sockets or rip my ribs apart. To eat me alive.

But it doesn't. Nothing happens.

Then, I notice a bluish glow emanating from the pocket of my costume. The Klujn reaches for it and tears the fabric with sharp claws. Its long white fingers pull out a shining wad of leaves. *It's the Moonlight Leaf,* I realize. The Klujn's body must have rubbed up against it. The glow isn't overly bright, but it's enough to see the creature's expression change, like a mood ring shifting from a hot surface to a cold one. Its monstrosity recedes like a tide, and it stands.

I'm released from the slimy trap of its legs. I edge backward slowly, my mind whirring with a hundred questions, but my only answer right now is escape. I climb over the slippery rocks, my eyes never leaving the creature, and when I've placed a comfortable distance between myself and the Klujn, I turn and sprint. Climb up the rugged shore toward that exit, imagining the Klujn's hand reaching out and pulling me back down, but it doesn't. My path is left unhindered.

When I reach the exit, I set down the little wooden hourglass, but it's too small and the chances that Wendy sees it from afar are unlikely. I put the gold one down instead.

I take one last look at the Klujn. It's still by the basin, cradling the glowing leaves like a miniature moon, completely captivated.

What is happening? But I don't exactly want to stick around and find out. When that light goes out, its new focus will be me.

With every remaining bit of strength I have, I throw my body out of the cave and into the sunlight.

22

There's solid ground beneath me, softened by the fallen leaves. The smell of dirt. The sun warming my skin. Something else, too, that my sixth sense feels: safety.

I will never step into another cave again, I think. *If I can help it.* I roll over and notice the congregation of surviving contestants, all wet and shivering, looking at me and the tiny wooden hourglass in my hand.

"*Ava!*" The ground shakes with a stampede of feet. I squint through my sodden eyelashes and see a tattoo of a pentacle in front of me. It's Willa's arm, reaching for me, supporting my head. Bindu and Rory close behind. They help me up. I try to stay upright, but my foot finally fails me, and my ankle rolls. They carry me until we've reached the rest of the group, and sit me down on a fallen log.

An amused Warwick and his guards observe us.

As my eyes adjust to the late afternoon's rosy light, which feels bright in comparison to the cave, I take a closer look around. Rory, the red-haired boy, has a broken nose. Willa's covered with scratches. Bindu clutches her abdomen, but is miraculously unscathed. Elizabeth, who watches from nearby, has a nasty bite mark on her arm. Most of the others have escaped with minor injuries—grazes, cuts, broken nails.

Some aren't so lucky. Ying Yue holds a bundle of reddened cloth to the stump of her left middle finger. Rachel's right eye is gushing more liquid than its makeshift bandage can absorb.

But everyone has an hourglass, each one of a different size. Some are large and glittery, others small and nondescript. Zoe's is by far the largest, almost as big as a flower vase.

"Twelve of us," I say, finishing my mental count.

"Thirteen, if Wendy makes it out . . ." Willa looks anxiously at the exit.

"That's everyone."

"I don't think they meant to kill us," says Rory. "Just ruffle our feathers."

"What *was* that Klujn in there?" Willa asks. "Was it actually wild or—"

"A paid actor?" he suggests. "Like the ghosts in those haunted house rides? Your guess is as good as mine."

"I saw a boy in there," I tell them.

"I saw him, too," Willa says. "I think he was a Hunter."

"With an Explorer's badge," Rory puts in. "That's what they give to all the brave idiots who volunteer to walk point in the First Patrol. He picked the wrong cave to wander in."

"He was so young," I say, thinking of Mercy, his poorly hidden fear of being sent into the wild.

"The ones our age are eager to prove themselves," Bindu says sadly. "They bite off more than they can chew. My older brother died that way."

"Does that mean that Hunters are nearby?" Willa is hopeful. "Maybe they're coming to get us."

"They could be miles away," says Rory. "It's like they say at Hunter's Camp: never get separated from your buddy. If you take a turn without them . . . walk a few feet in the wrong direction . . . you can get really lost really fast and never find your way back. The wild is tricky like that."

Elizabeth comes over. Throws a suspicious look at Rory and Bindu. "I didn't realize we were recruiting."

"I didn't realize we had a group," I retort. Turning my focus back to Rory, I say, "You know a lot about Hunters," although it's more a question than a statement.

"My parents made me go to Hunter's Camp. Every single year. Even though I hated it."

"Beats baking cakes," I say.

"Not to me, it doesn't." Rory goes quiet. There's something on his mind, but whatever it is he doesn't share it. He scratches nervously at his chin, no stubble there despite our lack of razors.

"Do the others know anything we don't?" I ask.

Rory shakes his head. "Everyone's in the same boat. The first two—Jade and Mabry—I think they're cousins or something. Mission Creek girls who've never set foot in the wild. The Military girl's Ying Yue—she's a first-year stationed at a Military base in Valor's Edge. She looks fierce, but I've caught her rescuing snails from the path. The silver-haired girls are all in the same underground weapons club in Brave Night. That's all I know. They don't exactly warm to conversation. Then there's her," and Rory indicates Zoe, sitting some distance away. "I can't figure her out."

"Zoe," I say. "She was my partner in the Deeper Woods. She said her father's a Hunter."

"Makes sense." To my puzzled look, Rory adds, "She has that need to prove herself."

"It's called survival." Elizabeth's voice is its usual bite.

"Have they said anything about us?" Willa wants to know.

"Bits and pieces," Rory says. Then he turns to me. "They think you're the leader. Are you?"

"We don't have a leader," I answer, the back of my neck heating up. I catch Elizabeth's annoyance out of the corner of my eye and work hard to suppress a smile.

"Well, group or no group, I like your vibe better than I like theirs. I don't like the way they talk. It's like they've drawn enemy lines."

"It's probably a good idea for us to stick together," Bindu says softly.

"I just find it strange that you're the only boy." Elizabeth's statement is laced with accusation.

Before Rory can answer, Diablo and the other guard arrive with our cloaks. They drop them in a pile. In the afternoon light, with his hood down, I can see Diablo's textured violet eyes and the ash-colored tattoos that decorate his hands, like the delta of a river that runs from somewhere out of sight. The other guards and the king, Warwick, feel somewhat unpredictable and chilling, but Diablo is different—a calm, introspective energy emanates from him.

In the distance, there's a scream followed by a splash.

Willa leaps up, and we all watch the darkened exit. Wendy's almost out.

There are more noises. Splashing. Thrashing. Grunting. The sound of a struggle. We all wait in suspense. There's another scream, and then a *thunk*. Whatever the creature is doing to Wendy, she's putting up one hell of a fight.

"Come on, sis," Willa whispers. I realize that she does care, more than she's willing to admit.

Then there is silence, and our hope diminishes with each passing second. The silence drags on, telling us all we need to know.

Tears track down Willa's cheeks.

I can't believe that Wendy might be dying in there right now, and there's nothing I can do about it. I swallow. *It's just like Wolf,* I think.

Rory puts a sympathetic hand on Willa's shoulder.

"No," she sobs. "Not Wendy."

Then, a gold hourglass sails from the cave exit like a whale spouting out a single jet of water. It lands on the forest floor and rolls a few times, but doesn't break. Following the hourglass is—Wendy! She climbs out of the hole and stands there, wet, disheveled, and panting. She's covered in mud and blood, her hair stuck to her face, her glasses broken, but despite all this, she manages a smile. She's missing a tooth—a central incisor. Either she doesn't know or she doesn't care.

Wendy's smile is knocked askew as a creature rams into her. It takes a moment for me to realize that the creature is Willa. Willa hugs her sister and chokes out a few teary apologies about the way she treated her.

After a moment, Wendy hugs her back and says, "Don't. *Ever.* Underestimate. Me."

Willa answers with a blubbery, "*I promise.*"

Watching them, I find myself wishing that I had a sister or a best friend. Someone who knows me inside out and still likes who I am. Mercy and I used to be that way, but as we got older, we grew apart. I can hardly blame him. I guess I'm weird sometimes, but it takes so much energy just to appear normal. Like the gears in a grandfather clock, working furiously to make the second and minute hands follow a steady rhythm that society, at some point, decided on.

When you've been left behind, it's hard to shrug off the feeling that you're disposable. That if you don't behave, it could all be gone tomorrow.

Willa walks over to the pile of cloaks, picks one up, and drapes it over Wendy's shoulders. I watch the sisters, wondering what it must feel like to have a real home.

There's a tugging inside me, a deep yearning to belong somewhere—or rather, to belong with some*one*. That way, home can be anywhere.

The sky rumbles with distant thunder. A few fat raindrops begin to fall. I'm glad. They'll mask the fact I'm crying.

23

As we head back toward the stand, Wendy recounts her story about how she beat the creature and found her hourglass. "It was right there!" she exclaims. "Waiting for me at the exit of the cave!" Willa has a proud smile on her face, and Elizabeth looks bored. After Wendy finishes describing the experience in gruesome detail, she looks at me. "It's strange, isn't it? How the hourglass was right there and you didn't see it."

"Weird," I say, biting my bottom lip to stop from smiling.

As Diablo takes us down an unfamiliar path, my mind returns to the Klujn in the cave. The look in its eyes when I pulled out the Moonlight Leaf. The way his expression became almost docile. *What was it about the light?* Lost in thought, I fail to notice a thick root sticking out of the ground. I trip but manage to stay upright.

Wendy looks down and her eyes double in size. "Oh, mortal horror!" she exclaims. I half expect another Klujn to jump out of the woods, but Wendy is staring at my foot. "That's one of the foulest things I've ever seen," she says, as I limp forward. "No offense."

"Worse than watching someone burn to death?" Willa asks dryly but leavens it with a small smile.

"Well, no. That is definitely up there," Wendy answers. I have to laugh—not at Reesa's death, of course, but at the expression on Wendy's face—she reminds me of the way a chicken fluffs up when you startle it. The more I try to suppress my laughter, the worse it gets. Maybe it's exhaustion or nervous tension or a delayed response to the awful trials we've been through. Who knows? Despite my damaged foot, I feel good. My body feels firm, no longer puffy or bloated. My mind, my blood, my energy . . . they all feel clean and light. It's like the late afternoon sun is shining straight through me.

And now I can't stop laughing.

The girls look at me like I've lost my mind.

"We've lost Ava," Willa says, amused.

"I'm sorry," I reply, through fits of giggles. "I don't know why I'm laughing." And I can't think of the last time I did. Had a wild, unrestrained, ridiculous fit like this.

"What was in that cave water?" Wendy adds. "Whatever it is—I want some."

As I continue to laugh for no apparent reason, the others crack smiles and roll their eyes, but there's nothing judgmental about it. Then, a pungent smell meets my nostrils, and my laughter simmers down. It's something like rotten eggs, and it's growing stronger.

Wendy makes a retching sound, and everyone joins in with their own take on the source.

"Ugh! Something smells like boiled feet."

"Did someone shit their pants?"

"It was probably Ava."

"Nope, not me," I say, cracking a grin. "Must be one of the silver triplets."

Looking at the front to the three in question, I get three identical cold glares in return.

"Don't tell me there's another challenge already?" Willa says defeatedly.

My smile fades. Well, the laughter felt good while it lasted. The path narrows between two large oak trees with flaming red leaves and descends toward an ice-blue river—and there, we discover the origin of the smell. There are individual bathing pools carved into the river's rocky banks, lined with purple crystals that color the water a cloudy lilac shade. Each is filled with sulfurous water, steam rising from its surface.

"Those look like Amethyst pools," says Wendy, squinting through her broken glasses. "Catrina Sherman wrote about them in *A Brief History of Klujns*, in the chapter about the Deeper Woods. Apparently some minerals in the water are responsible for the smell. I can't believe they're *real*!" she squeals. The pools bubble with hot water from deep within the belly of the earth. A gentle aroma of lavender and eucalyptus begins to mask the foul odor. "There are oils and minerals in the water that are good for a lot of things," says Wendy, indicating my foot. "Natural antiseptics."

Diablo and the other guards order us to undress, but they don't have to tell us twice. I take off my costume, less self-conscious than I was when we first arrived at Circo. I like this new confidence that flows through me. Soon everyone is down to their underwear, leaving their discarded clothes and hourglasses in small piles. Wendy is the first to slip into an Amethyst pool. I choose the one next to hers, which borders the river. The water is not lukewarm, like the showers back home, but blistering hot. My eyes roll back in my head, in pure and utter ecstasy—a pleasure so intense, I have never felt anything like it. Better than sitting by a fire after a long winter walk or a big meal after a day of sports.

"Oh. My. Stars," Wendy murmurs. "I've died. This is three cubic meters of heaven."

I couldn't agree more. I submerge the back of my head, and the velvety water massages my scalp. It fills every icy room in my body, making me forget what cold and pain are. I let the first challenge drift away. Floating in my pool, eyes closed, ears underwater, listening to the deep volcanic rumbling of the jets.

When I open my eyes, I flip to my belly and reach over the narrow stretch of earth that separates the Amethyst pool and the river. I dip my fingers in the icy water, enjoying the contrast of temperature. Down in the deep blue, I see a school of fish swimming past. *Don't go south*, I want to warn them. *The river there is no home for you.*

Across the river, about a hundred feet away, a pine forest rises royally into the sky. The sun sets behind it and the sky begins to fill with pink cotton candy clouds. What would happen if I hopped over the edge and let this river take me downstream? Where would it lead me? Home?

I feel like I'm floating in a dream, and in this dream, bad things cannot happen. How could they? Look where we are. In these crystal ponds, there is no yesterday, no tomorrow. No Red River or the reality waiting for us when we get back to our quarters. There is only now, and now is blissful ignorance. *If this exists*, I think. *Imagine what other beautiful things are out here in the forest, waiting to be discovered.*

We float there for who knows how long, in pure and complete rapture, too tired and exhausted by our pleasure to talk. Eventually, Wendy speaks, but her words are muffled. I lift my head out of the water.

"Look," she says, awestruck. The sky is darkening now, and there's a flickering across its canvas—waves of pink and purple light, ebbing and flowing. "They're Lumina. I've only heard about them. I never thought I'd ever actually see them." The Lumina dance like flames, licking at the oxygen of the night. Nature is performing just for us.

"It's magical," Willa says, from two pools over.

"It's science," says Elizabeth, ever the skeptic. She tries to pin it on dust particles or the angle of the earth or another explanation that doesn't do the marvel justice.

As I watch the Luminas' cosmic dance, I realize how far removed we are from the human world. From safety and laws and the protection of the fences. But also . . . from blackened forests, ash-filled skies, and a fear that everybody inhales but never exhales. Even though the last two days have been nothing short of horrific, it feels sort of good to be away from it all. I can't help but think that life on the other side of the fences is somehow bleak in comparison, dead in that anthropogenic way.

Diablo announces that it's time to leave. I pull my hands out of the misty purple water and look at them. My fingertips are wrinkled and swollen. I use my last ounce of energy to lift my body from the pool, wanting to return to it almost at once. But the cold is just a brief inter-mission—as I slip back into my leathery cloak I am warm once more. I feel like I could fall asleep and sleep for a very long time.

My bad foot hardly bothers me on the walk back. The girls discuss the Amethyst pools and why the Klujns brought us there. If we are here to participate in hideous contests, why bother bathing us? Giving us a pleasurable experience? Elizabeth has a theory that the reward was in-tentional, the way that some animals are primed and pampered before they're killed so that their meat tastes better. Our long soak might not have been for our own enjoyment but as a means of softening our flesh. I find this thought disturbing but say nothing. It feels too ugly for the beauty of this place.

As the sky grows darker, the forest comes alive with glow-in-the-dark creatures—fireflies, dragonflies, and other mysterious insects flit around. Little bioluminescent cars, flying between skyscraper trees.

"That's the biggest butterfly I've ever seen," says Wendy, as a glass-winged one the size of her head flutters by.

"Would make a nice brooch to go with my skirt," Elizabeth remarks.

Amid the fanfare of plant and animal life, I'm reminded of José's stories about forests and oceans and their creatures, and I let my mind drift into the memory as we walk.

* * *

"Ecosystems are as fragile as a house of cards," he said one afternoon, emp-tying a can of whale lard into a large saucepan. He stacked it on top of a pyramid of identical empty cans. "You remove a single card—a single species—and the whole house comes tumbling down." José removed a can from the bottom and, not surprisingly, the whole structure collapsed. "Be-cause in Nature, balance is crucial. Every creature plays an important role in the success of the ecosystem. Take worms for example—humans thought they were pests and killed them with their pesticides. As it turns out, worms were crucial to soil health.

"But humans don't want to see this," he continued, gathering the fallen

cans and tossing them into the garbage. "They don't want to work with Nature for the good of the whole. Working with Nature would require listening to her, nurturing her, taking less. And moderation is not a word that humans have ever liked."

* * *

Back in the forest, the creatures continue to carry out their nightly tasks, unbothered by us. I breathe in deeply, and beyond the living scent, there's a feeling. That this forest is happy.

Maybe Red River was like this once, I think. *Maybe the whole Territory used to be.*

* * *

When we reach Circo, Diablo and the guards lead us on an unfamiliar route. "I was hoping we were going home," says Wendy. "I'm craving that white fruit."

Elizabeth throws her a dirty look. "Did you say *home?*"

"You know what I mean." The path leads halfway up the hillside before veering right. As we curve around the mountain, the summit looms to our left, a few hundred feet away. I look up at those unexplored heights and that forbidding black tent at the very top, curious to know what goes on in there, but it isn't our destination for tonight—which might be a good thing.

The path winds back to the main face of the mountain, becoming more populous with trees and tents. Everything looks enchanting in the dark. We cross a number of circular plazas where parties are being set up: little bazaars with stalls that sell magical-looking toys, luminescent potions, and snacks. There is a Sideshow Alley of Klujn games, and children have their faces painted in glowing makeup while adults talk among themselves. I see Klujns balancing on slack wires strung between the trees, while others are twirling hoops of fire. It reminds me of the Klujn Fairs back home, only here there are no bloody contests.

No birds tied to strings. The birds here are free, perched on branches among the hanging green lanterns.

Diablo takes us down another street, this one quiet and away from the festivities. We arrive at a black tent, unexceptional from the outside. Diablo lifts a flap of fabric, and I cross into another world.

From the striped ceiling to the opulent fabrics draping the walls, we are surrounded by lush shades of gold and purple. Candles in sconces give off a pleasing scent of vanilla or coconut. Everyone's silenced by the largest surprise: thirteen dressing tables with makeup stations, vanity mirrors, and elegant chairs. Next to each table is a rack with costumes, shoes, headdresses, and jewelry. The makeup stations have bowls and brushes, paints and powders, glitters and pastes, and trays of lustrous crystals, shimmering seeds, and piles of bright leaves.

I'm dizzied by color; more color than I have ever seen in one place, aside from Nature. This is an artist's workshop, a treasure chest brimming with wondrous things.

Wendy shakes her head. "If this is a craft challenge, I'm shit out of luck."

I'm not. My hands are itching to pick up a brush, to hold faceted jewels.

A purple-robed Klujn stands at the center of all this magnificence, near a basin of dark water on a pedestal.

"What does her cloak represent?" I ask Wendy.

"Green is for plant workers," she murmurs into my ear. "Indigo is for guards, yellow for educators—I think—and red is the king. But I don't know what that shade of purple means."

The Klujn is roughly my height. As she pushes back her hood, I see that she is very old. A crown of gilded roses rests on her cropped white hair. She has the same violet eyes as Diablo, only hers are astonishingly bright, like a stained-glass window filtering sunlight. They sparkle, but her expression is somehow far away, as though between this world and another.

"Yesterday, the king allocated your symbols," she says, her voice gentle but self-assured. "Tonight, you will be given your corresponding crystals. These will be your identities for the remaining challenges.

"As a species, we Klujns believe that repressing our true self and our emotions only leads to great suffering. The Blood Race, whether human or Klujn, is about discovering who we are and learning to celebrate the individuality that exists inside each of us. Here, at Circo, you are performer and observer, artist and canvas. To thrive in the Blood Race and in life, your outward appearance must match the being who resides inside."

A few of the others are especially interested in what the old Klujn is saying. The expression on Rory's face lies somewhere between joy and melancholy. "Like crystals," she continues and reaches into the black basin. She pulls out a shiny, wet stone. "Formed in the earth over millions of years; shaped differently by pressure. Each crystal is unique, with its strengths and attributes, and that's what makes them precious."

She returns the crystal to the basin. "Tonight, my apprentice will assign you your particular crystals. After, I will meet with you all individually. As you wait, you may begin to experiment with paints," she says, indicating the dressing tables. "When I call you to my tent, please, do not keep me waiting. An old Klujn waits for no one."

And with that cryptic announcement, she turns to leave.

"That's *it*?" Elizabeth asks. "You're not going to give us a better explanation?"

The old Klujn turns back to Elizabeth, an eyebrow slightly raised. "You want a better explanation?"

"How about—*why*? I mean—costume or no costume—what difference does it make? This isn't a fashion show. No one's voting on who gets *best dressed*. We're all going to die anyway."

"With that attitude, you most certainly will." The Klujn's voice is steely, but there's dark humor in her eyes. "Sooner rather than later."

There's a fizz of nervous laughter from the other girls. I wouldn't want to be on the receiving end of the look Elizabeth gets from our leader. She may be ancient, but her strength defies age or size.

She walks toward Elizabeth, who visibly loses bluster as the distance closes between them. "Does a Klujn get an explanation when she is thrown into a human Coliséa?" she asks, her voice as steady as her steps. "Does a spotted wolf get an explanation when he is shot for his meat and pelt? What about when a thousand-year-old Mother Tree feels the first strike of the logger's ax? Who will explain to her that she is dying for the farms that Hunters wish to build on her land?"

For the first time, Elizabeth goes truly quiet.

"Perhaps the king likes to indulge humans with facts," the old Klujn continues. "Perhaps he gets a thrill out of dangling the rules of his favorite game above your heads. I, on the other hand, do not wish to waste my words on narrow minds. I have very little patience for your entitlement. I believe knowledge is a privilege that you have not yet earned. Humans who don't believe in our magic will never be convinced. And those who do believe need no convincing."

Again, she turns to leave, but this time pauses. A wry smile dances across her lips. "If you must know," she tells us, "tomorrow, you will fight each other. The tests will continue until only three are left. Those who survive will reveal a prophecy written by our gods. At least, that's what the king likes to believe. I personally think our gods are too busy to concern themselves with humans. You are merely characters in a game. Whatever he may have told you about learning is true, but along with that brutal apprenticeship of truth will come bloodshed."

Elizabeth glares. "So you're playing dice . . . with our lives? For what? A bit of entertainment? A prophecy? Your stupid gods who aren't even real?"

The old Klujn answers, with the slightest trace of sarcasm, "More like *cards*."

She retreats behind a curtain of dancing crystal beads, leaving us to stew in her words. I lean forward, trying to glimpse what lies in the adjacent tent, but the curtain settles into place behind her.

"Hi! I'm Glory!" Someone steps out of the shadows, smiling at us with bright white teeth. One of the girls screams.

Glory is female, I presume, judging by her sweet chirpy voice, although she looks neither male nor female. Her green cloak seems a little large for her small, undeveloped body. Her eyes are violet, like the old Klujn's and Diablo's. She wears spirited makeup on her brown, freckled face—purple eyeshadow, black lipstick, and gold dots along her cheekbones.

I catch my breath when I realize that all of Glory's fingers have been amputated right above the middle knuckle. A necklace of small crystal claws dangles around her neck, like charms. There is a horrible story there.

I look at her face again and realize that her smile is genuinely friendly.

"Who's first?" Glory gestures to the basin as if she's rounding up friends to play a game of Wolves and Townships. She looks around, excited by the look of us, as if we're exotic in our plainness.

Jade gingerly steps forward, crinkling her nose in revulsion at the sight of Glory.

Ignoring this—or, perhaps, not noticing it—Glory reaches into the water and pulls out a dark blue crystal.

"Lapis lazuli," she announces, depositing it in Jade's palm. Then, after explaining the properties of the Lake god's stone, Glory indicates a particular dressing table covered with makeup in more shades of dark blue than I knew existed. A rack holds blue costumes and shoes alike.

As Jade hurries over to it, Mabry, whose turn is next, saunters up to Glory, avoiding eye contact. Glory reaches into the water and draws out a stunning aquamarine, the crystal that matches the symbol of her River god. I wouldn't have believed a river could be that color if I hadn't just seen one this afternoon.

One by one, the others are allocated their crystals, from black obsidian to amazonite, clear quartz to opal. Each captive approaches Glory with caution, and all she can do is smile, as fascinated by us as we are wary of her. Rory gets fluorite, with hues of pink, purple, and green. Bindu, who still hasn't cried today, gets a citrine as yellow as her toenail polish. Willa has a dazzling dark red garnet.

Elizabeth's is a silvery-gold rock. "Pyrite," Glory says, delighted, handing over her stone. "Also known as fool's gold." *Fitting*, I think.

Then it's my turn. As I approach, I make sure to keep my expression neutral. My pendant warms through my clothes, almost in apprehension. Glory reaches into the basin and removes a crystal. As she gives it to me, our eyes meet, and I look deep into hers, curious about the pattern in her irises, as distinct as a fingerprint.

A startled Glory drops the crystal.

Quickly, she bends down to pick it up. "I'm sorry," she says, and our eyes meet again. This time, I see a mixture of emotions behind them: confusion, curiosity, fear. She gazes into me like a crystal ball.

I break the eerie contact and look down at the cold, wet stone in my hand. I dry it with the edge of my cloak and see that inside the pearl-white crystal is a gorgeous flash of blue.

"Moonstone," Glory tells me. "It represents strength, femininity, growth, and intuition. It's a favorite here. Quite lucky, really . . . although, our kind don't believe in luck." She winks.

"Thank you," I say, a bit confused and not sure what to make of her kindness. I walk over to the moonstone vanity. Now it's Wendy's turn, and Glory gives her a sunstone, which is a horrendous burnt orange color.

"Just my luck," my friend gripes as she settles at the table next to me. "I'll die looking like a steamed carrot."

I can't help but laugh. "It's not *that* bad," I say, trying to sound reassuring, but I catch her looking longingly at my moonstone.

Wendy looks over at Glory. "Why do they soak them in that black tub, anyway?"

"It's to neutralize them," Willa replies from two seats down.

"Neutralize them? Why do they need to be neutralized?"

Willa balances her garnet on her palm. "Crystals are like containers that store energy—both good and bad. Soaking them in purified water removes any bad energy they might have absorbed."

"How do you know all that?" asks Wendy.

"My *extracurricular* activities," Willa replies. "That Klujn—Glory—was right. Different types of crystals have different properties. Some attract love, some protect, while others heal. Each is unique to the environment it was formed in. After they've been neutralized, charging them in moonlight or sunlight brings out their best qualities. It returns them to their natural state—a positive one."

Her words take me back to the violent Klujn in the cave, and the way his eyes changed when he saw the glowing Moonlight Leaf. The plant was emitting *moonlight*. Was the light "charging" him, as Willa put it—returning him to a natural state of some kind? Something sparks in me: *Klujns have crystals in their bones.* What if their fascination with the moon is something more than mindless worship? What if it physically affects them somehow?

Glory clears her throat awkwardly, and we all look in her direction.

"Daciana will see you now," she tells Jade, who reluctantly disappears through the beaded curtain.

After a few minutes, Jade emerges, the curtain clicking behind her. She hurries to her table and leans in to whisper to Mabry. I notice that a pink claylike paste has been applied to the spot where she was branded.

When Glory calls for Mabry, I turn my focus to the makeup station in front of me.

Daciana's words echo in my mind: *In order to thrive in the Blood Race and in life, your outward appearance must match the being who resides inside.*

I mix a white cream with a shiny blue powder, the closest color to a moonstone I can get. Then I take a sponge and begin to smooth it on my forehead and cheekbones, painting the top half of my face with the glittery mask. I use a stencil to spray a blue glimmer on my eyelids and temples, then glue on tiny crystal beads along my hairline. I finish the look with light blue lipstick.

Even though I don't wear much makeup, I've always liked playing around with it. Sneaking into Diana's room and trying on the lipsticks she hasn't worn since she was my age. This is different though. There's something exciting about being permitted to be feminine. To express myself. It's like, with the palette in front of me, I can finally figure out who that is.

A few of the others also seem to be enjoying the task, including Rory, who dove into the makeup challenge with zest, now immune to the snickers of the silver-haired girls. He must feel my attention, because he catches my eye in his mirror and smiles, something cheeky and alive, and I smile back.

Next to me, Wendy is struggling. Her glasses are off, and her eyes look out of focus.

"I look like a circus clown," she groans, having applied a contour paste in all the wrong places. Her face is full of wild, brown brushstrokes. "Someone get me a flaming hoop and a tiger."

"You have to start by choosing the right color."

"I thought I had."

"That bright green with that purple makes brown," I tell her. "Try this shade of red, with that yellow." She does as I say, and begins to blend the colors. "More red," and she adds a dollop to the bowl, until it's the right shade of orange. "Okay, now clean the brown off."

"I hope you know what you're doing," she tells me, and grudgingly follows my orders.

When she's ready, I pick up a paintbrush and dip it into a bowl of white paint. "You have to make sure you're accentuating the right areas," I say, as I contour her face. "You want to work with the muscles and expressions that are already there." I paint two half-moons under her eyes. A line on her nose. Little circles on her brow and chin, moving with the curves of her face, adding definition. Then I take the dark orange paste and daub a line under her cheekbones. I wet a brush and begin to blend the strokes until Wendy's face is no longer a clown mask, but something a little more theatrical. A little more *Circo*.

When I finish the base, I do her eyes. Gold eyeshadow. Black eyeliner and lashes. Dramatic eyebrows. Then I glue crushed orange leaves to her temples and spray them with gold mist.

She looks more like an exotic bird than a human girl.

"There," I say. When Wendy looks at herself in the mirror, she doesn't look disgusted. She looks puzzled.

"How did you *do* that?" she asks wonderingly.

"Magic."

Willa overhears and chuckles in appreciation. On the other side of the tent, the silver-haired girls have painted their faces to resemble the Executioner's mask: blue with silver triangles under the eyes. It's eerie, this feeling they give off—like we're on opposing sides.

"You know, I hate to agree with one of our captors, but being in makeup does make me feel kind of different," says Wendy. "Like I'm wearing armor or something."

I try to keep my eyes on my own makeup, but they keep darting over to that crystal curtain as girls walk hurriedly in and just as hurriedly out, all sporting some kind of bandage. The Military girl, Ying Yue, emerges with a leaf dressing over her missing finger. Silver-haired Rachel comes out with a compress over her eye. When Rory slips back into the seat at his vanity, his broken nose looks straighter and less swollen, and though his face shows relief, there are tears in his eyes.

"It makes no sense," Wendy says. "Why are they healing us if we're only going to get hurt again? Do they want to make their meat tender *and* aesthetically pleasing?"

She has a knack for saying the wrong thing at the wrong time, but I find Wendy's humor amusing.

I think about my foot. It's going to take more than a leaf or a bandage to fix it—that is, if it's not already beyond repair. The girls continue to go in and out until Elizabeth returns, but she gives nothing away.

"Who's next?" says Glory. Her eyes fall on me, and it's as if she can barely contain her excitement.

My heart speeds up. Not wanting to keep the old Klujn waiting, I step through the curtain.

24

A dark passageway leads to an even larger tent. It is like an indoor forest, its walls covered in sundry plants and flowers. The tent has been built around existing trees, their trunks acting as living beams. Their lower branches reach outwards, providing clever solutions for storage.

Around the room are birdcages of different shapes and sizes, inside of which are brightly plumed birds. One of the cages' residents is, unmistakably, a blue sparrow.

"Sit down," says Daciana from her work table in the center. She crushes a plant with a mortar and pestle. I sit on a mat, and she kneels beside me. The old Klujn pulls up the right sleeve of my robe and seems startled by the scars on my arm.

I try to pull away out of habit, but she traps my wrist in the circle of her thumb and index finger.

"Don't move." She places the pestle on a nearby tray and takes a brush. Dips it into the paste and starts to paint the crescent moon brand on my forearm. The pinkish-gray paste is cool and soothing, relieving the itch at once. As she works, I watch the blue sparrow sleeping peacefully in its cage. And then I notice something strange. All the birdcage doors are open.

"Why do you leave them open?" I ask before I can stop myself. I wonder if, like Elizabeth, she'll have no patience for my questions.

She continues her work and I realize that, despite Daciana's outward severity, there's something innately calm about her, a gentle energy. "So they can leave at any time."

I decide to keep going. "Why don't they fly away?"

"Why would they do that? They're safe here, and they can go in and out as they please. It's the creatures who are deprived of freedom who most seek escape," she says. "The more freedom one has, the more comfortable one feels staying in place."

As Daciana finishes painting my burn, I notice that her claws have retracted; the fingertips are nailless and smooth. "What happened to your claws?" I ask.

"It would be impractical to always have them on display," she says.

"I thought . . ." I stammer. I don't know what I thought. I've never given the matter of claws much thought before, beyond being ground up for fertilizer or strung on necklaces. What is it like to actually *have* them?

"Viaţăs emerge when we need them," Daciana tells me. "When we are angry, when we feel threatened, when we experience passion or desire, and sometimes merely to show off." She finishes covering my brand. As the paste begins to dry, it pulls at my skin, tightening like clay. The feeling is unusual, but I like it. "Let it flake off naturally," she advises.

Then, before I realize what's happening, she has removed my right shoe. I flinch. My foot is dark purple, engorged and festering, even worse than it was before.

Daciana's reaction is subtle, but it's there. A mix of concern and amusement. "Where did you get that?"

"A trap," I explain. "I've had it for a few days."

"I can see that." There's a sly smile on her lips, like she's impressed by the sheer gruesomeness of it.

"Do you have something that could help?" I feel stupid for even asking. There's nothing that could mend it aside from a saw, and I'm not in the mood to have a limb amputated.

"I may," she says, surprising me. She takes a glass decanter filled with bright purple liquid from her work table, removes the cap, fills it up like a shot glass, and hands it over. I look at it quizzically. "Drink," she tells me.

I smell the liquid and cough; just the smell alone corrodes my throat. "What is it?" I ask.

"Violette liquor," says Daciana. "Nature's pain relief. Not to be confused with violet, the flower. *Violette* is a plant." I throw back the shooter and it burns all the way down to my belly. After this morning's challenge, the Amethyst pools, the hikes, and no food, it hits me almost immediately.

Daciana, who is evidently not squeamish, holds my foot in her bare hands. She turns it from side to side, inspecting it from different angles. "Someone treated this?" she asks.

"The guard—Diablo—he wrapped it in some leaves right after it happened."

"*Hmmph*," she says to herself, then pinches the skin on either side of the first hole and squeezes hard, as though trying to pop a giant pimple. An angry spray of thick green pus spurts out, covering her hands. Daciana doesn't look like she minds. She continues to squeeze until my foot begins to expel a triangular metal shard. "*Hmmph*," she says again, as though this was exactly what she expected. She gently pulls it out the rest of the way and drops the foreign object onto the tray with a *clang*. The skin of my foot immediately looks less puffy.

Daciana catches me looking at the bottle of Violette liquor.

"Humans," she *tsks*, then wipes her hands and pours another shooter of the stuff. This time, it burns less. Daciana moves on to the second hole, and then the third, until she has pulled out five identical pieces of metal. She wipes my foot clean and paints on more of the pink clay. "I don't know how you managed to walk on that thing for days," she says, with a shake of the head, "let alone compete in the first challenge."

"I didn't exactly have a choice," I say dryly. "It was kind of a life-or-death situation."

"They're a cruel invention, those traps," she says, with another shake of the head. "The bullets they expulse are filled with a poison that causes slow paralysis; they're meant to lodge in your flesh. The Violette leaf Diablo wrapped your foot in not only subdued the pain but confined the poison and stopped it from spreading to your heart. The same plant as the liquor you're drinking now. You have him to thank for his plant knowledge and quick thinking—without it, you'd be dead. It's cruel," Daciana adds, "like most things humans build."

"It was a human trap," I say. "Built by Klujns."

"Is that what they taught you in school?" she jeers. "That, my dear foolish human, was a *Klujn* trap, built by humans."

"But it was in the Deeper Woods . . . on your side of the fence."

"You think humans respect the fences? That's adorable." Her voice sharpens even more. "Those fences weren't made to keep us out, my child. They were made to keep you in." *Keep us in?* But we're not trapped. They are. Everyone knows the fences were built to keep Klujns away from human townships. If not, they would invade. Abduct us. Eat us.

Daciana indicates that we are finished. Carefully, I get up and put some weight on my foot. It's still numb, but blood begins to flow back down. "Why are you helping us?" I ask.

"The king may have a taste for violence, and he may have a taste for games, but Klujns always fight fair. If only the same could be said about humans."

"*Some* humans," I correct her. "We're not all the same." I don't know where it comes from, this desire to not be lumped in with the Colls and the Mr. Mogels of the Territory. What am I trying to prove to her? It's all moot. I am a prisoner, competing in the Blood Race. Then, something she said gets through my defensive front, and I blurt, "You said *the king* has a taste for violence . . ."

She picks up the tray with the mortar and pestle and brings it back to her work table. "This is his stand, and I must obey," she says. "But where I come from, it is not in our nature to capture the wayward human. If a person demonstrates no threat and wishes to learn about our customs, we welcome them in. It has happened many times over the years. Being in contact with humans allows us to acclimate to their wide variety of *diseases*"—a sharpness here—"and to learn their customs and languages. Knowledge is, in my opinion, more powerful than any weapon. But every stand is different, and the leader determines the climate of that stand. The king's heart is set on spectacle and vengeance, and so, Circo has become a vengeful place."

This is the biggest surprise of all. She doesn't condone the violence. I just stare at her in shock.

"Give it a night," she says, nodding to my foot. "It should heal in time for tomorrow's fights."

"Thank you," I murmur. There is so much more I want to ask, so much that I don't know where to start, but in my hesitation, I miss my chance.

Daciana turns away, and I put on my shoe and head back to the other tent. My foot feels lighter already. She may have just saved it.

I'm in the passageway between the tents and have almost reached the beaded curtain when I hear a growl. It's a long, deep animal sound that escapes from another room. Following it, I peer into a small sleeping chamber with a large mattress on the ground, plush pillows, a rug, and a fireplace. The room is decorated with black flowers. A huge wolf of the same color sits on the bed, a single white spot on its back, ears pricked, on alert, its nose testing the air. The wolf growls again, showing wicked fangs. *Stay away*, it's cautioning me. *Get out of my mistress's tent.*

But I don't leave. Instead, I step forward, drawn in by the blue eyes that remind me so much of the wolf back home. I take another step and its hackles rise, its jaw opening in menace.

I reach out a tentative hand and show it my palm, slowly holding it under the snout like an offering. The wolf smells it. Then, to my surprise and delight, its face relaxes and it rolls over, showing me its furred abdomen. It's a girl.

"What are you doing?" Daciana's voice startles me. I turn around and see her in the doorway.

"I'm sorry," I stammer. "I heard growling."

"And your instinct was to investigate?"

I say nothing.

"You should not be in here."

"You're right," I say, and as I'm about to wrench myself away, the words come spilling out. "I used to have one. A white one, with black spots. Well, he wasn't mine, but he used to visit me."

The old Klujn studies me and the now-submissive wolf on the bed. Her expression is still stern, but she seems intrigued.

"What happened to him?"

"He died," I say, pushing down my emotions. "He was trying to protect me."

"How can you be sure he's dead?"

"A man shot him. I was there." Daciana nods with an expression almost like regret.

"They are the most loyal creatures," she says gently. "They remember friends, like they remember enemies." Daciana's wolf yawns as she balances on her spine, four paws reaching toward the ceiling.

"Can I?"

"Who am I to deny an old wolf the pleasure of a belly rub?" Daciana's voice is laced with amusement now. "Rhea is affectionate—almost *too* affectionate at times. When she meets someone she likes, she won't leave them alone."

I smile, crouch down, and rub the wolf's stomach. She moans, eyes rolling back in her head, tongue lopping out of her massive mouth. Her paws are the size of a lion's, her claws the length of a bear's.

"How old is she?" I ask.

"She's as old as me, and I'm no new moon."

"How old is that? If it's not indiscreet to ask."

Daciana sighs. "I stopped counting after a thousand cycles. I supposed that's about eighty in human years. I know, I look old for my age, but I've lived a full life and it has tired me."

"Eighty? How can a wolf be eighty?" I splutter.

"Spotted wolves live to be as old as their masters. Royal Klujns are given a cub at birth." She holds up a hand. "Don't let that impress you—about one-quarter of the Klujn population is born royal. The royal Klujn and wolf are bonded together by ancient blood magic. That bond lasts a lifetime. Of course, your kind don't believe in magic."

"I think . . ." I begin, "that those who believe need no convincing."

There's a flicker in Daciana's violet eyes.

"Spotted wolves are fascinating creatures," she says, her voice warming. "They are our lifelong protectors. Once they're bound to their master or mistress, the Klujn and wolf operate as two parts of one whole. It is a symbiotic relationship—one of love and sacrifice, unparalleled in Nature." Rhea groans, in a state of relaxed euphoria. "You should have seen the other girls," Daciana titters. "As soon as Rhea growled, they fled. It was funny, really." Then, surprisingly, she adds, "You're not like the others, you know. You're curious."

"I've been told that curiosity's a bad thing," I say truthfully.

"Depends what kind of life you want to have. A mind that's curious about the world is one that's willing to grow. There is remarkable bravery in admitting you don't know everything. In my opinion, there is nothing more dangerous than a person who believes they have already learned all that they need to know, and who is convinced that their limited knowledge is the ultimate truth." Daciana's eyes are intent on mine. "What did you say your name was?"

"I didn't," I say. "It's Ava."

Again, Daciana seems startled. "Ava? Who named you?"

"My biological mom and dad, I guess. But I don't know who they are."

"Your mother?" For a long moment, there's something in her expression, like a billowing white curtain giving onto a dark garden. Then her face reverts to its harsh mask. "Send the next girl in," she says, and her voice is strict and cold.

I have overstayed my welcome.

Did I do something wrong? Did I offend her? I think, sliding back into the seat at my vanity. I realize that everyone is staring at me, even Glory. Elizabeth's is the most pointed look of all.

"What took you so long?" Wendy wants to know. "You were in there for a good fifteen minutes."

"She had to take care of my foot. It's really infected." It's not a total lie.

"Ying Yue lost a finger and she was out of there in five." Glory beckons Wendy, and her volley of questions cease.

I hope her visit with Daciana will be a long one, so the others can focus on someone else, but after less than five minutes Wendy breaks through the curtain, triumphant and beaming. "I got contacts!" she exclaims. "They're some kind of crystal disks." As she adjusts to her new sight, Wendy blinks more than usual, looking at everything through new eyes. "Woah. I can't believe this is what the world looks like. I can even see my *pores*!"

Glory informs us that it's time to remove our makeup. I almost feel sorry to have to see my face return to normal. I clean everything off except the pale blue lipstick. Across the room, Rory keeps his eyeshadow on. Glory tells us that we'll be back tomorrow before the fights; tonight was just a practice round. We leave our crystals behind.

Then Diablo arrives and leads us back to our quarters.

We cross through the plaza where the Ceremony of Fire took place. Tonight, it hosts a lively performance. A group of Klujns play various instruments while others in brightly colored robes and copper masks dance in a circle. A man blows a trumpet made from the dried spiral husk of a plant. Next to him, a pregnant Klujn with white hair weaves a song. Her voice is haunting, and even though I don't understand the words, they are charged with emotion. Beauty. Pain. When she sings the higher notes, her pale toes curl into the earth. I stop walking, rooted to the spot, entranced.

It's *music*.

The dancers are the living embodiment of her song—a story I can only guess at. The light of the ascending moon bounces off the filigree of their masks as their claws trace sparks through the air. Klujns of all ages sit in a ring around the performers, their skeletons almost visible through their translucent skin. Skulls the same size and shape as a human's.

My heart flutters like a bird in a locked cage. I feel a strange excitement; a desire to discover everything there is to know about this place. The feeling is tainted, as my life in Red River flashes before my eyes. A new memory appears, like a black tumor in my brain.

Now that I am starting to remember, I want desperately to forget.

* * *

It's later in June, the longest day of the year. General Santos invites himself over at the last minute. He comes in from the sticky summer heat carrying the smell of burning things, and brings a peace offering: a bundle wrapped in recycled paper.

As the men catch up in George's study, Diana cooks in silence, the vein in her temple pulsing for three straight hours. Mercy and I know better than to bother her. He plays with his trains and I with my coloring books.

Finally, we gather around the table, which is lit with yellow citronella candles. The roast sits on a nest of vegetables. There is a green salad and a loaf of fresh-baked bread; there's wine for the adults and juice for us children.

"May I?" Santos asks Diana, and she hands him the electric carving knife. It buzzes like a miniature chainsaw. "Have you ever had young kanum bone-in roast before?" he asks me, as he begins to slice it expertly. The general seems to be taking a special interest in me—more so than he does with Mercy. I wonder if it has anything to do with the Hunt I ruined. If this is a test of some sort.

I shake my head.

"This is a choice cut, a real delicacy," he says over the whir of the knife. "The bone enhances the flavor of the meat. A pound of young kanum is worth more than most people make in a month, and this has to be seven pounds, at least. Born in the Loudhouse. Nothing beats wild-caught kanum, but our Breedingroom has revolutionized rapid kanum production."

"Our children have never eaten kanum," Diana says, to which Santos raises an eyebrow.

"And why is that?"

"Diana doesn't eat animals," George tells him, smiling, trying to defuse the tension. "She's vegetarian. All these vegetables? They came from her garden."

Santos adds to the growing pile of sliced meat on the platter. "Eating meat is in our DNA. It's who we are as a species."

"That's not entirely true," Diana responds. She addresses Santos but includes me and Mercy in the conversation. "Our ancestors were foragers—they survived mainly on fruits, roots, and greens. Meat was hard to come by and usually reserved for special occasions. When people settled down and began to farm animals, almost everyone turned carnivore. But the world couldn't house eight billion carnivores, especially with the amount of meat

they ate. That's one of the main reasons the natural world collapsed. The forests, the oceans."

"Luckily, we aren't eight billion anymore," says Santos. "So now we can eat whatever we want." He smiles thoughtfully. "A vegetarian who once worked in my Loudhouse. Now, that is peculiar."

"Briefly," Diana says, her hand tightening around her butter knife.

George pipes up again. "She had to work somewhere. The land and water taxes won't pay themselves."

"Not on your teacher's salary." Santos slices off a bit of meat and deposits it on my plate. "The loin is the most tender part," he says. "Juicy, supple, and dynamic."

"You don't have to eat it if you don't want to," Diana tells me.

"Why on earth would you deny her the best thing she'll ever taste?" Santos asks. His voice is kind, but for some reason, I feel a chill, as though a draft just blew through the window. But the window is closed, and outside, humidity is at its thickest.

"Is kanum Klujn meat?" I ask.

Santos nods. "Yes, it is."

I can feel Diana and George listening intently.

"Then why is it called kanum?"

"Because Klujn is the beast, and kanum is the meat."

"Why do they have two different names? Why not call them the same thing?"

Santos wipes the carving knife. "A curious one you've got there," he tells my father. "Mine's more of an introvert. Keeps to themself. Go on," he encourages me. "Eat."

The slice of kanum is pinkish-white, like the spotted wolf meat. I pick up my knife and fork. Cut off a bite and raise it to my lips. The meat is tender, herbed, and flavorful, with a slightly smoky aftertaste.

Around me, the others begin to eat the roast—everyone except Diana.

"Klujns are our saving grace." Santos talks with his mouth full, masticating with as much gusto as he speaks. "If it wasn't for this here, half the Territory would have starved to death." He swallows.

"Half the Territory did starve to death," Diana answers, finishing her *glass of wine. I like this less-restrained version of Diana. It feels . . . dangerous. George throws her a look of warning, which she chooses to ignore.*

"Then the entire Territory would have starved," Santos says.

I remember what José said about wild dog meat tasting rancid because they feed on rotten meat and garbage. "I thought animals are what they eat."

"They sure are."

"So, if humans eat all sorts of dead meat, then isn't that what we'd taste like?"

George cuts in: "I hardly think this is appropriate dinner-table conversation."

"I assume we would," says Santos. "Fortunately, humanity hasn't had to resort to cannibalism just yet."

I follow my thought to the end. "But if our meat tastes rotten, why would Klujns want to eat us? Wouldn't we taste disgusting?"

The general doesn't answer right away. The only sound is Mercy crunching voraciously on a bone.

Finally, he says, "The only one who could answer your question is a Klujn. You know any?" *At that, a cackle escapes his lips. Sharp, electric.*

Outside, there's a flash of lightning. Rain starts to patter on the roof.

"How do they kill them?" *Mercy asks casually, tossing the bone onto his plate. He plucks a hair from his head and uses it to floss the bits of meat stuck between his teeth.*

Diana shoots him a look. "Mercy, not at the table."

I watch General Santos, his face made spooky by the candlelight. "We kill them quickly and painlessly," *he says with a touch of pride.* "The creature hardly feels any pain. A bolt to the head, slit the throat. This one"—*he indicates the remains of the roast—*"was taken from its mother only a few hours after birth. It was drowned in a marinade of citrus and vinegar, to fill its lungs with flavor. A peaceful death! The mother's milk is used for ice cream and bath products. Nothing goes to waste." *Santos forks up a chunk about the size of a brussels sprout.* "Try this."

"What is it?" *I ask.*

"The heart."

Diana scrapes her chair back loudly. "I forgot the Forest Cake!" *she tells us and leaves the room. When Diana returns, she drizzles the dark brown cake in maple liquor and lights a match. The flames devour the alcohol before settling down. She sinks a knife into the chocolate mud, serves each piece with cream and berries, then distributes the plates without a word.*

* * *

The general's return home is delayed by the storm. He and my father head downstairs again, talking in low voices over cigars and lumber liquor made from hundred-year-old trees.

"You were our lucky charm," Santos says. "What's it going to take to bring you back?"

"A new leg," my father replies.

"I've seen you on the one you have, and it's not half-bad."

I help Diana load the water-saving dishwasher. In the living room, Mercy plays with his toys.

As my stomach begins to process the meal, I feel sick. I barely make it to the downstairs bathroom before my dinner comes back up. I empty my stomach into the toilet bowl again and again until there's nothing left inside me but one big vacant space.

As I catch my breath, someone enters the bathroom, closes the door, and locks it. Gentle hands pull my short hair back into a ponytail.

"Shh. It's okay." It's Diana. I look up and see that her hair has come loose. She has given me her own band. She looks like a different person with her curls down, much younger—like the girl I imagine she was before the world changed.

"Respire." French for breathe. She fills a glass of water as I take a deep breath in, my lungs rattling. Then she hands me the glass, and as I drink she strokes my hair. "It's to create a distance between the animal and the food we eat," she says, and for a moment I don't understand. "That's why they're called by two different names. If we forget that the animal has a soul, we can forget how similar they are to ourselves."

I go to bed with my empty belly growling as the rain intensifies and shakes the house. Here in my den, I am safe, but I feel cold for Wolf outside.

I dream of flooded forests and creatures swept away. Of orphaned animals stranded in the branches, calling out for family members that are no longer there. I dream of trees cleared and black brick buildings built on that land. Of Klujns in tiny cages that are barely larger than coffins. Of pregnant females and babies drowned in marinades.

I dream of humans gathered around tables eating and drinking, safe and warm and unaware.

When I wake with a start in the middle of the night, my glowing moon lamp assuages my fear, calms my racing heart. Diana's voice is in my head. "Respire." With slow, steady breaths, I am able to quiet my mind and put myself to sleep.

* * *

Back in the circular plaza, the memory fades but the feeling of revulsion remains. I realize that my fingernails have been digging into my crossed arms through my cloak, leaving identical crescents of raw flesh.

I watch the pregnant Klujn as she continues to sing. I imagine the life inside her: How many pounds does it weigh? How much is that life worth? She reaches a haunting high note. I didn't even know Klujns could speak. Why didn't anyone tell us they could sing?

The audience is filled with parents, children, families. A young male Klujn holds a baby in his arms. It reaches for his nose. The baby's fingers are tiny and smooth, without claws or fingernails. Still, they look just like a human's.

I think about that dinner. The words *Klujn* and *kanum*, and the difference between them.

All this festivity and laughter . . . it all feels very human.

25

The girls and Rory were all ravenous at the scant dinner—blue bean soup with crispy vegetable chips, rainbow corn, warm bread, a black cabbage salad, and fruit. I could barely bring myself to lift my wooden fork.

"They're starving us," Elizabeth said as we left the mess tent. She snagged a few decanters of dandelion wine on her way out and didn't even try to hide them.

We're grouped around the bonfire now, the dark mountains to the west like the silhouettes of sleeping giants. Wendy and I share a log and a blanket, and Willa is cross-legged on the ground, shuffling her occult cards. At the back of our quarters, the silver-haired girls train on the jungle gym, doing pull-ups and crunches. I don't know what their strategy is, other than to avoid us. Alone as usual, Zoe sits in one of the tire swings and fiddles with something that looks like a red-and-black Rubik's Cube. Everyone else is in bed.

Dawn, our new bedtime, is still a few hours away. Despite the hour and everything that has happened, my mind feels wide awake.

Elizabeth finishes one of the decanters of sparkling wine and gets started on a second.

"Hey—pass it around," Wendy says, and Elizabeth raises an eyebrow. "What? If we're going to be fighting to the death tomorrow, we might as well enjoy tonight." Elizabeth hands over the wine. "How many did you take, anyway?"

"Enough for a party. So far, it isn't much of one." Her attention turns to Willa. "Are you ever going to explain why you're staring at those cards like they hold the answers to the universe?"

"They're tarot cards," Willa says. "We use them for divination."

"In English?" Elizabeth presses.

"Predicting the future. Each card has a distinct meaning. There are different ways to use them, but the most common is a three-card spread." Willa deals out three cards, facedown. Then, she turns them over one by one. "It's a reading of the future."

"It's like the Blood Race," I think out loud. "The king said that we're characters in a game. A prophecy of some sort."

"Only, instead of cards, they're using us?" Wendy stipulates, taking a drink.

Willa shuffles the deck. "I always knew that Klujns were occult creatures, but now it's undeniable. The banishing stick the king burned at the Ceremony of Fire, the sigils in the soil, the crystals, their Nature gods. It all aligns with witchcraft."

"Well, abracadabra!" Elizabeth declares sarcastically. "Klujns are witches!"

Willa keeps her cool. "Magic isn't *abracadabra*. It's not about worshipping the Devil or drinking the blood of virgins. It's about learning to control the existing forces in the world and bringing things from the invisible world into the material one. It's just science that hasn't been proven yet."

"What are you saying?" Elizabeth asks, her tone accusatory.

Willa chooses her words carefully, aware of her audience. "That Klujn behavior aligns more with good than evil. Creation over destruction. That's what magic is."

Elizabeth looks thoroughly disgusted. "Come back to earth. Klujns exist to terrorize humankind and close in on vulnerable human populations and drive us into extinction."

"Really? Then why have they never attacked us? They don't care about the fences. It's like they just want to be left alone."

Elizabeth takes a deep drag from her vape. "Why?"

"I don't know," Willa answers. "To do their work . . . to grow things."

"If they're all about creation, then how do you explain the human Blood Race?" Elizabeth wants to know.

"I'm still trying to figure that out," Willa says. Wendy passes me the dandelion wine and, as I drink, I consider telling them what Daciana told me: that not all stands are violent. But I don't know how that would go down.

At that moment, Bindu and Rory come back from the toilet and join us.

Rory slips onto the log next to me, his breath minty. "We discovered a sink-area back there with some kind of charcoal toothpaste if any of you are interested. And toothbrush sticks." He may have wiped off most of his makeup, but Rory looks different—more comfortable in his body, more self-assured. "I know it sounds weird, but I feel loads better now that I've brushed my teeth."

I run my tongue over my own furry teeth.

"There are *absorbent* plants, too," adds Bindu. "I, um—I got my period."

Elizabeth shoves the vape into her pocket. "This is ridiculous. We might all die tomorrow, and we're sitting here talking about some stupid tarot cards and our periods when we should be *taking action*."

"I'm open to suggestions if you have any," Wendy says dryly. "But in case you failed to notice, we're always surrounded by guards."

"Not always," I blurt. They all look at me. I feel my cheeks heat up. Maybe it's reckless to say these things out loud—after all, they are new thoughts, not yet ripe and ready for harvest—but the others look at me with such expectancy and hope. "Last night—or this morning—when we went to bed," I begin, "there was no guard at the gate."

"Maybe he went to take a piss," Elizabeth suggests. "Or sharpen his teeth on human bones."

"I think the gate was unguarded all day," I continue.

"So we're not prisoners?" Rory ponders.

"Think about it," I tell them. "We haven't been in shackles since we got here. Not since the Deeper Woods."

"What are you saying?" from Elizabeth. "That we're free to roam around?"

"What would be the point of capturing us, only to let us escape?" from Willa.

"Because they know there's no way out?" Wendy asks.

"Exactly," I say. "Not above ground, anyway. After what happened to the first girl, Reesa—the way she was possessed after inhaling the smoke—I wouldn't trust that barrier we passed on the way in. It might be electric, or cursed, or something. But there might be another way."

This is totally insane, I think, but I feel my certitude growing with each passing second. I don't know what the others expect—a thrilling speech? An intricate plan? All I have is a hunch.

"The Katacombes," I announce. They stare at me. "Remember the morning we arrived . . . the cave-like tunnels we passed? The little Klujn said they connect the different faces of the stand. North to south, east to west—in and *out*."

"That's where the wild dogs live," squeaks Bindu, grimacing as her body works through a cramp.

"At the Ceremony of Fire, the king said that when the dogs are fed, they stop growling," I tell them. "Listen. Do you hear anything?"

Dead silence.

"What if they're sleeping?" Willa asks, in response. "Or they're too far away?"

I shake my head. "They're not growling. Which means they've been fed."

I think about the soundness of my improvised plan, and that familiar push and pull feeling returns. On one end, I'm curious about Circo, but staying here is not benign. It means the Blood Race; it means probable death. Judging by the green moon in the sky, there are only three nights left until the Blood Moon, and whatever that entails. I've been lucky so far, but it's only a matter of time before that luck runs out. I can't imagine what would happen if I walked out into that arena tomorrow and my opponent was Wendy.

On the other end, assuming we make it out, how will everyone get home? What will happen back in Red River? Will Mr. Mogel be waiting for me with a raised rifle?

Do you even want to go, Ava?

My emotions are a whirlwind that I can't make sense of, but hope has sparked in the others' eyes and I feel a certain pressure to continue.

"We passed an entrance on the way in. If we can get to it, I think I might be able to get us out of here," I say.

"You *think*?" Elizabeth jibes, fixing me with a skeptical glare. I wrap my hand around my crystal pendant, warm from my skin.

"I'm almost certain." I could be completely wrong, but something tells me I'm not. It's a hard thing to put into words, this feeling I have, this instinct. "When Klujns built those tunnels, they must have needed a way to navigate them," I say.

"Like a map?" asks Wendy.

"Somehow, Pockets, I don't think Klujns are the mapmaking kind," Elizabeth retorts. "Look at anthills and fossils of beehives. They're elaborate, but they don't come with instructions. Animals are architects by design."

"But they *aren't* animals," I say. "That's the thing." She stares at me like I've officially lost my mind. "They speak English. They have their own complex society and beliefs. They even *sing*!" I take a steadying breath. "Klujns are artists. They have the same genus as us—which places us in the same family."

"But not the same species," Elizabeth counters. "'Human' is a very, very large family that covers everything from Neanderthals to apes to other archaic beasts."

Elizabeth is impossible to sway. "All I'm saying is . . . maybe their minds work more like ours than we think."

"I'm not trying to discourage your plan," says Rory. "It's a solid plan. But if there *was* a way to escape, how come no human ever has?"

"The king said that was a question for humans."

"So you're taking a Klujn's word over Grouse's?" Elizabeth's eyes burn into me. "You know on the other side of the fences, the DSO would have your tongue for thinking that. Add in an eyeball for saying it out loud. I would know . . . my mother works there."

"But we're not on the other side of the fences," I say. "We're here. I'm not saying I trust the king, but why would he lie to us if we're all going to be dead in a few days?"

The girls and Rory mull over my words.

And something shifts.

"Okay, so let's say you're right—and we can get to the Katacombes," says Willa. "The dogs are sleeping, and they don't devour us. How do we navigate those tunnels without a map? The small Klujn said we could get lost in there."

"Trail markers," I say, delivering my final proof. The others wait. "The glowing red symbols in the woods that the head guard was following. If we follow those red symbols, we can find our way out."

"I don't remember seeing any trail markers," says Elizabeth.

Wendy makes a face. "You were too busy regaling us with facts. Your head was so far up your own—"

"I don't know about this," interrupts Willa.

"It's dangerous," Bindu peeps.

"What other choice do we have?" I tell them.

After a moment, Rory nods. "Ava's right." His support comes as a surprise. I know he's torn like I am—his mind battling with his heart. But he chooses to put his trust in me, which is flattering but also makes me nervous. "Tomorrow we have to fight each other. I don't know about you, but I don't like the sound of that."

"Easy for you to say—you're a guy," Elizabeth snipes. "There's an unfair advantage if I ever saw one."

I see it as it happens—how Elizabeth's words make Rory shrink into himself. All of the poise and confidence he had in the makeup tent, and even afterward, is gone. I know that feeling—of being misunderstood.

I press my shoulder into his, and Rory looks at me. "What did the old Klujn say to you?" I ask. "When you walked out of her tent you looked relieved and . . . sad."

"Not sad," says Rory. "More . . . *conflicted*." A flicker of the new Rory returns as he speaks. "You know, I was with three guys when I got caught. The Klujns didn't even look at them. They just took me without question. It's like they *knew* . . ." Rory trails off. "They can sense who we are. Something deeper than our bodies."

"Females-only?" I question gently, repeating the words that Oak had sung. Rory nods, slowly, eyes flooded with the same relief as earlier. The relief of being seen.

"The old Klujn knew exactly who I was," says Rory. "I feel like I've been carrying this weight my entire life, and in her tent, for just five minutes, I could put it down. That's why I'm torn. Because this place is brutal, but it's beautiful, too. But I know that it can't last. I know that we need to try to get home, I'm just afraid of going back to my old life, and the lies."

"Do you have to?" I say.

"There's no place back there for people like me. People who don't fit into a box that's neat and tidy."

My heart breaks for Rory, and the weight he must carry every day. No, not *he*—that word feels wrong and ignorant now—because it's plain as day who Rory really is, and I feel stupid for not having noticed it before. Rory is right; there is no place in the world for people like *her*. People like us. People who don't fit into a mold. Not that I can compare my problems to hers; mine are trivial in comparison.

Rory and I look back at the others, and the conversation that has continued even in our absence from it.

"We got lucky in the cave," Wendy says to the group, her face illuminated by the dancing flames. "But it'll only get worse. I really do not want to find out what they have planned for us."

"Neither do I," says Willa.

Another shift. This time, it's Bindu. "How do we get to the Katacombes?"

"I saw some Klujns wearing neutral cloaks like ours," Rory offers. She clears her throat of the emotion that's lodged there and continues. "Can we blend in?"

Elizabeth shakes her head. "They'll smell us from a mile away."

"Their sense of smell is normal," Wendy says. "It's their eyesight I'm worried about."

"We don't have to worry about that," I tell them. My voice sounds confident, but I feel as conflicted as Rory. "Because we wouldn't be leaving at night."

Now they are surprised.

"What are you saying?" Elizabeth asks me. "That we leave in broad daylight?"

"Yes."

"This is total suicide," Willa moans.

Elizabeth says, "Even if we do make it out, we still have the woods to think about."

"One thing at a time," I say. I look at Wendy, then Rory, and they nod. I didn't realize just how unsure I was until this moment, but now that I have their support there's no going back.

"This is the best chance we have," Wendy says. "I don't know about you guys but I'm done being a sitting duck." There are a few murmurs of agreement. In the silence that follows, our insecurities shout unspoken questions: *Can we do this? Is it worth the risk? Or is this totally absurd?*

It might be the dandelion wine talking, but defiance fills me. I suddenly feel brave. Or is it reckless? I tell myself that staying is nothing but a fantasy. The loud voice of logic in my brain has never been more convincing.

"When do we leave?" Rory asks.

"At dawn," I say. "Just after lights out."

She nods. "Who else is in?"

Wendy is, but that's a given. Willa looks unsure but finally says, "Screw it, okay. I'm in."

"Me too," Bindu squeaks. Elizabeth shrugs in a way that says—*Fine, I'll go, but only because I don't have anything better to do.* I know she just doesn't want to get left behind.

Then I notice Zoe, rocking on her swing.

"There's someone else I want to ask," I confess.

"Not the weird Hunter girl," groans Elizabeth. "There's something off about her."

Rory seconds her. "We should keep our number small. The more of us, the riskier it is."

"Imagine if it was you," I say. "Wouldn't you want to be included?" They don't agree, but they can't disagree, either.

I go to Zoe before they change their minds. She rocks on the swing, black-and-red cube still in hand, twisting it around as if trying to unlock a hidden treasure. She doesn't look at or even acknowledge me, but I know she senses my arrival. "We're leaving in the morning," I whisper. She still doesn't look up. "Zoe?"

"I heard you," she says.

"It might be our last chan—"

"I'm staying." I try again, but she cuts me off, faster than before. I don't know why she's so intent on staying.

Finally, I admit defeat and return to the fire. Elizabeth looks at me like I've betrayed the exclusivity of our group. Crossed enemy lines. "It's just us six," I tell them. "We should try to get some sleep before we leave." They nod and start to head toward the sleeping tent. Elizabeth hangs back.

"You know, for a shy girl you sure know how to persuade a group," she says.

Provoked by her words, I straighten my spine and square my jaw.

"I never said I was shy."

26

As we leave the sleeping tent at dawn, swathed in our black cloaks, I feel like I'm swinging on a rope across a valley without a safety net to catch me. But what is the alternative? Stay and fight? By the time the next challenge is announced, it will be too late for exit strategies.

The gate is unguarded. "Will you look at that?" Rory says. "Ava was right." The sun is slowly rising, but the day is not yet bright. Wendy picks a handful of Moonlight Leaf from a branch that meanders down the fence and stuffs them out of sight, inside one of her many pockets. The others look at me expectantly.

"Here goes," I say. Slowly, carefully, I place my hands on the gate of sticks and vines and push it open. It creaks. I freeze, expecting a guard to come out and put a premature end to our escape—but nothing happens. Our quarters remain desolate and still.

I slip through and hold it open for the others. Wendy. Willa. Elizabeth. Rory. Bindu.

What are you doing? The voice inside me urges. Thoughts flash like a strobe light. How much time do we have before someone notices we're gone? What will happen when we get to the woods? Where will we find food, clean water, shelter, warmth? How will we make our way back across those dizzying mountains and locate the fences? Not to mention predators. We didn't even pack bedding or weapons or supplies!

Panic clamps down on my throat, and for a moment I struggle to breathe. It's too late for what-ifs. I reassure myself that Wendy has the survival skills I lack and can take over by the time we leave Circo, and that leaving is our only real chance at survival.

We are in the alleyway that leads toward the circular plaza. "Where to now?" Willa asks.

"The Katacombes entrance," I say. "On the other side." They nod and follow me toward the plaza. We're halfway there when, up ahead, I notice a Klujn in magenta robes coming toward us.

I shoot a look at Wendy. "You said Klujns have better vision than smell?" She nods, looking more unsure by the second. "Well, better hope you're right."

We draw the hoods of our cloaks low over our faces and keep our heads down. I try to walk with purpose, but nerves turn my gait into marmalade.

The stranger passes us without a second glance and disappears into a small tent. Pulls shut its door. We let out a collective sigh of relief.

"This way," I whisper as we enter the plaza. Then I stop short.

Filling the plaza where the performance was last night is a large mandala, made from soils of different colors. Plants and flowers have already begun to sprout in a striking mosaic. How did they grow so quickly?

I tell everyone to stay close, and we edge around the circle. All of us but Elizabeth, who walks straight through the plaza, crushing the delicate flowers under her shoes.

"Stop it," I say, quiet but sharp. Elizabeth keeps going, uprooting the plants and destroying the intricate artwork that must have taken hours to make. "*Stop!*"

Finally, Elizabeth does stop, but only because she's bored of the destruction. She leaves the circle and joins us, a stupid grin on her face. The mandala is a smeared, broken mess, a cemetery of baby plants.

My hands ball into fists, and anger swells.

Wendy tugs at my cloak. "Ava?" Her soft voice startles me. I manage to uncurl my fists but it takes all the self-control I have.

"Our leader's dozing off," Elizabeth says mordantly. I force myself to look away from the plaza and lead them toward the Katacombes instead.

A nauseating smell greets us, letting us know that we've arrived.

"Here it is," I say, peering into the Katacombes entrance. There's no visible trail marker, but perhaps there are some inside, or perhaps they're like stars: invisible in daylight.

"What now?" Willa asks. I monitor for any sound, but all is quiet.

"We go in," I answer, turning to look at the five anxious faces around me. "We need to make a line."

"Shotgun not being first," says Elizabeth.

"Shotgun not being last," Wendy adds.

"I'll take the front," I say, even though it's the last thing I want, but as the designated "leader" it's my responsibility. We form our line. "Breathe through your mouth if you have to. Keep your voices down, and hold on to the person in front. We can't get separated."

I follow my own advice and breathe through my mouth, pushing away any thought that does not belong to the present moment.

The Katacombes are wet and muddy. The ceiling is higher than I imagined and I can stand, albeit with my back slightly curved. One by one, the others enter and we start walking. After a few bends, I realize our mistake. Leaving in broad daylight, I didn't even consider how dark it would get in here.

There's a sound like the tip of a sparkler catching fire, and a little orb of green light fills the tunnel. I turn and there's Wendy, holding a bit of Moonlight Leaf in her hand. "Wendy, you're a genius," I say.

"Here," she says, giving me some of the plant, which is moist in my hand. "We have to move fast."

"What about me?" Elizabeth barks.

"I don't have enough for everyone," Wendy answers. "Ava's the leader, so she gets the light."

Even with the Moonlight Leaf, I can see only a few feet ahead. Still, it's better than nothing. No trail markers so far. The ground slopes beneath our feet, descending deeper into the belly of the mountain. The ceiling gets lower and I have to duck even more. I can hear breathing and rustling behind me, as everyone tries to keep up—Wendy tails me, her hands clutching my robes, then Willa, Elizabeth, Bindu, and Rory.

After only a few minutes, the light begins to dim. Wendy passes me more Moonlight Leaf, but she's running low.

"Why didn't you take more?" Elizabeth scolds.

"My pockets weren't big enough."

"That's irony if I ever heard it, *Pockets*."

Willa cuts in. "Elizabeth, your attitude isn't exactly helping. You could have taken some as well."

Then, Rory's voice—"What should we do, Ava? Wendy? Should we turn around?"

Wendy answers for me. "We've come this far. We must be getting close to an exit."

The new bunch of Moonlight Leaf begins to dim until I can't see more than a foot in front of me. I hold it further into the darkness, but the darkness wins. The light goes out and we find ourselves blinded, deprived of our most vital sense.

Wendy steps on my heel, then Willa crashes into her. In a domino effect, each girl bumps into the next.

"Ouch!"

"Watch it."

"Stop breathing down my neck!"

The words bounce off the invisible walls. I turn around, but I can't see Wendy's face even though she's right next to me.

I take a few cautious steps forward, my hands reaching out, feeling for the walls, and find them. The earth is cool and mushy under my fingertips.

"Hold on to each other," I say. Wendy's grip tightens around my robes, pulling the fabric against my neck. "Not that tight," I croak, and it loosens slightly.

Soon we reach a fork in the path.

"Okay, leader, what now?" Elizabeth asks, cloaking her fear in sarcasm.

This can't be happening, I think. I haven't led them this far only to get lost when we must be close to the end.

I squeeze my eyes shut and open them, desperate to see something, anything, in this debilitating darkness.

And then it kindles above the right-hand passage: a small symbol like those in the woods, glowing the color of raspberries. *Yes!* I rejoice. *I knew it!*

There are two symbols. The one on the right is the mountaintop I remember; on the left is that familiar *X* with a tiny circle above it. *North and West?* I wonder. *Could it be as simple as that?*

The morning we arrived, the sun was rising on our right—from the east. That means we were at the southern edge of the stand. But we don't have the option of going south. If we follow the west route, that'll get us closer than if we choose the north one. "This way," I tell the others, taking the left-hand path. I hope my instinct is right.

Bindu's voice is very quiet from the back. "Are you sure it's this way?"

"Almost certain," I tell her. "It's just like in the woods."

"What are?" Wendy asks.

"The markers," I tell her.

"What markers?" Elizabeth wants to know, but the glowing shapes are already behind us.

We keep going. I can't wait to see the looks on their faces when we get out of here. I smell mud and leaves, and my legs move faster. I smile, imagining that victorious moment when we'll emerge in the forest night.

We round another corner, and I trip over something and fall, and Wendy falls on top of me. Willa knocks into the obstacle but manages to stay upright.

"What is it?" she asks, from somewhere above us. "What's happening?"

My robes are soaked. I smell urine. I reach out sheepishly, exploring the damp earth around me. Wendy and I have fallen into a bowl-shaped hole.

"Is it a dead end?" Rory asks from the back.

"Should we turn around?" Bindu squeaks.

"Ava?" It's Wendy's voice now. My fingers touch fur. A small, warm body. Four legs. Two ears. A muzzle. Its tiny claws already sharp. It's a wild dog pup—and, beside it, another two, three, four, five, six bodies. I snatch my hand away. *We're in a den. Run!*

Before I can let out the warning, I feel her hot, rank breath on my face. And then I hear her growl.

The mother. She knows we're here, and she's not happy about it.

27

Black. It's so black I can't make out any shapes. All I hear are sounds: A growl. The click of claws on dirt. Then the dog's thin, powerful body springs, knocking me aside. I hear it land on someone. A slash of claws. A sound, like fabric ripping. There are screams. It's hard to tell who is screaming the loudest.

A flare of green light in the tunnel. Wendy, who's standing now, holds a few remaining bits of Moonlight Leaf in her shaking palm. She raises the light and we see—

The wild dog. It's tawny, scruffy, lean. It moves away from its victim's body.

Bindu. Face colorless, a scream caught in her voice box.

The animal takes Bindu's leg in its dangerous jaws and whips its head violently from side to side. Bindu is thrown against the wall. A cracking sound. Her limp body falls to the ground.

Now I can see that there is a wall behind the den—it's a dead end. I led everyone into a trap. I must've gotten the symbol wrong. The only way out is the way we came in, and the mother blocks our way.

I'm frozen in horror. Then I remember something.

I reach under my shirt and fumble for my crystal pendant. There is that tiny hole carved through it, and a memory sparks: *It keeps wild dogs and wolves away.* I bring the flat base to my lips, pucker them and blow.

The sound is sharp and shrill, so high it's almost inaudible.

Almost immediately, it happens. The wild dog withdraws. She abandons Bindu's body and cowers, as though physically affected by the sound. I blow again, and this time, she lies down.

Everyone stares at me. *What the hell did you just do?* But now is not the time for questions.

Willa rushes to Bindu. "We need to get her out of here. *Now.*" Bindu's dark brown eyes are glazed. "Keep her legs up," Willa tells Elizabeth, who for once does not protest. They lift Bindu. "How much light do you have left?" Willa asks her sister.

"I don't know. A few minutes, tops."

"Then we need to go fast."

Wendy darts to the back—now the front—of the line, and starts leading us out. Rory follows, then Willa and Elizabeth with Bindu. As they disappear up the dark tunnel, I'm paralyzed, hand clutching the crystal, watching the still-cowering dog. The others round a corner and the light starts to fade in the distance. A moment more and I'll be left alone in the dark with the angry mother. Who knows how long I have before the effect of the whistle wears off.

I force my legs to wake up, to *move*—and at last, they do.

Hearts beating in quick time, we race uphill, following the bends in the path. It's my legs that guide me. My mind is far behind, back in the den. *Run. Don't stop running.* After a few minutes, we find a way out, a different one, surfacing in a different part of the stand.

It's hard to get my bearings when everything looks the same—black tents and decorated trees and plazas. I realize that Circo is much more enchanting at night, when the sky is dark and the streets are filled with luminescence. The blazing daylight feels too bright and unforgiving for the scene unfolding before my eyes. As though bad things should only happen at night.

Willa and Elizabeth gently place Bindu on the ground. Her eyes are shut, her skin ashen. "Go get help!" Willa orders her sister, but Wendy stays rooted to the spot.

"W-who?" Wendy asks, mortified. "W-we'll get in trouble. They'll kill us!"

"If you don't," Willa says curtly, "then you can stand here and watch her die."

Rory steps forward. "I'll come with you." Wendy nods, still in shock. The two of them pick a direction and run.

From where I stand, I take in the extent of Bindu's injuries. Her right leg has been mauled and shredded, and her yellow-painted toe-nails curl in spasm. Her belly is torn open, innards spilling out like a doll's cotton stuffing.

There is blood everywhere. Willa yanks off her own cloak then pulls her shirt over her head and ties it around Bindu's right leg like a tourni-quet. Then, half-dressed and shivering, she drapes the black cloak over Bindu's body and cradles the girl in her naked arms.

"Don't fall asleep," she says, rocking her gently. "The others have gone to get help."

Elizabeth takes hold of Bindu's wrist. "Her pulse is slow."

Bindu's eyelids flutter open, showing only the whites. "It hurts," she manages. "It hurts so badly everywhere."

"It's okay," Willa says softly, like a mother nursing a sick child. Tears dangle like tightrope walkers on the rims of her eyes. "Wendy and Rory should be back any second now." Bindu shudders, fighting off another wave of pain. Her irises roll down and I see those dark orbs and all the fear they harbor.

"I don't want to die." Her voice is a thin thread. *She's so young. It's not fair.*

Willa swallows, steels herself so that she doesn't frighten Bindu—Bindu, who may not realize how badly she has been hurt, that these are the kinds of injuries you can't mend. Willa is covered in blood that isn't hers, but she doesn't care. She strokes the girl's hair. "You're going to make it, I know you are."

Everything takes place in the spaces between breaths. "What do you think happens to us . . . when we die?" Bindu asks. "Do you . . . think it's just . . . over?" Her words come out more slowly now, each one an immense effort.

"Of course not," Willa tells Bindu, her voice full of tenderness.

"We're all made from stardust—you, me, everyone, and everything. We come from different galaxies, and when we die, that's where we return. Because a soul is energy, and energy can't be destroyed. It just changes form." She pauses. "Some people even say that when we die, our souls become their very own constellation."

"Really?" Bindu's eyes are wide, looking up at a starscape only she can see, threaded with comets and planets and distant galaxies that we can't see in daylight.

"Yes," says Willa. "How else do you think all the other constellations got there?" She caresses Bindu's clammy forehead.

"Thank you," Bindu says. She mutters something else, something incomprehensible. She's lost so much blood. I see the moment the life force leaves her, the air rippling outwards and upward. Then her muscles release, and a patch of urine forms around the two of them. Elizabeth's fingers are still on Bindu's wrist as she mutters—

"She's gone."

Willa closes Bindu's eyelids. Gently lowers her limp body to the ground.

Then, she lets out the sob that she was holding back. It cracks the air like a whip, unrestrained and unapologetic.

Elizabeth pulls up the black cloak so it covers Bindu's still face. The only bits of her visible now are her little yellow toenails. *Just an hour ago*, I think, *she was so vibrantly here.*

In the silence that follows, I finally notice the Klujns. A crowd of them has gathered around us like a blood clot, carefully keeping their distance, whispering in a hiss of sounds. Some peer out from tent flaps, eyes still adjusting to the new day. Their eyes are different colors—purple, bright green, yellow. Not many red eyes to be seen here near the bottom of the stand.

"Why are they watching?" Elizabeth asks. "What do they want?"

"They look . . . concerned," I answer.

Willa looks up. "What now?" As if in answer, there's the sound of hurried footsteps. The crowd of Klujns parts, and Wendy and Rory come through, followed by Diablo and one of the two red-eyed guards.

Diablo's eyes move from us to Bindu's covered body, and he visibly tries to fill in the blanks.

Around the group, there's only silence. The others turn to me. They don't say anything, but they don't have to.

Diablo notices. "You—come with me. Palo—take the rest back to their quarters." As the other guard leads them away, Wendy avoids my gaze.

Diablo takes me down an alleyway so narrow that my cloak brushes the tents on either side. Colorful fabrics are draped between them, the bright sun casting richly hued spirals of purple and seafoam and orange-gold on the ground like oil on a wet road. There are the smells of apples and roasted nuts and baking bread—perhaps some early risers already at work in their outdoor kitchens.

I feel so ashamed.

We wind through the labyrinth of tents for another minute until, when he seems to feel that we are completely alone, he stops. We're in an outdoor workshop, with costumes laid out on large stone slabs, bowls of tiny crystals next to them, ready to be embroidered.

Diablo is less than a handspan away. He towers over me, and I feel some kind of energy charge the air between us. The look on his face is terrifying.

I take a step back. The wooden trunk of a tree beam presses against my spine. I'm cornered—there's nowhere to go, and no way to avoid him.

It's clear he's figured some things out, and by all rights, I should be scared. But, for some strange reason, I'm not. Just like Daciana, there's an energy that radiates from his body . . . something that, despite his best effort at intimidation, lacks hostility.

"What happened?" he asks, his voice still husky from sleep. Only a few moments ago he must've been inside his sleeping tent. It's a strange thing to imagine him in pajamas.

I sense that if I lie, he'll know it, and the consequences of lying might be more severe than those of owning up. "We tried to leave."

His face tightens. "You can't leave," he says simply. "Not until the end of the Blood Race. Only a Klujn can cross Circo's barrier. Any human who tries it without viaţăs is cursed."

"We didn't go that way," I say, secretly delighted that I was right. "We went through the Katacombes. Well, we tried."

Diablo's anger shifts to something else. Confusion, maybe. I answer the question he's asking with his eyes. "By following the red trail markers. The same ones you followed in the woods. We thought, maybe, if we did that . . . that we could find a way out of here."

"We?"

"*I*," I admit.

Diablo says nothing. His eyes search mine, more inquisitive than furious. His nose twitches slightly, like my humanity is a smell that nauseates him.

"What are you going to do?" I ask, bracing myself.

He deliberates for a long moment, not taking his eyes off me. Then he answers:

"Nothing."

Nothing?

This was not the outcome I expected. Bring me to the king and have him execute me in public. Throw me to the dogs, banish me to the woods, or have me participate in some gruesome test. But do *nothing?* This has to be a trick.

"You were an uneven number," Diablo says pragmatically. "Tonight, before the challenge, the king was going to eliminate one of you by chance. Now there are twelve, for an even number of fights. I will tell him what happened: that the girl tried to escape *on her own*. All you have to do is keep your mouth shut." His violet eyes narrow. "Warwick has no patience for ignorance. And believing you could escape through the Katacombes was very ignorant indeed."

I am stunned. Not by the insult, but by his actions. It may be another misstep, but I have to ask: "Why are you helping me?"

Diablo looks away, at the costumes around us in the workshop.

"I'm not helping you. If you recall, I'm responsible for you. I'm helping myself." But I don't believe him. When people lie, they avoid your eyes, which is exactly what he is doing right now.

"What about the Klujns who saw?"

"They're not from Circo," he says. "They will stay quiet."

"So that's it? You're just going to let me go?" Clearly, I won't be getting a real answer from him, so perhaps I shouldn't test my luck.

"Consider this a warning," he says sternly. "If you want to survive, trying to escape is not the way to do it. Play the king's game, and play by his rules. Don't start inventing games of your own." Diablo grabs my left arm and pulls me along, back toward our quarters. At first touch, I feel a buzz like static electricity, but it quickly fades. His grip is not as tight as it could be. I get the feeling it's more for show than anything, should we pass anyone, but on the ten-minute walk back to our quarters the streets remain empty.

My nose is level with his chest, and I can smell something, coconut or vanilla, like the scented candles in Daciana's workroom. A smell that evokes images of a beach—the beach of my fantasies. Of turquoise water and white sand and a warm breeze. But the ocean is hundreds of miles away, at least.

When we reach our quarters, Diablo lets me go. I take one last look at his eyes, and the confusion still orbiting there. Then he leaves, and the smell goes with him. The feeling of his hand around my upper arm remains for the briefest moment, like words written in sand at the foot of a crashing wave.

28

In the sleeping tent, the silence is heavy. The tension so palpable you could cut it with a knife. I sit on my mattress, wrapped in a blanket, pulling at its threads. Anything to keep my hands busy. Willa braids Wendy's hair into a fishtail braid. Elizabeth paces the narrow gap between our beds, sucking on her vape. Rory has returned to the other side of the tent, claiming Reesa's bed, and I don't blame her. The silver-haired girls are sleeping, or feigning sleep. Zoe's eyes were a question mark when I returned, speckled in blood, missing the last member of our party. But, as usual, she kept quiet, in perfect control of her curiosity.

Bindu's empty bed is a cruel reminder of something still so fresh and recent.

"I can't get the image out of my head," Wendy says. "It's the most horrible thing I've ever seen. Just when I think this place can't get any worse . . . it surprises me."

"Try not to think about it," Willa answers, combing her fingers through the knots in her sister's hair. Elizabeth's eyes keep darting over to me. They burn into me like ultraviolet rays, like Glory's did when she gave me the crystal, only nothing about this inquisition feels friendly.

I'm nervous that she'll bring the spotlight back to me. To what happened.

"You were great," Wendy tells Willa. "I don't know how you managed to keep your cool like that. I can't imagine what would have happened if you hadn't been there."

"I did what any of us would have done."

Elizabeth snorts. "Any of us. That's funny." Her eyes find me. *Here we go.* "Where did you get that whistle?" she asks accusatorially.

"My father gave it to me," I say.

"He's a Hunter?"

I shake my head. "He's a teacher."

"Then where did *he* get it?" Elizabeth wants to know. "A claw that pure costs more than a teacher's seasonal salary."

"He worked for the Military."

Elizabeth's glare could burn a hole through the ozone layer. "If you had it this whole time, why didn't you tell us?" she demands.

"I didn't know it was a whistle."

"But you figured it out—in the tunnel?"

"Yes." I feel myself cracking under her relentless questions. Why do I have to explain myself to her? The more I try, the guiltier I sound. "I had a feeling."

"A *feeling*?" she says with mock wonder, like she's hearing the word for the first time. Her jaw clenches. "Like you had a *feeling* about the trail markers?"

"Yes," I say again. Elizabeth's eyes dart over to the others like a prosecutor to a jury, presenting an airtight case. And she's just getting started. "So you have this *whistle*—that you don't know is a whistle—and you somehow figure out how to use it at the eleventh hour. Then this wild beast backs off like you're fucking *Grouse* or something."

"I don't know why it did that!" My eyes fill with tears. I don't want to cry, don't want her to think I'm weak, but my emotions win out. "I swear."

"If you had used your *whistle* earlier, that girl might still be alive."

Wendy leaps in. "Her name was *Bindu*. And don't make this Ava's fault. She didn't lead us into a death trap on purpose. Everything just went . . . *south*."

Thank you, Wendy, I think silently. But it's not enough to convince Elizabeth of my innocence.

"Maybe not," Elizabeth says, "but it was her great idea to leave in the first place."

"Yeah, and if we'd made it, we'd all be celebrating her right now."

"But we didn't make it out," Elizabeth takes a step closer to my mattress. "What did the guard tell you, anyway? When he dragged you away?"

I pull the blanket tighter. "He wanted to know what happened."

"Okay, but why did he let you go?"

"Because I told him the truth. And he said that we're an even number now—that if Bindu hadn't died, the king would have had one of us killed at random."

"That seems convenient." Elizabeth stares at me for a long time, as if I am a riddle that needs solving. "You know, *Ava*,"—she says my name like it's a lie—"there's something off about you, but I can't quite put my finger on it. What are you hiding?"

"Nothing." I sit there as tears dribble pitifully from my eyes. Under her barrage, I am stripped of words, defenses. An animal with its tail between its legs. It's frustrating to be so misunderstood.

"Leave her alone," says Willa. "We've had enough trauma for one night."

Elizabeth ignores her. "I can see right through you, Ava," she tells me. "When we arrived, you acted like a sheltered girl who knew nothing. Now you're getting a little too cozy for my liking. I don't trust this shy-girl act you have going on, not for a second."

"I'm not shy and it's not an act," I say. How can I tell her: *This isn't who I am. This is who I am* around you. *You bring out the worst in me.*

Elizabeth looks like she could strangle me. Wring my neck until the truth she wants to hear escapes my lips. I can see the red storm inside her. "You know what?" she says. "I hope I get to fight you tomorrow. That way I can make you feel even just an ounce of what you put that girl through."

Elizabeth goes back to her mattress and throws her body down. Willa finishes Wendy's braid, and the two sisters lie side by side, their backs to me. I turn to face the other way, but find myself staring at

Bindu's empty bed. I roll onto my back. It's the first time since arriving at Circo that I feel lonely.

Why didn't I act faster? I had a feeling about that crystal ever since I saw the little hole bored through it. It was only in the tunnel that I remembered George's words. But I wasn't fast enough. I acted too late. Because of me, a girl tragically lost her life. Not just a girl. *Bindu.*

I close my eyes. The image of Bindu's body haunts my closed eyelids—her shuddering and moaning, in unimaginable pain. The fear in her eyes. The way Willa had sprung forward, and Wendy and Rory had gone to get help. Even Elizabeth had made herself useful. Not me.

I look down at my hands. The wrinkles have smoothed out after the Amethyst pools, like fabric under a hot iron, but my fingers still feel swollen and fat. They ache from trying to pry the trap open and climbing over rocks in the cave and falling on the floor of the den.

What is Circo doing to me? To all of us? My body has felt different since we arrived. As if the fog in my brain is lifting, my senses sharpening, my mood less volatile than it is back home. It's like a whirlwind has swept me up into the air, but I'm not exactly sure where I will land. Yet I feel grounded, too, anchored in the confidence I feel. Or, rather, that I was starting to feel before this nightmare of a day happened.

Elizabeth's question knifes through my brain: *What are you hiding? Am I hiding something?*

Yes, the voice in my belly replies. *Then again—aren't we all?*

29

The woman's heart races as she stands by the edge of the cliff.

In the distance, through the thick smoke, there's a glow of orange. A fire crackles as it devours leaves and timber. It is only small, but growing larger.

I let out a cry, not understanding where we are or why we're here. Sensing . . . danger.

"Shhh, Ava," she says urgently. "Please be quiet."

I hear a crunch on twigs, and then he's there, silhouetted by the flames behind him. His face is all shadows, but I notice his uniform—gray and powerful; something of honor.

The man is a Hunter. A high-ranking one, judging by the bayonet of viațăs atop his rifle.

"Let us go," says the woman.

"You know I can't do that."

The Hunter lifts his rifle.

The woman tucks my blue blanket more tightly around me. My eyes sting from the smoke and turn her features blurry. I take in the vague details of her—the hood of her cloak, her long brown hair, her dark blue eyes.

My mother.

"I'm so sorry," she says. There is a brief burst of warmth on my forehead as she kisses me. Then, she tosses me over the cliff edge, into the jowls of the waiting current.

I fall, seemingly in slow motion, the night air thickening, slowing my descent.

From up above, a gunshot splits the night open. Her body collapses. But she doesn't fall over the edge, and the distance between us grows.

Smack. *My body hits the surface of the water. A cold shock of white water immediately trickles into my blanket, piercing my skin, dragging me*

down,

down,

down.

Bubbles swirl in underwater tornadoes. A delirium of panic sets in and I gasp for breath. I hyperventilate.

Water in my lungs. I am drowning.

In my last seconds of life, I catch sight of something swimming toward me. It's Wolf.

* * *

The afternoon sun pierces through the crack in the tent wall. I roll into it, enjoying its warmth. Still in that twilight between dreams and waking, I'm conscious enough to know that I'm safe, that what I saw wasn't real. *Or was it? Why do I have the feeling that it happened?*

My senses are still saturated with my mother's panic. How did she end up at the cliff edge with a weeks-old baby? Why was the Hunter chasing her? And why did he want me?

Was it really my biological mother, or a wild woman who snatched a baby from its crib?

Her hooded cloak, I realize, is just like the one at the foot of my bed. Black, like all of us human hostages. *Did she get captured? Was she here? A contestant in the Blood Race?*

As my eyes clear, the first thing I see is Bindu's empty bed. It is smooth and neat, not rumpled by a sleeping body. Horror and self-loathing wash over me.

My mind picks at the scab of my memories, replaying Bindu's death in my head over and over. I wish I could roll back into sleep, but even sleep offers no reprieve. Our failed escape attempt this morning feels like yesterday, and yesterday's cave challenge already feels like a lifetime ago. Because of the Klujns' inverted schedule, the regular rhythm of time is gone.

I want to tell Wendy and the others that they can trust me, that I'm not the liar Elizabeth has made me out to be, but she's always there, listening. Why did I come up with that half-baked plan in the first place? What drove me to enter the Katacombes despite the risks? Was it a desire to impress the others, or the attempt to outrun that quiet inner voice I should have listened to?

The same one that told me I could trust the red trail markers, and how the crystal whistle worked.

The voice of *instinct*.

Across Bindu's bed, Zoe lies on her back, already awake, black-and-red cube in her hands. She turns it over and over, four of its six sides now showing black and red stripes. She looks much closer to solving it. Her eyes are fixed on the ceiling where puddles of rain have gathered. On my other side, the sisters share a mattress. The steady tide of Willa's snoring is comforting.

I sit up and bring my right foot toward me. The pinkish-gray clay has begun to crack, and the pieces peel off easily. The swelling has gone down significantly, and the five holes in my skin are healing. I see the beginning of new skin, soft and pink as a baby's.

The guards come in to wake us.

There are no costumes at the foot of our beds.

As I stand up and stretch and flatten my hands over my crumpled pajama skirt, I avoid the others' eyes. Something feels different since Bindu died. Like the bond we had is gone.

* * *

At breakfast, conversation is sparse. No one comments on the unusual food. We pass the bowls silently, sharing what there is without argument or complaint, making sure everyone gets enough.

No one looks my way.

Rory is back at the other table, talking to Ying Yue. Guess she didn't like our vibe after all. What is she telling the Military girl about our failed escape? When we arrived at Circo, we were fourteen individuals who branched off into two sides. Right now it feels like me against everyone.

My muscles are sore after yesterday's cave challenge, but I would take physical pain over the agony of the silence that has formed between me and the others.

We walk to Daciana's quarters as the yellow moon rises. There is a moment of disquiet as we pass the Katacombes. I say a prayer for Bindu under my breath, although I'm not sure who I'm praying to.

I consider the moon, watching over us. I think about the stillness and the peace I feel in her presence, like I am in the arms of a great protector, one who is both strong and serene, powerful and calm. She has a dark side I will never see—like my parents' story, like my mother. Like Warwick said at the Ceremony of Fire.

Maybe I am *like the moon*, I think. *Duplicitous. Showing a bright face. Hiding the darkness that threatens to swallow me whole.*

* * *

Sitting at my dressing table, I try to concentrate on the treasures before me, but I can't focus, gripped by the fear of what lies ahead.

Bindu's vanity is just as she left it, her citrine costume hanging limply on the rack, unworn. *What did they do with her body? Will her family ever know that she died, or will she always remain a photograph on a Missing poster?* Candles burning at a vigil. A bedroom turned into a shrine.

I force myself to study my reflection. My painted face, eyelashes frosted with cyan mascara and tiny, dew-like moonstone beads. The crystal ear clips that curve from lobes to cartilage. I apply one last layer of cobalt lipstick. Finally, I brush out my thick, brown hair and try to braid it, but it's too short. My pendant grows hot against my skin.

"Do you need help?" Glory's chirpy voice almost makes me jump out of my skin. Reflected in the mirror is her odd freckled face, her warm painted smile, red today.

"No, thank you," I tell her. Glory's smile fades and I regret my reaction, but the last thing I need is to attract more attention from the others.

As she leaves, I unravel my half braid and use a clear gel to slick my hair back, then twist it into a knot at the back of my head. Then I turn to my costume, a stunning moonstone-colored jumpsuit with short sleeves, a tight-fitting bodice, and loose, flowy pants. A chest piece is studded with iridescent crystals—more moonstone. I slip on a matching pair of thin leathery flats. Their ribbons curl around my calves, licking at my skin and the prickle of hair that's growing.

I look over at Wendy, whose costume fits her curves perfectly. She looks more grown up somehow, more womanly, whether she realizes it or not. I want to say something, but a compliment seems out of place at a time like this.

And there's Rory, too, whose transformation seems complete.

I pick up the chunk of moonstone from yesterday and squeeze it in my hand. Draw in a few deep breaths. The costume and makeup feel like armor. The crystal in my hand gives me courage while calming me down. Strength, growth, femininity, intuition, I remember Glory saying. The attributes of moonstone.

I'll need them all.

* * *

The twelve of us are silent as Diablo leads the way to an amphitheater on the east side of the stand, about two-thirds of the way up the hillside. As we enter from the top, I hear the crowd before I see them. A buzz of excitement and activity. We are looking down at a space carved directly in the earth like a five-tiered cake turned upside down, with the lowest—and front—row about six feet higher than the stage. At the very bottom is a ring, thirteen strides across, covered in rich green soil. It is smaller than a Coliséa arena, but the smaller setting somehow feels more intimate—and terrifying.

The arena is filled with Klujns in a rainbow of cloaks—at least three hundred. From where I stand, I can see crystals change hands. Are the

Klujns placing bets? A child in a plum-colored cloak holds an object that resembles a grenade. He tosses it and, as I recoil, it explodes in a burst of multicolored dust on stage.

Not a real grenade. A *toy*.

The whole scene feels strangely convivial, the mood relaxed and playful. The word that comes to mind is *surreal*.

We reach the bottom of the packed-dirt staircase. Guards stand around the perimeter of the ring, wild dogs at their heels.

"This way," Diablo says, and we enter a tunnel below the first row of seats, away from the hungry watch of the crowd. The underpass leads to a dugout with one long bench and two foreboding doorways on either side. Diablo and Palo—the red-eyed guard from yesterday—seat us in our order, from Jade in her dark blue costume to Wendy in burnt orange. A large, rectangular window gives us a view of the stage and a portion of the crowd.

Across the ring, on the first tier of seats, sits the king. He wears coral lipstick and an extravagant costume, his scarlet cloak revealing a spangled waistcoat, billowing pants, and jewel-encrusted shoes. His face is alight with anticipation.

Beside him is the stunning female Klujn I saw with her friends—the one who was giving Diablo the eye. Her long brown hair is piled on top of her head in a complicated nest, studded with little moon clips; her makeup is simple, gold, covering only the top left quarter of her face. Her striking red eyes look bored. I am surprised to see Daciana and Glory nearby, to Warwick's left. While Glory seems to have dressed for the occasion, Daciana wears her plain violet cloak. Her face is bare.

On the far right-hand side of the ring, Poppet holds a large horn that looks like a twisted root. Oak smokes from his glass pipe, puffing out little clouds of green smoke—Klandestine, I remember. A spark lands on his costume and catches fire. Poppet hits him once—firmly—to put it out.

"That must be the king's daughter," Wendy says beside me, and I look again at the teenage Klujn by Warwick's side. "Gold cloak. That means she's royalty."

"So she's a princess?"

"Catrina Sherman says that Klujn royalty is determined by when in the lunar calendar a Klujn is born, sort of like the zodiac. If you're born on or near a full moon—you're royal. That Klujn"—she points to Warwick's daughter—"won't inherit the throne. When the king or queen dies, trials are held where all the royal Klujns battle it out to see who's going to become the new leader."

"So they kill each other, too?" I ask.

Wendy shrugs. "I guess it makes sense. They love games so much—why stop with humans?"

I snort, feeling grateful that she still wants to talk to me after what happened. Our banter makes me feel less lonely.

By now, the crowd has finished trickling in. There must be at least four hundred Klujns, from babies to the elderly, most of them red-eyed. Their irises are so bright that I can see them from here, a crimson constellation. Only a few dozen have eyes of a different color, most of them in the nosebleed seats.

The king stands up to address the crowd. He looks relaxed and has the air of a jolly ringmaster. The amphitheater carries his voice up to the highest seats.

"Welcome, welcome!" he cries. "To our first public event. These performers were chosen by our gods, selected by the stars. That, or they have a terrible sense of direction!" The crowd laughs. "Now, now," Warwick continues, "let us not be too harsh on our guests. Tonight, they perform in the spectacle of their lives."

The crowd crackles excitedly with a quick tap of tongues against palates, in what sounds like applause or cheering. Warwick puckers his lips; twirls a tendril of his bone-festooned hair. "This morning, one of our performers was feeling particularly adventurous and decided to try to leave by her own means. Unfortunately, she died without an audience." The crowd's crackle turns into a deep slow hiss that I can only imagine is disapproval. I search the king's face for a trace that he knows something—that I was the one responsible for our failed escape attempt—but I find nothing. So Diablo didn't tell him?

"Tonight, twelve remain," Warwick continues. "A dozen souls on a journey of awakening. Each performer will be allowed to choose a weapon before going on stage. When the first horn sounds, they will enter the ring. After the second horn, the fight will begin." Warwick gestures toward Oak and Poppet and the root horn they're guarding.

"On this night, our young set off on their arduous journey, through the wall of death, past the underground river and the painted caves. They bring with them only what they can carry. They choose tools and weapons without knowing the battles ahead. What they choose to bring with them into the arena of the wild can mean the difference between life and death."

Wendy's voice is in my ear. "I don't get it. If they're leaving tonight, then who are we supposed to be fighting in the ultimate challenge? I thought the Blood Race was meant to involve a fight between a human and a Klujn."

This is news to me, too. "I don't know. Maybe they'll be back in time?"

She shakes her head. "Nope. He said that their Race can last right through the winter, until the Ice Moon or whatever, when they find the new stand and choose their mate."

Warwick goes on. "The fight will end when one performer has been defeated or surrenders. However, surrender is not to be taken lightly." He points to the guards' salivating dogs. "Those who surrender will be promptly taken care of."

Bindu and the wild dog. There's a lump in my throat that won't go down even when I swallow. I feel sick at the thought of more unnecessary death. I don't want to have to kill a girl, but I don't want to be torn to shreds by the dogs, either.

"So place your bets," Warwick sings. "Today, we watch our gods battle it out under the light of the moon, and our prophecy is narrowed down by half."

The crowd cheers as he sits down. In our dugout, Palo approaches Jade. He holds a black bag in front of her.

"What do I do?" she asks.

"Pick a crystal."

Jade's trembling hand sinks into the bag. *Please don't be mine*, I think. *I don't want to go against her.*

All of a sudden, I'm hit with the reality of what's about to happen. It felt like an idea, something distant and far away. Reesa and Bindu's deaths could even be considered unfortunate accidents.

But this is all too real. We have to fight each other, and we have to kill one another, in front of a slavering crowd. There are twelve of us in the dugout. By the time we return to our quarters, only six will remain.

I have never killed anything, not even an animal. I've learned the theory of it, but the eleven people next to me are not silicone dummies. They have lives and families and dreams and beating hearts.

Jade's fingers close around a stone. She pulls it out. All eyes are on her as she uncurls her fingers and shows us the color of the crystal in her palm.

30

It's black obsidian, the crystal symbolizing the Seed. I look down the row of girls to see who wears that costume—Number Three, Ying Yue, in her jet-black, sparkling costume. *Oh, no.* Jade may look strong next to her friend Mabry, but she is no match for the Military girl. Judging by the look on her face, she knows this as well.

"It's time," says Palo. Jade clings to Mabry until he pries her away, practically dragging her through the dark doorway on our left. Diablo leads Ying Yue through the other one on our right.

After they leave, the dugout is quiet. The only sounds are Mabry's sobs and the anxious tapping of Elizabeth's foot. *Who will I get? Who will get me?* I feel horrible even thinking it, but with Bindu gone—the smallest, the easiest to beat—there is no good option.

Beyond our dugout, the moon hides behind the clouds and the stage grows darker. Tall lanterns of Moonlight Leaf cast their strange patterns onto the ground.

The first horn sounds, slicing through the anticipation like a newly sharpened knife. Finally, Jade appears from the left, holding a spiky wooden bat. She walks with heavy steps, like her legs are filled with sand. Like I walked before my trip to Daciana's tent. Ying Yue emerges from the right, in her hand a magnificent double-headed ax with red blades.

Wendy's damp hand crawls along the bench sideways, like a crab, before closing around my own. I don't pull away, but free a few of my fingers and squeeze hers back.

The two girls on stage look so human . . . and by "human," I mean frail. Not warriors or robots or seasoned Hunters, but mere girls who should be in school or at Military training right now, had they listened to the warnings and stayed on the right side of the fences. Or perhaps it wasn't their fault that they were caught. Regardless, here they are. And now one of them has to kill the other.

At long last, the second horn sounds . . . and the fight is on.

Nothing happens. Both girls are motionless. Ying Yue with her gleaming ax. Jade, with her bat raised in unconvincing confidence. Finally, Ying Yue takes a step forward.

"I don't want to die," Jade cries.

This is the real thing. Not the weird, delirious ecstasy Reesa experienced before she jumped into the flames, nor the terrible accident of Bindu's death. There's nothing to cushion this blow, no Violette leaf, no anesthetic. It's desperate and ugly.

"Neither do I," says Ying Yue. She's not a killer, but a person put in an impossible situation. Still, she takes another step forward, hand tightening on the handle of the gleaming ax.

"Please," whimpers Jade. Her makeup runs in blue rivers down her face. "Have mercy."

"One of us has to die." Ying Yue's voice is not menacing, but almost contrite, like a TV newsreader announcing the headlines. *A bad storm has led to the sinking of ships and a devastating oil leak around Mission Creek. A fire has wiped out an entire forest and neighboring township. Another island is lost to rising waters. When will the wrath of God end?*

Ying Yue is the largest and most well-trained of us all, but she's still an eighteen-year-old girl. She doesn't want to be here any more than Jade does. She isn't a fighter, a performer, or a character determining some Klujn-god prophecy for the king's amusement. She's probably only held a weapon in the safety of her Military training. Doesn't mean she's ever used one in the real world.

She advances toward Jade. When there is only a few feet of space left between them, Jade holds up her free hand. *Stop.* "Not like this," she says.

Then, Jade—our first girl, our Number One—does something that shocks us all. She tosses her spiked bat away. It bounces and rolls, then comes to a stop inches from Ying Yue's feet.

Jade sinks to her knees and bows her head. "Please, make it quick," she says. Eyes closed. Body bent in defeat. Bracing herself for the blow.

Ying Yue doesn't know what to do. Finally, she kicks the bat away.

"The ax will be quicker," she tells Jade. She raises it above her head with the solemnity of an Executioner.

"I can't watch this," Wendy says, covering her eyes.

"I'm sorry," Ying Yue mutters, then she brings the ax down to meet Jade's tattooed neck. I look away. There's a wet *thwack*, and then a yelp. The crowd becomes agitated, excited. It's hard to tell why: Is it for the girl—or the god she represents?

I look back to the arena, expecting to see Jade's lifeless body, but Jade isn't dead. The ax has only gone partway through her neck.

She lets out a bone-chilling scream. Ying Yue, panicked, yanks the blade out of Jade's neck—there is a horrible *crunch*—and swings again. This time, it sinks a little deeper, but still Jade does not die. She writhes and wails like a tornado siren.

The king leans in, looking eager, licking his lips. This is the spectacle he wanted.

Ying Yue swings again and again, desperate to put Jade out of her misery. But the more she swings, the messier things get. Jade wriggles around like a tenacious cockroach that's been squished a dozen times but just won't die. An angry jet of blood drenches them both.

The crowd crackles. Wendy pulls her hand off mine and covers her ears.

Jade is twitching, still alive. A desperate Ying Yue changes strategy. She strikes at the girl's back, the ax coming down in flashes of red— once, twice, a third time, a fourth.

I force myself to keep watching. *This is what I am going to have to do.*

Finally, after a few dozen jabs, Jade stills.

Her lifeless body is face down in the soil, her costume shredded. There's so much blood. It surrounds her, glistening like a red moon in a black sky.

Ying Yue wipes her brow. Turns to face the royal seats and, in particular, the king. "Is that what you wanted?" she yells. Her voice trembles. "To turn us all into murderers?"

Warwick smiles. "Why, you already are. Only, you are so far removed from your actions that you do not see it. You let others kill for you, but you are murderers no less."

The final horn sounds. Then a grenade lands at Ying Yue's feet. It explodes in a cloud of sparkling black dust. More and more grenades join it until she's completely engulfed.

The crowd chants: "*Să-mâ! Să-mâ! Să-mâ!*"

Ying Yue throws down her ax and marches offstage. A guard drags Jade's body away by the feet, her half-decapitated head bobbing in her wake. Another guard rakes the arena clean, readying it for the next fight.

Diablo brings Ying Yue back to the dugout and seats her in Jade's spot.

"I didn't want to kill your friend," I hear Ying Yue tell a crying Mabry, but the girl doesn't respond.

Palo offers Mabry the black bag. "No," she says, shaking her head.

"If you don't fight, you will be eliminated," he warns, although his voice bears no malice.

Mabry reluctantly reaches in and selects a crystal.

Garnet—that's Willa. Wendy's body goes rigid next to mine.

Palo takes Mabry away. There is no interlude to recover, nothing to temper the bloodshed.

As Diablo leads Willa out, Wendy grabs her sister's hand. "I really hope you've got some magic up your sleeve."

Willa's smile is pained. "That's not really the point of magic," she says. "But I'll see what I can manage."

After the first horn, the girls come onstage. Wendy bites her thumbs, alternating between closing her eyes and deciding to keep them open.

Mabry has chosen a sword that's too big for her. Her wrist trembles under the weight of the object. Willa holds a sharp spear that's thorny along the stem, like a rose.

The second horn sounds, and they throw their weapons around in a haze of red and aquamarine. A dance of fire and water. Something theatrical and hypnotic. Mabry is erratic, while Willa is poised. Focused.

Then, after a few minutes, Mabry swings turbulently at Willa and loses her balance, falling awkwardly to the ground. An uproar from the crowd. Laughter.

Willa stands over the shaking girl.

"Please, make it quick," Mabry manages, echoing Jade. The crowd hisses in disappointment. This is too easy. They want blood and carnage.

Willa looks anguished, but she has no other choice. She aims the tip of the spear over her opponent's belly, then closes her eyes as she uses her weight to drive it down. Mabry's body seizes and her eyes snap open. The last thing she sees before dying is the arras of the night.

Then her muscles release, and she is gone.

Next is Benilda, the first of the silver-haired girls, in her blue-green amazonite costume. She draws pyrite—Elizabeth's stone.

Benilda wields a chain with a spiky ball attached to the end—"a flail," says Wendy. Elizabeth comes out empty-handed. It would be like her to show off, to make sure we know she can win without a weapon.

They are evenly matched—it is clear from the start that both have had combat training and neither of them will go down without a fight. The crowd leans in with a hiss of excitement. Elizabeth is faster and stronger and more powerful than I could have ever imagined. She moves swiftly around Benilda's forceful blows, slowly tiring her out. After one particularly brutish swing, Elizabeth ducks under the flail's arc, grabs Benilda's waist, and tackles her down. The weapon falls into the dirt.

Elizabeth is unforgiving and terrifying. She plunges a hand into the girl's neck, her muscles swollen. Her skin like tracing paper, showing the network of veins beneath the surface. She reaches for the flail's chain—finds it—and swings down hard, smashing the spiked ball into Benilda's face.

One hit. That's all it takes. The girl's skull cracks and her brains spill out like a watermelon dropped on pavement. I cover my eyes, but it's too late. The image is already burned into my mind. As Elizabeth strides offstage, her face betrays the faintest hint of triumph.

"One mistake," Wendy tells me. "That's all it takes. There is no margin of error."

Next, Palo approaches Rachel, the second silver-haired girl. She's lithe but menacing, with long straight hair and feline eyes, one concealed behind a bandage. Her opal costume sparkles as she reaches into the bag without so much as a tremble. She draws a stone.

It's a moonstone. It's mine.

31

I am not in my body anymore, and time no longer feels linear. Images flash by—separate scenes, not connected by causality. One moment, I'm sitting in the dugout; the next I'm in an underground chamber; the next I'm judging the weight of a small spear. Diablo is somewhere behind me, near a black curtain.

"You have two minutes," he says. "Choose wisely."

The room is lit by candles in colorful glass jars. Before me is a long table laden with weapons: axes, daggers, swords, clubs, hammers, and other lethal instruments.

I don't know Rachel's strengths, nor, I realize, do I know my own. I never went to Scouts and practiced knife-throwing or archery. I don't even know what half of these weapons are called. The weapon I choose could be useless against my opponent's. *In a few minutes I could be dead*, I think. *Or I will have killed someone.* These hands were made to wield paintbrushes, not slaying tools. To spread glue and glitter, not blood.

I set down the spear and run my fingers over a beautiful dagger; its blade is black crystal, sharp as a wolf's tooth. There's a slingshot next to it, and a whip wrapped in spirals of wooden barbed wire.

Near the end of the table, I notice other kinds of weapons that don't appear to be weapons at all—torches, jewelry, glass vials filled with lurid potions which must be poison. I somehow doubt I can convince Rachel to open wide and drink herself to death.

"One minute," warns Diablo.

There is no way I can choose, yet I have to make a choice. Remembering the other fights and Mabry's much-too-heavy sword, I think I ought to opt for something lighter. My fingers are about to close around the black dagger when I get an idea.

"What would *you* choose?" I ask Diablo.

He blinks and his eyes widen in surprise. He recovers quickly and says, "The choice is yours." But as he speaks, his gaze flickers to the edge of the table nearest him where a weapon sits. Something I overlooked because it's so small and doesn't look like a weapon at all.

It's a ring.

There's something sinister about the small piece of jewelry. A smooth rose gold band with four sharp spikes on top where a jewel should be. Their tips have been dipped in some kind of pink dye. I slip the ring on the middle finger of my right hand. It's a perfect fit.

"This one?" I ask Diablo. Something passes across his eyes, something that says, *Yes. That one.* Even though his lips don't move. "What does it do?"

The guard doesn't answer. That's all I'm getting.

The first horn sounds.

Stick to my strengths, I think. But, like Elizabeth, my strengths don't involve weapons. So I keep the ring on and let my hand fall to my side.

I move to the doorway, and Diablo's violet eyes travel down the length of my arm to the choice I am already beginning to regret.

"Ready?" he asks. There's a landslide in my chest, a flight of rocks tumbling from throat to stomach. *No, I'm not. I need more time.* But I don't have that luxury, so I take a deep breath and nod. He draws back the curtain to reveal the empty stage. The circle of dark green soil. The glowing lanterns. The dogs and guards.

"Any words of advice?" I ask, and Diablo's lips curl into something that almost resembles a smile. There is the slightest trace of mischief in his eyes.

"Don't die."

As I step onstage, my costume becomes phosphorescent under the glow of lanterns. I run my thumb over the smooth underside of the ring, wondering if I have made the right decision. The audience is a blur in my peripheral vision. My focus is on one thing only: the dark doorway on the other side. When Rachel emerges, I immediately regret my choice of weapon.

Her makeup is an Executioner's mask, but opalescent instead of blue, so it matches her costume. She holds a long, wooden blowgun painted with sparkly green geometric shapes. The smile on her face tells me she knows exactly how to use it; otherwise, she wouldn't have chosen such a specific weapon. A belt of large darts is fastened around her waist. They're as long as pens and as sharp as knives.

I wish I had taken the dagger.

The second horn sounds. A deathly silence fills the amphitheater. Nothing in my life has prepared me for this, not even Mr. Mogel's punishing classes.

Rachel isn't the worst opponent I could have—she isn't one of my friends, and one of her eyes is bandaged. But there's something unnerving about the way she looks at me. A half smile, her visible eye unblinking. *Is it an intimidation tactic she learned in one of her weapons clubs? Or is she just bluffing?* Something tells me the former is more likely.

"Bold move," she remarks at my apparent lack of a weapon. "You know, you won't get a medal for playing the martyr. They'll never even find your body." My hands shake. I ball them into fists so that Rachel won't notice, but it's too late. "It's okay," she says, her tone condescending. "We all have to die of something. Tell you what—why don't you surrender? I'll make it fast, I promise."

Then, without warning, Rachel brings the blowgun to her lips.

A dart flies toward me at high speed. I duck out of the way. The dart misses my shoulder and hits the wall of packed dirt behind me, below the first tier of seats.

"So much for mercy," I say.

"You took too long to answer." Rachel smiles. She quickly loads another dart into the chamber and blows. This time, she aims lower. It flies toward my feet. I jump, and the dart misses me by less than an inch, landing in the green soil. The crowd laughs uproariously.

"You know, sooner or later you're going to run out of luck," she says.

"And sooner or later you're going to run out of darts," I answer.

She snickers. "Let's see which comes first." Another dart. I duck, and this one clips my shoulder.

Out of the corner of my eye, I notice the king, leaning forward in his seat. This is the kind of spectacle he has been waiting for. A game of cat and mouse. *I'm the mouse*, I realize. If I don't do something soon, one of Rachel's darts will get me.

I don't want to die on my knees like Jade or Mabry. I don't want my face smashed in, like Benilda. I don't want to die before getting to experience all the things I want so badly to experience, even the ones I'm too embarrassed to admit.

I don't want to die, period.

Another dart flies toward me. I try to dodge it, but it grazes my face. Then another, and before I can jump out of the way it plunges into my thigh like a syringe, only its tip is a dozen times thicker than any needle I've ever seen. I scream, and yank it out quickly in case it's poisoned. Rachel's darts continue to come with increasing velocity, but her ammunition doesn't seem to be diminishing. She was right. It's only a matter of time.

"You don't have to kill me," I tell Rachel, stalling. Her fallen missiles litter the ground. I back up carefully. "They're trying to make enemies out of us. I don't want to hurt you, and you don't have to hurt me."

"And then what?" Her voice is caustic. "We both get fed to the dogs? No thanks."

My shoulder blades touch the wall of packed dirt behind me. Rachel smirks, thinking she's got me right where she wants me—cornered, at point-blank range. From this close, with the force of her blows, Rachel's next dart could pierce my eyeball. Sink into my brain.

And yet there is one thing she doesn't have, and that is the element of surprise.

"Don't give the audience what they want," I say, as Rachel raises the missile to her lips.

"I don't have a choice," she says.

"Then neither do I."

Adrenaline floods through me, and the rest happens in a flash. I spring forward and grab the wooden shaft. Rachel blows just as I manage to push it down. The dart rockets into the ground, plunging into my shoe. But there's no pain; somehow, the dart has landed in the minute gap between my toes. I grab her weapon with both hands and shove it into her mouth as far as I can. Rachel stumbles back, gagging.

Her grip on the weapon loosens, and I rip it out of her hands.

When someone has a weapon pointed at you and you can't escape, Mr. Mogel had said once, *your best chance is to run toward them. It's the last thing they'll expect. If you don't charge, you're a dead man anyway.*

Whoever thought I'd be grateful for anything Mr. Mogel said?

"No," Rachel groans. I swing the blowgun and whack her in the side of the head. She staggers and falls. I pin her down, but she's already reaching for the darts at her waist. The next step is to get the weapon as far away as possible, so I yank at the belt and toss it wildly; it goes flying toward the other side of the stage.

Without the darts, the blowgun is not as dangerous. I turn it sideways and press down on Rachel's neck, blocking her windpipe. The tables have turned.

"Please," she croaks, her face turning red. "You don't have to kill me."

The attacker will beg for their lives, Mr. Mogel told us, pinning down the silicone female. *Don't listen to them. As soon as they get the upper hand again, they'll finish what they started.*

I push down harder on her neck. "And then what?" I throw her line back at her. "You kill me? Or we both get fed to the dogs? No thanks." Rachel's face begins to turn purple.

But right as she's about to pass out, the wooden tube cracks in half.

Rachel pulls in a raspy breath. "Spoke too soon," she grates, swinging me around and pinning me down, proving Mr. Mogel right. The broken pieces of the blowgun fall out of my hands. Rachel's long fingers wrap around my throat and squeeze tight.

The oxygen in my lungs is running out. The lanterns are a yellow blur. *Stars. I see stars.* Five more seconds and I'll be unconscious. And unconscious is just as good as dead.

Then, I hear a chant: *"Lu-nah! Lu-nah! Lu-nah!"*

My head tilts slightly, and I see them, the audience, all chanting the same word.

I remember Diana looking at the sky: *la lune*, in French.

And José, when we'd bake moon cookies for Hunter's Day: *luna*.

It's me. They're cheering for me.

Their wild chorus lends me a bit of strength—and that's when I remember the ring.

Somehow I manage to make a fist and bring up my right hand. With a last-ditch surge of energy, I drive the four pink spikes of the ring into Rachel's neck.

The crowd's chants intensify. *"Lu-nah! Lu-nah! Lu-nah!"*

"What the—?" Rachel swats my hand away like a mosquito, and I'm able to suck in a bit of air. Oxygen has never tasted this good!

The sharp corners of the ring have left four dots on Rachel's neck, and four drops of blood rise to the surface. They look innocent enough, like the bite of a strange insect, but their effect is instant.

Rachel looks down at her arms. Her eyes bulge and her hands loosen. "What did you do to me?" she spits.

"I don't know," I say, edging out from under her, careful to avoid the scattered darts.

She begins to scratch at her arms, seeing something that only she can see. "Bugs!" Rachel shrieks. "There are bugs under my skin!"

I glance over at the dugout and catch Wendy's eye. She mouths the word *Wilderweed*, and I remember the fuchsia-pink berries in the Deeper Woods. Of course.

My opponent stands up. "Whadjadotmeh?" she says again, slurring her words now. Her tongue hangs from the side of her mouth, her saliva thick and frothing. She begins to race around the stage, scratching at herself, trying to tear the imaginary critters out from under her skin. Rachel becomes frantic, bumping into walls, clawing at the dirt, and trying to climb them.

"Lemme ow-a ere!" she yells. But it's not the stage she's trying to escape, it's herself.

I continue to edge backward, trying to get as far from her as I can get. When I hit the wall that surrounds the stage, I can go no farther. I'm forced to watch as Rachel's predicament goes from bad to worse.

She claws at herself so violently that her arms begin to bleed. "Maeit-stoppp!" she shrieks.

I wish the stage was made of quicksand. Wish I could sink into the earth and emerge somewhere else, another world where actions have no consequences.

Rachel continues to run around the arena like a blinded animal, bouncing off the walls. She steps on a dart that goes straight through her foot. She falls to the ground but continues tearing wildly at the insects we can't see. "Ge-ow-fffmeee!"

The crowd watches, eyes unblinking.

When the scratching doesn't alleviate the bone-deep itch, Rachel begins to pull off bits of her flesh. She tracks an invisible bug as it climbs up her arm and into her neck. Then—Rachel's fingernails dive in with determination and she rips it out!

Only there's no bug in her hand.

Rachel's assault on herself has opened the skin and nicked a vein. A major one. Blood pours out, faster and faster as Rachel curls into herself, rolling pathetically in the soil, cradling her pockmarked arms.

"Hurts!" she cries, sounding like a toddler now.

Soon the girl stops resisting, stops fighting, and lies still.

Diablo watches from the right-hand doorway. Why didn't he tell me it would be this bad? I'm angry at him, but angrier at myself for listening to him. Angry that, once again, I have made myself a target for suspicion.

Sure enough, everyone in the dugout is watching me. I can almost hear their thoughts from here: *First the dog whistle, now this; what other knowledge does she have?*

How can I tell them that I didn't know? That Diablo helped me choose.

I don't know which is worse: siding with a Klujn, or telling them it was instinct. I imagine Elizabeth's smirk if I dared to say that word again. She probably hates it just as much as she hates the word *magic*.

The crowd goes wild. It's chaos. An onslaught of moonstone-colored chalk bombs rain down from the audience. I let it swallow me, wishing that once they disperse I could also be gone, like the star of a magician's disappearing act.

"Well done!" the king's voice booms. "Now that was something!" He is exhilarated, almost euphoric.

Some of the Klujns whoop and howl like wolves at the moon, chanting ever louder, "*LU-NAH! LU-NAH! LU-NAH!*"

And I realize: I am that Moon.

The cheering is overwhelming. It is not a triumph. No cause for celebration. It is scornful. Spiteful. Vindictive. A girl is dead. *A girl I killed.*

I pry the ring from my finger and hurl it as far away as I can. In the stands, crystals exchange hands as Klujns cash in on their bets.

In the midst of it all, I spot Daciana, in her violet cloak. She's not celebrating like the others. Her bright purple eyes are on me, but it's like she's gazing through me, at a vision or a memory. Even through the haze of sparkly dust, I can see the tears in her eyes.

32

When I return to the dugout, no one acknowledges me. Diablo seats me beside Elizabeth, and before I can even contemplate more fights—and more deaths—Palo is in front of Coco, bag in hand.

She draws a sunstone. *Wendy.*

In this limbo of shock and emotional exhaustion, I don't know if I manage a goodbye. Wendy is gone, and I'm staring at the stage, waiting for the horn to sound.

When it does, Coco comes out holding a regular ax. Her assertive stance doesn't make me feel very good about Wendy's chances. When my friend emerges, I'm surprised to see that she has chosen a caltrop. It is ugly and lethal—ill-fitting to her personality. It's comprised of four thick nails sticking out in different directions like a pointed star, positioned in such a way that no matter how it lands, one of them always faces up.

Wendy took my advice and stuck to her strengths. Picked a weapon she could throw.

The fight begins. Coco and Wendy seem to walk in an invisible circle, keeping the same distance apart. Their movements are slow and measured, a spell of clear quartz and sunstone. Then Coco steps forward and enters No Man's Land.

Wendy's hand tightens around the caltrop. *One throw.* That's all she has. No room for error. Her focus is intense.

Then, decided, Coco raises her ax and charges. She yells like a knight charging toward the front line of battle.

The crowd chants, "*So-a-ra! So-a-ra! So-a-ra!*"

Soara—is that Wendy?

Wendy's face shifts lightning-fast across a spectrum of emotions: Fear. Uncertainty. Confidence. Resolve. Her eyes pinned to her moving target, Wendy pulls her arm back and launches the caltrop.

The weapon's path is straight and true. It rotates on its axis like an asteroid careening through space—and one of the sharp metal nails sinks into Coco's chest. *Thunk.* Bullseye.

Coco takes a few more steps, almost in slow motion, like she's running in a dream, bound by invisible strings. She underestimated Wendy, and that was her mistake.

Coco looks down at her chest at the fatal object. Touches it with a single finger. Then the ax drops from her hand, and she's dead before she hits the ground.

The crowd goes wild, repeating their chant: "*So-a-ra! So-a-ra! So-a-ra!*"

The Sun.

I let out a sigh of relief—not because Coco is dead, but I'm relieved it's not my friend.

No bag of crystals is needed for the final fight: there are only two untried performers. Rory, in fluorite, versus Zoe in her tree agate costume. It's hard to pick a side. Zoe was my partner in the Deeper Woods, but Rory has become a friend. This is why people form sides, I realize. Without sides, slaughter is impossible to justify.

They face each other, Rory with a small sword and Zoe a Hunter's knife. Like Elizabeth and Benilda, the two are evenly matched. Both performers know how to use their weapons; they manipulate them like an extension of their arms, swinging, striking, dodging, grunting, their blades colliding in a fury of sparks. It surprises me that Zoe—quiet, serious, keeps-to-herself Zoe—is so skilled with a Hunter's knife. Then again, she's a Hunter's daughter. Guess her father taught her more than mine did.

Minutes pass. A test of speed and technique soon becomes one of endurance. Even as they begin to tire, neither loses focus. Their eyes are locked. They are like two animals fighting over a piece of meat; in this case, the prize is survival.

Rory is on the offense, Zoe on defense. Her arms begin to tremble with the effort of each block she has to yield. Then Rory lops off Zoe's knife hand—the other girls in the dugout flinch—but when the hand falls to the ground, there is no blood. It's her prosthetic. It lies out of reach, clutching the knife. Zoe is now unarmed.

"What the—?" Rory is confused.

"Wait," Zoe says, between breaths. "I can't fight without a weapon."

Rory stops, also winded. "What do you mean?"

"I can't win." Zoe's eyes fill with earnestness and grief. She drops to her knees, her body shaking. She's surrendering.

"No," I say. Barely louder than a whisper, but Zoe hears me. Her head turns, and she feels so incredibly familiar in that moment, but I'm not sure why. Rory moves toward Zoe, fingers tightening around the hilt of her sword.

"You need to say it," Rory tells her.

Zoe opens her mouth, her quivering lips trying and failing to shape the word *surrender*.

"I don't want the dogs to eat me alive," she finally says. "Please, have mercy."

Rory looks wrecked, perhaps hoping that Zoe would give herself up to the dogs so that she wouldn't have to do the deed herself.

"I beg you," Zoe says with increasing desperation. She bows her head, waiting for Rory to come and give her deliverance.

Rory wavers, then realizes that the sooner this fight is over, the better. She takes a few tentative steps toward Zoe, who is crying now. Zoe's tears are ceaseless, pouring down her painted face like a flash flood, showing more emotion now than she ever has.

Rory raises her sword, her kind face full of sympathy and dread. She is about to bring it down on the back of Zoe's neck when Zoe spits out three chilling words.

"Go in peace." Then, Zoe springs into action.

Rory doesn't have time to register what's going on. Neither do I.

Zoe has the skill of a Hunter, her movements quick and precise. She throws herself at her prosthetic—its plastic fingers still clutching the dagger—snatches it up, and stabs Rory in the thigh. The blade hits an artery—either a lucky stab or a frighteningly accurate hit. Zoe isn't finished. She stabs Rory in the other thigh, hitting her other artery.

Rory's legs collapse. She is stunned, and Zoe pushes her back and climbs on top of her, bringing the knife down into her jugular. Then she sinks the blade into Rory's chest, puncturing her heart. The crowd goes wild as Zoe stands. With four clean stabs, her opponent is dead.

Rory, who finally looked at home in her body.

It is a tragedy. But if she had won the Blood Race, what then? In our world, it is too dangerous to be different.

Rory's head lops to the side, and I see her empty eyes. Gone. A dark tunnel with no light at the end. But something in them looks . . . free.

At least at Circo she got to be herself, however briefly.

* * *

Zoe turns toward Warwick and takes an exaggerated bow. Her tear-streaked cheeks are a lie. She wipes her arm over her face, smearing sweat and makeup, and I see a scar above her lip that I hadn't noticed before.

Who is this girl? Where did she come from?

The way she tricked Rory . . .

Voices bleed into my reality, chants from another place and time. Suddenly the past takes harrowing form around me.

I *do* know Zoe.

* * *

"Kill the Klujn! Kill the Klujn!
Whichever way you choose.
Then send it to the gallows, and
We'll have a bar-be-cue . . ."

A game of Kill the Klujn is underway. I look over at the mass of jeering children standing on the perimeter of the chalk triangle, with Coll in the middle. He fights another kid—a little Black girl with clumps of missing hair and a stump for a left hand. They both clutch sharpened sticks.

With one easy blow, Coll knocks her down. She lies on the ground, whimpering, as he laughs. Blood covers her upper lip, which has split open.

Miss Hidgins comes over. "Get up, Orphan," she scolds. "You stay down, you die."

* * *

Another memory, the following spring:

We're in the cafeteria and the tables have been pushed aside. It's Adoption Day. Children are lined up, bathed, and groomed to look their best. Families come and go, but none look at me twice.

Coll stands tall and hopeful, his cheeks rosy and his hair slicked back. He is full of secret yearning, although he would never admit this to his friends. The little girl with a stump for a hand is at the end of the row. She looks downcast, as though her expectations aren't high. Well, no wonder, I think. Everyone knows that the cute and the healthy are always the first to get chosen. She is none of those things, so she compensates by being well-behaved.

That's when I see them. George, Miss Hidgins, and a tall, commanding man in a Hunter's uniform. General Santos.

A few days later, George takes me home. We cross the gravel parking lot. Through the fence separating it from the orphanage courtyard, I notice Coll alone, kicking rocks.

He looks up and stares at me, the fence casting diamond-shaped shadows on his face, framing his sad blue eyes. No one came for him this time.

He'll eventually be adopted by Mr. Mogel's sister, Gora Mogel-Newhouse, and her husband, Garrison Newhouse, but by then, it will be too late. That hope in Coll's heart will have already shriveled up and died, mutating into something ugly, like healthy cells turning cancerous.

"What are you looking at, freak?" he sneers, throwing a rock at me. It hits the fence and bounces off, falling to the ground. Coll's loathing for me is born that day. It's the kind of hatred someone has when they envy what you have.

"We can walk home from here," George says, and I turn my attention away from Coll, feeling sad for him. My new father nods at the uniformed man, General Santos, who is leaving with . . . Zoe.

* * *

"*Ava.*" Wendy nudges me, and the memories dissipate like the clouds of sparkling green dust in the arena. "Are you okay? Your eyes looked weird and far away."

"Fine," I say.

"Well, I wouldn't expect you to be fine," Wendy says. "Just wanted to make sure you didn't have a stroke."

Zoe slides back into her seat, and I watch her surreptitiously.

Does she remember me?

The orphanage was a long time ago, and we were only little girls. Maybe I'm not the only one whose past has been forgotten or erased, banished to the tenebrous basements of her subconscious. Maybe Zoe *does* remember me—remembers that I saw her at her weakest—and that is why she avoids me.

But I thought Santos had a son.

It was Zoe, then, that I saw in the woods when George took me camping. Dressed as a boy, with a bandanna over her mouth. It was Zoe who spotted the blue sparrow's nest and went to retrieve the eggs.

I would talk to her, but I'm unsettled by the look on her face. By the way she betrayed Rory. She is her father's daughter—cunning, conniving, not here to make friends. Her father, the Loudhouse owner and Grouse's Head Hunter. But why is she here at all? And what are the chances that we would both be caught on the same night?

What is it about Circo that's bringing these memories to the surface? And how am I supposed to trust anything about my past, when the continent of beliefs I was standing on is now rapidly shifting?

"That concludes the first round of fights," Warwick announces to a mostly satisfied crowd. He turns to the six of us. "You are invited to a feast in my quarters at midnight. The invitation is, of course, mandatory. Come with empty bellies and open minds. Oh, and please do not forget your hourglass."

33

Back in our quarters, Diablo and Palo wash us down, one icy ladle of water after another. It's far from the luxury of the Amethyst pools, but I'm grateful to remove all traces of my fight with Rachel. In the sleeping tent, we change into new bralettes and underwear and black clothes and retrieve our hourglasses. Then we are led out in three rows of two: Ying Yue and Zoe; Willa and Elizabeth; me and Wendy. In that order. No more Rory. No more Jade or Mabry. No more silver-haired girls.

A steep path ascends toward those unexplored heights of upper Circo. The air becomes thinner as we go, and the temperature drops by a few degrees. As we approach the highest part of the stand, the avenues widen.

I wonder if this is where the royal Klujns live. That if, by the luck of their births under a full moon, they are afforded more luxuries. The tents are larger and made from more opulent fabrics. A yellow lantern hangs outside each one. As we continue up toward the king's quarters, I see it—the black diamond at the summit. *An arena?*

But, once again, it is not our destination.

At the front of our line, Zoe gazes off into the mountains to the west. I want to talk to her, ask her about my memory, but how can I do that with Elizabeth nearby? The last thing I want is to give her access to my private past. Also, I don't want the others to think I approve of what Zoe did to Rory. If Zoe does remember me, her eyes give nothing away.

The breeze carries Zoe's voice down to me. "Where are they?" Her words are barely louder than the rustle of our cloaks.

"Who?" Ying Yue asks, startled to hear the girl speak.

Zoe's eyes scan the darkness of the distant mountain range with a saturnine stare.

"Forget it," she says curtly. "I was just talking to myself."

* * *

Warwick's tent is lavishly adorned in hues of red and gold, brimming with autumnal smells and decorations. A large round table fills the circular living space, a chandelier of acorns and Moonlight Leaf above it. At the back, a doorway leads to what must be his private quarters, cordoned off by a curtain of sunstone beads.

"Come, make yourselves at home," says the king, rising from the round table. We pass a fireplace where an auburn wolf with black spots sleeps by the hearth; nearby, curled into one another, are a pig and a young bear.

"Please, take your seats." Warwick indicates six high-backed chairs around him, each bearing one of our symbols. Ying Yue is to Warwick's right, then Zoe, Willa, Elizabeth, me, and finally Wendy, who looks on edge as she slips into the chair at the king's left. His scarlet eyes study her with a combination of curiosity and hunger. She looks anywhere but at him, as if trying to convince herself that she's not the guest of a wild human-eating king. This is a challenge, after all. Will we be poisoned? Or is this just a harmless dinner invitation?

At the center of the table is a large, round elevated platter, laden with the usual colorful buffet that I have grown to enjoy during my time here. Beneath it is a revolving disk as big as the table itself.

Warwick pours himself a flute of a green fermented drink and suggests we try it. We pass the decanter around until we have all been served.

"To you," he says. "And your remarkable progress in such a short amount of time." We raise our glasses and I sip the curious liquid. It's fizzy, a little sweet, but not unpleasant, like sparkling wine aromatized with pine.

"Did you see my companions on the way in?" Warwick asks, like a jovial host wanting to show off a rare collection. "Maré, Mimas—come," he calls, and the pig and bear get up and waddle over. He takes a few orange spirals from a nearby dish. As the animals gobble up the treat, Warwick grins. "They love marinated carrots. I didn't mean for my quarters to become an animal shelter," he adds, "but when a creature in distress arrives on my doorstep, I find it impossible to turn them away. Now"—his voice changes tenor, turns businesslike—"I take it you've all brought your hourglasses."

We set them on the table. The hourglasses all vary in shape and size. Mine is by far the smallest. Elizabeth's is a little larger. Wendy's—the gold one I left in the cave—is second-largest, after Zoe's humongous one.

"Good," says Warwick. "By now, I'm sure you've noticed how fond I am of games. Especially games of chance. For this next one, you will all want a little bit of that on your side. Because now, you fight not with your hands, but with your stomachs. I very much hope that you will learn something new in the process.

"I find that food is a gateway to a culture," he adds. "Learning what a population eats tells you everything you need to know about them."

Diablo, Palo, and the other red-eyed guard emerge from the doorway carrying dishes. There are six gold plates, covered with gold lids. The Klujns set them carefully down on the outer edge of the revolving wheel, one in front of each of us.

"Do not touch," chides Warwick—and this is directed at Wendy, who is already reaching for her dish—"before you are invited to do so."

She pulls back her hand and studies the mysterious dish with a burning interest. "I have a little sweet craving," she says. "Whatever it is, I hope it's fresh."

"The game is simple," Warwick tells us with a smile. "Spin the wheel and eat the dish that lands in front of you. You will have the amount of time in your respective hourglasses to finish eating. There must be nothing left on your plate, and you must keep it down. If you fail, you will be eliminated. This game will be completed in reverse order," he adds, turning to Wendy. "I invite you to start."

Wendy reaches out to give the wheel a spin. The gold dishes flash by with a *clink, clink, clink*. I hate to imagine what lies beneath their lids. Somehow, I don't feel as optimistic as she does. The wheel slows down and eventually stops. A dish settles in front of my friend. Diablo uncovers it, and the eagerness on Wendy's face vanishes.

It's a questionable lump about the size of a meatball, deep-fried and garnished with green herbs. Diablo turns over Wendy's hourglass.

She eyes the dish with great suspicion. "What is it?" she asks the king.

"Mountain oysters," Warwick replies. "Inspired by human cuisine."

"That sure as war doesn't look like an oyster."

The king's patience is fraying. "It's meat."

"What kind of meat?"

"Does it matter?" When Wendy doesn't answer, Warwick *tsks*. "You humans are such fascinating hypocrites. You make the strangest distinctions between the animals you kill and the ones you keep. It is a paradox I'll never understand. Life is life, and meat is meat."

"That's rich coming from a creature that eats humans," mutters Zoe.

Warwick points a murky white claw at Wendy's hourglass. A quarter of the sand is gone.

"Hurry up."

Wendy gingerly picks up her fork. "I don't like the look of it."

"You don't have a choice," I tell her.

She nods with resolve, sinks the tines of her fork into the meatball and brings it to her nose. Sniffs it.

"Don't smell it!" Elizabeth scolds, revolted.

"Sorry . . . force of habit." Wendy takes a small bite. "It's crunchy," she remarks, then takes another bite. "And tender on the inside. But I *really* don't like parsley."

Willa is bemused. "That's your main concern?"

We watch as Wendy continues to chew with closed eyes, reacting to the new tastes and textures. After a long minute, and too much chewing, she can no longer delay the swallow. The last grains of sand fall and she opens her eyes.

"See how easy that was!" Warwick exclaims, as Diablo takes her plate away.

"It kind of tastes like veal." She wipes her mouth. "But stinky."

Warwick beams. "Who would have thought that human testicles would be such a treat?" Wendy clutches her napkin. "These were kindly donated to us by our wayward Hunter in the cave. By the way, the Klujn you encountered was not an actor," he says. "But a criminal. You may think we are all barbarians who sit around picking human meat from our teeth"—and he grins—"but we have rules as well, and Klujns who commit crimes are punished for them, and sometimes banished from the stand."

An ashen Wendy looks like she's going to throw up.

"Keep it down," cautions the king. "It would be a shame for you to be eliminated after all your hard work, simply because you suddenly developed a fussy appetite."

She reaches for her glass of sparkling wine. Drinks it in one go. I top her up again. She drinks this one, too. After about a minute of deep breathing, Wendy's nausea seems to pass.

"Good work," Warwick tells her. "I find that these things are often a case of mind over matter. A little trip to a street market on the human side of the fences, and you'll find things far more sinister than you'll ever find at Circo. I never did try baked puppy heads or bull penis. Can't say I see the appeal. Now," he continues, "who do we have next?" His eyes land on me. "Ah, yes. The Moon. You were in the running for Most Vicious Kill. Who knew that Wilderweed was in your narrow human repertoire of knowledge?"

The king's insults don't bother me; there is something darkly humorous in his delivery. I survey the glass wheel in front of me. *The faster I get this over with, the better*, I think, and give it a spin. The dishes flash by, one by one. After about ten seconds, the wheel slows then comes to a stop.

I look at the gold lid of the dish in front of me. Wonder what it's hiding. *Please don't be something foul or something big*, I hope silently. My hourglass is tiny. I probably have about twenty to thirty seconds of sand, tops.

Diablo lifts the lid to reveal a glass filled with a thick red drink. He turns my hourglass over.

I blink, and half the sand has already fallen. There is no time to waste. I grab the glass, pinch my nose, and tip the liquid down my throat. Chug. Swallow. Gag. It's foul, but I keep drinking as it oozes down my chin and finish just in time.

The taste lingers on my tongue. Not metallic, like blood, but more . . . earthy.

Warwick applauds. "Beet juice! The *look* on your face. This is why I love this game!"

"Seriously?" Elizabeth snaps. "Wendy gets balls and you get beet?"

"It could have been blood," I say.

"Yeah, but it wasn't." She sounds angry or suspicious, as if I had control over which dish I received. Warwick said it himself—this is a game of chance. It strikes me that Elizabeth seems more irritable than usual, if that's at all possible.

And of course, her turn is next. She spins and winds up with a bowl of soup decorated with a floating eyeball with a brown iris.

"Our eyes," says Warwick, "are the way we *perceive* reality." Elizabeth is clearly disgusted, but there's no chance she'll let herself get eliminated for this. She goes for the eyeball first, wincing as it bursts between her teeth, then drinks the cloudy broth.

Willa's dish is a long, pink tongue. As she finishes eating, Warwick smiles broadly and informs her that it was pink jackfruit, which flourishes here; even if a plant is not endemic to a place, we learn, some Klujns are able to grow it.

After that, it's Zoe. She spins with minimal effort, and the wheel stops before completing a full rotation. Diablo takes off the golden lid. Our mouths drop as we see what is on the plate.

It's a heart, a little larger than a fist. And it looks human.

The heart has that sickly blue-black tint that the dog meat had.

Zoe chokes. "I'd like to spin again," she says, even though she knows that's wishful thinking. At least her hourglass is large.

Warwick playfully shakes his head. "'Love In Disguise,' an unusual name for an unusual dish. Garnished with breadcrumbs, to give it that extra crunch." The color has drained from Zoe's face. "In Klujn stands," says Warwick, "when the king or queen dies, trials are held to determine the new leader. The winner of these trials can only be crowned once he or she has eaten the heart of the previous leader, inheriting its strength, its power, its memories. This, however," he concludes, "is just a regular human heart. Just a cold, sickly Hunter's heart, glazed with some herbs from my garden."

Diablo steps forward and turns over Zoe's hourglass.

She looks at the heart. "I can't," she says.

"You don't have a choice," Willa tells her.

Zoe struggles with herself. Picks up the organ and brings it up to her mouth. She catches a waft of its fetid flesh and gags. "I . . . really . . . can't."

"If you don't do this, you're dead," says Ying Yue.

"I suggest you begin eating," Warwick says in a singsong way. "Time is of the essence."

About one-tenth of the sand in Zoe's hourglass is gone, and a minute elapsed. She picks up the heart again, and closes her eyes. "I'm sorry," she whispers, like the prayer I always see her muttering. And then she takes a bite.

"Pretend it's something else. Anything," Willa tells her.

"It could be a chicken heart," Wendy puts in, trying to be helpful. "From a very, very big chicken."

Zoe gets through the first few bites, chewing and swallowing, chewing and swallowing. She eats like a machine. After a few more minutes she finishes, her hands wet with blood. In her hourglass, half of the sand has fallen.

"Good job," Willa says.

Zoe sits silently, processing her newly received meal.

Then her body rejects it.

In an impressive fountain, she vomits the chewed-up heart onto her plate. Zoe covers her mouth with the back of her quivering hand, stunned by the way her well-trained body has betrayed her. "No . . ." she utters.

Zoe doesn't deserve my help after what she did to Rory, but I wouldn't be able to live with myself if I didn't at least try.

"Wait," I tell her. "There's still time." She looks at her vomit-covered plate, then at me, understanding my implication. "For your life."

The remaining sand in the hourglass seems to be falling with increasing speed; I can almost hear the rush of grains hitting the bottom. *Three minutes. Two minutes and a half.* Zoe doesn't have any time to waste. She cups her hand and scoops up the contents of her stomach.

Around the table, the nauseated girls watch.

"Nope."

"She won't."

"She can't."

"She doesn't have a choice," I say.

Zoe takes a bite. Retches. Takes another. She continues to eat the clumpy heart-puke like oatmeal, gagging and heaving.

As she finishes the last mouthful, her time runs out.

"Keep it down," I caution her.

Zoe wipes her mouth and closes her eyes. Tears leak from their corners. She waits, she prays. If she throws up again, it's over. Finally, after about a minute, Zoe opens her eyes. Her body has accepted the meal.

"You did it," Willa says feebly as Diablo takes the plate away.

Zoe isn't in the mood to celebrate. Instead, she withdraws to a secret room inside herself. A miasma of despair hangs in her eyes like a ghost town. Power turned off, no one in sight.

Finally it's down to Ying Yue. She rotates the wheel until the last gold dish is in front of her. Palo takes off the lid. Just when I thought that things couldn't get any worse . . .

It's Bindu's head. Half of it, lying sideways, hair and all, used as a bowl for the real delicacy . . . a chunk of her brain. The right hemisphere is there, the cerebral cortex and cerebellum and brain stem that

I remember studying in biology. Nestled in the frontal lobe, just behind where the bridge of her nose would be, is a dark orb I've never seen before. It stands out against the pinkish-gray tissue.

Not. Real. Not. Real. Not. Real. The words pound inside my head to the rhythm of my throbbing heartbeat. It can't be.

My throat tightens, eyes flooding with tears of rage and sadness for Bindu, whose fate was to end up on this table for the King's sadistic game.

"The third eye!" exclaims Warwick. "The way we see *beyond* our false perception of reality. This happens to be my favorite dish in the game." That's when I realize . . . the thing in Bindu's brain is actually a withered *eyeball*.

I look at the dead girl's face—the side of her face that's there. With her soul gone, nothing there looks human, simply a vessel for something now far away.

"Our third eye affects dreams, memories, inhibition, as well as *sexual maturation*," says Warwick, smiling roguishly at those last words. "This small but powerful organ connects us more deeply to Nature and to ourselves. It is a sixth sense, if you will. Our *instinct*. But these organs are not exclusive to Klujns. Humans have them too, only they do not even know it. So, if you have found your senses sharpening since you arrived at Circo, it is perfectly natural. Your third eye is beginning to stir."

"That's the most absurd thing I've ever heard," Elizabeth says. "We don't have eyeballs in our brains."

"I could show you," Warwick tells her good-naturedly. "But by the time you'd believe me, you'd be dead."

The other four girls don't look as skeptical as Elizabeth. Willa shifts in her seat uncomfortably. Ying Yue is clearly disturbed, but it's unclear whether it's due to the king's words or the dish in front of her. Wendy massages her brow, perhaps trying to see if she can feel the eyeball with her fingers. Zoe's eyes are blank. She has armor around herself, shields and breastplates that Warwick's lessons will never pierce.

I mull over his words. *Dreams. Memories. Inhibition . . . Instincts.* They hit the nail right on the head. *Never mind the last thing he said.*

"In the human world, the third eye has become a sort of myth.

Something laughed at by scientists," he continues. "The same scientists who discount magic, who believe that the reality around them—the one observed with their five senses—is all there is. But that reality is just the beginning. A broom closet in the great palace of consciousness."

Elizabeth snorts. "I don't believe this," she says to the table at large. "He's actually insane."

Warwick doesn't seem to hear her. "How do you control a population? Through fear. Because people who live in fear are easy to manipulate," says the king. He looks around the table, focusing on us one by one. "Have you never wondered why your world is so small?" he asks. "It is because your leaders don't want you to know the truth— that there's *more* out there. They want to keep you sick and stupid. Because the sick and stupid are easier to control than the healthy and enlightened."

I feel an uncomfortable restlessness—a need to move, to escape this stuffy tent and run deep into the crisp night. I don't know if I want to know where the king is going with this, but isn't knowledge all I've ever craved? What if there really is something there—something dormant in my brain? A third eye?

"What is the truth, then?" I have to ask.

Warwick looks delighted that I'm showing interest. He takes a sip of his drink, puckers his lips.

"The truth?" He savors the word like it is a piece of candy on his tongue. "The *truth* is that you are what you eat, and the food you eat is dead. Fertilizers, pesticides, poisons . . . the government is quite literally killing you with every bite. Cancers, learning difficulties, birth defects, depression, contagious rage . . . their only goal is to keep you sick. By adolescence, your third eye has already shriveled up. You have lost your memories, your creativity, and the ability to think for yourself. You worship those leaders who have no regard for your life."

There is quiet around the table and Warwick's voice gets louder, falling into a rhythm.

"Have you never wondered where your food comes from? Perhaps, deep down, you don't want to know. The cost on the land. On your bodies. On *us*. Because it is easier to close your eyes and pretend that these things aren't going on at all.

"However, it is never too late to awaken! Here, at Circo, the water is pure, the soil is healthy, and the food is alive. So, if you have felt different since you arrived—if you have found yourself experiencing new memories, or feel the fog in your brain clearing—it is because your third eye is healing. We have not been starving you, but *detoxifying* you. Perhaps if you stay with us a little longer, you will finally see things *as they really are*."

A smile dances across Warwick's lips. "So much talk has made me thirsty," he says, topping up his glass. "Now, I believe we have a game to finish."

The focus turns back to Ying Yue and what is on her plate. The black shriveled eye does not look appetizing at all. As Ying Yue's hourglass is turned over and she begins to eat Bindu's brain, I can hardly concentrate, so numb to the horrors before me that they stop registering.

Is it true? That we're all being poisoned? That Circo is awakening us to a reality beyond what our senses can perceive? I think about how sick so many of the orphanage kids were, how disease and aggression ran rampant. How, growing up, I always felt exhausted and unfocused all the time, forgetting things, feeling dumb.

Despite the horror of Circo and the king's bloodlust, the truth is that I do feel slightly better, physically. My body is strong, my senses sharp, my memories vivid—like an ash storm clearing, giving way to bright blue skies.

Then, I remember something else: Diana's determination that we eat only what we grew ourselves. How angry she would get if I had junk food or forgot to filter my drinking water. When I had mood swings and broke things or failed classes or complained about my night terrors, she always refused to put me on medication. Instead, she made changes in my nutrition, as though all these problems could be rectified by diet. She is an agriculturalist. She worked in Greenhouses and Loudhouses.

Does she know something?

I realize that Ying Yue's plate is empty. She's completed her task. She looks nauseated, which is to be expected. I feel for Bindu, but I'm glad that it's over, that Ying Yue has succeeded, and therefore won't be eliminated.

Warwick claps his hands elatedly. "Clearly, my story has made you hungry for the truth," he says. "There are six of you left. Tomorrow, when the moon glows orange, you will undergo the final round of fights before the Grand Finale. I suggest you return to your quarters and rest your bodies, minds, and eyes . . . because tomorrow, the rules may change. In true Circo fashion, we always like to save the best spectacle for last."

"You're animals," Zoe snarls through clenched teeth, unable to hold back any longer.

"Are we?" A dark flame flickers behind his eyes. "Or is that another human lie?"

"You're savages," she says, without a trace of caution.

"And so are *humans*." Warwick sizzles like oil in a frying pan. His breezy demeanor is gone and his voice raises to a frightening growl. "We speak your languages. We have been in contact with your kind for years. Long before your government "discovered" us. They depict us as wild beasts, and you drink up the lie. Because the more you fear us, the less guilty you feel about burning the forests *we* grow, building your farms, and wearing our claws as trophies.

"Let me tell you something, *human*," he says, and that word has never sounded as insulting as it does now. "I hope it will enlighten your ignorant mind: we only began to capture you for the Blood Race out of vengeance for your ruthless acts. You think our intelligence is inferior to yours? We have magic that far surpasses your science. We are not predators, but the only hope the planet has. Stop gorging yourselves on the hatred your leaders serve you on a platter. *Open your eyes.*

"Klujns are not *cannibals*," thunders Warwick. "We do not eat our own, and we do not eat humans. We eat plants. But most of the time"—a significant pause—"we lunasynthesize."

There's quiet around the table as the king delivers his final words. I shiver in a way that only something true can make you feel, like those dreams I've been having.

"We feed on *moonlight*."

34

After brushing our teeth with the minty charcoal toothpaste and getting changed into pajamas, we leave Ying Yue alone in the sleeping tent—meditating in her usual corner—and go sit by the fire. We should be in bed, getting as much rest as we can, but none of us can sleep after the feast. Still digesting the king's words. My mind whirs with the new information.

Zoe rocks on her tire swing, a little distance away, where she's been ever since we returned. Elizabeth vapes, pacing frenetically. Wendy and I share a log again, curled under the same blanket. Behind me, Willa combs my hair with a nurturing hand, and I enjoy the feeling of her fingers on my scalp. It's my turn for a braid.

The silence feels weighted, but at the same time I savor the feeling of being part of something, no longer on the outside, looking in.

Finally, it's Wendy who speaks. "Catrina Sherman went in and out of Klujn stands for years," she begins. "That's how she got all the material for her books."

"If I hear Sherman's name one more time, I'm going to gouge your eyes out," spits Elizabeth.

"Well, good luck getting to the third one!" Wendy bites back. After her triumphs with the cave challenge, the fight, and the feast, she holds herself with newfound confidence. "We only ever hear about Quest,

259

Logic, and Frost, who wrote about Klujns from the outside looking in. But when Sherman was younger, before the AK era—before it became illegal for women to be in the wild—there were so many great female explorers. Like Sherman's friends: Shirley, Faryn, April, and DK! Sherman wrote about Klujns like someone who knew them. She forged relationships with them, relationships based on mutual trust."

"Until the day they captured her and ate her for lunch," Elizabeth retorts.

"They're as intrigued by us as we are by them. They know more about our planet than we do."

"What's your point?"

"My point," says Wendy, thinking out loud, "is that if Klujns really are these fierce, merciless beasts . . . why didn't they kill Sherman right away? Why let her get close at all? What if . . ." Her eyes gleam, like one of the female explorers she mentioned, sailing up uncharted rivers. "What if the king was right? What if Klujns *don't* eat humans? What if all they really do eat are plants and moonlight?"

Elizabeth sucks on her vape. "Moonlight," she scoffs. "Right."

"Maybe Sherman knew," Wendy goes on. "Maybe she wrote about lunasynthesis in her earlier books, and *that's* why they were all burned. Not because they were lies . . . but because they were true."

Elizabeth bursts out laughing. "First of all, that's absurd. Second of all, we all know that Klujns are vicious, hu—"

"—human-eating beasts," finishes Wendy. "I know, I went to all my Klujnology lectures, too. I read the textbooks written by the same three men. Who, by the way, were employed by Grouse's father. But something doesn't add up."

Willa finishes my braid and sits on my other side.

"Wendy's right," I say, thinking of the book George lent me—one of Sherman's original, illegal works. Black cover, gold-edged pages. I wish I could remember something specific about its contents, but all that comes back are abstract shapes—potions and rituals and dances. Something beautiful in the way they were depicted, not the sensationalized monsters we see on television with sharpened teeth. I dig deep, but I can't recall anything in there about eating humans. *Why would they?* I think, remembering the night General Santos came over. *We probably taste disgusting.*

"I'm beginning to think we only got half the story," I say.

"Have you guys seen a Klujn eating a human since we got here?" asks Wendy.

"I saw Klujns cooking these meaty skewers on the grill," Elizabeth says.

"They could have been plants," Wendy answers.

"When we got to the stand, the little Klujn asked for a bonus," Willa chimes in. "And when he said it, he was looking right at me."

"He never called us *food*," I tell her. "He probably just wanted a toy to play with."

"Ava's right," Wendy says. "I mean, I don't necessarily think they want to eat us, but that doesn't mean they want to come to our birthday party."

"Why would the government lie about something this big?" Willa asks.

"To invoke fear," I say. "They want us to fear Klujns so we're not tempted to go beyond the fences." Daciana's words echo. *The fences weren't made to keep us out. They were made to keep you in.* "Humans have created an image of Klujns as the perfect predator, but it isn't real."

"Why go through all that trouble?" Willa asks.

"As a distraction."

"A distraction from what?" she wants to know.

Another memory, this time of José and his impassioned lectures. "Because God didn't destroy the planet," I say. "Humans did."

There is silence as it sinks in.

"Klujns are the perfect scapegoat," says Wendy. "Think about it. Humans can make up whatever lies they want and no one can ever prove them wrong. It's all one big spooky story to cover up what Hunters are really doing out here."

"Which is?" Elizabeth demands.

"Klujns are trying to reforest the land," I say, feeling as impassioned as José. "But humans are Hunting them. Burning down their new forests to build Loudhouses. It's a quick fix."

"If Klujns really do eat plants, and we eat kanum," Willa starts, "that makes *us* the cannibals." Her forehead sinks into her hands. "That is so messed up."

"We're not cannibals," says Elizabeth. "We'd only be cannibals if we ate the same species as us, and Klujns are not the same species. Klujns are animals. Kanum is meat. That's it."

"Animals don't talk," Wendy says. "And don't give me that spiel about dolphins."

"You think it's right? To eat kanum, after being here?" I ask Elizabeth.

"If it's not, then why is it legal?"

"Because it's easier for humans to Hunt them than to try to understand them, let alone work with them," I shoot back.

"It doesn't make the Blood Race okay," Willa says, her face knotted with conflicting ideas.

"I'm not saying that I agree with the king and his idea of fun," I say. "But if I were trying to do my work, trying to reforest the Territory, and someone kept destroying my progress, my home, *eating my people*—I can understand the desire for revenge."

I think about the last few days. Despite everything, we've been treated with a kind of respect. We've been bathed, clothed, and fed; kept warm and comfortable and out of the elements. We've been given the courtesy of knowing what was going on, even though they didn't owe it to us. We're not caged. And even though I don't entirely understand—or agree with—every aspect of Klujn culture and the king's sadistic ways, it's not that different from many of the things humans do for sport or entertainment.

How different is the Blood Race from a Coliséa?

Daciana said some stands aren't violent at all; that they are intrigued by humans and welcome them in. The relationships Klujns had with the French and Indigenous people who were here before, in the century before the AK era. Maybe some Klujns are evil, but aren't some humans?

"Believe what you want, but they're still animals to me," Elizabeth says.

"What's your problem?" I snap. "Have you *seen* nothing? *Felt* nothing since you got here?" I don't mention my dreams, but I know that Wendy—and possibly Willa—understands my implication.

"I *saw* a wild beast in a cave that tried to eat me alive," she answers. "And a psychotic king who forced us into cannibalism. When I get out of here, that's exactly what I'm going to tell the media." Has Elizabeth truly felt nothing since we arrived, or is she lying? She thinks it's something to be proud of, this resistance to having her beliefs changed. But is it strength, or is it ignorance? It's a hard thing to admit you've been wrong about something your entire life. Easier to keep pretending you're right.

"There's something else," I say quietly. I know I should be staying out of the spotlight after the failed escape attempt that cost Bindu her life, but I can't keep it to myself. "What if the king wasn't lying when he said that if we win, we might be free to leave?"

"Then where are all the humans who were set free?" Elizabeth asks.

I repeat what Warwick said at the Ceremony of Fire: "That's a question for humans."

"What if Sherman wasn't killed by Klujns?" Wendy says. "What if she knew too much, and the government wanted to silence her? That much knowledge is dangerous."

A flash of my mother in her black leathery cloak, running from the Hunter.

I shiver.

I want to tell the others, but it's too risky, too nascent a thing to vocalize, especially when so much of it relies on instinct.

Was my mother here? Was she Hunted for what she'd learned?

"It's official. You guys have been possessed," says Elizabeth. "You better hope the DSO never gets wind of this conversation. Straight to the Sweatbox or the Nailroom."

"Even if there's a chance we can be set free," says Willa, looking between Wendy and me, "only three of us can survive the Blood Race. No matter what, at least half of us are going to die tomorrow."

And on that grim note, the conversation comes to an end.

"I need to go to the toilet-hole. That time of the month is starting," Wendy says. "It's funny—I've never been regular before."

"That's because you synched to a dead girl," Elizabeth mutters.

"I'll come with you," Willa tells Wendy, keen for a distraction.

After the sisters leave, I go over to Zoe. She sits in her tire swing, raking her feet in the soil, the red-and-black cube in her hands. Five sides are complete, and she's working on the sixth. I thread my legs through the other swing and we rock for a moment in silence.

I try to think of something to say, but Zoe beats me to it.

"I didn't think it would be this hard," she says without looking up. An odd remark.

"No one thought it would be this hard. None of us got captured on purpose," I say.

Zoe stops swinging. "Do you miss your home?" she asks.

"I'm not sure I have one anymore."

"That's a shame." She fiddles with the cube, rotating the black and red squares, incredibly close to solving it. "It's a Klujn toy," she explains. "My father brought it home from one of his raids. There's a secret compartment inside. He likes to hide little surprises in there. You need all the stripes to align for it to open," she says. "When I was younger, I used to be fascinated by the Klujn artifacts he'd bring home. But then I realized there's nothing fascinating about Klujns. They're vile creatures who want to see us suffer."

"Not all Klujns are bad," I offer.

She still refuses to look at me but her expression shows dismay. "Whose side are you on?"

"I think this is more complicated than sides. I think sides might be the problem."

Zoe's eyes finally meet mine, for the first time since the crossing in the Deeper Woods. The look in them is unnerving, as though she's drilling into me, mining for crystals or coal. "You remembered the orphanage, didn't you?"

I nod slowly. "You, too?"

"The moment we arrived. That's why I went to sit with the others.

Not that I wanted to be near anybody, but it was better than being close to you." I look at her, wounded by her words. In response, she says, "We sort of know each other, and that just makes things harder."

"It might make things harder," I say, still recovering from what she said. "But I wouldn't have survived without Wendy and the others." *Rory*, I want to say, to see how she would react to the name, but this is the longest conversation we've ever had and I don't want it to end prematurely.

"I guess I was scared of seeming weak," says Zoe. "When everyone else seemed strong."

"It's just a front," I tell Zoe. "Everyone's terrified. If I had to pick, I'd say that Elizabeth is probably the most frightened of us all."

Zoe cracks a smile. It feels like a colossal achievement, not that I was trying. "Oh, yeah? Why's that?"

"Because that kind of confidence isn't real. It's protective armor." I pause. "I'm starting to wonder if real strength isn't physical, but something else—something to do with emotions, or vulnerability. Anyone can act strong, but it takes a lot of courage to show the world who you are, and to be honest with yourself about who that is."

Zoe takes in my words. "My father trained me to be strong," she finally says. "Elizabeth's definition of the word. He taught me to Hunt, even though I wasn't allowed to, because—well, you know. But he believes in me, and I want to make him proud."

"I'm sure he is proud," I say, remembering that this is, of course, General Santos she's talking about. That unsettling question returns: How is it possible that we were both caught on the same night?

Zoe twists her cube one more time, and all six stripy sides align. She presses a square in the center and the cube clicks open like a jack-in-the-box. But before I can glimpse what her father hid in the secret compartment, Zoe snaps it shut, almost like she already knows what's in there.

"Did you know that Ying Yue's adopted?" she says. I shake my head. "I overheard her telling the boy."

The boy. So that's all she thinks of Rory.

"Two of the silver girls were adopted, too. What are the chances, huh?" Zoe says. "Five out of fourteen."

"That *is* strange," I remark. "I guess there are a lot of abandoned kids out there." I don't know where Zoe is going with this. Her eyes continue to search mine, and I feel more and more uncomfortable.

"You don't know, do you?" she finally asks.

"Know what?"

"I guess your father wasn't as honest with you as mine was."

"Honest about what?" I ask Zoe. She looks at the rose gold chain around my neck.

Then she says something surprising: "It's not just a whistle."

"Then what is it?" I want to know.

"It's not my job to tell you." With that, Zoe hops off the swing and disappears into the sleeping tent.

I pull out the pendant and look at it. There's the minuscule airhole, but nothing else stands out. Zoe's statement nags at me. What am I not seeing?

"Hey, check it out!" It takes me a moment to find Wendy near the mud-wall toilet, close to the front gate. She and Willa are looking through the fence, at something beyond our quarters, and I join them. There's a rush of movement in the distance—a river of costumed bodies cascading down the hillside. Excited shouts and laughter drift over to where we are.

"It's the young Klujns," Wendy says, awestruck. "They're leaving for their Blood Race in the wild."

Among the group, I see her—Warwick's daughter. She looks even more regal in her black costume and makeup, her small claws dipped in black, a sun crown on her head, like the one in the Coliséa. Tucked in her belt is an elegant black machete, maybe obsidian. She looks so free as she runs and laughs with her friends. She doesn't have a backpack, and her spotted wolf is not there.

I don't know where it comes from, this pang of jealousy. At her popularity, her confidence, her sense of belonging. This great adventure that lies waiting. This Race. *Make it back to the stand before the Ice Moon, and choose your profession and your mate.* A winter filled with parties and celebrations.

The young Klujns reach the bottom of the mountain and that invisible barrier. Warwick's daughter is first. She reaches out her black-tipped claws, finds the invisible curtain, and shoots out a dazzle of red sparks. The protective curtain parts and she passes through, followed by her friends—or *competitors*. When the last teenage Klujn has passed through, the red light dissipates and the barrier is closed again. Their excited laughter echoes as they disappear into the dark valley.

Their lives are just beginning, but ours may soon be over.

35

José wears a little pin on his bloodied apron—a black circle with a gold symbol I don't recognize. He talks about his homeland as we chop wild dandelions to make a salad, the stories so vivid I can almost smell the salt air. When I ask for more, he tells me that my curiosity will only end up getting me into trouble. Or, worse, heartbroken.

"The world isn't what it was," he says with a shake of the head. After his island disappeared underwater, he fled to the mainland; his biggest regret is having gone north, not south. He was one of the last ones to arrive before Pepito Silver closed the borders, exiled the desperate climate refugees, and turned his ambition to Canada, with its abundant lakes and electricity and those timber factories called forests.

Those who refused to give up their land or culture were killed. Those who complied were forced into Military training, serving the government that had slaughtered their families. He used natural disasters as a way of making millions of people disappear. Other countries tried to stop the massacre with sanctions, but Silver's Military was unmatched.

And so the North American Territory came to be.

Silver's popularity saw a significant drop in subsequent years. Rebel groups began to sprout, and when he died, Atoll Grouse took over. He used his mother's maiden name as a way of differentiating himself from his father. Grouse had the task of rebuilding the Territory in resources, population, and morale.

After his inauguration, rebel groups were quickly eliminated. Grouse established the DSO, the Department of Societal Order, whose goal was to regain control of its citizens by imprisoning, torturing, or killing anyone who spoke out. When rebels found other ways to spread their messages—through books and music and art—Grouse had it all burned. Free speech would cost a person their life.

And then Klujns were "discovered," and the narrative of fear began. Grouse ordained the erection of the fences—and women, who had been at the heart of the rebel movement, were allowed nowhere near them. "It was all smoke and mirrors," says José. "A way to make people forget about that family's crimes against humanity and nature. And they did. Most of them. Because Grouse is a genius. A powerful, sadistic, manipulative genius."

I realize that José is crying. "Why are you sad?" I ask.

"Because we destroyed it all. The natural world. The animals. And the few good souls who tried to protect it. All because of our greed. Our stomachs. We ate the world."

I want to know more, but José won't tell me. "Please," I beg. "I'm almost ten. I can handle it." Eventually, he admits defeat, and I sport a smile.

"There are two kinds of people in the world, aside from you, princesa.*" He opens an enormous can of Fisherman's Mix, and the room reeks of salt and decay. "The evil and the ignorant. Evil, like our leader and his herd of Military and Hunter sheep. And the ignorant, like every other soul on this godforsaken Territory. Because willful ignorance is its own form of evil."*

"I thought Grouse was supposed to be good."

"Good?" José fills a huge pot with the reeking stew. "If that's what you want to call it. We had brilliant agriculturalists and activists with long-term plans for wildlife protection and soil rejuvenation and climate change, but they all ended up with bullets in their heads. Grouse and the general . . . they are Military men trying to combat an environmental problem, a humanitarian problem, with weapons.

"In my lifetime, I have watched the complete collapse of the natural world. Human activity has pushed almost every creature into extinction—for what? Food? The success of our species? What is victorious about being the only survivors in a dead world?"

I don't know if the question has an answer.

He stirs the thick soup, then lowers the heat after it starts to boil before continuing, "Forests keep our weather systems stable—they carry moisture from the coasts to the deserts."

"So when you cut down a forest," I put in, "that would mean that the moisture can't travel."

"Exactly," he says. "You end up getting a lot of rain in one place—and none in another. Floods and droughts. And trees keep carbon in the ground, so when you cut them, it's released into the air. It raises the earth's temperature—the oceans warm, the coral is bleached, and the sea life dies. It's one big vicious cycle. But humans couldn't take responsibility for their crimes. They looked out their windows and complained about the weather. Called it a 'War against God,' or Mother Nature. But it wasn't a war against God. It was a war of total human ignorance and inaction.

"Did you know," he continues, "that before the Amazon was a desert, it was a rainforest?"

"Really?"

José nods. "With slugs the size of your hands and butterflies the size of your head. Howler monkeys, jaguars, birds, snakes of all colors . . ."

It sounds too good to be true. I stare at the chef in wide-eyed fascination, wanting to know more.

"Now the Boreal's the only thing we have left, and Grouse is coming for it."

My gaze falls to the ground as I feel my hope for the future fading, like the moon fades with every passing night. Like a sunflower that managed to grow through concrete, only to be squished back down.

José pats me on the shoulder. "I'm sorry," he says. "I shouldn't have said all that. But you asked for a story, and this is the most important story of our time."

"What about another story?" I ask. "A happy one? Like . . . how you became a chef."

"Maybe tomorrow."

We go back to our silent chopping and grating and stirring. Flies buzz around, and I wave them away.

A blue fly lands on the counter in front of José. He grabs the swatter that's always at hand and brings it down hard. Wham! The table shudders. When he lifts the swatter, there is no blood, no twitching wings or legs. Just a tangle of wires and a tiny blue light where a heart should be.

I look at it curiously, but before I can ask any questions, José says, "I'm almost finished here. Why don't you go play with your friends?" His tone is suddenly severe, and I see that the contempt on his face has been replaced by something I can't name.

I fold up my little apron, wash my hands, and politely oblige, not wanting José to know that he is the only friend I have.

* * *

The next morning, I am awoken by a commotion. Kids are running out of the dormitory, calling to each other, whispering urgently.

I follow them to the other side of the courtyard, past the little fence between the kitchen and the river. People are already there, Coll and Zoe among them, hovering like wasps around a hive. Their bodies form a membrane that blocks the river from sight.

I nudge my way through to the front and that's when I see him. José. He lies facedown in a rock pool, a wet tea towel in his hand. There's a large round hole in the back of his head. One kid says he saw a silver van drive away at sunup. Another says she saw three letters painted on the side.

I force myself to step closer. José's head is tilted to the side, his mouth open and filled with water, his eyes already clouded into a milky quartz. The bullet's exit wound is located directly between them. Frigid water stings my bare feet, and I realize I'm standing in the river. Shock slows my thoughts, cushions the blow, makes me feel like I'm not in my body anymore, no longer Ava. I lean down and peer into my friend's eyes.

Where have all his stories gone? *I wonder.* And who will tell them now?

36

I wake up screaming. Wendy leans over me, pinning my arms to the bed. They're badly scratched, almost bleeding. The braid Willa gave me has come undone, my short curls all around me.

"Shh, Ava, you're okay. It was just a bad dream."

The room takes shape—her worried face, Willa close by. The other three watching from their beds. When Wendy feels it's safe to let go, she does. The nightmare evaporates, but the truth of it remains. *José was killed for speaking his mind. For telling a story to a nine-year-old child.*

"I can stay, if you want," Wendy says. I nod. She smiles and lies down next to me.

On our backs, we look up at the ceiling. Her shoulder presses into mine, and the fact that she doesn't pull away at the touch is heartening. She smells like an apple tree, sweet and woody. "What was that about?" she asks. "If you don't mind sharing."

"A memory," I answer. "Not a nice one."

"I've been having some of those as well. Almost makes this place feel like the dream." Wendy smiles ironically, but she looks forlorn.

"Are *you* okay?" I ask.

"Never better," she says with forced lightness. Then she switches gears, deciding to release whatever she's been keeping in. "My dad is Métis," she starts. "Half-Indigenous, half-French. He comes from a community near Good Earth. I always thought he moved to Justice Falls after he met my mom"—she draws a deep breath—"but I've been seeing things in my dreams. Hunters and Military . . . coming onto his family's land, lining them up, tying their hands . . . killing almost all of them."

Wendy collects herself, then continues. "Sherman says that Klujns like to anglicize their names, because to them it's exotic. Whereas humans like simple, old names because it makes them sound *less* exotic. I never realized the significance of a name. *Wendy*. A name to make me just like everybody else. A name that says nothing about who I am, who my father was, and the language he lost. The one I've been remembering in my sleep.

"I wish my dad had told me who he was," Wendy says sadly. "Who I could have been. But I understand why he lied. The truth is dangerous. There are so many kids back home who look like me, who have no idea where they come from. It's all one bland culture. It's . . . unnatural."

No one has ever trusted me, confided in me, before. But now Wendy is.

"The night I was caught," she continues, "I was so frustrated, seeing all the boys leave for Hunter's Camp. *Again.* And there was my dad, preparing to take me and the other Scouts on our stupid little mission in the acreage behind the school to earn our 'Independence' Badges. I was so angry that I found a part of the fence that was broken and went out into the forest. I was ready to die that night if it meant being free for just one second.

"Dad realized I was gone and sent Willa to look for me," she continues. "Then we got caught . . . and the rest is history. Truth is," she muses, "these last few days—I don't feel trapped anymore. Funny, isn't it? I'm not even scared. If it's my destiny to die tomorrow, then at least I'll die having lived something."

She shakes her head. "*Wendy*," she repeats. "It feels so arbitrary. It's a cute name for someone else, but it's not me."

"I didn't know," I say. "About any of that. The day I met you, you seemed happy. Almost *too* happy."

"I guess we're all good at pretending. That's the thing about this place. It's so intense. *In-tents*, get it?" Wendy jokes, and I have to crack a smile at her ill-timed humor. "It's stripping away all our layers," she says, more serious now. "You and me, we barely know each other, and I feel closer to you than anyone, except maybe Willa, but that's different—we're sisters. But you know what I realized?" She turns her head and our eyes meet. "True friendship has nothing to do with knowing everything about a person, like their favorite ice cream flavor or sideshow game or what subjects they're good at. It's about *being there*, knowing that another person has your back not only when things are good, but—more importantly—when they're bad. And you have."

Something releases in my chest—a flood of warmth and appreciation for my friend. "So have you," I tell Wendy. Then I add, "Coconut. That's my favorite flavor."

Wendy smiles. "Mine's fruit punch."

For some reason, that doesn't surprise me at all.

* * *

The horn wakes me. It feels like mere minutes since I closed my eyes.

The tent is unusually chilly. I look for my usual ray of light but don't find it. Groping for the slit, I see that outside, the afternoon sky is a melancholy gray, as if the weather echoes my mood. Or maybe it's the other way around. They mirror each other, like ocean and sky.

We are taken to eat, but my stomach won't settle. My dream—it's unfair that I should remember José, Wolf, and my mother, only to be reminded that they're all gone. Maybe forgetting is a good thing, after all, like a warm blanket keeping out the saw-toothed cold.

Since there are only six of us left, we share a table. The others nibble on fruits and freshly baked bread packed with nuts and apricots, still warm from the fire it was cooked on. None of us are very hungry, or perhaps our appetites have shrunken. There are no more teams or sides, which makes the prospect of tonight's fights that much more daunting.

After we eat, we are taken to Daciana's quarters so we can put on makeup and change into our costumes. Black obsidian. Tree agate. Garnet. Pyrite. Moonstone. Sunstone. By the end, there will be only three of us marching into the arena at the top of the stand to face the final challenge, and whatever lies waiting.

Diablo and Palo lead us to the same amphitheater as yesterday. I feel like a sleepwalker. My eyelids keep closing, like a pair of broken shutters. There's a cold humidity in the air, the kind of chill that makes you want to crawl back into bed—but you couldn't pay me to go back to that nightmare.

The outdoor theater isn't packed this time. There are a few empty seats, and the hubbub is less lively than yesterday's rowdy stadium vibe. Again, we sit in the dugout, facing the stage and the orange glow of lanterns. Even Warwick looks tired as he stands to address the crowd.

"Welcome back," he says. The seat that had been occupied by his daughter is now empty. Daciana is not there, and neither is Glory.

"When our young Klujns enter the wild, as they did last night, they must adapt to life without four walls. Dangers are ever-present, and emotions become heightened. Here, a Klujn's nature begins to emerge. As they unearth the truths of the world and their life's purpose, they discover who they are: strong or weak, honest or deceitful, brave or cowardly." He addresses the six of us. "As you were forewarned, the rules have changed for this challenge." We glance nervously at one another. "In this round," says the king, "it is the performer who must decide whom she wishes to face."

We have to choose our opponent? I must have misheard. But Warwick's face tells me that he isn't joking. Beside me, Wendy is chalk-pale. The other girls are equally dismayed. Going second to last has never been more of a disadvantage. Ying Yue will pick the girl she deems the weakest—is that Wendy or Willa or me? Then Zoe will choose next. Willa—if she wasn't already picked—will take whoever's left. Elizabeth, Wendy and I are helpless to our fate.

"These seats await our victors." Warwick gestures to three empty seats to his right. "Today's winners will move to their own quarters in the upper part of the stand, where they will be well taken care of in the lead-up to tomorrow night's finale. A win today means you are that much closer to freedom."

I look at those empty seats and what they represent: three lives, and three lifeless bodies tossed to the dogs. "We've got this," I tell Wendy, but my encouragement rings false. It's us against who—our comrades?

"Now they all know I'm good at throwing," she replies. She holds up her trembling hands and spreads her fingers. "These hands . . . they don't know how to fight. And they don't know how to kill."

Palo stands before Ying Yue. Asks her for a name. She keeps her eyes on the ground as she deliberates.

Clears her throat and says: "Zoe."

Zoe? It's the last person I would have expected. Who would want to face her after the heartless way she killed Rory?

Wendy's voice is in my ear. "I can't believe it. She didn't pick me. Why didn't she pick me?"

But then a thought strikes: maybe Ying Yue didn't pick the easiest, but instead chose the strongest, the most dangerous, making it the closest to a fair fight. Perhaps it's the only way she could live with herself, should she survive.

Zoe's eyes give little away. If we had been given more time, there's so much I could have asked her—but no, we'd had plenty of time. She just never let me get close.

Diablo leads her past me, and I'm not sure what to say, if anything, but it's Zoe who speaks. Her voice is faint but determined as she says, "If you see my father, tell him I held on until the end." And then she is gone.

A few minutes pass as the girls choose their weapons. Then the first horn sounds. Ying Yue wields an ax more impressive than yesterday's. Zoe clutches the same little Hunter's knife.

After the second horn, you can immediately tell that something has changed. Today, there is no kneeling, begging for mercy. Today, the girls fight like warriors. Or, at the very least, like girls who are desperate for that seat by Warwick's side, even if they have to kill for it.

The fight seems to stretch on for hours. Where Ying Yue is strong, Zoe is fast. She tries to tire her opponent, but Ying Yue stays focused, moving deliberately, dodging easily, and reserving her energy. They twist around each other in a whorl of black and green. Sharp blades, slicing through the air. A few close calls. It's only a matter of time before—

Thunk.

Zoe freezes, facing us. A thin red line becomes visible, running horizontally across her neck. The blade of Ying Yue's ax has sliced right through it.

Her expression is panicked, but then that panic recedes and is replaced by something else. Calm. Relief.

Ying Yue pulls the ax back, and Zoe's head wobbles and falls, rolls a few times, then settles faceup. Her dead eyes stare at the orange moon while her body stands there for a moment, headless, then sways and crumples.

A single cry escapes me. *Zoe is dead.* My partner in the Deeper Woods. The general's daughter. Gone, when moments ago she was here, alive, breathing. Soon her body will be picked at by the dogs. In a few hours, only the bones will be left.

I didn't like her, but I knew her.

The final horn sounds. Ying Yue tosses down her ax and storms offstage. Palo escorts her into the stands and she takes her seat by Warwick's side, not looking at him.

The crowd chants, "*Să-mâ! Să-mâ! Să-mâ!*"

The Seed.

There are four of us left. I try not to think about who my opponent will be, but it's impossible. I don't want to fight Wendy, who befriended me without knowing a single thing about me and who I have watched flourish. I don't want to fight Willa. Cool, kind, nurturing Willa, who saw Bindu through her death. I don't want to fight Elizabeth, either. Elizabeth who, for some unknown reason, has been waiting to sink her claws into me from day one.

The person Willa chooses will determine everything. If it's Elizabeth, then I have to fight Wendy. But Elizabeth is unstable, tapping her leg, chewing her nails, almost vibrating. It makes the most sense for Willa to choose me. Elizabeth will be up against Wendy, but I may not be alive to see that happen.

Willa's spine curls with the weight of the decision she must make. Four girls. Two fights. And only two seats left.

The red-eyed guard steps in front of her. "Make your decision."

Wrung out and devastated, Willa looks like her heart of glass is shattering into a hundred pieces. She looks up at the guard and says a name that shocks us all.

"I pick Wendy."

37

As far as betrayals go, this one gets first prize. I thought that Circo had brought her closer to Wendy. Clearly, Willa had an agenda all along.

Now she has chosen the girl she deemed the weakest competitor—her own sister. Warwick was right about deceit. You think you know someone, only to realize you don't know them at all. *Which leaves Elizabeth and me*, I realize.

"I'm sorry," Willa says, as Palo takes her through the dark doorway and into the weapons room. Wendy refuses to acknowledge her. She rises to her feet defeatedly.

"Guess I'll see you around," she mumbles.

"Wendy—" I take hold of her hand, but it slips out of mine too quickly. "Thank you."

Two words, with a world of meaning packed into them. They aren't adequate for what she has meant to me, for what her absence in my life will mean. It's like when I pushed Wolf away, and the six years of solitude that followed.

One person's absence can fill a room more than a hundred strangers.

We share one last look. "Likewise," she replies. One word. I hope it stands for as much as mine did.

I can't watch this. I can't watch them fight.

"Looks like it's just you and me," says Elizabeth, and it's clear that she can't wait for our fight to start. But I know that her outward strength hides something else. Something broken and boiling inside. A rejected child, like Coll with the diamond shadows on his face.

All too quickly, the first horn sounds and the sisters are onstage. Red and orange, like a bleeding sunrise. Willa holds a black object that could be the Klujn equivalent of a flashlight. Wendy carries no weapon.

Willa doesn't look like an Executioner, here to deliver her sister's death sentence. She is sobbing. "I'm so sorry, Wendy! I didn't know what to do. I panicked." Wendy is uncharacteristically speechless. The second horn sounds. "Please, Wendy, look at me."

Wendy raises her eyes. Her face is wounded. Gutted. Betrayed.

"So how are you going to do it?" she asks, her voice dripping in sarcasm. "Are you going to stab me, or club me to death with that thing, or make me beg for mercy? Which one is it?"

"What?" A stunned laugh escapes Willa's lips. "No." She shakes her head and laughs incredulously through her tears. "No, Wendy, that's not what this is. I had to make sure you'd be okay, and this was the only way." Now Wendy is confused. "I couldn't let you go up against them. You're strong—I can't believe how strong!—but so are they. I had to make sure you would get that chance of escape, and get home, and see our parents again, and this was the only way." Willa's voice shakes. "Mom and Dad . . . they don't deserve to lose us both. They deserve to know what happened."

Wendy stares at her sister, still befuddled, not processing a word she says.

"I'm sorry," Willa cries. "I'm sorry I couldn't protect you the night we got caught. We wasted our whole lives hating each other, but this week—these past few days—I'm so glad we had them, Wendy. That I got to know you, and see how brave and beautiful you are. There's a warrior inside you. Once she finds her cause, she'll be unstoppable."

Willa presses a button on the side of the black weapon and a green flame ignites—an electric current. I realize what Willa's doing. Why she chose Wendy. *She's not betraying her. She's saving her life.*

"No," Wendy says, catching on. "Willa—don't!"

"It's okay," Willa smiles through her tears like she did when she held a dying Bindu; staying calm and strong to protect the sister she loves. "I'm going to be okay. Now I want you to promise me that you'll be okay as well. That you'll be strong, and that you won't waste your life." She pauses. "I love you, sis."

Wendy screams and charges toward her, but it's too late—

Willa turns the weapon on herself, and the current shoots through her body. She lurches into the air, like a rebellious marionette—

Up, up, up. Then down, down, down.

With an angry slurping sound, the life is ripped from her. By the time Willa falls back to the ground, she's dead. Wendy arrives at her side, seconds too late.

"Don't touch her!" I yell. Wendy hears me and stops mere inches away, as her sister's body continues to pulse with green rivulets of electricity. Her clothes are scorched, and a bit of smoke escapes her lips.

Wendy drops to her knees, her entire body rocked by grief. The horn sounds. Her wails are louder than the tumult of the crowd. She lies down as close as she can to Willa without touching her.

"Thank you for following me into the forest," she weeps. "I promise you, I won't waste my life." When Willa's body finally stops pulsing with electric current, Wendy breaks the invisible barrier and strokes her sister's cheek. "Goodbye." She gives Willa a farewell kiss. "I'll see you among the stars."

I realize that I am crying, too. Elizabeth looks stoic. I know she must be affected, how could she not be? When Wendy takes a seat next to Ying Yue, I see the inferno that blazes in her eyes. A deep hatred— or a fierce resolve.

She is not the same Wendy I met in the Deeper Woods.

38

It's already time for the final fight, and I'm not ready. "Well, this was fun," Elizabeth says as she follows her guard through the left-hand door. Her composure seems inhuman.

Diablo leads me into the weapons room. I'm grateful for the dark, quiet space, even though I don't know the first thing about weapons. I've never held a crossbow or a sword. Last time I got lucky with the ring, if you could call that luck. What will Elizabeth choose? A double-bladed ax like Ying Yue, or a torch that produces a fatal spark like Willa? Surely something flashy and cruel, to make my death as spectacular as possible.

The table of shiny weapons is there, with its spiked clubs and crystal knives.

For the first time, I realize that there are no guns.

"Guns are a coward's weapon," Diablo answers, and I realize I've spoken aloud.

My eyes settle on a weapon. It's similar to the machete that Warwick's daughter was carrying; bigger than a dagger, smaller than a sword. I recognize the whitish-blue crystal of the blade—it's moonstone. The machete is light in my hand, easy to maneuver. Practical, and not too showy.

Despite all this, it still doesn't feel right, but it's the best I can find.

I reach the doorway and Diablo eyes my choice. I search his face for a clue; something to assuage my doubt, but there is nothing. "No words of wisdom today?" I ask.

"Good luck."

"I thought your kind don't believe in luck." The guard's eyes flicker as the horn sounds. My right hand closes around the weapon's hilt. *Get yourself together.* Elizabeth will smell my fear. She probably already has.

I step out.

The arena is dark, bathed in an orange glow from the lanterns and the moon. I feel the crowd's attention on me. Elizabeth emerges from the other side of the stage—and, like yesterday, she is unarmed. The absence of a visible weapon fills me with dread. *What is she hiding?*

"Nice machete," she sniggers. It's an eerie, unnerving sort of snigger, too self-assured for my liking.

I feel stupid. Self-conscious. The weapon is awkward in my hand. I should have chosen something else, but what? I don't know how to use anything other than my hands!

"You want to make this a fair fight?" she asks.

"How?"

"Hand to hand," Elizabeth says. "No weapons. So the most *deserving* person wins."

"That's easy for you to say. You're not armed."

"As you wish. But, judging by the look on your face, you don't have a clue how to use that thing."

She's right, I don't, but I hardly thought it was tattooed on my forehead.

"No weapons," Elizabeth says again. "No cheap tricks."

"Let me get this straight," I say. "You make me drop my weapon and then you attack me with whatever's hidden in your costume?"

"I don't have anything to hide," Elizabeth says, turning out her pockets. "Do you?"

I don't trust her. Never have. Yet the machete feels unnatural in my damp palm. If Elizabeth manages to wrangle it out of my hand—which is likely—she'll plunge it straight into me.

Maybe she's right. Maybe a fair fight is better.

I decide to follow my instinct. Abandon common sense. So I toss the weapon into the empty dugout. On the first tier of seats I catch Wendy's eyes. She looks at me, tear-stained. Smudged makeup. *What are you doing?* she mouths. I ignore her. Turn back to face Elizabeth.

"Good," my opponent says with a smile. "Now it's fair."

She moves forward, an animal fixed on its prey. Her hands ball into fists. Her arms are thick and strong, her biceps well-defined, more muscular than I ever noticed—*How did I not notice?*

Her eyes are hungry. She steps into the lantern light, and I see that they're red. Not the colored irises of the Klujns, but bloodshot, like a junkie.

"What did you take?" I ask in horror. She smiles a wicked smile. And then it hits me—Elizabeth didn't hide a weapon on her body. She *ingested* it.

The conversation we had during our first meal at Circo returns.

"It's the green herb that dwarf was smoking. You can smoke it, drink it, sniff it. If you take a little bit, it makes you stronger and fiercer. It makes you more Klujn. *"*

Klandestine! There must have been a vial at the end of the weapons table. Those colored potions I thought were poisons.

"How much did you take?" I ask.

She shrugs. "Oh, you know . . . just enough to get a buzz." It all makes sense: her lack of a weapon, her distended muscles. The constant, frantic pacing. Judging by her bloodshot eyes, she's had more than a little—enough to have a serious advantage over me. It'll be like going up against a machine. Flesh against metal. Human against beast. I regret throwing my weapon into the dugout.

"You cheated," I say.

"Did I?" Elizabeth comes closer. "Or did I make things even?"

"What are you talking about?" That familiar frustration flushes behind my cheeks. It travels up to my eyes and down to my fingertips.

"Ever since we got here, I knew there was something off about you," she tells me. "But I couldn't quite put my finger on it. A *feeling*," she sneers, as she continues to edge toward me. She is close now. Too close.

Her breath is in my face, laced with the vestiges of Klandestine's herbal smell. "If there's one thing in this world I can't stand, it's liars. People who pretend to be something they're not."

"I'm not a liar," I say, frustrated at being constantly misunderstood.

"Yes, you are," Elizabeth replies. "And I know what you're hiding." She slaps me with an open palm. The pain shoots up my face. She's trying to provoke me. I take a step back. "*Fight me!*" she yells.

That's exactly what she wants. A fight. A provocation. A reason to attack without feeling bad about it. That's what all bullies want. But the best self-defense is, after all, no fight at all.

Elizabeth shoves me. I stumble but manage to stay upright. She swings her arm, trying to hit me again, but this time I block her wrist. She looks at it, clearly impressed by my speed. This is the show she was waiting for. A fresh piece of evidence for her grand jury. I wrench her arm around, pin her wrist to her shoulder blade, and push. Elizabeth staggers then falls facedown in the dirt. She lies on the ground, rubbing her shoulder, smiling in a sort of maniacal way.

"What I don't understand, Ava, is why you look so normal. Well, normal enough," she amends. I kick at the soil, and it flies into her open mouth. Elizabeth's smile is knocked askew and she gags.

Then, without warning, she swings her legs around in a Tiger Tail sweep and brings me down. I fall on my ass, hard. The soil does little to cushion the blow against my tailbone. Elizabeth lunges and we grapple, fists flying at each other's faces. She manages to get on top of me and pin my arms down with her knees. Then, she launches a fist at my cheekbone, and I duck out of the way. Her knuckles hit the ground instead. *Crack.*

Before I can take a breath, she wraps her other hand around my throat and squeezes. She's strong . . . stronger than I ever imagined. It's not her strength, though, but the strength of the drug in her bloodstream. I look up into her malevolent face, her reddened eyes. Elizabeth's hatred for me bubbles and boils, but why? What did I ever do to her?

"You know what the dead giveaway was?" she continues. "Those red symbols you kept harping on about. The ones you saw in the forest and the Katacombes. The ones that *no one else saw* but you."

Elizabeth whacks me in the ear with her free hand. My eardrum flares like a solar storm. Then she releases my neck and bashes my head from the other side, and that eardrum ruptures. The world is drowned out by an incessant ringing.

I suck in as much air as I can with her weight on me, and scream—a long, guttural scream.

My pain isn't coming from my ears anymore, but from somewhere else, somewhere deep inside me. It is sharp, excruciating, worse than anything I have ever felt before, like an inner fire concentrated in my eyes and hands.

I free a hand from under Elizabeth's knees and see that my fingertips are red and swollen. They throb, the feeling of molten lava pressing at their ends, looking for a hole, an opening, but there is none.

Elizabeth looks frightened and grips my throat again, cutting off my screams. I try to break free but without air, all strength abandons me. Blood rushes to my head, the sound of rivers in my ringing ears.

Elizabeth leans down and whispers, her voice a raspy echo: "You know who else sees colors that humans can't? *Klujns.*"

Shut up. Shut up! Anger vibrates through me like an earthquake. My limbs shake like shifting tectonic plates. I want to wipe the smugness off her face. Send her words back into her throat and back into her mind, back to preexistence.

The hatred I have for the girl on top of me fills every last corner of my body with adrenaline and rage. Letting her win is not an option.

I can't. *I won't.*

Determination races through me like a lit match held to a trail of gasoline.

I find my second wind. Suck in a breath. Pull up my legs and hook them around Elizabeth's neck, then yank her down to the ground. Her ribcage hits the ground with a *crack.* My hands are freed.

I straddle her, pinning her legs down with my own. Grab her wrists in one hand and trap them over her head. My other hand presses down on her chest—in that moment, I notice that my veins are also bulging. But, unlike my opponent, I didn't take anything.

"Looks like shy little orphan girl isn't so shy after all," Elizabeth croaks, undaunted.

"*I'M. NOT. SHY!*" I scream.

In that moment, I want only one thing: to wipe that wretched sneer off her face. So I grab one of her ears and tug. *Rrrrrip*! It comes off in my hand. Blood gushes from the side of her head. *Like turning a doorknob*, Mr. Mogel had said, as he tore the ear from the dummy's silicone head. This time, the black hole of the ear canal isn't ornamental; it's real.

Elizabeth manages to free one of her hands and reaches for my face. I bite down on her finger and—*crrrrack!* It severs in my mouth. Elizabeth grunts in pain. I spit it out, gagging at the taste of her blood. I swing my right fist and punch her in the side of the head. Her cheekbone disintegrates. *There is power in these hands.*

I swing from the other side and my fist meets her temple, leaving a dent in her head.

Side to side I go: *right, left, right, left.*

Unleashing the fury I have inside. Elizabeth begins to plead now, a last-ditch effort to save her life.

"*STOP!*" I roar, and tears stream down my cheeks. But I don't know who I'm talking to.

I'm not swinging at Elizabeth anymore, but at every bully and every enemy—even the less obvious ones like my family, and every lie they ever told me, every truth they ever withheld. I'm swinging at Rodrigo and Zoe, who took the blue sparrow's eggs. Zoe, who betrayed Rory. Swinging at Mr. Mogel and the bullet that killed the wolf, *my* Wolf, and the one that took José.

My fists take on a life of their own. I'm battering at the world and its injustice, its cruelty, and all the things I am powerless to change. I swing at Warwick for the Blood Race, a game of vengeance that only justifies what humans do to Klujns and perpetuates this vicious cycle of slaughter.

Right, left, right, left. I lose myself in my wrath. My fists ache, but it's my fingertips that are on fire, burning with an unfamiliar pain. My ears are still ringing, but I keep going, keep pounding.

Until, from under me, there are no more sounds at all. Until Elizabeth is a limp mass of silvery-gold fabric between my legs.

Until Elizabeth is dead.

Then, when my anger has reached its summit—a blinding whiteout where I can see nothing but pain—I hear a sound. A *pop*, like a needle bursting through flesh. Then, after it, there are nine identical sounds.

I look down at my hands, and can't believe my eyes.

Ten crystal claws have pierced through the tips of my fingers.

39

My head swirls. The crowd becomes a blur. The world tips upside down and I'm plummeting through space, flying through galaxies. My human form no longer exists and I am stardust—everywhere, nowhere. The only thing that anchors me to reality, that binds me to the planet like a golden thread, is Elizabeth's limp, bloodied form between my legs.

Reality gradually returns, one fragment at a time. I see the crowd. The bleachers of screaming Klujns, yelling and hissing in surprise. I try to focus on individual faces, and when I do, they are the faces of the humans in the Coliséa as the Klujn was being electrocuted on stage—their mouths open with mashed beaver dogs in them, their bared teeth and mustard-stained hands. The faces become Klujn again. They are painted, colorful, but just as bloodthirsty.

Warwick is stunned, but at the same time, he's grinning, clearly entertained. The ringmaster has been tricked in his own ring. Diablo's usual indifference is tinged not with surprise, but concern. Then I glimpse Wendy's face, and it is this face that devastates me the most.

Stupefied. Shell-shocked. Betrayed. Like I am not Ava anymore. Like the Ava she knew is dead.

My eyes land on a reflective panel in the wall, beneath the first row of seats. I catch a glimpse of my reflection, only at first, I don't recognize the girl I see. She looks like a wild creature, hunched over Elizabeth's corpse. Shuddering, panting, her every intake of breath making a sick wet rattle. She is pure animal. Her face—*my* face—is a white-blue painted mask, only it looks nothing like me. I am unrecognizable. And then I see them, fringed by frosted eyelashes.

My eyes. My *violet* eyes.

I am flooded with disgust, horror, shame. How am I this? How is this me? I want to smash that reflective panel and shatter the lie. I want to reach inside my body and tear out the darkest pieces. I want to run into the woods and find that river, jump into it, and let it carry me home so that I can go back to being just a girl, just Ava, who goes to school like any other girl her age. Who does combat and science and goes to Home Studies and bakes cakes for the boys—and does so happily.

What is this wild thing?

Nausea fills me, and my head whirls. I want to close my eyes—my ordinary *brown* eyes—and vanish. But just like Rachel during our fight, it's not the stage I want to escape . . . it's myself.

Beneath me, it's as if a trap door opens and I'm thrust into a not-so-distant memory.

* * *

Wolf's blood stains my sweater, a widening circle on my chest that grows bigger and bigger. He lets out a final breath, and then he's gone. His eyes are left open in a milky glaze.

"You didn't have to kill it," I say to Mr. Mogel.

"The law is the law," he responds.

"What happened?" Mrs. Mogel-Newhouse asks her son. Coll is drenched in sweat—still alive, but barely.

With hatred in his eyes and disgust in his voice, Coll says, "She's one of them."

"What are you talking about?" I stammer, standing up. All eyes are on me.

"I saw it," Coll says. "I don't know how it's possible, but her eyes . . . they changed color."

* * *

Strong arms scoop me up and carry me. I am a child who has fallen asleep in public, being taken home to bed. My head bobs with the soothing rhythm of each step. The scent of the beach is in my nostrils, exotic yet familiar. Not a memory of the beach—for I have never seen one—but something deeper, in my blood or genes. Exhaustion washes over me like the shadow of clouds, and fighting sleep is an impossible task.

I am vaguely aware I've been brought inside now, and a wrinkled hand cups my chin. My vision is thin as a nail clipping, blurred by eyelashes. A gentle voice asks me to swallow the liquid they've poured in. I do, and the pain disappears at once. I sink into the soft mattress that surrounds me like my own private island. Dreams come and go. The bed becomes a raft.

* * *

I'm drifting down a river under a dark, moonless sky, watching the landscape of memories play out on either side. The air carries the sound of crackling flames, the feeling of danger.

On my left are the woods. My mother is running, holding a bundle wrapped tightly in a blue blanket. A wolf pup chases at her heels. She reaches the edge of the cliff. I cry—not the me on the raft, but the one in her arms. The Hunter corners her. I take in my mother's long brown hair, her panicked blue eyes.

"Let us go."

"You know I can't do that."

"You killed my wolf five times," she tells the Hunter. "Five." She says this like she's surprised, like she expected more of the man holding the rifle.

There are footsteps; someone else is coming. My mother looks for an exit, but she is trapped.

The Hunter raises his rifle. "Give me Ava."

"No!"

"She's mine too."

"She'll never be yours."

The footsteps grow closer. The potent beam of a flashlight pierces through the trees, illuminating my mother. I see her eyes—not human-blue, like I thought—but violet.

The Hunter tightens his finger on the trigger as another Hunter steps up behind him, the one holding the flashlight.

"Give her to me," the first Hunter says again, more firmly this time and without emotion.

My mother looks down at me. Speaks words that are foreign but comforting, like a lullaby from far away. "Apolojhia, mehja lunah," she whispers. "Forgive me."

Then she tosses me over the edge, deep into the jowls of the waiting current. The wolf pup doesn't hesitate. He jumps in after me.

Then, a gunshot splits the night open.

My bed-raft continues to float down the dark river. It's not clear how much time passes—moments, or is it hours? It's hard to tell, but the river is calmer here. I see a green sign that reads RIVIÈRE ROUGE in fading white letters. The words have been painted over with new ones—RED RIVER. There are no fish here. Nothing lives in these waters but the blood of trees.

Then, on my right, another scene unfolds.

The wolf pup drags my body out of the water by the wrist, and onto the river bank. He is small but strong, with four black spots on his white fur. It's him, my Wolf. We are both babies. He lets my wrist go, and licks the injury clean. Then he uses his muzzle to push away my soaked blue blanket, which has somehow stayed wrapped around me. Wolf inspects my face. My skin is purple. My eyes are open, brown, but empty.

Wolf howls sadly. He tugs at my blanket. I don't stir. He covers me with his warm body and waits. Checks on me. Nothing. It's too late. I'm dead.

Then, as though guided by a voice inside him—a whisper of instinct— Wolf positions his head over my own. He brings his muzzle up to my mouth and exhales. I see the transfer of breath, like a twinkling breeze traveling from his body to mine. As it does, one of the four spots on his back vanishes and color slowly returns to my cheeks.

"Hey—what are you doing?" someone cries. A man runs toward the

bank, a bloodied tea towel in his hand. His face comes into focus—it's José, although of course my baby self doesn't know him yet. "Get away!" he yells at the wolf. Wolf—too small to defend himself, and not strong enough to bring me with him—flees toward the river and the Military fence on the other side.

José continues to shoo Wolf away until he's gone. Then he picks up the little blue bundle that is me and examines my face. "Not another one," he says sadly as he carries me into the kitchen. He has only just made it inside when a shrill cry fills the early morning. Mine.

Wolf watches from his hiding place. He howls that low, sad cooing sound of his. From where he is, he can no longer protect me.

40

When I come to, I'm lying on a mattress by a blazing blue-green fire. I feel so comfortable and warm. My ears have stopped ringing, but my hands still throb. I look, and my claws are still there—small and smooth and curved; half an inch of the clearest crystal. Their swift birth has split the skin around them open, which is red and tender, but the blood has been wiped clean. My remaining fingernails have started peeling away from the skin.

The disgust I felt in the arena returns, followed by an avalanche of questions.

A groan.

I look past the mess of my hands and see a black wolf with one white spot watching me. When she sees that I'm awake, her bushy tail thumps the bed excitedly.

It's Rhea, Daciana's wolf.

"You're awake," Daciana says from the doorway. "I tried to keep her out, but she refused to leave."

"How long"—I clear my throat—"how long did I sleep?"

"The fight ended a few hours ago," she says, adding a log of sparkling timber to the fire. She sits at the end of the bed. "It's early morning."

"How did I get here?"

"Diablo brought you in." *Diablo, the guard?* Then I remember being carried in strong arms, and how light and comfortable I felt. "You can come in," Daciana tells someone right outside the door.

Glory bounces in. Against my chest, my pendant becomes warmer. "Thank goodness," she squeaks. "For a moment, I was scared you wouldn't wake up at all."

I arrange myself against the lush purple and gold cushions until I'm propped up in a seated position as Glory sits on a rug by the hearth. Suddenly I feel the oddness of lying in a Klujn's bed, a spotted wolf at my feet, with these two creatures who are practically strangers. Although the word *creature* doesn't fit.

"What did you give me?" I ask Daciana, remembering the soothing liquid that helped me sleep.

"Violette liquor," she tells me, "for the pain. With a few drops of blue lace agate."

"What does that do?"

"It relaxes the barriers of your mind. Helps one peer inside."

"Peer into . . . my mind?" I say, suddenly feeling the intrusion as a physical one. An invasion of privacy. *If it's even possible*, I think. *Which it isn't.* There is no science or technology that allows someone else to see into your head. Maybe a test in a lab, with a monitor lighting up different areas of the brain, but not image for image.

Then again, fires don't glow green.

"I hope you won't mind the intrusion," says Daciana. "Usually I would ask for consent, but you were fast asleep and time is limited. I needed to see."

"See what?" I ask.

"Only what your mind was willing to show me," she answers. "Your mother and the Hunter. And the wolf who saved your life."

"So you were really in my mind?" I ask, baffled and weirded out, but fascinated, too.

"Don't worry," she reassures me. "The blue lace agate will wear off in a few hours, and then I'll be gone completely."

It's an uncomfortable feeling to imagine someone in my brain seeing things that I don't even want to see myself. I hope there was nothing too embarrassing in there.

"Our blood magic can do remarkable things," Daciana says. "I wish I had the time to show you, but right now there are more important matters to discuss."

"What happened?" I ask. "Why did Diablo bring me here?"

"Because I instructed him to do so," she tells me. "The king was confused, but I explained the situation. He felt foolish—that he did not see it, and that none of his guards did. You hid it well, your true nature."

I am wide awake now, even though this entire scene feels out of this world. "I wasn't hiding," I say. "I didn't know."

But how could I not have known? I always had a feeling that I was different, not like the others; that I was in the wrong body or the wrong township. But never this. A *Klujn* . . .

Images flash across my mind. More and more flashes.

The kanum roast that General Santos brought over. The way Diana watched me eat it, and the way I couldn't keep it down. *Did she know? Did George?* If they did, then why did they adopt me? And Wolf, my sweet Wolf, who always kept an eye on me in the only way he could— from a distance. How alone he must have felt after I shooed him away, having to live in forced solitude for so many years. Then, on that dark Military road, when he came back to protect me, only to get shot.

I feel so ashamed of what I am.

An animal, a monster, a beast.

But I swear I had no clue, just an inkling that something wasn't right. A little voice in my gut, no louder than the rational one in my mind. How can I be blamed for something I had no control over? How is that my fault? I wish I could go back, back to not knowing.

Glory takes a poker and stirs the logs in the fire. The sea-green flames crackle and spark.

I look at Daciana, who seems more tired than I remember. She must be dizzied by the speed of my thoughts—my mind a carousel, a whizzing machine that screeches and spins and gets nowhere. "I know this must be quite a shock to you," she says. "It was a surprise to us as well." And she cuts to the chase. "I'm sure you've gathered by now that your mother was a Klujn."

A surprise? To say the least. My world is upended.

"Did you know her?" I think about her—*our*—violet eyes. Daciana nods slowly. "Is that why, the other day, when you asked my name . . ." I trail off. "And after the first fights, you looked upset." Daciana looks pained. She nods again. "Why didn't you tell me?"

"A person cannot be forced through a door," she answers. "They must decide to cross over the threshold on their own, in their own time."

"How do you know that she's my mother?" I say. "That I'm her daughter?"

"I didn't feel it right away," Daciana replies. "My second sight has weakened with age. It was Glory who saw it, the very first time she looked into your eyes." I remember that first trip to Daciana's tent. The look on Glory's face when she saw me. How she dropped the moonstone. "She's a gifted ochimime," Daciana explains, seeing my confusion. "It means she can read eyes."

"Yours were a different color than your mother's, of course, with that beautiful, exotic shade of brown, but the constellations in them were a dead giveaway," says Glory, pleased with her insight.

"Constellations?"

"The black spots in your eyes," she explains. "Every Klujn bloodline has a unique pattern. It's like a map. A way of knowing where they come from, what their lineage is, and what their gifts are. When I looked into your eyes, it was uncanny. I knew straight away that you were Adria's daughter."

Adria. My mother has a name. All this time, she has been nothing more than a shadow, a running woman. Now she is real. And she is dead. Shot by a Hunter who knew her name.

"Does she have a last name?" I ask.

Daciana smiles. "Klujn last names are very long and oftentimes unnecessary. They detail the lunar conditions at the time of birth, as well as any other notable details about the weather and constellations and planets. Most of the time, we don't go by names at all."

"What about my father?" I ask.

"That, I don't know," says Glory. "I'd have to be standing in front of him in order to read his eyes."

"When Glory told me who you were, I had my doubts," Daciana puts in. "I haven't seen Adria in almost twenty years. But when you told me your name—Ava—and then I saw you on that stage, with those symbols on your arms, I realized she was right. That, despite your human traits, you are well and truly your mother's daughter."

"My arms?" I am perplexed. "What do they have to do with anything?"

Daciana holds my wrists down gently so I can't pull away. "Our symbols are our language," she says, tracing her finger along the pattern of my scars. "Our language is how we create, a spell cast in the soil. They are how we grow things, how we heal the earth. It is our artistry as Klujns."

"I thought it was agriculture."

"Agriculture is art," she answers. "Look and you'll find those three letters hidden in the word." Daciana turns toward the fire, the flames reflected on her face. "If we don't allow ourselves the freedom to create and express our true selves, then the force inside us becomes destructive. This language is in your DNA, Ava," she says.

I can't keep up with all this new information. My night terrors, my compulsions . . . the way I clawed at my arms . . . it was all something inside me, trying to emerge? A language of some kind?

"Today, on that stage, we witnessed the violence that occurs when Klujns repress the essential parts of themselves. There is nothing wrong with you," she tells me. "You are not to blame for your behavior. You have been raised in the wrong environment—an environment that values loud acts of destruction over quiet acts of creation. A world whose toxic imbalance of masculine sun energy has tipped the scales and made both men and women stray from their true nature—that of nurture, discovery, and love."

"You said my *human* traits," I start. I remember that last Klujnology class, when George said that Klujns and humans couldn't mate. "But it's impossible to be both. If I was both, that would mean that Klujns and humans . . ."

"Belong to the same species?" Glory finishes.

Daciana picks up the thread. "A species is defined as a group of organisms who can reproduce with one another and produce fertile offspring. While I have observed—on only a few occasions, mind you—Klujn and human partnerships, never before have I heard of any offspring. If humans discovered that we could bear mixed children, that would be cataclysmic. Because if Klujns and humans belong to the same species, then how can one continue to Hunt and eat the other?

"The Sun, the Moon, and the Seed," she says—and I realize she's talking about the outcome of the fights. Wendy, me, and Ying Yue. "Humans, Klujns, and rebirth," Daciana explains. "The human Blood Race may be a frivolous game to the king but, once again, our gods have reminded us that the only way we can heal the earth is if we all work together."

My mind boils with a million questions, but I don't know where to start.

"I suppose we should start at the beginning," says Daciana, and I realize that she's still in my mind. "Before the king comes to pay me a visit."

I look at her.

She answers my unasked question. "I suppose he will think I was complicit somehow. And he will want to banish me for it."

I remember the Klujn in the cave. "He can't do that! You had nothing to do with this."

Daciana holds up a hand to silence me. "There is no point dwelling on the things we cannot change. Now, do you want to hear about your mother, or do you not?" At my nod, she turns to Glory. "Do you want to tell the story?"

Glory is enthusiastic yet grave, as if she has been entrusted with a great responsibility. "Your mother comes from a stand called Estrella. It's where Daciana, Diablo, and I are from," she begins. "He's my brother. Estrella was an island stand off the coast of the Gaspesia peninsula, with beautiful beaches and caves and coral—"

"A little less detail, Glory," Daciana cuts in. But I would gladly listen to every single detail, no matter how long it took. I have waited my entire life for this—to know who my parents are and where I come from. Although, this is only my mother's side, and it's not at all the image I expected.

"One night, eighteen years ago, there was a raid," resumes Glory. "I was three and Diablo was six. Our queen was traveling at the time, as all queens do, to visit other stands. It was a new moon, so the stand was naturally a bit anxious, as Klujns tend to be when moonlight is scarce. Hunters surrounded our island on their ships and closed in. Most of the stand was killed. Only a handful of us managed to escape. Diablo saw our father get shot," she says straightforwardly, "and our mother captured. Adria—who was a friend of our mother's—managed to get us out through our network of caves beneath the ocean. She saved our lives."

"How old was she?" I ask.

"Eighteen," says Glory. "She had already completed her Blood Race, so she knew the wild, a little. But when we reached the mainland, that was the true beginning of our struggle. The wild is a dangerous place—volatile weather. Poison plants. Traps. Hunters. Poachers. And traffickers who recruit Klujns for Coliséas and other nasty business. Even your own mind can quickly turn on you."

I remember my time in the Deeper Woods. The irony that I could never have survived had I not been captured.

"Luckily, we stumbled upon a small stand. They let us stay for a few days while we got in touch with our queen."

"How?" I want to know.

"With Nature's internet," explains Daciana. "A web beneath the soil and in the air that binds all things. It may seem impossible to you, but I've always been just as captivated by human technology. The idea that you can pick up a phone, dial a number, and hear a person's voice across the world. That there are telephone lines under the sea! Now *that* is magic."

The image of Daciana using a landline telephone gives me a brief smile as Glory continues the story.

"Our queen had heard about the raid and taken refuge at Circo," she says. "We needed to travel west to join her. One night, as we were crossing through the swamplands, Diablo and I were resting in our tent. Adria and her spotted wolf were keeping watch, but up to that point, we'd all been awake for days, and she was starting to hallucinate. Diablo and I were woken by the sound of boats. We went to hide. When we came out, Adria and her wolf were gone and our camp had been raided. We never saw them again." There are tears in Glory's expressive eyes. She takes a moment to collect herself.

"We were in the wild, alone, for weeks. I don't know how Diablo did it—he was so young!—if it was instinct or the need to survive, but he managed to guide us to the Deeper Woods where we eventually found Circo. We were reunited with our queen, who struck a deal with Warwick: we were allowed to stay, but she had no power here. Even though she didn't agree with the way Warwick ran things, Circo became home. We could have gone to look for other stands, but our queen was getting older and the wild was crawling with Hunters almost year-round. So it was safer that we remain with the stand.

"When Diablo came of age, the king selected him as a Blood Race guard, since he had proven so capable in the wild. He continues to travel every chance he gets. I think, deep down, he hopes our mother is still out there somewhere."

"As for your mother," Daciana says, "I tried for many years to see into her mind, to communicate with her, but she must have been too far away. And my magic is not as strong as it used to be." *Then where was I born? What happened in that two-year gap between the raid and the day I washed up in Red River?*

"I don't know for certain, but your memory confirmed my fears," Daciana continues, once again answering the questions in my mind. "Adria must have been captured by Hunters, who decided to keep her alive. Not all Klujns are sent to slaughter; some are wasted for science, and others are used for myriad tasks. Some time after her capture, you came into this world. Whatever happened to Adria, it's safe to assume that she wasn't thinking clearly. The Adria I knew wouldn't have thrown her child into a river unless she had a very good reason.

"Like all Klujns, Adria belonged with her stand," Daciana says. "All Klujns need a balance of freedom and security. We need moonlight to charge our viaţăs and our bones, and a diet of freshly harvested plants. If we are deprived of any of these vital things, our fragile internal harmony is disrupted and we become the monsters that humans think we are. Which is how they make us into monsters—by throwing us into cages, keeping us in the dark, and depriving us of these things on purpose.

"It is not our wildness that makes us dangerous," she says. "But forced domesticity."

Just like the female Klujn in the Coliséa.

Just like the lone one in the cave, banished from his stand.

If I wasn't in bed, my knees would be buckling. I'd be falling. I feel about as solid as water. I could keep pouring onto the floor, and into the earth, until it drinks me whole.

"So she went mad?" I ask. "That's why she threw me off a cliff?"

"If I could take a guess," says the old Klujn. "I would say that Adria ran away from where she was. She bonded you to your wolf so that, if anything happened to her, he would keep you safe. When she found herself trapped on the edge of that cliff, she decided to throw you over the edge. Not because she didn't love you, but because she would rather you chance death than end up in a Hunter's hands."

"*Apolojhia, mehja lunah,*" Daciana says, and I remember the words my mother spoke. "'I'm sorry, my little moon.' It is a term of great affection. Not the words of an insane woman trying to drown her child."

I spent my entire life thinking my mother didn't want me. That she didn't love me. In any other circumstance, I would be relieved. "I can't be Klujn," I say, voice quiet but on the edge of breaking.

"Unfortunately, you don't have much of a say in the matter," Daciana tells me. "You are what you are, and your soul was placed in this body for a reason."

Rhea the wolf groans and rolls onto her side. She reaches out her paws, pedaling an imaginary bicycle. I notice the spot on her back and am reminded how Wolf's four spots dissolved into three when he saved me from drowning. "Spotted wolves are fascinating creatures, aren't they?" Daciana muses.

It's unsettling, this feeling that she's still in my head, but it's oddly comforting, too. I'm too tired to articulate questions, and I know her presence there comes without judgment. "Once they're bound to their master, that bond lasts a lifetime. I say *master*, but as Klujns we do not believe we are superior to any plant or animal, no matter its size. Our culture is not based on hierarchy or violence. It is circular, like the moon, like the earth, like a womb, where everything is a cycle, and everything is one."

"What about the king?" I ask, who seems to embody both hierarchy *and* violence.

"Years ago, Warwick was captured and spent a decade with a human circus. Tortured and beaten and forced to perform night after night." She shakes her head. "His need for vengeance has turned his heart black. He has led his stand away from their true nature—one that is innately good, because Klujns are, at their core, moon creatures . . . creatures of creation."

Rhea groans again, and I continue to pet her. "Did you know that spotted wolves have five lives?" Daciana tells me. "If their master dies, they can give up one of their lives to save them. The cycle is repeated until they are down to their final life. Then, if the master dies, the wolf accompanies them in death. It is a bond unmatched by any other species. One cannot live without the other."

"What if the wolf dies first?" I ask.

"That usually doesn't happen. Five lives tend to last a while. So—whatever happened to your wolf—as long as his body remains, chances are he's very much alive."

Alive? That's impossible. I watched him die. No technology in the world can bring the dead back to life. Then I remember my dream, my own lifeless body by the riverside. My heart leaps. But spotted wolf meat is a delicacy. Chances are, he ended up in Mr. Mogel's swollen belly.

I caress Rhea, and her eyes roll back in her head, showing only the whites. "How many lives does she have?"

"We're both on our last," says Daciana. "A thousand cycles. Sometimes I catch her watching me and I wonder if she isn't praying for my demise."

My mind cannot process all of this new information. *I am half Klujn? Wolf and I were bonded? My mother was the one who did it? My father may still be out there . . . a human? A Hunter.*

A high-ranking one.

Then, I remember something else. "What about the Queen of Estrella? Is she still alive?"

Daciana gives Glory a small nod. "She is," says Glory. "And she took me on as her apprentice."

My eyes go straight to Daciana. I take in her violet cloak, her bright eyes, and the crown of gilded roses on her head. The strength that emanates from her, despite her age and size—something emotional and intuitive and gentle and powerful, all bundled into one.

My eyes widen in disbelief. Daciana smiles.

"The king educated you on the third eye," she says, "which is good for personal development—learning about yourself, your past. What he failed to mention is that the queen of a stand has a fourth. An eye that not only benefits the individual, but the planet. We call it *second sight*. With this fourth eye, a queen can travel without leaving her tent. Of course, real travel is still important. She can see past and future and peer into the hearts and memories of every human, animal, and plant—alive or dead. She can hear the heartbeat of the earth and, if she becomes powerful enough in her lifetime, she can attempt to heal it."

Daciana opens her cloak so that I can see the center of her chest. And there, over her heart, is an actual eye. The lid closed, no eyelashes. Seemingly asleep.

I gasp at this weird, beautiful thing. I can't believe it.

Daciana is a queen.

41

"You're a queen?" I say, stunned, staring at the closed eye on her chest.

"You can't be a queen without a stand," she clarifies. "Although some who oppose Warwick's leadership look to me for guidance, I cannot govern here. I haven't been queen in almost twenty years, not since I left my stand."

The curtain ripples, and Diablo enters. "You asked for me?"

"Yes," Daciana replies. "Just a moment." She turns to me. "Glory has volunteered to take you to your new quarters and help get you settled in. It is customary for the finalists to move to the upper part of the stand before the last challenge."

"Glory should leave now," Diablo cuts in.

Daciana gives him a look, good-humored yet stern. "Glory will help Ava settle in, and then she will immediately come back here." There is a silent exchange between them that I do not understand.

And then something occurs to me: "Do I still have to compete if I'm half Klujn?"

She nods. "The king still sees you as human, if only half." Again, she picks up on my thoughts. "Ava, I'm not sending you to be slain. It is important that you see this through, for many reasons that will one day become apparent."

"What do you need from me?" Diablo asks Daciana. I want to stay, to hear their conversation, but I know I'm not allowed.

Glory helps me up and leads me from the room. We're a few steps down the tunnel when she stops abruptly, slapping her forehead. "I forgot the Moonlight Leaf. Wait here." She runs off toward the tent with all the plants.

I am alone in the dark tunnel, Daciana and Diablo's voices barely audible through the wall. I peer through a hole in the fabric. Daciana's back is to me. I hear her say my name and then the words "home" and "safety."

"That is an order," she finishes. Diablo shuffles his feet. He doesn't agree with whatever she has commanded. "I know how you feel about humans," Daciana tells him. "But don't forget—Ava is Adria's daughter. You and Glory both owe Adria your life."

"She's human," Diablo says, incensed.

"If you believed that, you wouldn't have protected her the night she tried to escape," says Daciana. "Or in the woods, when you tended to her injury. You helped her because, deep down, you have always sensed what she is, and you know that there are so few of us left."

"Ready?" Glory is back, beaming, carrying a bunch of leaves. I quickly move away from the hole and we step out into the rainy morning.

* * *

Glory leads me to my new quarters in upper Circo. The tent is a smaller version of Warwick's, striped in green and gold. The thick canvas blocks out the daylight. There's a lit fireplace in the center, a large mattress on the floor to the right, a black dividing screen to the left. Against the far wall is a dressing table with makeup and a rack of moonstone clothes, shoes, and accessories.

"I hope it'll do," says Glory, bustling around, distributing Moonlight Leaf to several lanterns. As she does, she tells me that the sap of Moonlight Leaf is what absorbs the moonlight and gives it its glow. It only burns for a few minutes, but if you add a sprinkle of alcohol, it can burn for hours. Even longer if it's in direct contact with moonlight. We call it *rebel ink*," Glory continues. "The sap is invisible, and only discharges the light when it's been activated by friction. It's good for writing messages you don't want anyone seeing."

"Is it like the red trail markers in the woods?"

"Not quite," says Glory, but without arrogance. "Rebel ink comes from the moonlight tree, and anyone can use it. Whereas our trail markers are made using energy from our claws, just like the barriers of our stands, and only Klujn eyes can see those."

"So that's why humans have trouble finding Klujn stands?" I ask. "They look invisible from the outside?"

Glory nods. "First, they'd need to track us, to know the exact location of our stand. Then, they'd need Klujn eyes to see the slight difference in atmosphere, which is almost impossible to detect even for us." I remember the ripple of the invisible curtain when Diablo ran his claws along it, and again with Warwick's daughter. "Then, they'd need our claws to get through the barrier unscathed. The gods all have different personalities, and some of them'll play terrible tricks on those who try to cross it without viaţăs."

It's strange to think that my eyes are made differently—that they can see certain things that others can't. It's lonely . . . this feeling that I'm between two worlds. Not entirely human nor Klujn. I remember something else that Daciana—the *queen*—had said.

"Is it true about moonlight?" I ask. "That Klujns need it to feel . . . sane?"

"As true as true north," Glory answers. I think about the restlessness I felt on the other side of the fences. The prickling discomfort in my veins. My mood swings. How I felt better when I was in my room, with the moon lamp regulating my inner cycles. Not as strongly as the real moon outside, but to some extent.

"We're more connected to the moon than humans realize. It impacts our natural cycles, our emotions. A full moon brings excitement and joy because when the moon is full and bright, Klujns tend to be at their most relaxed; a new moon brings anxiety and darkness because our energy sources are depleted. We can get restless and sometimes aggressive then, but it's an altered state, like a crystal that's been charged with bad energy. Moonlight helps us return to our true nature."

"This whole time I thought there was something wrong with me."

"There's nothing wrong with you, Ava," Glory smiles. "You were in the wrong environment, that's all, with people who don't see the world the way you do. When we feel misunderstood, it makes us question the very essence of ourselves."

After she folds back the black screen, I see a bathtub level with the ground, its surface covered in smooth Amethysts. Next to it is a cauldron perched atop a small stack of logs. Glory lights the logs with a green-tipped match. As the water in the cauldron heats, it gives off the familiar aroma of eucalyptus and rotten eggs.

I remember the word Mercy scratched onto his notebook, when we played our game of Hanging Klujn. *Enemy.* "I'm the enemy," I murmur.

"I guess that depends on which side of the fence you're standing on," Glory remarks. "Sides are only a matter of vantage point. A mirage." She tips the boiling water into the tub. I watch the clouds of vapor as they rise and dissipate. "I have to go soon," she says. "Daciana needs me."

I have to ask: "Why didn't Diablo want you to come here? What's going on?"

She gives another smile. "It's just Klujn business. Relax and focus on finishing the Blood Race. The rest will be taken care of."

Relax and *Blood Race* don't exactly belong in the same sentence.

"Glory," I say, as she's about to leave. She stops in the doorway, and without saying a word follows my gaze to the baby claws protruding from my fingertips. I don't even know what to ask her. I feel embarrassed. Like the first time I got my period and had to ask Diana for a cloth pad. It was years ago, when I was around eleven, I think. Diana looked surprised—she said most girls didn't get theirs until they were fifteen, if they even got it at all. Something about hormones in the food, which hadn't made sense at the time.

"The minerals in the water will help with the pain," Glory offers.

"But—are they supposed to go back in?" It feels like such a stupid question, but they're so alien to me. Like malignant tumors growing out of my skin.

She doesn't seem to think it's stupid at all. "They'll go back in when you calm down," she reassures me. "In the beginning, they can be a bit unpredictable. They'll have a mind of their own. You'll be sensitive for a few weeks, but eventually the swelling will go down and you'll get used to them moving in and out. When you see what they can do, you might even begin to like them. So I've been told."

Her smile is sad. I look at her hands, their amputated fingers and thumbs. Then at her necklace, where I count nine baby claws.

"It happened on the night of the raid," she says quietly. "I was only three, so of course my first claws hadn't grown yet. They chopped my fingertips off instead. I guess they thought they'd dig them out."

I can't help it; I shudder. "Are those them?" I say, indicating the necklace.

Glory nods. "There was a diversion, and that Hunter left. Your mother helped me find them. We got them all except for one."

"Do they still work?"

"They're just decorative," she says. "Viaţăs need to be attached to a living Klujn in order to work. It's not the crystal alone that's powerful, but the way the Klujn channels the energy of the earth. If the crystals are separated from our bodies, the energy in them usually dies after a few hours. Sometimes it remains longer, warming or cooling. There is a memory there, to some extent, but their magic heightens a thousand-fold when their Klujn is alive."

"So it really is *magic*?" I ask Glory.

"Isn't everything?" Glory answers. "The way a seed grows into a plant. The color of a sunset. The way a mother bird knows how to care for her young, and a baby bird flies on its own? Isn't it all magic?"

"I suppose."

"We Klujns are happier with less. We can walk through an old-growth forest without needing to possess it. There is so much more value in things alive than dead," Glory says. "Humans choose not to believe in magic, but magic is everywhere in the natural world, and worth pro-tecting."

"Do you wish you still had your viaţăs?" I ask, and want to take it back immediately.

Her smile is haunted. "That's like asking a bird if it likes having wings. Or if I asked you if you want to keep your heart."

My face is hot. "I'm sorry."

"It's not your fault," Glory says gently.

"Yes, it is." I reach up and unclasp the rose gold chain. In my palm, the crystal is hotter than it's ever been and emits some kind of magnetic charge. *Virgin crystal*, George had called it, *taken from its hands before they grew.* Used to make a trinket.

The crystal is practically scorching now.

And that's how I know that it's home. That it was never mine at all.

I feel sick with myself. With my father, too. How could he not realize? An intelligent, sensitive man like him. A Klujnology professor.

As Glory watches, I open my hand and offer her the crystal. "This belongs to you," I say.

She's confused at first. Then tears begin to pool in her eyes. It takes her a while to answer, but when she does, her voice isn't angry. It's filled with something like forgiveness.

"I don't want it," she says. "It isn't mine anymore."

"I'm so sorry. If I had known, I would have—"

"Shh, Ava." Her large eyes are compassionate, and even though this was her tragedy, she is more composed than I am. Beneath her innate friendliness is a kind of strength I've scarcely witnessed, the strength of kindness. "We can't live in the past," she tells me, and she closes my hand around the pendant. "That'll get us nowhere new."

42

After Glory leaves, I move over to a mirror. It's the first time I've seen myself since the reflective panel in the amphitheater, and I'm relieved to see that my eyes are brown again—but how long will they stay that way? What will happen if I lose my temper again? Could I attack someone else the way I attacked Elizabeth?

It's difficult to remove my cloak with my new claws. My moonstone costume is covered in dried blood. Elizabeth's, or mine? A bit of both, perhaps. I unstrap my shoes and pull them off; slip off the dirty costume and let it slide to the ground. In my bralette and underwear, I study my body. My arms bear the symbols of a language I don't yet understand, but that makes a little more sense to me now.

I remember Wendy's face when she saw me—like I was a stranger, like the person I was had died. I want to talk to her, explain that I didn't mean to kill Elizabeth like that; I lost control, I exploded. That I'm still me, I'm still—

Who am I? I touch the scar on my right hand, the bite mark from the wolf. *My* Wolf. The one my mother bound me to before she died. *I'm a Klujn.*

A royal one, too.

I strip the rest of the way, trying not to scratch myself. The claws may be small, but they are scarily sharp. At long last, I lower my body into the steaming purple water.

I could die of gratitude at the pleasure I feel, but I am unworthy of it. I should be outside in the cold and rain, shivering like the animal I am. But *animal* is not a fair word. Wolf was an animal, and he deserved no such thing.

The water is hot and the minerals sting, entering my every cut, scratch, and wound. After a moment, the pain in my fingertips begins to subside. When I close my eyes and inhale, I am back in the forest by the river, looking up at the glorious clouds. Floating in a dream, pink and purple Lumina lighting up the night.

It feels like a lifetime ago. Of all the possible scenarios to unfold at Circo, I could never have predicted this one.

The weight in my chest begins to disperse, like water eroding rock over time. My anxieties and doubts melt away until I am just a body, stroked by the warmth's lovely hands.

I lift my own hands above the surface. They are still red and swollen. The nail on my left index finger has almost completely peeled off, next to its already nailless neighbor. I wiggle it like a milk tooth and—*snick*—it's gone, my finger pink and smooth as a baby's. I drop the useless nail into the tub. Grab the claw of that finger and push.

I push, push, *push*, trying to force it back in. Soon I'm screaming in pain, excruciating pain, but the crystal doesn't budge. It remains where it is, on display for everyone to see. I want it gone. Gone, so that I don't have to feel ashamed anymore—ashamed of what I am, when I never asked to be this way. I push again, harder this time, and the pain is unforgiving, but nothing happens. I drop my hands under the water in surrender. The minerals greet my fingertips like an old friend.

I sink into the tub and wet my hair. Let the water into my ears, hoping they might silence my thoughts, but nothing can. How can I trust myself or anything I've been told? The entire image I held of the past is shifting. A kaleidoscope. Same colors, different shapes. Same people, different landscapes. Nothing makes sense anymore.

I should have let Elizabeth kill me. Slipping into oblivion would have been easier than this. Even if I survive the Blood Race, how am I going to go back home? How will I even find my way there on my own?

If humans find out what I am, they'll kill me. They'll hang me at the gallows in the public square and roast me, and broadcast it on television.

I stay in the tub until the water has turned lukewarm and my fingers wrinkle like cranberries in the sun. It takes all my remaining energy to lift myself out of the water and wrap myself in a black robe. The bath has knocked me out, taken whatever little strength I had, and I feel so tired, as though I've gone on a days-long trek.

A peek outside, where the rain falls in relentless sheets. I love the sound. I let the canvas close and the inside of the tent is dark like the dead of night. I lie down on the mattress, my wet hair soaking the pillow, and fall into a sleep that is anything but dreamless.

* * *

"George!" I yell, banging on my father's basement door. "Are you in there? Open up, please!" No one answers. I peer through the frosted-glass window, but all I can see are some gadgets and a row of black books with gold-embossed spines on his bookshelf.

"Ava?" I hear from above. I tear back up the stairs and see Diana and Mercy on the porch. "What's wrong?" Diana asks. "Are you hurt?"

"It's not mine," I say. "Where's George?"

"With Rodrigo. They went to patch a hole in the fence. Ava, what happened?"

"They're coming," I take a gasping breath. "Coll attacked me. Then a wolf came and attacked him. I tried to stop it, but they killed it."

Diana's eyes narrow. "Why are they after you?"

There's a muted rustle, like boots on leaves.

A sting at the back of my neck.

I reach up, my movements already slow, and my fumbling fingers find the source: a dart. Confused, I look up at Diana, and that's when I see them.

Mr. Mogel, rifle raised. Dayn and Justine on his heel.

Mercy takes a step back toward the house, but Diana surprises me by running down the porch stairs and charging at Mr. Mogel. "Get off my property!" she yells. "You have no right to be here!"

"Move out of the way, Diana," says Mr. Mogel.

"No."

Mr. Mogel shoots over Diana's shoulder. The bullet crashes into a wind chime, which explodes into a hundred pieces. A real bullet, not a dart. Diana doesn't flinch. "You know the consequences for harboring one," he says. "I guess the question's why?"

"You shouldn't believe every word that comes out of that boy's mouth," Diana hisses. If she was an animal, her hackles would be raised. "I don't know what he told you, but he's lying."

"Yeah?" says Mr. Mogel. "Then where'd she come from? A baby who washed up on the riverbank. You know where that river comes from, don't you? There's nothing north of the orphanage aside from mountains."

Everything is spinning. My spine is turning liquid. My tongue heavy in my mouth. I try to form words, but they don't come out.

"What is he talking about?" Mercy cries.

Diana ignores him. "You small township people are all the same," she says to Mogel. "Spreading cruel rumors at the expense of others. Ava's parents were forced to abandon their second child because of our leader's laws. That's all." But she's lying. I feel it.

"Di-anuh?" I manage. I feel tired—so tired.

She looks at me, and she appears different all of a sudden. As if the woman I have lived with for almost six years was wearing a mask, and the real her has been hiding beneath the surface.

"Don't worry, Ava," she tells me. "Everything's going to be all right." Then she turns back to Mr. Mogel. "It's time you went home. Before I call the authorities."

"The DSO is the authority."

She squares her shoulders. "If you want to get to her, you'll have to go through me," she says, with a confidence I didn't know she was capable of. "Mercy, get the rifle."

Mercy is frozen, unsure what to do, but then he goes inside.

"Very well," says Mr. Mogel, aiming his own rifle at Diana's chest.

No. She can't die for me. I try to take a step back, but it's like my feet are stuck in cement, and I can feel the poison racing through my veins. The lights of the house pixelate. All sounds turn to echoes.

Diana is there, close to me now, her eyes fixed on a point over my shoulder.

Mercy, back on the porch now, clutches a rifle—his face shows shock, confusion, horror.

Mr. Mogel, Dayn, and Justine are nearby, but they didn't shoot me, they didn't shoot . . .

The earth tilts up and takes the place of the sky. My head hits the ground.

My attacker walks toward me, with an almost-imperceptible limp. "Show's over," he tells Mr. Mogel. "This is between us and Grouse."

From where I lay, I can see my attacker's face and the woods behind him. His kind, green eyes—although they don't look so kind right now.

It's George.

43

George shot me. The thought fills me with confusion. Like fog rolling down into a valley, thick and impermeable. George, my greatest ally? George, who fought with Diana for so many months after he brought me home from the orphanage? George—the only father I have ever known. *Why would he shoot me?*

I lay in my cot, still digesting my dream.

The dart. It was poison. It must have muddled my memories, erasing George's face from my brain. Maybe it was my mind trying to protect me from a truth so horrible, so unimaginable . . .

How could it be him?

Then, another memory fights its way to the surface, this one quite recent—at the Feast Roulette. Warwick saying that Klujns had not been starving us, but detoxifying us. That if we stayed a little longer, we would finally see things as they really are.

A chill. My blood is ice. I roll over, not wanting to have to deal with the implications of my dream and the fact that the one person I trusted more than anyone else utterly betrayed me. I cannot process it. It doesn't make any sense.

There's the aroma of coffee. A hand nudges me. I open my eyes.

It takes a moment to adjust to the dark tent. I have no idea what time it is, nor how long I slept. Diablo stands by, watching me. His face is its usual unsolvable riddle, although I feel I can read him a little better now. He is a child who lost his parents and watched his stand destroyed in front of his eyes. Who, at six years old, became responsible for his little sister. "You need to get ready," he says. "The final challenge is about to start."

"Okay," I say.

"Okay," he echoes back. He lingers for a moment, watching me. My mind fills the gap between us with childish fantasies—his strong hands reaching out, picking me up, making me feel weightless again. There's a shiver inside me, although it isn't icy. It's a warm burst that invades my lower abdomen like internal bleeding.

I feel something stirring. A dark, primal, animal longing. A hunger to be touched, but not in the way Wendy touched me. My cheeks grow hot and I push the thoughts away. I'm not thinking straight. Even if Diablo broke that invisible barrier—which would never happen—I wouldn't have the faintest clue what to do next. My sexuality is a great, deep ocean that I stand on the shore of, not knowing how to swim.

I meet Diablo's piercing violet eyes and pray that he can't read my mind the way Daciana did. I wonder if he longs for anyone, like Warwick's daughter, or if that part of him is dormant because he has bigger things to think about. Toward me, he has shown only revulsion, but beneath that revulsion is something else.

I wonder if he is about to say something, but then he leaves and I'm left there feeling stupid.

I pour myself a bowl of coffee—*Diablo must have brought it*, I think—and take a grateful sip. Then, I station myself in front of the vanity.

My costume is another comfortable, artfully cut jumpsuit dripping in crystals. It is even more dazzling than the one I saw in the display case before entering the Coliséa. Its light blue fabric is so soft I could sleep in it. But its sleeves are shorter than I'm usually comfortable with; there are only a few inches of fabric on each shoulder.

I tie my hair back in a loose knot and select a moonstone headdress. The jewels are heavy but not cumbersome. I decide not to paint over my arms and leave them as they are. There is a story in these scars.

Putting on my makeup has become a ritual. I am a performer, getting ready to go onstage. I have no idea how I will fare on this unknown final test, but I can't think that far ahead. I need to remain in my body. Finally, I pick up my crystal pendant. Glory's claw, which is cool again. I hate what it represents, but instinct tells me to slip it into my pocket.

Made up, dressed, and adorned, I take in my reflection. How different I look. I am no longer the girl from Red River, drugged and dumped in the wild, forced to grow up all at once.

I am Ava. A capital *A* versus a lowercase one. Two people at war inside the same flesh. Despite this feud of identity and belonging, I find my reflection beautiful.

Am I a wild thing domesticated? Or a domesticated thing made wild?

* * *

Diablo leads me through upper Circo, where the sun has set and the moon is rising. The Blood Moon. She is red, full to bursting point. In the streets, there is a bustle of activity. Food, drinks, games, and music— the usual fanfare of color and movement. There are fewer Klujns than I would expect, seeing that this is the most important night of all.

I imagine the teenage Klujns in the wild, and what they must be doing right now. Heading toward their chosen landmark, a months-long journey. That feeling of risk, of excitement, of camaraderie. I suppose it's not too different from what I've experienced here.

We reach a plaza right before the highest point of the mountain. There are Klujns of all ages here, old and young, bathing in moonlight, playing instruments, wearing masks. The pregnant Klujn I saw a few days ago hums a wordless lullaby. Two royal children run with a luminous red kite, and their spotted wolf pups give chase, trying to bite the kite's glowing tail.

"This way," Diablo says, pulling me through the plaza and around a cluster of trees. And that's when I see it. The arena. The black diamond I have only ever glimpsed from afar. From this close, it is even more terrifying than I imagined. Unlike the amphitheater on the east side of the stand where our fights were held, this structure rises into the sky with impressive height. Three sails, like black flames curving into one another, open on top so the moon can witness what goes on inside. A front-row seat to the bloodbath.

"We're here," says Diablo, leading me through an entrance to the right of the main spectator gate. Once inside, we twist around a dark tunnel, sandwiched between two black walls. I feel like I am in a Loud-house, being led to the Killingroom. A room of shrieks and blood and final words.

Suddenly, I realize how totally unprepared I am for all of this. I do not want to fight a full-blooded Klujn in an arena, or face whatever is about to happen. I do not want to be torn limb from limb in front of a cheering audience. But if that was the intention, why would Daciana send me here and force me to compete?

Finally, we arrive at a black canvas door. On the other side, the crowd awaits my arrival.

"I'll come back when this is over," Diablo says.

"Are you going to tell me what's going on?" I ask, but he ignores my question. He appears impatient. "Wait—what about a weapon?"

"No weapons. You won't need one."

A horn resonates from inside. Diablo pulls the curtain back. *I'm not ready,* I think. But I'm out of time.

Before I can gather my thoughts, Diablo pushes me out onto the stage.

44

The stage is round and looks to be about thirteen strides across, surrounded by a circle of glowing red Moonlight Leaf. Not individual lanterns like the previous fights, but one solid line, like an eclipsed sun, sealing me in. Just the color alone feels ominous. The tiers of seats around me are about half-full, and the audience is eerily quiet. The hoods of their cloaks are pulled up, shadowing their expressions.

What's going on? Who am I fighting? And how am I meant to see anything in the dark?!

As I walk forward, the silhouette of an object becomes visible. I stop dead. Catch my breath when I see the grotesque thing that stands in the center of the stage. Its trunk is thick and charred, its black branches reaching out like the tentacles of a giant sea creature. Some sweep the ground, while others reach up toward the opening in the roof. Vines of sinister colored roses are curled around the branches.

It must be a Carniflora.

My brain swims against the current of the last week, sorting through memories. Finally, it finds one in George's classroom. Reesa. Before she died. Before all this. When she was just a know-it-all in my Klujnology class.

"These black trees in the Deeper Woods that eat humans alive. If you get too close, they trap you with their roots. Their thorny branches have

roses that release a toxin that basically digests humans alive. It's like getting slow-cooked by acid."

I gulp. Take a step back. The tree's branches sway slightly, although there's no discernible breeze. Nothing to move it other than *volition*. Its roots slither like snakes. It's as if they're waiting to grab my ankles and pull me in. But how can a tree be alive in this way? Why does it feel like it's watching me, even though it has no eyes?

Then, across the stage and to the left, a curtain ripples, drawn open by a guard's hand. A figure emerges: Wendy, in her sunstone costume. Then, from a third doorway, this one to the right—Ying Yue, in obsidian. I try to catch Wendy's eye, but she deliberately looks away.

My heart begins to pound, blood moving like rapids. Am I supposed to fight the two of them? Is it two against one?

Or human against Klujn?

I swallow, my throat like sandpaper. I hear the king's voice before I see him.

"Please, come," he says. Warwick stands to my left by the first row of seats, just outside the perimeter of Moonlight Leaf, his guard behind him. On the soil inside the circle, our three symbols have been traced in red luminescent ink: the Sun, the Moon, and the Seed.

Wendy takes her place on the left, Ying Yue on the right. I fill the space between them, standing behind my crescent moon symbol. We face the king and the dark crowd behind him.

"You have made it this far," Warwick says, stepping across the circle of Moonlight Leaf and into the arena. He continues until he's standing near the Carniflora's trunk. His back is close to the tree; his feet inches from its exposed roots. "And now we have reached the end. But the end of the night is just the dawn of your new journeys back home." He seems tired and distracted, nowhere near the ringmaster he has been. It's as if he is only conducting this ritual out of obligation or formality. "Along the way, there were surprises and upsets. But overall, you put on a thrilling show. You three are here because you have fought well, and because you did not resist change. You allowed your minds to be awakened and planted with new seeds. So," he announces, "let us begin the final test."

"Are we fighting each other?" Wendy asks tersely. The fire that kindled in her eyes after Willa's death still burns like the peak of summer.

"*Fighting?*" Warwick splutters. "Who said anything about fighting? The physical tests are over. This is a test of the brain. It is theater of the mind."

"I thought the Blood Race was a fight between a human and a Klujn," says Ying Yue. She, too, nervously avoids my eyes.

"It is, in a way," Warwick replies. "The Blood Race is many things, as I told you on your very first night: it is a game, a prophecy, a feast of moonlight, a battle between human and Klujn *ideas*. When our young return from the wild, they have witnessed the state of the world. Yes, the Ice Moon is a very exciting time in a young Klujn's life, but with fun also comes hard work. For life is not only about personal pleasure, but purpose. Unless," Warwick adds playfully, "you want to fight some more."

Wendy asks, dead serious: "Are we going to be fed to the tree?"

"Fed to the tree?" Warwick guffaws, laughing uproariously now. "*Fed to the tree!* Why, where did you hear such a stupendous lie?" The crowd laughs along with him. The king walks up to the Carniflora, reaches out, and strokes its bark. The black giant's thorny branches sway in response, stirring like a sleeping beast. "Trees are alive, yes, that much is true," says Warwick. "They do not walk, but that doesn't mean they don't feel danger or pain. They communicate to one another in complex underground fungal pathways and pass knowledge down from generation to generation. They help their sick and look after their old. But they don't eat humans. They don't even have any teeth!"

A ray of moonlight shines down through the gap in the ceiling and touches the Carniflora. The tree responds to the moonlight by reaching toward it, its roses sparkling in the light.

Warwick reaches out and plucks a blue rose from one of the lower branches. He holds it up for us to see. "The Midnight Rose. This is the final challenge in the Blood Race. You will each pick a rose and eat it. After that, you will be free to go."

"F-free to go?" Wendy stammers. "What happens when we eat it?"

"The Midnight Rose is the ultimate bearer of truth, accelerating the journey you have begun in your time at Circo. Your third eye will be opened—and you will finally see everything you could not see before."

"It sounds too easy," says Ying Yue.

The king nods. "It is as simple as it sounds. But the truth is not for the weak," he adds. "For, once you discover it, there is no forgetting."

"Then why don't you eat it?" Wendy probes.

"I have, on many occasions," says the king, twirling the blue rose between his thumb and index fingers. "I know my past well enough by now to have no desire to revisit it. It's not exactly my idea of a good time." He smiles wryly.

I look at the Midnight Rose in Warwick's hand. The final puzzle pieces. All my unanswered questions. The whole truth. At my fingertips.

I take a step forward. Ying Yue stares at me, and I'm surprised that her expression isn't mean or judgmental. We are, in a way, teammates now. *Don't do it*, her eyes warn. *It might be a trap.* But Warwick won't let us go unless we eat the rose, and my curiosity feels as destructive as a cyclone. The faster I do this, the quicker it'll be over with.

"Well, it looks like we have a volunteer!" Warwick announces happily. "Come right up, pick a rose, any rose; which one will it be?" He sounds like a Sideshow Alley barker. If only this was as simple as throwing rings around the necks of bottles or winning a goldfish in a plastic bag.

"What do I do?" I ask when I am beside the tree.

"She likes hugs," he says as if this is normal. "But if you're shy, I suppose a stroke will suffice."

I reach out tentatively and touch the Carniflora's scratchy bark. I stroke her once, twice, three times, like I'm patting a cheetah. Something rumbles from deep inside the trunk, vibrating like air through vocal cords. The deep organic chant that sounds at dawn.

Warwick was right . . . the tree *is* alive in its own way. It—*she*—lowers a branch toward me. On her outstretched arm are a few roses of striking colors. I pluck a ruby red one, gently. It looks like a regular rose, dipped in glitter.

"Remember . . . every journey is unique," says the king. "Now, please, when you are ready."

I look down at the rose. What can it show me? About George, and why he shot me? About my mother, and my father, and where I come from? Will it even work? Or could I see something else entirely?

First. I'm going first. It's terrifying. But I'm fueled by a need to learn, to know, to see. So I bring the Midnight Rose up to my lips and take a bite.

45

The rose is bittersweet, like a mixture of cherry and vinegar. As I bite into it, its nectar drips down my chin. After I finish, I wipe my face with the back of my hand and return to my place. Ying Yue goes after me, picking a stripy pink-and-white one, the color of raspberries and cream. Wendy deliberates for a long time before choosing a black one.

"Very well," says Warwick, when we are back in front of our symbols. "I must issue one final warning, because the truth is a dangerous thing, and some people would go to unspeakable lengths to have it silenced. If you manage to leave Circo and make it back to the fences, I caution you to be wary of whom you trust. The real monsters are not always apparent," he says. "Most of the time, they are the ones who pretend not to be monsters at all."

Warwick steps out of the ring and returns to his seat in the front row. The three of us are left alone onstage with the Carniflora.

I wait, checking to see if the others are affected by the rose in any way, showing symptoms. *But what kind of symptoms?* Then, slowly, it begins.

Black splotches appear in front of my eyes, like I've stared at the sun too long. I blink, but they don't go away. More and more appear, bleeding together until I am completely blind. My eyes are open but I can't see a thing.

"Ava?" Ying Yue sounds afraid. It's weird to hear a stranger call my name. Her voice seems to echo down a long tunnel to where I am.

Then, my eyes fuse together. I try to open them, but they're stuck together. I reach up and touch them, but can't feel where they begin and end. It's as though my skin is made of wax that has melted and solidified into a new shape.

In my frontal lobe, a white light begins to pulse. I don't know how I know the light is white if I can't see it, but I just do. It grows bigger and brighter until it flares and explodes, like a wave of radiation from a bomb site.

And there, inside, just above the bridge of my nose, there's a wet *crunch*. Something crusty opens, like a jar of pickled vegetables that was sealed over the winter. *It can't be!* I think. But it is. My third eye blinks slowly, as though roused from a long sleep. The lens is covered in a milky film that makes the world look cloudy. My actual eyes are still shut but, all of a sudden, I can *see*.

* * *

I'm in the Deeper Woods, in the same exact spot where I came to five days ago. The sky is filled with thousands and thousands of glimmering stars. I look down: blue corduroy skirt, pumpkin-leather boots, white sweater. The circle of Wolf's blood is there, still warm to the touch. Then I see Glory's crystal. It lies on the forest floor in front of me. I pick it up and study it. The stone feels cold and lifeless.

That's when I notice a tiny imperfection in the crystal. It looks like a single piece of blue glitter. From the side, it is flat and almost invisible. From the front, it is still tiny but round. The minuscule thing starts to pulse with a blue light that is not natural at all—faster and faster, until the crystal sends an icy chill into my hand and I drop it. Back away. I close my hands around wet leaves and earth to erase the memory of how it felt.

Beyond my pumpkin-leather boots, on the forest floor, the blue light blinks faster and faster. Like the heart of the mechanical fly in José's kitchen. Like the one that landed on the windowpane of George's classroom.

The tapestry of stars above my head transforms into something else. Like a hall of mirrors, Zoe's face is reflected a hundred times. Her voice is loud. Harrowingly loud.

"You don't know, do you? Maybe your father wasn't as honest with you as mine was."

"Honest about what?" my own voice echoes back.

Then Zoe's face morphs into a fiendish grin. "Why we're here."

Those three words pound in my brain. All around me, the trees mutate into her face, which now wears an Executioner's makeup, blue with little silver triangles under her eyes.

Why we're here. Why we're here. Why we're here.

The forest blurs into a cacophonous ocean.

I don't think I'm ready for the truth after all. But, ready or not, it's coming.

Zap.

It's Adoption Day at the orphanage. Families come and go, but none look at me twice. Down the end of the row, Zoe is there, obedient and discreet.

There's a sting in my hand, and I uncurl my fingers to reveal José's black pin. My eyes are turned liquid by the memory of his death. The anesthetic of shock has faded, and I am awake on the operating table, the cold surgeon's scalpel of grief pressed to my chest.

That's when I see George. He stands next to Miss Hidgins and General Santos. The three of them speak. George's eyes scan the room like the beacon of a lighthouse, and when they land on me, they stop. I read the words on his lips. "Who is she?" Miss Hidgins follows his gaze and notices me. She mutters something—words of caution or discouragement—but this does little to curtail his interest. He walks toward me, squats down so that we're the same height, and drinks me in with his eyes.

"What's your name?" His voice is warm and calm, not shrill like the ones I'm used to hearing.

"Orphan," I say.

"Your real name."

"Ava."

"Who gave you such a pretty name?"

"It was sewn on the blanket they found me in."

George's eyes flicker like a green-flamed fire. He introduces himself, then notices the crown that I drew on the misty window behind me. "If I didn't know any better, I'd say you're a princess."

Princesa. That's what José called me all my life. But a princess has parents, doesn't she? Now that he's gone . . .

"I'm a queen," I answer.

"A queen?" George's eyes fill with delight. "I've never met a queen before. I don't even know the proper etiquette."

"What's that?"

"Etiquette? It's a code of behavior. A proper way to act."

"People usually bow to queens," I explain. "But no one here knows I'm one, so they don't bow to me."

George takes off his hat, holds it to his chest, and bows. "Don't worry, my queen. Your secret is safe with me."

The clock on the wall behind him dissolves into a moon. It's not the real moon, but the lamp in my new bedroom. It's my first night with the Sparrows. I lie on a canopy bed with a mosquito net and brand-new stuffed animals. A cool breeze blows through the open window. I walk over to close it.

Down on the porch, Diana's angry voice drifts up to where I am. "This is a bad idea, George."

"Trust me."

"Trust you?" she answers, aghast. "I trusted you, but now I'm pretty sure you've lost your mind."

I run back to bed and bury myself under a mountain of blankets and pillows. José used to say that my curiosity would get me in trouble, and I don't want to get in trouble on my first night.

But as my little body lies in bed, my third eye now takes me over to the window, and I drift down to the porch where Diana and George continue to argue in whispers.

"Did Rodrigo put you up to this?" Diana asks. "I don't trust that man."

"Don't say it."

"He's a bad influence on you. Always has been. I don't understand why you went back to him. After the Estrella raid, you said you were done."

"I was," George says. "But it's not up to me. They haven't had a significant raid in years and Grouse is getting anxious. The ones they bred aren't producing offspring anymore. The ones they tried to clone were diseased. Grouse is desperate for a fresh batch, and he's convinced I'm the answer to giving him Circo. You and I both know—nobody says no to Grouse."

George lowers his voice even more. "The cyborg dogs didn't work . . . they couldn't pick up a scent. Drones don't work. No human technology can locate or infiltrate their tribes. They used Klujn cells to grow eyes that can see their invisible barriers, but you have to be within a few feet of a settlement for them to work. They figured out that viaţăs can get a person through the barriers unharmed, but they still need a way to find those settlements in the first place. It's like looking for a needle in a haystack."

"What does this have to do with us?" Diana asks.

"Grouse came up with another plan. Something more . . . grassroots."

"Orphans?" she says.

"If they raise ten, twenty, fifty unwanted children, and send them off at the right time of year, over the next few years . . ." George trails off. "Grouse wants to give it a try. And he wants us all to be part of the experiment. If it makes you feel any better, Rodrigo's taking one, too."

"Great," Diana says, her voice dripping with sarcasm. "That makes me feel so much better."

"Think about what this means," he tells her. "A few years of work, one more raid—the big one—and we can finally be free from Grouse. He's offered to give me my Military pension, even though I left ahead of time. You can stop working in that awful Greenhouse, have more time at home."

"You and I both know that nobody is ever free from Grouse," Diana says. "After this raid, there'll be another one."

"I'm asking you, but I don't have a choice. All we need to do is raise her for a while."

"And then what?" Diana demands. "We wait until she turns sixteen? Then we send her into the woods—as bait?" A beat. "That's sick."

"I need you to understand how big this is. We need that little girl."

"So why not get a regular human girl?"

"We could have," George says. "But I found a Klujn instead. We hit the jackpot. Two birds, one stone. I can spend the next few years studying her, seeing how she responds to our world, and then, when the time comes . . ."

"You send her off to slaughter."

"You and I both know that the Blood Race isn't necessarily a death sentence," George answers. "We can keep her under control, with moonlight and physical activity and a healthy diet. Take her to the woods and see how she responds to it. But no one can know what she is. Not Rodrigo, not Mercy, not her. Especially not her."

"She's not a science experiment," Diana fizzes. "A test of Nature versus Nurture. She'll want to know where she comes from. Who her parents are. She'll want to be like the other children, and explore, do Scouts! You can't deny these things to a child."

"If she really is what I think she is, Diana, not only have I got a Klujn . . . I've got a royal one."

"How do you know that?"

"You know how I know?" George says, and his finger points toward the woods. "The spotted wolf that follows her around."

"What spotted wolf?"

"The one out by the fence who's been keeping an eye on her."

Diana sighs heavily, disturbed by what George is asking of her. "If you help Grouse get Circo," she says. "Such a big, important tribe . . . that will be the beginning of the end."

"Circo is not what it was," George says. "It's a loss we can afford. The most violent tribe, aside from Muja, but we haven't spotted them in years. Grouse knows about the heart now, and he won't stop until he's got it. What he doesn't realize is that he's going after the wrong one."

I am back in my bed, covered in a patchwork blanket. The moon lamp watches me from the wall. A face without eyes, a nose, a mouth. But still, it watches.

The floorboards creak, and George knocks on my door.

"Can I come in?"

The room starts to rock gently, pieces of it slipping away, replaced by *new ones, until an entirely different landscape surrounds me.*

I'm in George's Jeep. We drive down a Military road. "Where are we going?" I ask my father.

"To get you X-rays," he says.

"Why do I need X-rays?"

"You know how you have those bad dreams and pick at your arms? We're going to make sure there's nothing wrong with your hands."

We come to a tall gate outside a Military facility. George reaches for his credentials, but a man in a blue uniform waves him through. "All good, Dr. Sparrow."

"I didn't know you were a doctor," I say.

"Not a medical one," he says with a laugh. "I'm simply an expert in my field."

We arrive at the facility, which is surrounded by gates of intimidating barbed wire. It used to be a petrol mine, George tells me, but the Military took over after there was nothing left to dig up from the ground.

Inside, we take an elevator down to a basement. I peer through the glass floor of the elevator, into the dark recesses of the shaft, as the ground gets closer and closer. Ding. *The doors open.*

George guides me to a door with a nameplate: Dr. A. Kaplin. He greets Dr. Kaplin with a handshake and a smile and whispers I can't hear. She is female, which is unusual. Then the doctor takes me to a room and asks me to lay my hands down on a machine. She lowers the lid, sandwiching them between two panes of cold glass. I enjoy the feeling.

There's a hum and a green light as the device scans my hands. Then the machine ejects a sheet of translucent paper and the doctor holds it up to a glass box on the wall. Turns on a light. Her silhouette blocks the image from view, but I see the way her neck and shoulders clench when she sees the image. Like she bit down on an ice cube.

Dr. Kaplin snaps off the light. She turns around and smiles at me, but the smile no longer reaches her eyes. It is polite but cold, like a teacher to a disobedient child. "Wait here," she says.

The doctor goes out into the hallway, where she speaks to my dad. He meets her concern with reassurance until, after a few minutes, she relaxes.

I notice the outline of the X-ray on the light box. In the hallway, my father and Dr. Kaplin are still talking. I squint with my new eye, my third eye, and that's when I see it—what I was blind to before.

The X-ray shows the outline of my hands, and my bones. And then I see, under my skin—ten tiny baby claws pressed up against my fingertips, like milk teeth. Beneath them, between the first and middle knuckle, are larger ones. Adult claws. Waiting for the day I will need them. Waiting for the day they will grow.

I hear sounds; George and the doctor are coming back. I blink the image away and plunge my hands under my thighs and out of sight. The door opens and George beams.

"I have an idea," he says. "Why don't we go camping?"

* * *

The arena comes back into focus. Wendy is across the stage, on the ground. "Let me out!" she cries, rattling the bars of an imaginary cage. "Get me out of here!"

Ying Yue is nowhere to be seen.

I am in a groggy purgatory somewhere between dreams and waking. The crystal pendant is on the ground in front of me, its blue light still blinking. My hands shake. My arms shake. My entire body shakes. It doesn't make any sense. Yet, all the evidence is there . . .

George adopted me. He raised me. He shot me with a tranquilizer gun and brought me into the Deeper Woods. He left me there as bait. So that Circo Klujns would catch me and bring me to their stand. So he could track me.

How could he do this to me? He was the kindest father I could have ever asked for. Was none of that real? Was I just an experiment to him? How could I have been so wrong about someone?

Beneath me, the earth trembles. There's a thrum of footsteps.

I think of Diana, who I thought had never warmed to me—when, in reality, she had been opposed to George's plan. The strictness that I had mistaken as dislike had actually come from a place of love. She was trying to shield me from an environment she knew was toxic. From what was to come.

I remember my last morning in Red River, the way she cried as she peeled the onion. The way the vein in her temple pulsed when she was forced to serve kanum. Every mouthful she watched me eat.

No one can know what she is, George had said. *Not Rodrigo, not Mercy, not her.* He kept me in the dark on purpose. Whereas Zoe had known all along what purpose she was serving. She had gone along with it, desperate to prove that she was worthy, like a child soldier or a suicide bomber, brainwashed into thinking that her mission was a noble one. Meanwhile, I had been clueless, naive, and blind, unaware of what was going to happen. *And yet, knowing less is what saved my life.*

The earth continues to shake. The footsteps grow louder. I hear a muffled *pop, pop, pop*. Gunshots. My body begins to sink.

That's when I realize . . . the stage is quicksand. I try to stand up, but my legs are stuck fast. I struggle and sink, sink, sink, until my entire body is submerged. My head goes under. I can't see. I can't breathe. I'm trapped. Drowning in the earth. And then, the soil's cocoon expels me.

I fall onto the stage. The *real* stage. I'm jarred awake. The rose's poison fades. The images around me are still blurred, forming trails of light as my eyes move from one thing to the next. But I'm lucid, my mind sharp, adrenaline running wild.

Wendy is still in her invisible cage, but she's given up trying to escape. All that's left of Ying Yue is part of her discarded costume: her headpiece, her cloak.

Hands on my arms, pulling me up. "Come on," a voice orders. It's Diablo. His usual confidence betrays the slightest trace of fear. "The Hunters are here."

46

Diablo hoists me up onto my feet. My legs are not yet steady. "We need to leave," he says urgently.

I notice the arena is almost empty. The last of the Klujns are fleeing. The king is gone, along with his guard. But why is Diablo suddenly in charge of me?

"Where are we going?" I ask.

"Daciana asked me to take you home. We have to use the north route. It's the safest. There are too many Hunters coming from the south."

"I can't go home! If they find out what I am, they'll kill me."

"You pretended to be human all your life," says Diablo. "You can pretend for a while longer."

I turn on him. "I don't *want* to go back!" Not after what I just discovered about George. I need a safe space, some time to think . . .

Diablo looks at me like I'm a child throwing a tantrum. "Don't look at me like that," I say.

"Like what?"

"Like I'm only human."

"A few hours ago you didn't want to be Klujn," he says. "You haven't earned your place among us. So either I bring you home, or you find your own way there." I realize that was the argument in Daciana's tent.

She asked him to look after me and he didn't want to, but he couldn't disobey his queen.

Diablo moves toward the exit. "Wait," I say. I look over at Wendy, who's still under the influence of the rose. Eyes glazed, in her own world. "I can't leave her."

"The Hunters will find her," he tells me.

"That's exactly what I'm afraid of."

"She'll slow us down," he says, but I see that he's on the edge of persuasion.

"Please." My voice is louder and more commanding than I expected. There's something conflicted in his expression. Then his hatred draws back, and I glimpse a flicker of mercy.

"Fine," he says. "But she's yours to carry."

I hurry over to Wendy. "Come on," I say, draping her arm around my shoulders. She leans into me, heavy and rose-drugged, her legs like jelly.

She blinks. "I was in a cage," she says, looking around. "Where's my cage?"

"No more cage," I tell her. Diablo looks at us impatiently. "I'm not leaving her," I answer his silent criticism.

"Then keep up."

Diablo leads us out of the arena. We have barely taken a few steps when I see—Circo is burning.

It's mayhem. Frantic Klujns flee in all directions, running for their lives as bullets spray up the hillside. Hunters march through the narrow alleyways, their faces covered in gray war paint, torching tents. Some of their rifles have bayonets of viaţăs glinting red in the moonlight, others just have metal. There are Hunters on robotic horses with silver hooves. Cyborg hounds with beady eyes that stalk with light, predatory steps, their metal muzzles sniffing at the night, their claws as sharp as knives. Everywhere I turn, there are gray uniforms. They look like an army of death.

Pop. Pop. Pop.

A shower of bullets misses me by mere inches. There's a thud and a thump, and I turn to see that one of the bullets has hit a Klujn child. The child lies on the ground on a bed of golden robes, eyes open, soul already gone. Next to her—or him—a spotted wolf pup howls as a cyborg dog closes in, preparing to finish the job.

"Don't look," Diablo warns me, but it's too late. My eyes take in every horrific detail.

Metal, teeth, flesh.

Screams, cries, and moans.

Blood, fire, and smoke.

Down an alleyway, a huge Hunter has pinned down a screaming Klujn. The Hunter's pliers close around one of the Klujn's claws. A sickening sound and the claw comes out, followed by a tail of nerve endings. The Klujn shrieks. The Hunter smirks. Adds his prize to a pocket full of crystals.

We are almost running. "This way," Diablo urges. "We need to go faster."

I try, but Wendy is a dead weight. My arms ache, and my shoulder is numb, but if I complain he'll tell me to leave her behind, and I can't do that.

I don't know what truths Wendy experienced during the Midnight Rose ceremony, what trip she had from the black rose, but Warwick wasn't lying about the lengths humans will go to silence them. And I don't think Grouse is fond of people who know the things we do.

We pass Warwick's tent, which is already ablaze. I slow down when I notice a creature in the front yard—badly burned, its breathing shallow. It's Warwick's pig, I realize. A little name tag on its collar reads: Maré. There is no one to help it, no one to ease its pain.

Diablo realizes I'm no longer behind him and turns around. "You can't save them all," he says.

I know. But my legs won't cooperate. It takes everything I have to pull myself away from that innocent creature in distress, and even more to keep up the pace while carrying Wendy.

Finally, we find an entrance to the Katacombes that hasn't been closed by fleeing Klujns. I follow Diablo down the dark tunnels. He pulls a small branch from his cloak, snaps it in two, and hands me half. The sap at the tip begins to emit a red glow.

The Katacombes are quiet. No Hunters have discovered them yet. And whatever Klujns escaped through these tunnels have already gone, the sound of their footsteps no longer echoing from the walls. With the bright light of our branch, I don't see any trail markers, but Diablo knows the way by heart. My shoulder is completely numb with Wendy's weight. A few more minutes of running brings us to a fork in the path. Going left will take us outside, while the right pathway continues underground, the ceiling uncomfortably low.

"Which way?" I ask, and Diablo points to the right. Of course.

Wendy's derangement is fading. Suddenly, she stops walking. Her eyes lock on me, then Diablo, then our surroundings. As the last of the rose's serum leaves her bloodstream, the drunk vapidity in her eyes fades and lucidity returns.

"*Get off me!*" she snaps, pushing me away. Her arms thrash out like insults; hurtful, unnecessary.

"Wendy—it's okay! I'm not going to hurt you."

She stops moving, but stays at a safe distance. Her eyes survey me with disgust. "Where are you going?" she asks accusatorily.

"We have to go with him," I answer.

"No." Wendy shakes her head stubbornly. "I need to go home. I need to see my parents."

"He'll get us home. But, Wendy, you can't trust the Hunters." She takes a step back toward the exit. "If they find you . . ." My voice cracks, afraid of the possibilities.

"We have to go," Diablo tells me.

"Just a minute." I hope that in my eyes Wendy can still see my humanity, can understand that I'm still the same Ava she met in the Deeper Woods.

I take a step toward her. Reach out and rest my hands on her shoulders. She recoils a little at the sight of my claws but doesn't move away. "You don't have to come with us," I say. "But please, don't let them catch you. Use the stars, follow them south. You'll hit the river eventually. The river'll take you home." I don't know if she'll listen to anything I have to say, but it's worth a try. "When you get home, talk to someone you trust. But don't trust anyone who works for Grouse. And don't say anything out loud . . . write it down, then burn it. They're everywhere, and they're listening, all the time."

A long moment passes.

"You're a good friend," Wendy says. "I didn't think I'd ever say that about a—Klujn. But you are. I wouldn't have survived a single day here without you, Ava." She takes a folded piece of paper from the pocket of her cloak and looks at it. "During the ceremony, I saw—"

"It's okay. You don't have to talk about it."

"It's not okay," she replies. "What they do to them in the Loud-house . . . it's horrible, Ava. No one deserves to live or die like that." She hands me the paper. "My entire life I've been told one story: that Klujns are the enemy. After Willa died"—and she chokes a little—"I wanted to believe it more than anything. But how can they be bad, if you're one?" In Wendy's eyes, I see a glimpse of the sweet, affable girl she was the day we met. The part of herself she gave away so freely when she thought I was human. It's only a flicker, but it's there. As promising as a pulse. "How could they be merciless," she continues, "if you risked your life to leave me that hourglass? I know it was you. I know you put it there. You saved my life."

"I couldn't let you die," I say, tears forming in the corners of my eyes. "You were so kind, right from the start."

"It's my weakness," she says ruefully.

"No, it's not. It's a great strength. I wish I could be more like you."

"It might take me some time to wrap my head around what you are. *Who* you are." She takes a breath and looks me in the eye. "But I'll try to get there, I will. One day."

"I'm going to miss you," I say.

"I'm going to miss you, too," she admits.

"I hope I get to see you again."

"I sure as winter hope that happens," Wendy mutters. I throw my arms around her. I don't care if she pulls away. But Wendy doesn't move. In fact, after a moment, she hugs me back. "Please don't scratch me with your claws," she squeaks through her tears, and I laugh through my own.

I squeeze my first, hard-won friend. She has been my lifeline here, my buoy in an ocean storm. In our embrace, I feel her friendship. A friendship that can only be measured in days, but spans a far greater distance than that. One that is blind to fences and sides. The way the earth looks from space, and the moon looks from here: two glowing orbs with no borders or territory lines.

After a moment, I let her go. "Follow the stars," I say.

"South," she answers, nodding.

Diablo speaks up. "Avoid the dirt roads. And the secret trails. They lead to Military and Hunter facilities."

Wendy looks at Diablo, deciding whether or not to trust him. After a few seconds, she nods. "Thanks."

Diablo nods ever so slightly in return. "We have to go," he tells me.

"Stay safe, Wendy," I say. "And please . . . be careful."

"You too." She replies and heads toward the tunnel that leads outside. Stops. Turns around. "Hey, Ava?"

"Yeah?"

"Break a leg," she smiles.

* * *

Diablo and I crawl through the low tunnel. My fingers close around the piece of paper Wendy gave me, but there isn't time to read it. I tuck it into the breast of my costume. Finally, the tunnel opens out into the frosty night. I look around, trying to get my bearings.

We have emerged at the bottom of the mountain on the north side of the stand, near the beehives. The hill rises up behind us, its neat terraces of rich soil sprouting plants where the symbols used to be. A full, blossoming harvest, now wasted.

I take one last look at Circo. The only part of the stand visible from here is the arena, which is being ravaged by flames. The canvas melts, revealing the Carniflora, which is on fire, crying out with a sound of distress, shattering the untouched magic of this place. By morning, there will be nothing left.

"I know you're tired," Diablo says. "But we have to keep moving."

My legs ache, my mind is exhausted and spinning, but I do the best I can. He leads me into the forest, to the same trail we took when we headed to the cave challenge. We walk quietly, making almost no sound at all.

Then, in the distance, I hear a sharp cackle of laughter. Diablo pushes me behind a tree, his body shielding mine. He looks around for anything out of the ordinary, reading the stillness like a map. The laughter is gone now, but an unnerving silence remains. I've walked these woods before, and they were filled with sounds.

"We can't stay here," Diablo whispers. "Follow me." He moves away, and I am suddenly cold, but the cold is something I have to face if I want to get out of here alive. He takes a careful step forward. I edge behind him. He continues along the path, one vigilant step at a time. I look up, searching the darkness. I take another step—

Before I understand what's happening, a rope tightens around my ankle and I'm thrust into the air. It's a snare. I'm hanging upside down, blood rushing to my head. Diablo looks up at me, his features strained with worry.

Then, behind him, I glimpse something.

"Diablo—run!" I yell. But it's too late. The Hunter takes the metal bayonet of his rifle and stabs Diablo in the back, and the Klujn falls to the ground.

The Hunter's boots crunch over dead leaves. Then, he aims his rifle at me—and shoots with military precision. The rope of my trap snaps and I fall to the forest floor, landing with a painful *thud*, my shoulder taking most of the impact.

"Got one!" the Hunter calls out excitedly. "Two, actually." His voice is young and eager. Familiar. I look up and see a teenage boy with dark curly hair and bright eyes, his build on the smaller side of average. Behind the confident front, there's a boyish softness in his eyes.

It's Mercy.

47

I snap my eyes shut. Squeeze my hands into fists. *Please*, I pray to my unfamiliar claws. *Please go back in. Don't let Mercy see me like this.* I hear a sound, a faint *slurp*, and my fingertips tingle momentarily. Slowly, I uncoil my fingers and see that my baby claws have retreated. *Thank goodness.* The only traces of their existence are infinitesimal slits at the tips, and my peeling fingernails.

I keep my eyes open but don't look up, watching Mercy's boots as they come toward me. His dark gray pants, the belt adorned with a crystal knife and grenade. A real one, not a toy. His body looks more sure of itself, bigger somehow.

"Ava?" Mercy comes closer. "*Ava!* I didn't recognize you in that ridiculous costume." He reaches me and helps me up. "I was so worried," he says. "I'm so mad at Dad. He told me he had no choice, but he did. Are you hurt?" he asks, his voice full of sympathy. What did George tell him?

I look up to meet his eyes, and his expression freezes over. It's the same look Wendy had when she watched me kill Elizabeth. *My claws didn't betray me*, I think. *But my eyes just did.*

Mercy goes rigid. He drops my arm and takes a step back. "W-what did they do to you?" he stutters, in total disbelief. "D-did they make you like this?"

"Mercy!" A voice booms, this one older and more assertive. There are footsteps, and a second Hunter arrives.

I can't believe it. It's George. But what is he doing in a Hunter's uniform? With a crystal bayonet.

He looks at Mercy. "Where's your buddy?"

"B-back at the camp," Mercy stammers, his eyes still on me, trying to make sense of what's happening.

"Go and find him," George orders. "And never leave his side again. You're never to go wandering off on your own."

Mercy doesn't budge.

"*Now!*"

Mercy finally peels his eyes away from me and starts to head back toward camp.

I stare at George defiantly, challenging him to look at me. To own up for what he did. He does, briefly, but the eye contact makes him ill at ease. *No shit.* He shifts his weight, his heavy boots cracking the twigs beneath them. Around his neck, he wears some kind of pendant, an eyeball with a red iris. One of his *gadgets.*

"Ava, I . . ." he starts. Then he's saved by the crackle of his radio.

A voice grinds through static: "Santos for Doc."

George presses a button. "Go for Doc."

"We got the king," he says over the sounds of victory behind him.

"Terrific," George replies, then adds, "Send backup. I got another one." I never realized how imposing my father could be. His green eyes are the only part of him I recognize. The uniform makes him look like a different person. It makes him look . . . ruthless. "It's a male," he adds. "A big one."

"Copy that," Santos replies.

"I need to leave," he says. "Family emergency." General Santos understands the coded message and gives George the go-ahead. The radio crackles off.

My father continues to study me. He reaches into his jacket and pulls out a small vial of blue powder, tips some in his palm. "I'm sorry that I have to do this, Ava." George blows, and the blue powder envelops me. It's in my hair, my eyes, and my nostrils. It's trickling down my throat, making everything numb, numb, numb. The world's edges are already blurring.

How absurd is this? I think. *I survived the Deeper Woods. I survived the Blood Race. Only to be taken out by my own father.*

I'm already drowsy. I surrender to the great fatigue that sweeps through me.

The last thing I hear is George's voice.

"The wild suits you, Ava," he says.

* * *

I'm not completely unconscious. I can still move my legs, but barely. As George holds me up, walking me somewhere, images flash by—the faces of Hunters. Old and young. *Too* young. Some of them are injured, but as long as they're alive, they're victorious, swigging liquor from flasks. Cyborg dogs drag the carcasses of wild dogs and spotted wolves and birds into a pile. A drone takes flight into the night sky, mechanical wings buzzing.

A Jeep door opens, and I am pushed inside. It slams shut. I try to pull the handle, but it's locked, and it's like my arms have no muscles or bones. No strength to pry my way out, to chance escape. The back seat is a little black cave with a single airhole on either side. I bring an eye up to the hole on the left passenger side and peer out, but the world is fuzzy and my mind can't make sense of what it sees.

Living Klujns are herded onto a black school bus with blacked-out windows. Dead ones are loaded onto another.

Two older Hunters carry Diablo's body. I bite one of my remaining fingernails, waiting to see where they take him. They load him onto the first bus. *Alive.* I'm flooded with relief until I realize that he may not be alive for very much longer.

My body feels heavy, so heavy. I can't keep myself upright. There is too much butchery, too much carnage. I sink into the back seat and relinquish control to the poison in my blood. I close my eyes.

Enough heartbreak for one night.

* * *

Still groggy from the Midnight Rose or the tranquilizer, I'm jostled awake. The Jeep is driving along a bumpy road. I look out the airhole, but the jerky movements make it hard to focus on any one thing. I glimpse keyhole-sized images—clearings in the forest, piles of sparkling timber, crates painted with large words: LIVING SOIL. HANDLE WITH CARE.

The Blood Moon, fading.

I already feel that itching in my body, the need to be outside. I lean close to an airhole and suck in a deep breath, my shaky lungs intoxicated by the cool night air. But the forest smell is growing weaker as the smell of dead things grows.

I wonder if I will ever smell the wild again.

The black school buses tail close behind. We drive through deep mud, across fallen logs. Most of the forest here has been cleared. It is a black cemetery filled with sepulchral stumps. There are no animal sounds, no luminescent insects, no blue sparrows hopping along low branches. Instead, there is machinery, abandoned for the night. Tractors and gaping holes in the earth and the skeletons of animals, those innocent bystanders.

As we cross a fence so tall and menacing it must be the Military fence that separates two worlds, the air thickens and becomes grayer, and the Blood Moon continues to fade in color and size. She goes back to being an ordinary moon. No longer a god, but a gray disk in the sky.

I lie down on my Jeep bench and tuck my legs into my body, anxiously chewing off my remaining fingernails. When that's done, I rest my head on my arm, using it as a pillow. I try to relax, but that restlessness inside me remains. *What if I forget again? Forget Circo, and what I experienced here? After all, I already forgot once.*

A few hours pass. I try to sleep, but slumber doesn't find me. My limbs cramp from being in the same position. I move around, bend, stretch, but my options are limited. Screams echo in my ears. Circo burning. Klujns dying. Claws ripped from fingers. Spotted wolf carcasses. Thousands of years of culture and magic . . . gone in an instant.

"*Ava.*" A voice speaks in my mind. It ricochets, like footsteps underground. I recognize it as Daciana's. Is she okay? Did she make it out?

"*I will visit you later,*" she says. I realize that there must still be traces of the blue lace agate left in my system; she is still in my head, although for how much longer I'm not sure.

"Diablo was taken," I tell her, my voice pitiful and weak. There is a pause.

"Try to get some sleep," she finally says. *"You're safe enough for now."*

Safe *enough.*

Finally, bouncing and bobbing with the ragged road, I manage to slip into a shallow sleep. It is the first time in almost five days that I don't dream.

* * *

I wake in the late morning as the Jeep and buses emerge from the dead woods into sloping hills. But these don't compare to the breathtaking vistas of the Deeper Woods. We pass mines and Military checkpoints and townships that look like larger versions of Red River, with public markets and gallows. There are abandoned bus stops with decades-old murals painted over sloppily in gray. Plastered on top of the paint are rows of navy blue posters with silver words:

REPORT UNUSUAL BEHAVIOR

A message from the Department of Societal Order

We pass Industrial Greenhouses and power plants. There are flat fields broken up by straight dirt roads—a perfect grid of sterile farmland. And then we near a road that branches off to the right, a long driveway that leads into a black wooded area. I can see the top of a black brick building poking out from the canopy, a silhouette that chills my blood. It's a Loudhouse.

Is that where they're taking me? As we come closer, I'm petrified. But the Jeep doesn't turn; it continues along the main road. The buses aren't as lucky. They turn down the gravel driveway, their tires sending up clouds of dust. When the dust settles, the buses are gone. *Diablo.*

We drive for another half hour or so; it's hard to measure time. The Jeep continues through Tremble Hills. We must have gone southeast from Circo, then taken a right after the fence and headed northwest on the human side. There's only one road that comes up here, like a hundred-mile cul-de-sac.

Finally, the tires crunch up a driveway and come to a stop.

I hear a single set of boots on the gravel. There's the twist of a key, the scrape of a handle, and my back seat enclosure is flooded with light. George stands there, looking tired after the long drive.

"I'm sorry, Ava," he says. "It was a necessary precaution. I had to get you out of there without attracting attention." George offers me a hand, but I don't take it.

I manage to get out of the Jeep on my own, lean against it, and look around. *I'm home.*

It feels like an eternity since I was here. The cherrywood house, the sprawling veranda, Diana's greenhouse with the crack from Mr. Mogel's bullet. It looks like the set of a house, not a real house that people actually live in.

George's eyes are full of apology. "I know you must have a million questions," he says. "And I will answer them all when you're ready. But now, we need to get you ins—"

Wham. The heel of my palm flies into his jaw. Teeth crack. George touches his bleeding mouth, but he doesn't look angry.

"You're a Hunter?" It's the only thing I can think to say.

"I'm not," he says. "It's just a uniform."

"It's not just a uniform," I answer.

"I know you think I'm the enemy. But everything I did, I did because

I had no choice. There are enemies out there far worse than me. One day, I hope you'll understand why I had to do what I did."

I have no words for him. No *I hate you* or *How could you* or *What you did is unfathomable.* I don't care what web of lies he wants to spin. I trusted him. He was my *father.* And he used me . . . he gambled my life . . . but it's worse than that.

He pretended to be nice. To earn my trust.

Primed and pampered.

He didn't have to do that.

I leave George standing there and take the steps to the porch. Go through the door and into the quiet house. Up the stairs, down the hallway, until I am in my room. It's just the way I left it. Moon lamp. Bed unmade. Nightshirt crumpled on the bathroom floor. A museum of the way things were, which only makes me realize how much I have changed.

I close the curtains and the bathroom door—Mercy is not there, thank goodness—take off my spoiled costume, and collapse onto the bed. A nagging voice in my gut says, *What now?* I don't want to be here, but what choice do I have? I'm angry at Daciana for sending me back. Angry at Diablo, too, for complying.

There's a gentle knock on the bedroom door. *No, please no. Don't let it be George.* Next time, I'll give him more than just my palm; I'll wring his neck until his eyes pop out. I've had practice.

The door opens, and I see Diana. She looks tired, her expression somber. *Guess some things haven't changed.* After everything I've learned, though, I can't help but see her in a new light. Diana didn't hate me. She never hated me. She hated what George was doing to me.

She gets right to the point. "I know that you probably don't want to talk to me, or anyone. I don't blame you. But there's something you need to know. Grouse is coming here. He heard you made it, and he wants to have a word. You were the only human found." I cling to these words. *That means that Ying Yue and Wendy weren't caught? They're still out there?*

"Does Grouse know that I'm half Klujn?" I ask Diana. She looks stunned—either that I know what I am, or that I dare to say it aloud.

"I don't know how much he knows," she says. "Maybe he does. Regardless, even as a human survivor, you still know more than you're supposed to."

"Then why did George bring me back?" I ask. "Why not send me straight to the DSO? Or a Loudhouse?"

"Because you're still our daughter."

I shake my head at that ridiculous word.

She presses her lips together before continuing. "We need to keep Grouse off your case while we come up with a plan."

"What plan?"

"Grouse will keep you around if he thinks you have information he needs. Especially if it could lead to further raids. You might have *options*," she says.

"Options?" I say bitingly. "I wish I had been given *options* before George sent me out into the woods to die."

Diana looks shattered, and she doesn't come to George's defense. "We live in a complicated world," she says with a sigh. "But there are still good people out there. People who remember the truth and who are fighting for the future of our world."

"Then where are they?" I say, raising my voice dangerously. "Where were they when the Hunters burned an entire stand to the ground?"

"You should use the words 'tribe' or 'settlement,'" Diana says. "Language can easily give you away."

I want to cry, but I'm too tired. Everything is still so fresh.

"Look, Ava, it's not safe to talk about any of this here," she tells me. "Before we find a place to have that conversation, I have someone who's been waiting to see you, and he can't wait any longer."

Someone? He?

Diana opens the door a little wider, and he pushes the rest of the way through. White fur, black spots, blue eyes. My heart leaps. Somersaults. Soars. It's Wolf. *He's alive.*

I close the distance between us in less than a second. He meets me halfway. I throw my arms around him, already sobbing, and Wolf licks my tears away. His breath smells like grass and roots and his fur smells like . . . our basement. *I've missed you so much*, I think. I look up at Diana. My lips curve into a silent word. "How?"

"That driveway is on our land," she explains. "So even if Mogel shot him, his meat was ours to keep. At least, that's what I told him. I might have also mentioned that our family friend and Grouse's right-hand man Rodrigo might want to know about his illegal poaching. The general has a reputation for being . . . unforgiving. That shut him up pretty quickly."

I never imagined I would ever think this about Diana, but right now she may be my favorite person in the world. I bury my face in the thick rolls of fur around Wolf's neck. *I'm so sorry for what you went through. I will never leave your side again.* Wolf howls in response. He understands. I am forgiven.

As Wolf and I nod off to sleep in the early afternoon, my mind is still swirling with questions. Cradling him in my arms, I feel a great sense of peace. Here is a creature who knows exactly who I am, yet we have never exchanged words. I trace my finger along his whiskers, his long eyelashes and eyebrows, and lift the tent of his lips to reveal those sharp white fangs. He lets me map his features with my hands, occasionally making small sounds of appreciation or licking my hands.

Two halves of one whole.

He is a stranger, and yet he is family. We have so much catching up to do.

But first, a nap. In my sleep, I am visited by another friend.

48

The queen sits on the edge of the mattress, watching the crackling blue-green flames, as her wolf Rhea sleeps by my legs. Everything in the room looks exactly as it did when I woke up here after my fight with Elizabeth, and yet I have the feeling that it isn't a memory.

"Where are we?" I ask Daciana.

"In my quarters," she says.

"What I mean is . . . is this a dream?"

"Let's just say that you are graciously hosting me in your mind, and I will not take up too much of your time."

"You and Glory made it out?" I ask urgently. "You're safe?"

"For now," she answers. "Although the woods are crawling with Hunters. More than we realized." I look around the tent, as detailed and rich in color as the real one, which must have been burned along with the rest of Circo.

"Humans are intelligent," says Daciana. "They have sophisticated science and technology. But I have something they do not: the ability to see things in the Unseen, to sense danger long before it's coming. I knew of the Hunters' presence for a while, laying traps around our stand, waiting for the right moment to strike. Their strategy this time was not to raid quickly, but to lay down more traps and get us as we fled."

"If you knew this, why didn't you do anything about it?" I ask. "Couldn't you evacuate the stand?"

"It is not my stand, therefore it was not my decision to make."

"But so many Klujns died," I say.

Daciana changes the subject. "Did you know that Klujn stands are usually matriarchal?" I shake my head. "Over many years of watching Mother Nature herself, we have found that female moon energy—no matter what body it is in—tends to make the best leaders."

"What body?" I ask.

"The body is only a vessel, like a lamp, and energy is the endless flow of electricity that gives it light—as you saw with your friend Rory. As Klujns," she tells me, "we know that the only way we can heal the world is by moving away from the imbalance of sun energy that has led to destruction and spectacles of horror, and adopting a more moon-based approach to the way we treat the world and its creatures. That is why Warwick likes to abduct girls for the human Blood Race," she says. "He believes that they are more susceptible to learning. Of course, this isn't always the case, but no belief system is perfect."

"I don't understand," I say. "If Klujn stands are usually matriarchal— then how come Warwick is king?"

Daciana sighs. "Let's just say that Warwick's experience on the human side of the fences scarred him deeply. Before Warwick, the Blood Race tradition was not violent, nor did it involve humans. When Warwick escaped and returned to Circo, he didn't agree with the Circo queen's gentle approach to humans. He challenged her, and he won. Ever since, he has led his stand astray from our very purpose as a species. Unfortunately, most are too afraid to challenge him. Now Circo is divided.

"When Warwick ate the Circo queen's heart," Daciana explains. "The knowledge that is usually passed down was lost on him. He wasn't on the frequency required for a leader to develop their second sight—the frequency of the earth, of creation. Warwick does not have any remarkable abilities beyond physical strength and a fondness for games and parties. When I warned him about the Hunters, he ignored my warnings. But it is not in my nature to sit back and do nothing"—Daciana snickers—"even in my old age. Diablo and I evacuated the stand slowly, without Warwick's knowledge. Many chose to stay, out of loyalty to their mad king. But about one-third left over the past two days."

I remember the subdued festivities, the half-empty arena. "Warwick could banish or kill me for going behind his back," says Daciana.

"He was caught," I say, remembering the crackle on George's radio.

"He escaped humans once," she says. "I wouldn't be surprised if he managed to do it again."

"Where are you going to go now?" I ask.

Daciana sighs, as though the idea of travel is exhausting. "That is yet to be decided. And winter is not my favorite season."

"I want to come with you."

"Ava—you can't." Daciana's voice is stern. "You are not yet one of us. While I don't believe in the senseless wasting of any life for sport, I do believe that a Klujn must earn their place in the stand. The original Blood Race tradition exists for a reason: a Klujn must get to know themselves and get to know the wild before choosing a profession and a mate. You have begun your journey, Ava, but you are not yet ready."

"What do I do in the meantime?" I ask. "How do I become ready? Diablo's in a Loudhouse . . ."

"Like I told him, this is the safest place for you right now."

"But what about him?"

She sighs deeply. "There's nothing to be done."

"No." I can't accept this. She expects me to sit back, return to my normal life, and pretend to be fully human while Diablo's in a cage awaiting slaughter?

Daciana turns away from the fire and looks at me, her purple eyes luminous. "Be strong, Ava," she says. "I couldn't protect my Adria, so forgive me for needing to protect you. Just because you haven't found your place yet, does not mean it doesn't exist."

I dwell on Daciana's words. "You said . . . 'my Adria,'" I stammer.

The queen's eyes twinkle in the firelight. "That's right," she tells me. "Because Adria was my daughter."

49

Wolf and I sleep for hours, curled into one another. His body is so warm that, despite the cold of my room, I wake up sweating.

My moon lamp glows, already waning. There's a tray on the bedside table. A plate with a sandwich—thick rye bread, bursting with grated carrot and veggie paste and sprouts. A glass of water with an orange slice. I'm not hungry, but I appreciate the gesture. There's care in the way it was made, something tender.

I go to the window and draw open the curtains. The sun has set. The sky is dark, no moon in sight. When I open the window, a cool breeze blows in.

Was my conversation with Daciana a dream? But it's a stupid question. I know the answer with every atom in my body.

I look over at my costume crumpled on the floor. Falling out of one of the pockets is a rose gold chain; Glory's pendant. I can't believe that thing followed me here, that I still have it. I don't care how much it's worth.

I throw on a clean oversized shirt and feel something scratching against my breast. I reach into my bralette and find the piece of paper Wendy gave me.

I unfold it. It's the first page of Catrina Sherman's book. *A Brief History of Klujns.* I study the piece of paper, looking for a message, a clue, the code Wendy was so intent on finding, but I find nothing. My moon lamp watches me, sparking a memory of something Glory had said.

My heartbeat quickens. *Why didn't I think of it before?*

I rub the piece of paper, creating friction the way I did with the Moonlight Leaf. *Please,* I pray, *let this be rebel ink.* I rub again, but nothing happens.

Did Wendy figure it out? I wonder. There's no way to know, because the ink only works once.

I sit down on the edge of the bed and try the bottom of the page instead, the editor's note. Maybe Wendy discovered it, and left me something to decipher! Otherwise, why bother giving me the piece of paper at all?

Please work, I think. And then, after a moment, it happens.

Glowing red words are scribbled all over the bottom half of the page. Entire sentences have been crossed out, replaced by new ones. Notes are scratched in the margins, changing the original meaning of the text.

The editor's note now reads:

Catrina Sherman ~~was~~ *is* an anthropologist, author, explorer, and scientist who devoted her life to the study of Klujns. After the ~~death~~ *murder* of her wife,*by Grouse's DSO* Sherman went *orchestrated her disappearance* *slain* to live in the wild. She ~~disappeared~~ in 16 AK while researching the ~~fallen~~ Estrella *stand.* ~~tribe, where she was likely killed and eaten by Klujns.~~ *While this book is government-approved toilet paper (at best), those* *with curious minds will find satisfying truths hidden between its pages. Sherman* *currently resides in the northeastern Boreal, although she believes that a balanced* *life is one in motion. Her door is always open to the wayward traveler.*

At the bottom of the page, a sentence catches my attention.

DK, the rebellion lives on in the wild. Knowledge is power. Stay safe, old friend.
Love, C.

50

I can't believe it. This entire time, Wendy was right! Catrina Sherman's final book *was* garbage, because she didn't want to attract unwanted eyes. But is every copy marked like this, or just this one? Who published it, and when?

I read the text again. DK—who's DK? The initials ring a bell. By my third read, the rebel ink is already fading. I rub the paper once more, but the words are gone. *If this page alone contains so much code, imagine the rest of the book!* I wish I could talk to Wendy. I pray that she made it home, to safety.

There's a crunch of tires on the driveway. A flash of headlights illuminates the trees. I stand up and walk back to the window. Wolf *humph*s in disapproval.

"I'm not going far," I assure him. A slick silver car pulls up in front of the house. George comes out to greet it, wearing formal Hunting attire.

The driver gets out. Walks around to the back passenger door and opens it. A cyborg hound hops out, wearing a crystal collar with a name tag that jingles. Then out comes a man in a silver suit covered by a spotted wolf cloak. There's something surreal about seeing him with my own eyes.

It's Atoll Grouse.

My father smiles, but it's a nervous smile. He waits for Grouse to address him.

"How's your daughter?"

"A little shaken, but she'll survive," George says too quickly.

"I'm looking forward to speaking to her."

"Of course," George replies. "But I'm afraid she's sleeping now."

I draw my blackout curtain shut, my heart thundering like a fast-approaching train. I want to run downstairs and confront the man responsible for all of this. I want to hurt him, knock reason into him, give him a taste of his own medicine. *Control yourself. If you do that, you're dead.*

I go over to my bedroom door. Before closing it, I watch the men downstairs.

"Are you happy with the outcome of the raid?" George asks, escorting Grouse into the kitchen. But our Territory's leader is distracted by his dog, whose black beady eyes are fixed on the staircase, perhaps smelling me or Wolf.

"We barely got half the tribe," Grouse says testily. "At least we got the king, so there's that."

"If the business about the king's heart is true," my father says, "this raid will lead us to more tribes than we could ever imagine."

"I hope you'll be part of those operations." It is not a statement, but a question. George is backed into a corner.

"Have you eaten?" he asks, keen to change the subject. "I think Diana's making potato gratin."

"I had my driver pick up something from Rodrigo's farm. The catch of the day," Grouse says, smiling broadly. "It's already been marinated and cooked, but needs reheating."

"Terrific," George exclaims with forced sincerity. "I'm so hungry I could eat a tribe."

"Come, Showman," calls Grouse, and the cyborg dog turns away from the stairs and follows his master into the kitchen. "I got him at one of the dog fights in Brave Night. He's vicious but loyal. You'll have to come see him compete sometime. Although, it's not much of a competition."

"That would be an honor."

I slip my door shut. Lock it. Turn to look at Wolf. His teeth are showing, his hackles raised. The train in my chest returns, thundering through various stations. Disgust. Terror. Rage.

I go back to my bed, my fingers absent-mindedly stroking Wolf's fur and the two spots that remain. *Two lives.*

I think about the last few days. I have seen things I never imagined. I don't want to go back to fogginess, to muddiness, to oblivion. To being sick and stupid, controlled by a system that wants me dead. I cannot hide who I am anymore. I do not want to live in a world where the simple truth of who that is will get me killed. My eyes have been opened.

What else is there to see?

There's a flush behind my cheeks. A warm prickling sensation. The flame of purpose, of mission, burning for the very first time. I stand strong inside my body. I feel that inner fire behind my eyes, my irises changing color, returning to violet. There's a sound. A quiet *click*. My claws emerge from the tips of my fingers. It hurts, but not as much as it did yesterday. I don't need a mirror to know what I look like. Less and less human. More and more *Klujn.*

I look out at the dark sprawling forest beyond my front yard. Somewhere out there, Circo is burning. Perhaps it is already only smoking ashes. I already miss this place that no longer exists. The taste of the food. The warmth of my cot. The bonfires. The cool evening breeze and that crisp forest smell. The sunrises and the sunsets, the sky ablaze with Lumina and cotton candy clouds. The Amethyst pools and costumes and music—and the color of the moon.

I miss that feeling in my chest . . . that burst of exhilaration, of adventure, of discovery, like everything around me was alive, and I was alive with it. Like life was big, and dangerous, and thrilling. Like I was part of something.

Maybe it's not the place that I miss, but its inhabitants and guests.
Daciana, Glory.
Wendy, Willa, Rory.
Diablo.

Even though Circo is gone, there are other stands out there. There are forests and animals and Klujns that can still be saved.

Wolf howls, his low, haunting *coo*. I look at him. He looks at me. His blue eyes are textured like a mountain range on an alien planet. Finally, I understand them. I know exactly what they're saying.

What are you waiting for?

ACKNOWLEDGMENTS

Blood Circus began as an idea I had back in 2008 when I ran away with a circus. It evolved into a film script before a few wise people convinced me to turn it into a short story and then a novel. It was a steep uphill slog the entire way, but luckily, I like to climb mountains. I am so grateful to all the people who guided me along the way and came into my life by chance or magic.

First of all, my parents. I am so lucky to have won this lottery of souls and ended up in the family that I did. Thank you for taking me to see *Jurassic Park* when I was five, and letting me read Goosebumps books, and showing me that it's possible to travel on an artist's budget. Thank you for being proud of me when I told you I wanted to take a gap year (that turned into a gap seven years) and see the world. You have always encouraged my writing and trusted my dreams, and never once did you tell me to get a real job!

Thank you to my sister Mathilde a.k.a Midi—from our feud-driven sisterly beginnings to becoming each other's biggest fans and most loyal supporters. The world would not make sense without you in it. I could write a novel about how much you mean to me, but this book is already long enough.

Thank you to my teachers along the way, who may not remember me but who deserve a mention: Ms. Craig at Montville who helped me publish my first "book" when I was nine; Ms. Poulsen at Kelvin Grove who inspired me amid a difficult year; and Rodger, Joyce, Gayle, and Jessica at VFS, where *Blood Circus* the script began.

To Woody, who taught me why it's important to care about our little planet.

To Ruby, my agent, who opened doors I only dreamed of and believed in my voice long before I even knew I had one. I am here because of you.

To my other amazing agents and lawyers and friends at CAA and beyond, whose excitement for the project was contagious—Darian, Berni, Lexi, Ashley, Ryan, Storm, Robyn, Spencer, Lauren, and Kim.

To Trent, my incredible manager and only other member of my imaginary coven.

Pause. Sigh.

Mollie and Abby, the world's two best book agents . . . Thank you for the call that changed my life when I was standing on a busy street and my phone was dying and I couldn't hear anything you were saying aside from the fact that you loved the story and wanted to represent me. You talked me into writing a book I didn't think I was capable of writing, and you read every draft. You have been so patient, and so kind, and I don't know what I did to deserve you. My writing path was paved with hard work, sacrifice, rejections, and setbacks, but you have been there, always, through all the growing pains. I love you both very much even though, at the time of writing this, we still haven't met in person!

To Sharyn, my lovely editor—thank you for cracking me up with your notes in the margins about human butcher charts and whether or not testicles would be "crunchy." As Stephen King said: to write is human, to edit is divine!

To everyone at Blackstone, my publishing family, who has been so good to me throughout this entire process—

Dan, for being my first YES and believing in this story, loving it fiercely, and having the courage to take a risk. You're the best!

Courtney, my manuscript editor, for going above and beyond! (She even edited this!)

Kathryn, for your talent and creativity in designing the cover of my dreams.

Sam and Isabella, my publicists. I never thought I would ever have a publicist!! It's so exciting.

And to Josie, Megan, Josh, Rachel, Bella, Ananda, Jeff, Lauren, Stephanie, all the proofers and compositors, and the production team. Thank you for all you do!

To Mamie, the greatest matriarch I know, and the rest of my family and the best friends that have become family—Audrey, Qaseem, Areli, Ari, and my Montreal pole community. The key to happiness is to surround yourself with people who uplift you and celebrate your success as their own (and vice versa).

To all the authors and artists I deeply admire, whose work shaped me in one way or another.

Specifically to Paulo Coelho and Suzanne Collins and Heather O'Neill and Charlotte McConaghy and Guillermo Del Toro for giving me my love of beautiful horror.

To all the writers who want to write but are afraid to. As the late Wayne Dyer said: don't die with your music still inside you. Give yourself permission to explore, write, fail, adventure, and find inspiration in unusual places. Writing is rewriting, and writing some more after that. Success isn't only about the end result, but the small daily efforts that eventually amount to something. It isn't about external validation and glowing reviews, but knowing you have something to say and saying it. The world needs artists. Your work is necessary.

To younger me, for working her ass off, not having a Plan B to fall back on, gambling her financial future and always staying stupidly optimistic. I have a lot of love and admiration for the dark, troubled girl she was who made it out of the darkness, who kept going no matter what.

To my homes—Quebec, Canada, and Australia.

And to my baby, my wolf, Flora.

Finally, to Mother Nature and all her creatures that desperately need protecting. It can sometimes feel like we're moving toward a bleak and meaningless future, but it's not too late to make a change. There is still hope. If we learn to consume less, eat healthier, educate ourselves, share the planet with our plant and animal friends, eliminate cruelty, and live more sustainably, there can be a future for us here, and a world worth living in. It's not about one person doing everything, but about everyone doing a little bit. We can't wait for our leaders to make changes—sometimes change has to come from the ground up. We have forgotten how to live in harmony with nature and be wild, but amazing things can happen when we step out of our comfort zones, come together, and learn to be wild again.

Perhaps then we, as a world, can heal.

Cami xx